# *The*
# SPITFIRE
# GIRLS

## ALSO BY SORAYA M. LANE

*Wives of War*
*Hearts of Resistance*
*Voyage of the Heart*

# *The* SPITFIRE GIRLS

SORAYA M. LANE

LAKE UNION
PUBLISHING

Published by Lake Union Publishing, Seattle

www.apub.com

Amazon, the Amazon logo, and Lake Union Publishing are trademarks of Amazon.com, Inc., or its affiliates.

ISBN-13: 9781503905030
ISBN-10: 1503905039

Cover design by Emma Rogers

Cover photography by Richard Jenkins Photography

Printed in the United States of America

*For Maureen, the best mother & grandmother in the world. Thank you for everything.*

*This is not a time for women to be patient. We are in a war and we need to fight it with all our ability and every weapon possible. Women pilots, in this particular case, are a weapon waiting to be used. Hence I am speaking up for the women fliers, because I am afraid we cannot afford to let the time slip by just now without using them.*

— Eleanor Roosevelt (1 September 1942)

# PROLOGUE

## TEXAS, 1940

## LIZZIE

'Sweetheart, what are you doing in my office?'

Lizzie looked up, pen poised above the words she'd so carefully written on the page. She smiled at her father as he collapsed into the armchair on the other side of the heavy oak desk. He always gave her the same look, as if they were co-conspirators in whatever she was working on, and today was no different.

'I'm writing to Mrs. Roosevelt to explain how women could assist the military,' she said, waiting for his eyebrows to shoot up in surprise, which they did almost immediately. 'Would you like to hear it?'

'You're writing to the first lady?' he asked, shaking his head, his eyes twinkling. Her father was always humouring her, always ready to listen to whatever hare-brained idea she might have. 'Lizzie, we're not even at war.'

'Yet,' she said. 'We're not at war *yet*, Daddy.'

'Well then, read away.'

Lizzie cleared her throat and sat back in her daddy's chair, letter raised slightly in her hand. She glanced at the framed photo of him in his uniform before reciting the words, imagining herself doing the daring things he'd described to her ever since she was a little girl, the adventures in the air during wartime that he had so vividly recalled to her.

> 'Dear Mrs Roosevelt,
> As an avid supporter of women's rights, I write in the hope of your expert assistance. I have thought of many ways to start my letter, but in truth I'm a straight talker and I want to get directly to the point. Although our country presently isn't at war, and I certainly hope it will remain that way, I want to be prepared to assist if required.
> Women can play a much bigger role in the event of war than nursing and supporting our men at home. As an experienced pilot myself, I believe women pilots could take over military flying jobs that don't involve fighting, to allow male pilots to be released for combat service. Women pilots could successfully ferry planes for the military and conduct support missions, and I would be more than prepared to personally train these women.
> To succeed, we need your support, and I would love to meet with you to discuss how I could assist the military to establish a squadron of brave, capable American women pilots.'

She cleared her throat and dropped the letter to the desk.

'So what do you think?' she asked, studying her father's face. He was always telling her that she could achieve anything she set her mind to, but this time she didn't want to be placated. This time she wanted his honest opinion. He was a veteran, one of their nation's most celebrated pilots from the Great War, and she wanted to know what the pilot in front of her thought, not the daddy trying to say what his daughter wanted to hear.

'Sweetheart, I honestly don't know what to say.'

She sighed and folded the crisp sheet of paper, placing it carefully in the envelope.

'You think I'm crazy for believing this could happen?' she asked. 'Is that it?'

He reached out and took her hand. 'Lizzie, it's not me you have to convince. I've seen you in the sky. I've been watching you and listening to you for years,' he said. 'But convincing men that you're every bit as capable as them isn't going to be so easy. You know that as well as I do.'

She squeezed his hand in return before gently letting it go. 'Mrs Roosevelt isn't a man,' she replied, knowing she sounded like a temperamental child. 'And I bet there were plenty of people who doubted how talented you were until they saw you fly first hand.'

'Getting what you want is never easy. Don't go thinking that I dazzled everyone from day one, Liz. It took me months before I had the chance to prove myself, but I always knew that one day I'd have the opportunity to show everyone what I could do,' he said. 'And it might be the First Lady you're writing to, but it's men you're asking her to convince on your behalf.'

Lizzie knew that – of course she did. But if she could get just get one person on her side, if she could get one foot in the door, she knew she'd be able to convince others that she was capable. Patience had never been her virtue, and she doubted it ever would be. But determination? She had that in abundance. And she didn't believe it had ever been as hard for a man to prove himself as it was for a woman to do the same.

'I'm not you, Daddy,' she said. 'You had the opportunity to show them from the sky, but I might never get that chance unless I fight for it.'

'One day, Lizzie, women will have all the respect in the world.' He sat back, puffing on his pipe. The strong, familiar odour was pungent, but it was a smell Lizzie had grown up with and one that would forever be associated with her father. 'For now, you need to bide your time, keep your flying hours up and wait for the opportunity to present itself.

And you need to placate your mother before she starts on at me again. You won't be going anywhere if you can't get her on side.'

'Mama isn't going to tell me whether or not I can fly if we enter the war. I'm a grown woman,' she retorted, pressing the seal on the envelope. 'She knows better than anyone that I can't just sit here and do nothing.'

'Keep writing those letters then. Keep fighting,' her father replied. 'And don't let anybody tell you that you can't fly a plane better than a man.' He laughed and puffed again. '*Your mother included.*'

Lizzie curled up on the chair and stared out the window, looking up at the bright blue sky as she smiled at her father's words. She *would* keep writing, and as much as she loved her mother, this was one thing she was more than prepared to defy her on. If Mrs Roosevelt wouldn't help her, then she would write to the president himself, and to the army, and then she'd write to Mrs Roosevelt all over again. She wasn't going to stop until someone took her seriously and gave her the chance to prove herself from the cockpit.

Her daddy was the finest and most decorated wartime pilot in Texas, and she'd show the world that she was every inch her father's daughter.

### Hatfield (north of London), 1940
### May

May Jones clenched her jaw tight, hand trembling with anger as she held the well-thumbed copy of *Aeroplane*. Once, she'd loved reading the aviation magazine, but she vowed then and there never to so much as touch another issue of it.

She cleared her throat and glanced up at the seven other women watching her before starting to read out loud from the page in front of her. They'd been waiting at the factory for almost an hour, and she'd been wondering why the usually chatty group of girls had been so quiet. Now that she'd read what her second officers had been whispering about, she understood why no one had wanted to show her. She took a deep breath and shook her dark hair back, still unused to the short crop.

'We quite agree that there are millions of women in the country who could do useful jobs in war. But the trouble is that so many of them insist on wanting to do jobs which they are quite incapable of doing.'

May paused, anger pulsing at her neck and setting her skin on fire as she read the words.

'The menace is the woman who thinks that she ought to be flying in a high-speed bomber when she really has not the intelligence to scrub the floor of a hospital properly, or who wants to nose around as an Air Raid Warden and yet can't cook her husband's dinner.'

When she set the magazine down, silence fell, and May slowly considered every woman in the room with her. The concrete floor wasn't helping the frigid conditions, and they all had their hands tucked into the armpits of their sheepskin jackets to stay warm, but she was burning with an anger so red hot she was no longer feeling the cold. They would never dare to say such things about men – but women? They treated them as second-class citizens no matter what they were doing, unless they were cooking dinner or holding some sort of cleaning apparatus, and she was sick and tired of it. They were all fighting for the same cause!

'Ladies, this is the biggest load of nonsense I've ever read,' she said, sighing and shutting her eyes for a beat as she tried to calm the fury pumping through her veins. 'This editor, this' – she took a deep breath – 'this *excuse of a man*! To think he can write about us in this way is absolutely appalling. I don't want to see anyone reading or talking about this ridiculous article ever again.'

Betty, one of her most experienced fliers, started to clap, and one by one every other woman followed suit until all of them were clapping and grinning back at her, their cold hands clearly forgotten. May held her head high as a mechanic walked in, a puzzled expression on his face as he looked at them, no doubt wondering what in God's name they were doing. She met his gaze and nodded, feeling sorry for the poor lad that he'd walked straight into a room full of furious women.

'He's right though. I can't scrub floors to save myself!' Betty called out.

'Scrubbing floors,' May scoffed, shaking her head as she scanned the page again. 'I'm not sure what he thinks we were doing before this, but I can tell you that women with more than five hundred hours' flying experience have better things to do than scrub bloody floors!'

They were fully fledged members of the Air Transport Auxiliary, a civilian organisation established to ferry new, repaired and damaged military aircrafts for the Royal Air Force, not silly girls pretending to be pilots! And today, on their first official flight, they were going to prove how much they were needed in this war.

Another of her girls, Penelope, cleared her throat, and May turned to her. She'd always been the quietest of the bunch, so it was good to see her joining in.

'My mother wrote to me the other day and said she chased a neighbour away with her broom when he questioned her about my pay,' Penelope said. 'Apparently it's a national disaster that *glorified female show-offs* are being paid six pounds a week. But she told him where to stick it and not to come back!'

They all laughed, and as May watched them, the heat that had spiralled up her neck and burst into her cheeks turned to warmth. She hadn't laughed in a long while, but it felt nice to be part of the camaraderie for once. It was lovely that Penelope's mother had been so forthright in defending them, and she knew her own parents would do the same. They were proud of her and wouldn't hear a bad word about their pilot daughter. *Even if it had been months since she'd been home to see them.* She pushed the guilt away.

'Excuse me, but do you have a match you could spare?' May asked, gesturing to the handsome mechanic in overalls, who was still hovering near the door.

He walked over, dark eyes searching out hers, his broad, straight shoulders and easy stance telling her that he wasn't in the least intimidated by what he'd heard. She watched as he reached into his pocket, and when he politely extended the matches and some cigarettes, she thanked him and took only one match, swiftly lighting it and placing it to the open page of the magazine.

'You can't light a fire in here!' he blurted, flapping his hands at the paper she still held as a low flame licked across it. 'What the heck do you think you're doing?'

'I don't want any of you reading this kind of rubbish again,' May insisted loudly, ignoring the poor mechanic. She dropped the paper to the concrete floor and he stomped on it to put the fire out. 'We have every right to be flying, and one day our fellow countrymen will look back proudly on what we did for the war effort.'

'Hear, hear!' cried Betty, stamping her feet.

'We are doing our duty and enabling men to go to the front and fight, and I will not hear a bad word said about any of you brave ladies. Do I make myself clear?'

'Perfectly clear, ma'am!' Sarah called back, saluting and giving her a big grin.

May received murmurs of 'Yes' and nods from the seven women gathered, and in that moment, as she saw how proudly they wore their flying suits while they waited to be assigned their planes, she could hardly believe what they were about to do. Their flying outfits might not be fashionable like their smart dark-blue uniforms, with their gold threaded wings and ATA insignia on their jackets, but they were practical, and they'd been made just for them. And she'd never been so proud to wear anything in all her life. To hell with their superiors, who'd thought they could wear skirts in the air in almost polar conditions – a pilot was a pilot, and they all needed the same protective clothing in the sky. She wasn't going to stand for men making decisions about her women, not if they were going to be taking to the sky to help defend their beautiful country.

They were the First Eight, and they were about to show the rest of England exactly what they were made of.

'It's time for wheels up, ladies,' she said, signalling for the women to follow her and shrugging at the mechanic's still-furious expression. 'Any questions?'

She received none, and she hadn't really expected any. She'd hand-picked the women herself, and with impeccable logbooks and thousands of hours of flight experience between them, their ability to do their job wasn't something she worried about. The weather conditions? *Yes.* She was constantly concerned about the cloud cover that England was so well known for. The chance of being fired upon when they had no bombs or guns to defend themselves with? *Absolutely.* And the fact they were flying without radios and instruments? *Every second of every day.* But not once had she doubted their ability to fly whatever plane they were asked to transport; and the slow, sturdy Tiger Moths weren't difficult by any means. It wasn't glamorous work, and no one else wanted to fly the sluggish aircraft in the middle of winter, but she was going to prove that her little squadron could fly every darn plane the military had. If they had to prove themselves in Tiger Moths first, then so be it.

'What's your name?' she asked the mechanic, turning her attention back to him.

'Benjamin,' he replied. 'I'm actually your flight mechanic, ma'am.'

She froze. 'You're *my* mechanic?'

'That's me,' he said, his dark gaze never straying from hers. She couldn't decide if she liked how forthright he was or whether it irked her. 'I've completed a thorough visual check of your engine; it's been uncovered and completely examined for leaks. She's warmed up and ready to fly.'

May hesitated before speaking again, wishing they'd got off on a better footing if they were going to be working closely together. 'Thank you, Benjamin. And if you're assigned to me, we should be a team – there's no reason for formalities. May will do just fine,' she said briskly. 'I hope you'll forgive me for my little stunt before.'

Benjamin raised a brow, still looking unimpressed. 'We'll see.'

She watched him go before turning back to her squadron. They all walked outside, with May in the lead, and she cast her glance skyward. The cloud had mainly cleared, which meant conditions weren't likely to get any better, so it was time for take-off. The planes sat in the gloomy morning like shining steeds lined up on the runway. They were a mixture of new and repaired, and May and her squadron needed to fly them to Scotland immediately, then bring back wounded, less able versions to be worked on at the factory. That was the flight she worried about most, because even the best pilot in the world was only as good as the engine and wings keeping him or her in the sky, and limping back in a damaged plane was never ideal. There would be no assigned flight mechanic at the other end to make sure they all made it home safely, that was for sure.

'I can't believe we're actually doing this,' said Amber, the youngest pilot of the group. Her voice wavered as she spoke, and May knew how she was feeling; her own bravado was more for the benefit of the other girls than a reflection of how she felt about their first real test. They'd waited all this time: so many months of her petitioning for women to have the right to assist the war effort in the sky, answering questions and refusing to take no for an answer, and then preparing the pilots to join her. Now they were finally going to be playing their part. This was it.

'See you soon,' May said, touching Amber's arm as she passed her, swallowing down a stomach-curdling wave of anxiety. 'You'll be great up there. We all will, and it's about time we proved exactly how we can help to turn the tide on this war.'

She winked at Betty and waved at the other girls before following the mechanic to her waiting plane. She'd been unsure whether to wait until last and wave her squadron off, or go first and lead the others into the air, but she'd decided that being first up would give the others confidence and cement her place as their leader.

The plane loomed, and Benjamin held out a hand to help her. She took it gratefully and climbed up, knowing she was being watched by every single male mechanic and ground crew member. Settling into the seat she took a deep breath and smiled as her gaze settled on the controls before her, zipping her flying jacket as high as it would go to stave off the cold and pulling her goggles down over her eyes. She was grateful for the leather hat keeping her head warm, and the fact that her big boots were lined with fleece.

*You're with me, Johnny*, she thought, squeezing her eyes shut and steeling herself as a wave of emotion shuddered through her, tightening in her chest like a knife piercing her heart. His death would not be for nothing. Her big brother had given his life fighting, and she was going to make certain that every plane the army needed was delivered to them until the day the Germans surrendered.

'*I'm sorry,*' she whispered. '*I'm so, so sorry, Johnny.*'

The loss, so recent and raw, gaped like an open wound inside her. But she was sure that however many weeks or months passed, or however long he was gone, it would never get any easier. And she still couldn't forgive herself for the way they'd parted, her so angry that he was allowed to fly for their country and she wasn't.

May sat tall, took a deep breath and put her hands on the controls, **pushing** down her emotions as she focused on her job, forcing Johnny to the back of her heart.

It was time to fly high and, freezing cold winds or not, she couldn't wait. Johnny's wings might have been taken from him, but she was doing this for him. She knew that wherever he was, she was making him proud: she was making it more likely that someone else's brother could make it home. Their boys needed these planes and nothing was going to stop her from delivering them.

# PART ONE

# CHAPTER ONE

## WASHINGTON DC, UNITED STATES,

## LATE 1941

## LIZZIE

Lizzie dug her nails into her palms as she waited to be called in to see Mrs Roosevelt. She was worried her heart might beat straight out of her chest if she had to wait a moment longer, but it had already been fifteen minutes and there had been no movement since she'd been greeted and invited to sit. Her father had told her to be patient and gracious, and she was determined to be quiet and not move an inch until she was asked.

'Miss Elizabeth Dunlop?'

Lizzie leapt up when she heard her full name, quickly smoothing down her skirt as she fixed her smile. A woman had appeared from behind a door and was now beckoning for her to follow.

'Sorry to keep you waiting,' the woman said pleasantly. 'Come right this way.'

Lizzie followed, surprised to find that her stomach was doing cartwheels. She'd been preparing what to say for weeks now, but knowing that this might be her one chance to convince someone influential to assist her was weighing heavily on her mind. She gingerly patted her hair, checking that her up-do was still in place, hoping she hadn't overdone her curls and make-up for such an important meeting.

'*Look everyone in the eye when they speak to you, but in a respectful way. Listen to them and give them your full attention,*' her father had said. '*And whatever you do, don't go interrupting anyone! You need to think carefully about every answer you give, Lizzie. No one likes a smart mouth or a know-it-all.*'

The door opened and Lizzie stepped in, her father's words filling her mind. Then she stopped in her tracks, taking in the scene in front of her: three people looked up, and only one of them was the woman she'd expected to meet. She immediately forgot all about her appearance.

'Elizabeth! It's so wonderful to see you again.'

Lizzie swallowed and propelled herself forward, forcing her feet to move and her mouth not to gape. 'Mrs Roosevelt, thank you so much for inviting me to lunch.'

She stepped into an embrace as the First Lady gave her a warm hug and a kiss to the cheek. They'd met twice before at various events, and both times she'd got the impression of immeasurable warmth. Today was no different.

'I could hardly not invite you after your last letter,' Mrs Roosevelt said with a laugh. 'Your powers of persuasion are rather impressive. And, please, while you're in my home, you're to call me Eleanor.'

'Eleanor,' Lizzie said with a nod, smiling as her hostess stepped back and extended an arm.

'Gentlemen, I'm pleased to introduce you to Miss Elizabeth Dunlop, the delightful young woman I've been telling you so much about.'

Lizzie held herself together as first the president rose and then the man in uniform beside him. She didn't know a great deal about military ranks, but for this man to be seated beside the president and sharing lunch with him, he must be extremely important.

'Lovely to meet you, Miss Dunlop.'

'Mr President, the honour is all mine.'

'My wife insisted that I clear time in my schedule to meet with you,' he said, one eyebrow raised as he spoke. Lizzie wasn't sure if it was a sign of amusement or not, but she guessed the president was too busy to mock anyone by making time to take lunch. 'This is General Henry Arnold. He's as curious as I am about this concept of women fliers, so I thought it best he join us.'

Lizzie's face was burning as she exchanged pleasantries with the general and sat down at the table, following the first lady's lead. Her father had talked about General 'Hap' Arnold, and she couldn't believe he'd come to meet her. Someone appeared with iced tea, and before long both men and Eleanor had their eyes trained on her. She was desperate to take a sip of tea; her mouth was parched as she tried to remember everything she wanted to say, but they were looking at her expectantly. For goodness' sake, she was about to share her ideas with the president himself!

'Miss Dunlop, tell us more about your thoughts on women fliers,' General Arnold said, taking the lead and shifting in his seat. Lizzie wasn't sure what to make of him yet, but the fact that he was waiting for her to speak was a good sign. 'I'm intrigued by what Eleanor has told me of your ideas so far, and I understand you've written quite a few letters to her on the topic. But I'd like to hear it from you.'

Lizzie sat up straighter, keeping her shoulders square and reminding herself not to speak too fast. This was her one chance and she wasn't going to waste it.

'I'm not sure if either you or Mr President are aware that we have almost three thousand women with pilot's licences here in America, according to government records. Many of these women would love to assist the military in the case of our country joining the war, including myself. I see our potential role as being non-combat pilots supporting the military.' She cleared her throat. 'I believe women fliers are capable of anything.'

It had been almost two years since she'd first started pushing the idea, and to finally be talking about it with someone who could make it happen was almost impossible to believe.

'And this support you're thinking of – it includes the ferrying of planes?' the general asked.

'Yes, it certainly does,' Lizzie replied, feeling more confident now that she'd got started. 'I would like to see women ferrying all kinds of planes, so our men are free to engage in combat. I envisage our women pilots doing everything possible to assist the military to ensure the smooth operation of our air force.'

'And what sort of girl would want to fly planes for the military, Miss Dunlop?' the general asked, exchanging glances with the president.

She paused, taking a sip of her iced tea and then levelling her gaze at General Arnold. He wasn't going easy on her, and she liked that. If he was, she'd know that he was merely humouring her, rather than taking her seriously – and, more than anything, she wanted to be heard. Her confidence rose as she prepared to answer him.

'A girl just like me, actually,' she said, giving what she hoped was a dazzling smile. 'One who has spent her spare time in the air for as long as she can remember, exploring the sky instead of playing with dolls and learning the piano. *That's* the kind of girl you'll find wanting to fly military planes.'

There was silence for a moment before the two men erupted into laughter, and Eleanor caught her eye, giving her a quick smile. Lizzie could understand that men had a difficult time with her love of flying – to them she was as feminine as could be, with her signature pink lipstick and her blonde hair curled and pinned. They thought that being a pilot was a man's role, and they couldn't fathom her desire to be in the sky when she should be consumed with thoughts of marriage and babies.

'She has you there, gentlemen,' Eleanor said, smiling and thanking a staff member who arrived with plates of sandwiches and a platter full of bread, cold meats and cheese.

'She certainly does,' the general agreed, nodding. 'Given that you're Lieutenant Dunlop's daughter, it doesn't really surprise me that you're so confident in the air, though. I suppose he had you up in a plane when you were knee-high to a grasshopper?'

'You know my father personally?' Lizzie asked, surprised.

'Miss Dunlop, every military man worth his salt knows *who* your father is,' the general told her. 'There weren't that many men awarded the Distinguished Service Cross in the Great War for five victories in the sky. It's one of the only reasons I entertained this meeting in the first place.'

She nodded, not sure whether to be happy her father's legacy had helped her, or annoyed that she hadn't been seen on her own merits.

'Now tell me,' President Roosevelt began, taking charge of the conversation, 'would you be personally prepared to train these women, if we allowed such a thing to go ahead? You genuinely believe you are up to the task of commanding a squadron?'

'Yes, absolutely,' Lizzie replied. 'I wholeheartedly agree with Mrs Roosevelt's recent comment that women are a weapon waiting to be used. With respect, Mr President, I honestly don't believe that you or the army could imagine how brave, talented and capable women pilots would be. You won't be sorry if you give us the opportunity – I can personally guarantee that.'

The president laughed. 'Miss Dunlop, my wife is a daily reminder of exactly how capable women can be. That's not something you need to convince me of, and it's the precise reason I'm sitting here listening to your ideas.'

'Who is it that I need to convince then? Because I'm not afraid of telling anyone what I want or why women should be included,' said Lizzie, as the others took their plates and slowly filled them with food.

Then she shut her mouth before she said anything too bold. She could almost see her father shaking his head in disapproval. She followed Eleanor's lead and took two small cut sandwiches, placing her plate in front of her even though the last thing she wanted to do was eat. Her mind was racing, her stomach still flipping back and forth as the enormity of what she was negotiating filled every cell of her body.

'Me,' General Arnold finally said, his voice deep and commanding. 'You need to convince *me*, Miss Dunlop, that I'm not a fool to be considering this idea of yours. I've looked into your flying credentials and I'm impressed by your skills and your passion, but the question is whether I want to put my reputation on the line for such a bold change in policy. And, frankly, whether you're the right woman for the job.' He shifted in his seat as he considered her, his gaze steady. 'Women have never been permitted to fly military planes, and in all honesty it might be best to keep things that way. We'd be taking jobs away from men who well need them, and I can only imagine what will be said to that effect.'

Lizzie nodded and took a delicate bite of her sandwich, forcing the mouthful down as she bided her time, a dry lump in her throat as words bubbled inside her. The last thing she wanted was him thinking she was hot-headed and incapable of taking criticism, even if most of the people who knew her well would describe her as exactly that.

'I respectfully disagree that we'd be taking jobs from men,' she said carefully, her heart pounding as she tried to keep her voice even. Her father wouldn't believe she'd responded so calmly. 'In the event of war, we'd be freeing men from those positions to allow them to fly in combat. We merely want to assist in any way we can, and put our flying skills to use. That's all I'm asking.'

'Gentlemen, perhaps we should eat lunch and then resume this conversation once you've both had time to consider the merits of Elizabeth's proposal,' Eleanor suggested. 'I think we can all agree that women would be more than capable of flying any plane the military might have, but it's a delicate subject.'

'With respect, Eleanor, we have planes that even some of our best men are frightened of!' General Arnold scoffed.

Lizzie bit her tongue. It took every inch of her willpower not to retaliate and argue with him, but she knew better than to cross a man in his position, who was giving her the time of day to present her case – especially when she felt she was so close to convincing him.

'How about you tell me more about your personal experience, Miss Dunlop,' the president said. 'I'd like to hear about how you won the Bendix Trophy Race. If I'm honest, that was the part of your resumé that intrigued me the most.'

Lizzie nodded in relief, feeling more at ease talking about her flying. 'It was probably the most exciting moment of my flying career, sir. It certainly made my heart race!'

Everyone seated at the table laughed.

'I'm well aware that you beat two men who are now general officers in the air force,' commented the general. 'Not to mention that you were also granted the world's most outstanding pilot award by the International League of Aviators. It's no mean feat to achieve such things.' He paused. 'And that, along with your determination over the past couple of years, means I will indeed be supporting the inclusion of women pilots, despite my inner conflicts about it, should the opportunity arise.' He smiled. 'Although something about you tells me I could live to regret that decision.'

Lizzie took a slow, deep breath. '*Should?*' she asked. The word continued to echo through her mind. '*Should* the opportunity arise?' She'd been certain he was going to **give** her the go-ahead then and there.

He nodded, frowning slightly. 'You heard correctly. We're not at war yet, so I don't see any need at this immediate stage to establish a squadron of women pilots to assist our military. But I do have a suggestion for you to ensure that we're well prepared.'

Lizzie held her breath. Her heart started to pound again and she dug her fingernails back into her palm, fist tightly closed. 'Oh?' she said, trying not to sound as if she were about to burst.

'Have you heard of the Air Transport Auxiliary in Britain? The ATA?' asked the general, glancing at Eleanor and receiving a nod in response.

Lizzie nodded too – she knew that women were already assisting the military in England. It was one of the reasons she'd hoped she was one step closer to seeing her vision realised.

'In short, it's a civilian division. They ferry planes all over the place, for the same purpose you've suggested, and I would like you to consider travelling to England to join the women's division for now – in an active role, of course. Primarily it will give you an understanding of their inner workings and experience of ferrying fighter planes and so forth. What do you say?'

Lizzie tried not to leap out of her skin with excitement, but it was impossible to suppress the smile that spread across her lips. 'What do I say?' she repeated, laughing as she traded looks with Eleanor. 'I say that's a brilliant idea! What plane shall I take to fly across the pond?'

'How about I make the travel plans and you follow orders,' he said gruffly. 'We don't want to send the army into collective heart failure over female pilots just yet.'

Lizzie beamed at the men seated in front of her. *England, here I come!*

# CHAPTER TWO

## LONDON, ENGLAND, JANUARY 1942

### RUBY

Ruby Sanders sat beside her mother and held out her cup for more tea, concentrating on keeping it perfectly balanced on the saucer. She reached for a cube of sugar and dropped it gently into the cup, cringing when she saw the look on her future mother-in-law's face. Carolyn sighed and pointed at the tiny tongs on the tray. Ruby didn't want a second sugar, but she smiled and reached for them anyway. The woman was a stickler for manners, and despite her best efforts, Ruby still managed to do the wrong thing almost every time she visited.

'Darling, if there's enough available, would you like silk and lace?'

Ruby nodded politely. 'Of course. Although I'm more than happy to alter my mother's dress if need be.'

'There's no need for hand-me-downs,' Carolyn said, visibly shuddering. 'I wouldn't hear of it!'

'Well, thank you,' Ruby said, squirming in her seat as she sipped her too-sweet tea. 'But only if it's not too much to expect, after the war.'

'If you want silk, we'll find silk,' Carolyn said with a curt nod. And Ruby believed her. She was certain this woman got everything she wanted in life, no matter how high the stakes. 'We certainly don't want this to be a *common* wedding by anyone's standards, now do we?'

'Mmmm, of course not.'

'But you wouldn't want to show too much skin. Modest is best, don't you think, dear?'

Ruby blinked away images of the pretty, deep V-neckline she'd been coveting, not about to disagree. 'Yes. Of course.'

*Tom.* That's why she was here. That was the reason she was even in this posh sitting room, pretending it was the most natural thing in the world to talk about silk and dresses and fancy cakes, despite the fact that her fiancé was away fighting, with his life on the line. The way Carolyn talked, it was like she expected the war to end and everything to go back to normal with a click of her fingers – almost as if they were pretending that Tom was away on business, and not part of a war!

'And white? Or cream? I think your beautiful peachy skin tone will look stunning no matter what you wear.'

Ruby smiled. She couldn't wait to marry Tom, but the finer details were lost on her. She just wanted him to make it home safely; however and wherever they got married wouldn't matter. *So long as I get my Tom back.*

'Ruby?'

She glanced up, realising how long she'd been in her own little world, daydreaming.

'Darling, you're a million miles away!' Carolyn exclaimed. 'We were just talking about cakes. Fruit cake with white icing, do you think?'

Ruby nodded politely, as she always did. 'That sounds perfect.' She was certain they'd discussed the cake every single time she'd come to visit, and they always all agreed on a fruit cake.

'Won't it be wonderful to see our two lovebirds finally united,' her own mother eventually said, giving her a strange look.

Ruby sat up straighter, trying to focus on the conversation. But she knew why she was so distracted. She glanced down at her bag, thinking about the advertisement she'd seen in *Aeroplane* magazine only a few hours earlier. It was burning a hole in her mind and she wanted to find the page again and make sure she hadn't dreamt it. It seemed an eternity since that scathing article she'd read about women pilots in the same magazine two years earlier; the tide was turning, and it wasn't so common to read negative feedback about women taking to the sky. In fact, everyone seemed to be applauding them now, after being so terribly mean to them in the beginning.

*Women pilots.* She'd read about May Jones and the First Eight with so much excitement at the time, but the idea of joining the ATA hadn't seemed like a real possibility to her, and she'd certainly never considered that she might be good enough. Flying for fun was one thing, but flying *warplanes*? She couldn't ever imagine being brave enough to put her hand up for that.

Ruby tried to imagine what it would feel like, climbing into a plane to deliver it to a military base, and almost laughed at the thought; it seemed so ridiculous. It would be incredible and so rewarding to help the war effort so boldly, but would she be capable of flying those types of planes? Was she cut out for flying so defiantly and taking risks like that? She sighed. Probably not. Not without Tom beside her in the co-pilot seat, guiding her when she needed him.

The wireless crackled into life, and Ruby jumped up to tune it, used to doing it for her parents, who were always glued to the news each night. She stood for a moment, listening, then shuddered when the announcer stated that Japanese aircraft had launched a surprise air raid on an airfield in Western Australia. Every bulletin **made** her fear for Tom, and she preferred to imagine him doing his job and coming home to her safely than worrying about every loss and casualty reported. She went back to her seat, hoping the Australian losses weren't severe.

'I pray to God they don't attack Australia like they did Pearl Harbor,' Carolyn said. 'It's unbelievable!'

'It sounds like a much smaller raid,' Ruby's mother replied. 'Surely we'll see some real progress in this war soon?'

'I'm certain of it. Now, Ruby, do tell me how your volunteering is going, dear? It must be very stressful trying to sort through all those letters.'

Ruby smiled politely, reminding herself that without this woman, she wouldn't have her Tom.

'Oh, it's going fine,' she said, deciding not to pull out the magazine and show them the advertisement. She found her role with the post office boring and nothing like her pre-war job as a flying instructor, but she was pleased to be doing her bit and getting on with things. 'It's nice to know I'm helping our soldiers stay in touch with their families.'

'Of course,' Carolyn said, reaching over to pat her hand. 'It's wonderful you young women are stepping up and being so brave.'

Ruby refused to look at her mother, knowing her expression would only make her laugh. She doubted her mother would ever think the job *brave*, but if Carolyn chose to think so highly of it, then so be it. *Necessary* may have been a better, more accurate description. Necessary to the war effort, but so very, *very* boring.

'Actually, talking about being brave,' Ruby said, choosing her words carefully. She paused to take a sip of tea before setting the cup and saucer down, rattling them with her shaking hand. 'I saw an interesting advertisement today, looking for more women pilots to join the ATA. You don't even need to be a qualified pilot to apply now.'

Carolyn's face froze for a second, then carefully composed itself again. 'Oh, well, no *wonder* they're having to advertise. They'd be hard pressed to find respectable women ready to brave the skies during wartime. It's hardly proper for women to do such a thing. Would you believe, I heard them recruiting on the BBC the other day? The *BBC* of all places!'

Ruby took a deep breath, deciding to contradict Carolyn for the very first time. How had she missed the recruitment messages on the

BBC when her father had the wireless on all the time, and why hadn't her darling mother-in-law-to-be thought to tell her about it in the first place? Anger flared within her; her cheeks burnt.

'I, um, well,' she stuttered, digging her nails into her closed fists. 'I was actually wondering whether or not I should apply.'

Carolyn's cup clattered to the floor with a smash. 'Absolutely not!'

The silence that followed was almost painful, until her mother dropped to her knees and started to collect the broken pieces of china from the small puddle of tea on the wooden floor. Ruby unfisted her hands, but she couldn't stop them shaking.

She bravely stared at the woman across from her as a wave of calm swept through her. It had only been a thought, something she might never have actually done; but the moment Carolyn forbade it, it was like a switch had been flicked within her. She cleared her throat and sat taller. She might not be good enough, but it wasn't for Carolyn to decide. That was for the ATA.

'Carolyn, I, ah . . .' she struggled with her words before forcing them out. 'I understand that it might come as a shock, but I'm actually a well-trained pilot and I'd quite like to give this a go. I have over three hundred hours of flying experience, and I think it would be amazing to assist those incredible women who are already . . .'

'What would Tom say?' Carolyn interrupted. 'If he was your husband, he wouldn't hear of any of this nonsense, I can tell you that. And *I* will not hear of it, for that matter. I'm speaking for him in his absence, and I expressly forbid you to register.'

Ruby bit her tongue and bent to help her mother to give her something to do. Short of saying that it was none of her or Tom's bloody business what she chose to do, and that they weren't married yet . . .

She scooped a piece of china into her mother's hand and touched her shoulder. She watched as a tiny prick of blood pooled on her finger where the china had pierced her, and tears filled her eyes.

'Mother, may I ask what you think?' she asked quietly. 'Would you be proud to see me ferrying planes to our boys fighting at the front? Or do you think I should ask Tom whether he forbids it or not?'

She was being rude, but she suddenly couldn't help it, even though she could feel how red her cheeks must be. Would Tom dare to tell her she wasn't allowed to fly? Was it so wrong for her to want to help her country with other brave female pilots? All those women were doing was helping their boys do their own jobs well by ferrying planes to them!

Her mother looked like she'd rather not answer the question, but she did so anyway. 'I wouldn't choose the role for you, but I'm very proud of those young women who've taken to the skies. It's your choice, if you'd like to apply.'

'Surely you're not going to let her do this, Sally?' Carolyn exclaimed. 'This is – well, it's, it's simply *preposterous*! I can't believe you'd allow it.'

Ruby sat down again and looked directly at her future mother-in-law, biting her lower lip before finally responding. 'Carolyn, I was a respected pilot before the war. Tom and I fell in love because of our mutual love of flying, and when he left, the hardest thing – other than not having him – was no longer being able to fly myself, when the airfield was closed to civilian fliers.' She spoke quietly and reached for Carolyn's hand, looking into her eyes, speaking the truth. 'I know in my heart that he'd be proud to see me flying again, especially if it meant helping the war effort in such an incredible way. And I *want* to do this. If I can be of service to the military, then I feel as if it's my calling.' She paused. 'Please can you accept my decision?'

Carolyn pushed her hand away, tears in her eyes as she stood and crossed the room to stare out the window.

'I won't allow it,' she said. 'I simply will not have my boy worrying about his fiancée doing a man's job when he's away serving. Would you dare to humiliate him like that, Ruby?'

She didn't answer, her eyes downcast. Her own mother had finished cleaning up the mess, and Ruby felt the warm touch of her hand on her back as she rejoined them.

'There are things our girls would never have dreamt of doing before the war, Carolyn,' Sally said gently. 'But we need to respect their changing role in society at this difficult time. It's not all about parties and flower arrangements these days, and we both know it. It'll be different when it ends, but everyone who can must step up.'

Ruby sat there, guilt weighing heavy on her shoulders. It wasn't in her nature to cause a fuss or upset anyone, but from the moment she'd seen the advertisement she'd known in her heart it was what she wanted to do, even if she wasn't sure she'd be accepted. She couldn't just sit by and listen to news of the war and do nothing! She was sick and tired of feeling so helpless, and of doing little but worry about whether Tom would ever make it home. She missed flying like she'd miss a limb, and with Tom gone it had been as if the two things she loved most in the world had been stolen from her. For years she'd flown at Stag Lane, where Tom had been her flying instructor, and the memories of being in the sky with him kept her awake at night, hoping and wishing that one day they'd be back there together. It had been the most exciting time of her life, learning to pilot a plane on her own, flirting with the handsome pilot four years her senior and eventually falling for him. When he'd first left she'd even gone on to work as an instructor for a short time, until all civilian flying had been halted.

'Will you at least ask my son's permission before doing anything dramatic?' Carolyn asked. 'Surely you need time to think about this, to at least get your father's permission if you're not going to seek Tom's?'

'She has *my* permission, and her father will be equally proud of her decision,' Ruby's mother said, her voice as soft as ever, but nevertheless filled with authority. 'I know everyone has their opinion about our female pilots, but they're doing our country proud and I'd be honoured for my daughter to be accepted to fly with them.'

'Sally!' Carolyn spun around, her eyes wide and her mouth gaping. 'You truly want to send your daughter to her death doing a job women shouldn't even be allowed to do? What good are women pilots when they'll never be able to fly as well as our men? It's ridiculous that the idea was ever entertained in the first place! And what do we do if women start getting thoughts in their head about doing men's work? We need them here, ready and waiting, for when our boys return!'

'Enough!' Ruby pleaded, looking from her mother to Carolyn. 'Please, can we just enjoy being together instead of arguing? I only wanted to share my ideas with you, not cause another war to break out.'

'Even if it means losing your fiancé?' Carolyn asked, her expression turning sour. 'Because lose him you will, Ruby. Mark my words.'

Six weeks later, Ruby held her breath as the train started to slow. She looked anxiously out of the window as they pulled into Maidenhead station, the anticipation almost impossible to bear. She smiled at the other two women seated across from her, wondering if they could hear her heart trying to hammer its way from her chest.

'Is it far from here?' a woman asked from behind her as the train slowed, then finally halted.

Ruby shook her head, the stranger's Australian accent taking her by surprise. 'No, not far at all. I'm Ruby,' she said.

'Polly,' the woman replied, holding out her hand.

Ruby shook hands with her and gestured towards the other two. 'This is Evangeline and Sarah.'

'Pleased to meet you both. I'm feeling a bit out of my depth here, so far from home.'

Before they had a chance to talk further they were signalled to disembark. Ruby collected her bag and headed for the door, her knees knocking so hard she could barely put one foot in front of the other.

They were to be met by cars and taken to the ATA headquarters at White Waltham, and she looked around the station, waiting for someone to step forward and show them where to assemble.

'Is it always so gloomy here?' Polly asked. 'I've been in the country for over a week and I haven't seen the sun yet!'

Ruby patted her shoulder. 'I'm afraid you'll have to get used to it. We're as famous for our thick grey clouds as you are for your sunshine in Australia.'

'This way, ladies!' A man with a clipboard gestured towards them. He called out all their names and then ushered them to three cars, lined up and waiting to ferry them away.

'Come on,' Ruby said to Polly. 'Sit beside me.'

As she climbed in and the vehicle pulled away, excitement mixed with terror started to pulse through her again. The last few weeks had passed by in a blur over Christmas, from sending off her written application to the ATA to being told within weeks that she'd been accepted, based on her flying credentials and references. And now she was here, about to meet May Jones herself and the other women she'd read about but never seen in the flesh before. Her nerves were still rattling, but she was heartened by the fact that some of the other women had never even flown a plane before.

'Have you been flying for long?' Polly asked.

Ruby turned to face her, liking her easy smile and bright blue gaze. 'Quite a few years, but nothing like this. You?'

'My father is mad on aircrafts, and I was the only child out of five that loved aviation as much as he did,' Polly shared. 'I've spent more time as a passenger than as the pilot, but I love being in the air.'

Ruby wondered if Polly was as uncertain as she was about making the grade, whether she was having the same flutter of nerves over climbing into a huge aircraft and knowing that the delivery of every plane could take them one step closer to winning the war. She shuddered at the thought, wishing she could clear her head and stop overthinking everything.

As the others in the car continued to chat, Ruby stared out of the window, her forehead touching the glass as they approached White Waltham. Would May change her mind and send some of them home before they'd even spent a day on base? What type of plane would she be flying? Would she have to undergo any formal tests or interviews?

'You look nervous,' Polly whispered in her ear as Ruby folded her hands tightly in her lap.

'I am,' she admitted. 'It's kind of hard to believe, you know, that we're actually here, that this could actually be happening.'

'Well, believe it,' Polly said, patting her folded hands as they pulled in. 'Because we *are* here and there's no turning back now.'

'Here we go, ladies,' the driver announced as he pointed out of the window. 'Head straight in there.'

Ruby pushed open her door and studied the flat-roofed, two-storey brick building that awaited them. She held up her hand to shield her eyes from the glare as the sun peeked from between the clouds, turning only when she heard a low wolf whistle.

She saw the men then, lounging outside another building, cigarettes in hand as they stared at the cars. *And at her.* She twirled the engagement ring on her finger, pleased she'd kept it there even though she didn't expect she'd be allowed to wear it for long. Or perhaps even *have* a fiancé for long if she didn't hear back from Tom soon. Clearly these men had been waiting to see the new recruits, and she knew that she'd never survive if she couldn't deal with a whistle or two in the field.

Ruby forced a smile and stood straight, waving a hand in their direction. 'Afternoon, fellas,' she said, hoping she sounded more confident than she felt.

Some of them waved back; others looked down at their boots as if they were embarrassed. *Serves them right*, she thought as she walked as determinedly as she could towards the nondescript brick building.

'I thought mechanics would be better-looking,' Polly whispered with a giggle.

Ruby averted her eyes, smiling as they made their way inside. The room was bare, with desks and chairs lining the walls and little else; and there they all stood, a growing group of women quietly chatting, until a strong voice cut through the noise.

'Welcome to our newest volunteers!'

Ruby turned as the room fell silent, and watched as May Jones herself walked towards the large desk in the corner. Her dark-blue dress uniform fitted her like a glove; the jacket was tailored to her frame and fit her perfectly and her tie was snug to her shirt. Something about seeing a woman so feminine yet so full of authority filled Ruby with both anticipation and fear, but the one thing she was certain about was that she wanted to wear that exact same uniform. And she'd do so brimming with pride.

'We need to get the basics out of the way first, so you'll all be having your medical check today, followed by an interview with me. I personally confirm with each new recruit that you've passed our tests, and our aim is to train you and get you in the air as soon as we possibly can.' She paused and took a quick sip of water, but Ruby still couldn't take her eyes off her. 'Once all that is out of the way, you will commence with ground school, which will cover everything from meteorology, map-reading, mechanics, navigation and so forth, and then you will progress to dual and then solo flights in the good old Tiger Moth. From there, you'll be required to fly a number of cross-country flights along fixed routes before being assigned to your ferry pool.'

May's dark gaze was steady as she appeared to study the room, her manner as perfectly composed as her uniform. The hopeful candidates all stared back at her.

'You're all doing something amazing by being here today, and I'm proud of every single one of you for volunteering for this role. If you have any questions, please ask me at your interview, and I'll be more than happy to discuss anything flying-related.'

Ruby expected someone else to take over now that the introduction was complete, but it was May herself who ushered a doctor into the room. She watched her check all the blinds were properly closed and then nod to the doctor, moving towards the front of the room to lock the door as they all looked on, wide-eyed like children who weren't sure what to expect. Her dark hair was cropped shorter than Ruby had imagined it would be – much shorter than the original photos she'd seen of her – and she wore barely a scrap of make-up, so she was much more serious-looking in real life. But she was pretty in a classic kind of way, with eyes as dark as her hair, full arched brows and a wide mouth.

'Ladies, this is Dr Arthur Barbour, the chief medic here at White Waltham, and you'll come to know him as Doc.'

He held up his hand in a wave and bowed to them. 'Ladies, it's a pleasure. I'll be doing our standard medical check today, so please come forward in an orderly fashion.'

Ruby followed him with her eyes as he set up in the corner of the room, pulling out a curtain attached to a metal pole. Not one of the women moved, including her.

'Who's first? I promise I won't bite,' he joked, although no one laughed back.

Ruby looked around, but still no one volunteered. She counted to five in her head, hoping someone else would speak up, and when nothing happened she slowly raised her shaking hand and gulped down her nerves.

'Um, ah, I'll go,' she said, clearing her throat and forcing herself to close the distance between herself and the doctor.

Doc's smile was wide as he looked her up and down, and Ruby suddenly wished she hadn't been so forthcoming. 'You'll find that my care for my pilots is second to none,' he said, his Scottish accent sounding friendly as he touched the small of her back, propelling her forward.

'If you'd please go behind the curtain and remove all your clothes, we can begin.'

Ruby's feet turned to lead. 'Excuse me?' she stuttered as heat flooded her cheeks. *No clothes?* She couldn't take her clothes off in front of a man!

'Your examination must be done naked. We have the same rules for men and women, no exceptions. I'm sorry, love.'

She turned to look at the women waiting in a group behind her, but the only one to meet her gaze was May. She walked forward, no doubt knowing precisely why Ruby was so ill at ease.

'It'll be over in no time,' May said briskly. 'I can be present if you'd prefer another woman . . .'

'No! No, I'll be fine,' Ruby said, regaining her composure. The only thing worse than the doctor seeing her naked would be having May herself watching on! 'It just took me by surprise, that's all.' She'd never been naked in front of a man before, not even their own family doctor. But if this was part of the job, it was part of the job, and she could either follow orders or get on the next train home.

Doc gestured again for her to disappear behind the curtain and she followed his instruction without hesitation this time, quickly taking off her clothes and folding them in a neat pile on the chair.

'Ready,' she called out.

He entered, and her face and neck burnt hot as his gaze swept quickly up then down, but she refused to do anything other than look straight ahead, no matter how tempting it was to cross her legs tightly and wrap her arms across her breasts.

Ruby endured the touching and prodding, the opening of her mouth and the eye check, and wondered why on earth she had to be naked for such a consultation. Couldn't she have kept her undergarments on, at least? If she were braver she'd have said something, but she couldn't have uttered a word if she'd tried.

Once it was finally over, and she felt more like he'd asked her to strip down to nothing for his own pleasure than out of any genuine medical need, she waited for Doc to leave her and blew out a breath she hadn't even known she was holding. Was that it? Had she passed? She was sure there was nothing wrong with her – no illnesses or disabilities – and her eyesight had always been excellent.

'Next, please,' she heard Doc request as she hastily pulled her clothes back on, not wanting the curtain to be drawn back to reveal her half-naked body to the rest of the girls.

Once dressed and back out in the room, Ruby took in the wide-eyed expressions of the other girls and felt pleased she'd got it over and done with. She cast a quick look at Polly and smiled, hoping she could tell that it hadn't been so bad.

'Miss Sanders, would you please follow me,' May requested.

Ruby jumped to attention and followed the woman she hoped was about to become her commander as she walked outside.

'Yes, ma'am,' she replied hurriedly, falling into step beside her.

'No need for such formalities – we all work together here, and I'd prefer you to call me May.'

Ruby nodded. 'I appreciate that. And you're to call me Ruby, of course.'

'Well, can I start by saying how pleased I was to receive your application,' May said, her expression hard to decipher as she stopped a short distance from the building and turned to face her. 'My only disappointment is that you didn't think to make contact with us earlier.'

'I should have, I know, but you all seemed so . . .' Ruby took a deep breath. 'What I'm trying to say is that I honestly wasn't sure if I was good enough, after hearing how talented you all are.' She sighed. 'I'm here now, though, and I'd very much like to be of assistance.'

'Indeed,' May said, seemingly unconcerned by her falter in confidence. 'I'm going to sit down and talk more closely with the other recruits, but I wanted to talk to you more directly and out of earshot.'

Ruby's heart beat a little faster. 'I'm not sure what I've done to deserve any special attention,' she said, but the moment the words left her lips she wondered if she'd been singled out because she was about to be sent home. 'Oh gosh, did I fail somehow already? Is that why you want to talk to me?'

'No! Oh no, it's nothing to worry about,' May said, finally cracking a small smile. 'Ruby, whether you believe it or not, you're one of the most capable and experienced pilots to apply in quite some time – well, on paper, at least. That's why I processed your application immediately.'

Ruby let the words sink in, surprised. 'I'm more than happy to fly with you now, if you need to see my ability,' she offered. 'I have no interest in overselling my skills as a pilot. I mean, I've only been flying for a few years and . . .'

'Stop,' May interrupted her. 'I don't want to hear you underselling yourself.' She gestured back towards the brick building. 'Those girls in there – they'll make great pilots if they have the will to succeed, and one or two of them have flown before. But it's going to take time to train the rest of them, time we don't necessarily have. One of the girls doesn't even have a licence to drive a car yet, and another has left her job as a professional ballet dancer to join us. They want to be here and I want to have them, but I need someone to join our Class II or Class III ferry pool that I can rely on.' She sighed. 'Almost immediately, in fact.'

'You don't have enough pilots in that division?' Ruby asked, confused.

'We *did* have enough, and now we don't,' May said, her disappointment clear. 'I've lost two of them just today. One is pregnant and had to be sent home, and the other simply didn't have the nerve for it. We don't have many girls leave once they've finished their training, so here's hoping today isn't the tide turning on my programme.'

'So you don't, well, *lose* any in the air?' Ruby asked, stumbling over her own tongue. Fear gripped her at the realisation that this wasn't flying for fun.

May's eyes met hers, and the commander tightened her lips. 'No – well, at least not yet. We've been lucky so far and I pray every day that the odds stay in our favour. We have to fly planes back from bases when they're marked as unserviceable, just to get them back to the wrecker's yards, and we have to fly every day without instruments or radios, so all my girls need to be vigilant and capable. We're a country at war, which means we're in danger every time we fly.'

When Ruby signed up, she'd known the risks; but hearing that no woman had yet died in the sky with the ATA was heartening, even if the lack of instruments and radios wasn't. She cursed the familiar, nervous shake of her hands and she clasped them tightly, hoping May hadn't noticed.

May took a step closer, studying her face. 'Tell me why you want to fly for us, Ruby. What made you write to me after seeing our advertisement?' Her expression was serious. 'Is it your sense of duty, your love of flying, or both?'

'Honestly, I read the advertisement and it hit me right here,' Ruby replied, fist to her heart. 'Flying is what I love most in the world, and since the war I've been grounded. The closest I get to it is reading my fiancé's letters about his work as an RAF pilot, and I'm sick of sitting around when I could be doing something truly useful, when *I* could be doing my part to help our boys instead of sorting mail and making cups of tea. Flying to me is like breathing, it's just . . .'

May's smile had a warmth that had been missing until then. 'You just want to get back in the damn plane, am I right?'

Ruby laughed. 'I suppose it takes a pilot to know one.'

May held out her hand and grasped Ruby's, palm to palm, fingers warm against hers.

'Ruby Sanders, will you do me the honour of joining the ATA? I want you up there flying every kind of plane we have before those other girls are even in a Moth, and within a few months I'd like to put you forward for Class V conversion so you can fly those four-engine bombers that every RAF squadron is so desperate for. Your record is impeccable and I believe that you're exactly what we've been looking for.'

'You're certain? Gosh, I feel like I should be asking for your autograph,' Ruby stammered, hardly able to believe the conversation she'd just had. *And a four-engine bomber?* 'Are you sure, are . . .'

'I'm no different to you,' May cut in. 'The only difference is that I've been doing this for longer and I was one of the first in the sky. Before long you'll have equalled my number of flights, and I'll be the one asking for your autograph.'

'I . . . I'd love to join you,' Ruby managed, finally voicing her answer even though her knees were knocking and she wanted desperately to tell May all the reasons she *shouldn't* be hiring her. 'Whatever you need me to do, the answer is yes.' She folded her hands together, excitement building as she thought about the adventure ahead. Part of her couldn't wait to write to Tom and tell him all about her new base, the uniform she'd be wearing and the ferry pool she'd been assigned to, but the other part was nervous about sharing her news with him. She'd already written to him when she'd been accepted, but his reply hadn't reached her yet and she felt anxious, especially in light of what his mother had said.

'Is there anything I can do to assist today?' Ruby asked.

'Just **walk** tall,' May said, as they headed back towards the building they'd been in earlier. 'I don't want anyone getting all fussy about your height.'

Ruby gulped and nodded. 'Will it be a problem?'

'Not if I have anything to do with it,' May muttered, holding the door open for her. 'As far as I'm concerned, it's nothing that a decent cushion on your seat can't fix.'

Ruby stifled a laugh. She had a feeling she was going to get on just fine with her new commander, but she still walked into the room as tall as she could to prevent anyone noticing just how short she really was.

# CHAPTER THREE

## ENGLAND, APRIL 1942

### LIZZIE

It wasn't very often that Lizzie was taken by surprise, but nothing had quite prepared her for the surge of anticipation that gripped her as their ship sailed closer to England. The four other women, pilots she'd hand-picked to go with her before the others joined the following month, had all enjoyed the crossing. Other than a brief diversion when, in the middle of a lively cocktail party, their captain had received instructions to change course due to submarine activity, the crossing had been uneventful. Well, that and the storm that had had them all heaving and clutching their stomachs.

It had taken nine days to reach England, and what with the plentiful food, wine and cocktails, and the company not only of her four travelling companions but also the others on board and the highly entertaining crew, she'd had little to complain about.

She went back inside her cabin to ensure her belongings were all packed, glancing briefly in the small mirror to check her make-up. The last thing she wanted was to arrive looking dreary instead of glamorous, though by all accounts England wasn't going to be anywhere near as exciting as she'd expected. Her girls had spent the past month living it up in Montreal at the Mount Royal Hotel, and she was certain they'd be envious of the fellow countrywomen they'd left behind, who still had plenty of partying time left. But she'd wanted to get her best fliers here as quickly as possible, because the sooner they made an impression, the sooner she could convince General Hap to give her her own flying squadron back on home soil. She gave her Mae West life vest one last look, the bulky safety device sitting forlornly on her bunk, grateful that she'd never had to get it wet. She still remembered laughing at the captain as he'd explained its name – it was aptly named for the actress's ample chest.

Back outside, the gloomy weather did little to dampen her excitement about arriving. She wanted to see what this May Jones had managed to **establish** here and figure out exactly how to build something bigger and bolder back home. America was at war now, too, and she knew how much women could do to help; and, of course, she longed to be back in the sky. The Japanese attack on Pearl Harbor had shocked her deeply, catapulting her country into the conflict, and she was more determined to fly than ever. All the training in Montreal had been good. It had given her girls a real taste of what they'd be facing on the other side of the pond, but now they were ready to put training behind them and help the Allies to win the war. A smile played across her lips as she imagined her first flight, showing off until she had all the ATA pilots standing in the field with their jaws slack. Doing their job and showing how useful women could be to the war effort was why she was here, but she also wanted to show everyone exactly what an American girl was made of.

'You've got a strong stomach,' commented Ann, coming out to join her. Ann was the first pilot Lizzie had chosen and she liked the friendly Southerner, her accent a nice reminder of home. 'The others are trying not to heave into the ocean.'

Lizzie laughed. 'I think perhaps it's the alcohol from last night and not the boat that's to blame,' she said dryly. 'But I'm sure the fish will enjoy it.' Her own stomach was heaving, too, but she wasn't about to let anyone see that.

Ann grinned back at her and held out a pamphlet.

'What's that?' inquired Lizzie.

'Apparently from the US War Department,' said Ann. 'Sandy discovered it earlier. I found her in hysterics. Want me to enlighten you on the *Instructions for American Servicemen in Britain*? I suppose we didn't qualify for an information pack, given that we're not service*men*.'

Lizzie smiled. 'Go on. I have a feeling this is going to be good.'

Ann cleared her throat dramatically. '*Don't be misled by the British tendency to be soft-spoken and polite*,' she read in a terrible British accent that made Lizzie chuckle. '*The English language didn't spread across the oceans and over the mountains and jungles and swamps of the world because these people were panty-waists.*'

Lizzie chortled, wiping at the corners of her eyes as she wondered who on earth had been charged with writing this propaganda. *Pantywaists?* She wished she could tell her father – he'd be in fits.

'Even more importantly, don't be a show-off. It says that here in bold,' Ann told her. 'The British strongly dislike bragging.'

'Well, honey, they're not going to like me one bit then, are they?' remarked Lizzie.

Her mother might have agreed with that point. She could still see her standing there, pleading with Lizzie not to go, imploring her to be happy with her own plane rather than heading off to prove herself to the world. Lizzie blinked the image away, refusing to let anyone, even her mother, sow seeds of doubt in her head.

Ann handed the pamphlet over. 'Enjoy the read,' she said, turning to go inside. 'Call me when it's time to finally put our feet on the ground.'

Alone again, Lizzie tipped her face back to the sky, wondering how the air could smell so different in a foreign country. She'd travelled far and wide in her own plane throughout America, but to be arriving somewhere by boat, at the mercy of a captain instead of her own piloting skills, was a different experience entirely. She'd thought leaving home would be so easy, and in some ways it had been, but waving her parents farewell and actually departing still played on her mind more than she'd expected.

An hour later their ship, the SS *Beaverhill*, had successfully docked. Lizzie was happy to be the first to head down the gangplank, her companions close behind, towards the crew who were lined up at the end of it, hats in hands. They'd been a fun and rowdy group to travel with; although there had been plenty of flirting and much drinking, they hadn't been anything other than respectful and Lizzie appreciated it as much for herself as for the women in her charge.

'I'm almost sad to say goodbye,' she said, laughing as the captain took hold of her shoulders and planted a big smacking kiss on her cheek.

Lizzie kissed him back, then walked down the line of men and kissed each one, enveloping most of them in big hugs. Some blushed pinker than she'd ever known possible.

'Thank you for the wild ride, sirs,' she said, smiling flirtatiously and watching the captain clutch at his chest as if she'd stolen his heart. She wouldn't miss the old converted coal liner – it hadn't exactly been the most luxurious vessel – but she would miss the jovialness of the crew.

Lizzie kept walking, looking for her point of contact. She'd been told that Commander Jones would meet them near the gangplank, but it wasn't until the crowd had thinned that she saw two women, both dressed in impeccable blue uniforms and looking very serious. She hoped this wasn't a sign of things to come after such an entertaining trip.

'Elizabeth Dunlop?'

Lizzie smiled and waved as she approached the slightly older of the two women. '*Lizzie*, please,' she said. 'And what kind of a welcome party is this? We expected bouquets and symphonies!' The two women looked at one another and Lizzie laughed at their puzzled expressions. 'I'm only joking. Sorry, we were warned how straight-laced you Brits were, weren't we, girls? Seems like the rumours were true.'

The four women with her were laughing, but the two women in front of her were not. She stared back at their bland, unimpressed expressions and sighed. This was going to be a long few months.

'I'm Commander May Jones,' the older woman said, with a frown. 'And this is Executive Officer Ruby Sanders. It's a pleasure to have you here to join us.'

Lizzie held out her hand. 'And it's an honour to join you ladies here, even if the laughs *are* going to be far and few between. Anyhow, it's good to have my two feet on solid ground again instead of lurching around at sea.'

They shook hands and she introduced the other four, noticing that her new associates still looked as though they'd sucked a lemon. 'This is Ann Foster, Sandy Freeman, Brooke Mayweather and Ruth Powers. They're my best four fliers and we can't wait to join you ladies in the sky.'

'Tell us about your crossing,' Ruby said as May led them away. 'We heard you were caught in a ferocious storm and had to pass by a German blockade.'

Lizzie shrugged. 'It was worth it to come here and fly, but I have to confess that knowing the last convoy lost six out of ten vessels didn't give us the most confidence.'

'You're telling us that now?' Ann shrieked. 'Those odds were terrible at best!'

'Tell me more about when we'll be flying. I hear we're to be put up at the Savoy in London,' said Lizzie, ignoring Ann's horrified question and stepping closer to May. 'I want to hear *all* about it.'

'Yes, you'll be at the Savoy. We'll be travelling to London by train in the morning, but tonight we'd like to invite you all to dinner at the Adelphi Hotel. We have a table booked for seven-thirty.'

'Sounds wonderful. One last fine dinner before we knuckle down and start work.'

Lizzie could almost imagine what they were thinking, these two prim and proper English roses. Was that what they called the pretty, porcelain-skinned women in England? They'd no doubt seen their brazen kisses and hugs of the ragged crew members, watched as they laughed and chatted and disembarked as if it was **all** an adventure, and were wondering what on earth Americans were about. Once they saw her flying, though, saw her determination in the air, they'd soon realise that any preconceived ideas were wrong. They weren't guests of the British government for nothing, and she was looking forward to showing them precisely why they'd been given such special treatment.

Lizzie walked through the restaurant and touched her hand to her blonde hair, gently patting her curls to make sure they were still perfectly in place. She was exhausted and ready to fall into bed, but she wasn't about to let her English sisters in arms think she didn't have the stamina to join them. She saw May and Ruby ahead, still dressed in their perfect little uniforms, and wondered if she'd dressed up a little too much for dinner with her new colleagues. Trouble was, she'd only packed one nice dress and a pair of heels to go out in, and as far as her hair and make-up went – well, she wasn't going anywhere without her trademark pink lipstick firmly in place. It didn't matter if she was flying or dining: she always wore a sweep of Chanel. She thought of her mother telling her to make herself look confident even if she didn't feel it, then firmly pushed away all thoughts of her and her sobs as they'd parted. Her daddy had held her tight, then given her a smile and a wink that told her everything she needed to know. '*You can do this,*' he'd whispered in her ear.

'Ladies,' she said as she approached the table. 'Sorry I'm late.'

They both smiled back at her, but May gestured to the vacant seats. 'We seem to be missing the others, too. Have you seen them?'

Lizzie grimaced. 'Oh, well, I tried to rouse them but it seems it'll just be the three of us.' It wasn't the best first impression they could have made, but they'd clearly been exhausted and she didn't want to be too hard on them yet. 'We had an intense training programme in Montreal and I expect they wanted a decent rest before travelling to London tomorrow.'

'I see,' May said abruptly, clearly annoyed. 'I expect they'll be more reliable once we reach our headquarters? We also have a rather intense training programme here in England, and I'd hate to think they're not cut out for it after coming all this way.'

'You won't have to worry about them. Drinks?' Lizzie asked, brushing the criticism off. 'What do you girls recommend on this side of the ocean?'

A waiter appeared and May spoke up. 'Three Pimm's, please.'

Lizzie noticed Ruby's raised brows.

'Since when do you drink?' Ruby asked.

'Since our American cousins stood us up,' May replied tartly.

Lizzie stifled a laugh at her rigid response. 'It's only dinner, May. Don't get your knickers in a knot. And do tell me what a Pimm's is, would you?'

May's stare was as cold as ice. 'That's *Commander Jones* to you, and I'll have you know that I wouldn't accept this level of tardiness from even my newest recruits. Your pilots should be here.'

'My apologies, *Commander*,' Lizzie said, giving her a mock salute before laughing; the look on the other woman's face was almost comical.

'A Pimm's is alcohol and lemonade mixed together,' Ruby interrupted in an obvious effort to diffuse the situation. 'Before the war we'd mix fruit with it – it's divine with summer berries thrown in.'

Lizzie sat back and considered the women in front of her. She wasn't sure exactly how Ruby fitted in, but May was clearly her superior, and from the way Ruby kept glancing at her, it was obvious she wanted to please her. Perhaps she was new to flying, or at least newly recruited. May was clearly the one she needed to impress, not her little sidekick, and they'd already got off on the wrong foot.

'So tell me,' Lizzie said, addressing May. 'What's it really like flying those beautiful big planes day in, day out?'

The look on May's face softened a little. 'The day you first fly a plane that you know scares the heck out of men? Nothing beats that feeling,' she replied. 'Knowing that you're delivering it, and that within hours it could be shooting at the enemy – it's incredible.'

'So what kind of planes will I be able to get my hands on?' Lizzie asked. 'Anything exciting?'

'Well, Spitfires to begin with,' May said. 'Depending on your aptitude, you may be put forward for the larger four-engine bombers, but we haven't had a woman cleared to fly one yet. Training is soon to begin at our all-female airfield in Hamble, and in fact they're making quite a big deal about who might be the first to officially fly one.'

'Sounds like just the job for me then,' Lizzie said with a wink, stifling a laugh when May's face turned to stone. 'If you're not earmarking the position for yourself, that is?'

'We'll see about that,' May muttered. 'But no, it won't be me. I'm too busy with administration to be in the running, but it'll be quite the honour for the chosen pilot.'

'Well, regardless of the aircraft, it must be amazing, flitting around in a warplane all day.'

'Flitting?' May asked, now openly scowling. 'My girls are hardly *flitting*. With intense flying schedules, multiple planes to deliver daily and weather concerns, my pilots are in life or death situations every time they report for duty. Not to mention that we're doing this because we're a nation at war!'

Lizzie held her hands up. 'Bad choice of words. I was only meaning . . .'

'You were only meaning what? That my ladies are out there having fun? Because they're not, Miss Dunlop – they're out there working hard to make sure we actually have a damn chance of winning this war and bringing our boys home safe.'

Her words were low, snapped almost, and Lizzie knew she'd probably gone too far. But if the English rose couldn't handle some teasing, then she shouldn't be running a squadron.

'So have you lost any pilots yet?' Lizzie asked, sitting back and crossing her legs at the ankle. 'In these *life and death* situations?'

'No,' May said, her eyes narrowing. 'We've had some close calls, but our fatality rate is zero and I'm extremely proud of that fact. And trust me, there's not a day that goes by that I don't pray to keep it that way.'

Ruby touched May's arm then, a gesture that took Lizzie by surprise. 'Tell her,' Ruby said softly.

Lizzie gazed back at them. 'Tell me what?'

'We fly with no instruments and no radios, so when I say that my girls are the best? I mean it. It takes more than good skills to fly that way, *Elizabeth*, it takes guts and a good dollop of determination.'

'No radios?' Lizzie asked. 'Is this a joke?'

'It's no joke that our superiors don't want our movements or whereabouts to be detected, and we're not trained to fly with instruments. We're at *war*, Elizabeth, in case you've missed that very important fact.' May's smile started slowly, like a match to a wick, spreading down the line. 'If that sounds too hard, you're more than welcome to board a ship and head home.'

Lizzie smiled straight back, clenching her toes, not about to let May see that she'd thrown her off balance. 'Radios, instruments, bad weather? Honestly, I don't know what you're making such a fuss about. I'm sure it's all in a day's work for you lot now, and the same will be true for us.'

Lizzie shook out her hair, tipping her head back as the waiter arrived with their drinks. She reached for hers gratefully and took a big gulp. What kind of fools would be expected to fly without radios? It was ridiculous! But she simmered silently, for now; once she was on base, then she'd start to make a fuss.

'I have a feeling you're newer to this whole thing,' she said eventually, to Ruby. She'd noticed how perfectly starched her uniform was, as if it were almost brand new. 'Am I right?'

Ruby's cheeks coloured slightly, but Lizzie pretended not to notice as she took another sip. The younger of the two women was tiny – so petite and short, in fact, that Lizzie wondered how she'd even passed the minimum height requirements.

'You're right,' Ruby replied. 'I haven't been with the ATA for long. Only months, actually.'

'So you're the commander's little sidekick then? Or are you her office girl?'

'*Office girl?*' Ruby spluttered. 'No, I'm a pilot, I mean I . . .'

'Ruby is no sidekick, nor is she relegated to office duties,' May interrupted. 'She might look like a doll – in fact I was told by our doctor that a gust of wind might blow her over – but put her up in the cockpit and she's got the heart of a lion and the bravery of a team of men. Not to mention she's highly experienced as a pilot.'

Now Ruby's cheeks were positively scarlet.

Lizzie laughed, and winked at her. 'I was wondering how she'd snuck in past regulation height. I'd have sent her home the moment I laid eyes on her, experienced or not.'

'We're not exactly drowning in women pilots with more than three hundred hours' flying experience, so when an application like Ruby's passes by my desk, I don't give a damn about height restrictions,' May said. 'Women were required to have more than five hundred hours' flying experience in the beginning, but the rules have eased somewhat. Now that we've proven we can be trusted not to break their planes, of course.'

Lizzie chuckled then, finally seeing something about the Brit to like. 'If a man had to demonstrate three perfect landings, a woman would be asked to do six just to prove herself, am I right?'

'Precisely.' May held up her glass, nodding. 'Lizzie, it must be frustrating not to have your own national women's squadron established yet.'

'After Pearl Harbor I expected to hear news immediately, but so far all they want is their best women pilots flying with you Brits. No offence, but I'd rather be flying American planes in American airspace instead of being sent on some glorified work experience mission on the other side of the world.'

May shrugged. 'No offence taken. I'd feel exactly the same.'

'Now, tell me, how did you start flying?' Lizzie asked, deciding to at least try to get along with her new colleagues. 'And how in God's name did you manage to convince a bunch of old men to let women ferry fighter planes? I've been petitioning for years – I want to wring all their wrinkly old necks!'

'Do you have all night?' May asked, brows arched high. 'Because I did the same. The only reason we finally received a green light was because they needed us, pure and simple. And to be honest, after the Battle of Britain, we simply didn't have enough trained pilots left. We literally ended up losing a quarter of our RAF pilots and they couldn't spare any for ferry work. It was suddenly a case of them looking foolish by not using us, and you'll no doubt find the same thing will happen in your country. They'll need you, and then it'll be the army chasing you, not the other way around.'

Lizzie waved the waiter over. 'Another round of these, please,' she said. 'And what are we eating, ladies? Is there steak on the menu? I'm ravenous! Please tell me you can do a decent steak here?' The waiter nodded. 'Well, steak it is then,' she continued, as the other two ordered. 'Now, Commander Jones, tell me about your first flight. When did you become a pilot?'

May settled back in her chair. 'I was what my parents called a flying addict when I was growing up. I was always trailing around after my older brother, begging him to take me up with him,' she said, a smile playing across her lips. 'When I finally started having lessons on my own, I learned at Brooklands, which was a pretty famous flying club here before the war. We both learned there. Then I went on to work for my uncle, taking punters up for joy rides. I suppose flying was in my blood.'

'And your brother? Is he a pilot?' Lizzie asked, intrigued. 'I bet he's one of the best in the air force now?'

'My brother is an excellent pilot,' May replied quickly. 'Better than I'll ever be.'

Silence fell, and Lizzie cleared her throat. 'The commander of her own squadron thinks a man is better than her? I expected more from you, Jones.'

When May's gaze met hers, it was cold, the warmth completely gone. 'I'm merely stating a fact, Elizabeth. He is a truly exceptional fighter pilot, and I give credit where credit is due.'

Lizzie held up her hands; she'd clearly hit a button. 'And I apologise. I didn't intend to get off so thoroughly on the wrong foot with you.'

May didn't respond, other than to cross her knees and fix her gaze on Lizzie, who wondered exactly what nerve she'd hit. She couldn't figure it out. She'd researched May Jones and her crew months ago, and there was little professionally that she wasn't aware of.

'So, tell me,' she said, changing the subject. 'What does this *Attagirls* saying mean? I understand it's a play on words, but . . .' She let the question hang.

'It's slang, something we say to encourage a young woman here. Like, that's a girl, you can do it,' Ruby explained, finally speaking up. 'So it's a play on that saying.'

Lizzie watched as May smiled up at the waiter when he arrived with their meals, seeing how warm she could be when she wanted to be.

'There's a bit of a joke here that ATA stands for *ancient and tattered airmen*,' Ruby said, leaning in a little closer. 'And they love nothing better than calling us the *always terrified airwomen*, because they know it drives us all mad.'

'And it couldn't be further from the bloody truth,' May swore.

They all laughed, and Lizzie picked up her knife and fork to eat her steak. It was served with mashed potatoes and peas, covered in a dark sauce that smelt delicious, and she suddenly realized how hungry she was.

'So what's next, ladies?' she asked, after a mouthful. 'We travel to London tomorrow and then what? Will I be in the air immediately? Will you have me flying the biggest, baddest bombers on day one?'

'We check you into the Savoy and then have you measured for uniforms at Moss Bros,' May said in a no-nonsense tone. 'And then it's off to White Waltham, although your lot won't be taking the train from Paddington like most of our girls. I have two borrowed Daimlers for you to drive up instead. Heavens, you can drive, can't you?'

Lizzie grinned. 'Honey, I can fly a plane. Of course I can drive an itty-bitty car. And my first flight? When will that be?'

'You'll have your first flight when you've proven yourself to me,' May said. 'I don't care whether you've been sent by the president of the United States himself, you will have to earn your stripes, Elizabeth. So, no, there will be no first flight in one of our expensive bombers on day one.'

'Here's to us then,' Lizzie said, holding her drink high and ignoring May's curt words. 'And all those brave girls who've followed the call of duty.' The empty chairs to her left caught her eye as they clinked glasses. Her girls had embarrassed her by not attending, but being tardy wasn't a mistake they'd make again – not on her watch, and not when she was up against a commander as straight as an arrow.

'To us,' May replied, with a slow smile. 'And to seeing what you Americans are made of in the sky.'

Lizzie sipped her drink, ready for the challenge. Commander Jones was going to swallow her words when she saw her in the air. *I'll make you proud, Daddy. Just you wait and see.*

# CHAPTER FOUR

## ENGLAND, APRIL 1942

### MAY

The train rumbled out of the station and May rested her head back against the seat, the motion making her crave sleep. She felt as if she hadn't slept properly in years: her eyes were burning, her bones aching, begging to rest for longer than a few hours at a time. She remembered thinking she was tired before the war, when she'd wake up and wish for just one more hour of slumber, but she'd never truly known what tired was, and she hoped never to know sleep deprivation like it again once the war was over.

Sleep had been hard to come by after Johnny had died; her nights had been full of horrific dreams that left her in a tangle of sheets, crying out for the brother she'd lost. Talking about him tonight, pretending he was still with them, had been stupid, but it had also been the only thing she could do to avoid falling to pieces.

'Why do you get to fly off to war, when I'm stuck here twiddling my thumbs?' she demanded.

'Because I'm a boy,' he teased. 'And you're supposed to be sitting at home knitting, waiting for your darling brother to return.'

'Ugh!' she screamed, throwing a book at him, furious when he caught it in one hand and calmly threw it back to her. 'I hate you sometimes.'

'The feeling's mutual.'

'But why? Why is it fine for you to go off and be a fancy fighter pilot, and I have to stay home? Why can't I fly? Why is it so impossible to imagine that women could do it too? Why can't women help to win the war if we can fly as well as men?'

'Not women,' Johnny said, his hands pushed into his pockets. 'Just you. I've never seen another girl fly like you, May.'

'Tell them about me,' she begged. 'Tell your superiors that I should be given a chance. I can fly a plane as well as you can and you know it. I can't just sit here and let our country get bombed to oblivion without doing something!'

'No.'

'Johnny!' she demanded. 'Please.'

'You think I could do that to our parents? And you think I wouldn't be laughed off base, for a start?' he muttered. 'Seriously, do you know how ridiculous that sounds?'

'Just go then,' she whispered, tears choking her.

'Come here,' he said. 'Give me a hug goodbye. I don't want to leave like this.'

May turned her back. 'Just go.'

She listened, knew he was still standing there in her room, that he was waiting for her. But when he came close and touched her elbow, she yanked it away.

'I love you, sis,' he called, as she still stubbornly refused to look at him, tears raining down her cheeks for the brother she couldn't bear to be parted from. 'I'll miss you.'

'I'll miss you, too,' she whispered to herself, as she fell onto her bed and cried. When she heard the bang of the front door, she went to her window and pressed against the glass, one hand raised as she watched her brother leave.

May clenched her jaw as she fought the memories, as she relived the last day she'd seen her brother before he'd been taken from them. Why had she been so stupidly immature? She quickly wiped at her cheeks, her body turned away from Ruby slightly, grateful that she had the window seat.

'Do you think it was unusual that the others didn't turn up for dinner?' Ruby asked quietly.

May forced her eyes open, not wanting Ruby to see how exhausted she was, or how much she was struggling. She'd never told anyone about Johnny, about how deeply the loss had cut into every part of her being, and she meant to keep it that way. She'd been quick to laugh, before he'd left; always the one to sit up late with him and his friends playing cards, go to dances, sneak off to run barefoot across the grass down to the river for a swim. But now it was so much easier to shut herself off and not feel anything, other than her determination to keep her girls alive and to help end this bloody war. Seeing Lizzie with her carefree attitude and easy smile had rattled her more than she'd realised. She'd never been rude or full of herself like the American, but something about her had reminded her of how fun life had once been.

'Highly unusual,' she agreed, clearing her throat. 'They'd only been at sea for just over a week, and they're not exactly here on vacation.'

'She was something else though, wasn't she?' Ruby commented, her eyes wide. 'I mean, the things she said!'

May raised her eyebrows and did her best to reply diplomatically. 'All we can do is hope that our newest pilots remember what we're all doing this for.'

'Well, I think it's all just an adventure to her.' Ruby sighed. 'I've never met anyone like her.'

May shut her eyes again, deciding it wasn't such a bad thing for Ruby to see her sleeping. If she were a man serving his country, would she be so concerned about getting some well-deserved shut-eye? Sometimes she felt as though she had to work ten times harder than any man, fly double the planes and do it all with a big smile and her lipstick perfectly in place. She imagined Johnny teasing her about wearing lipstick for a flight, asking whom exactly she was trying to impress. It was a weird, bone-deep pain, knowing that he was gone, but still feeling like he was with her.

She heard a rustle of paper and opened her eyes, but it was only Ruby unfolding a letter.

'From your family?' she asked politely, glad of the distraction. It wasn't often she let her thoughts drift to Johnny, and she wondered if it was the alcohol bringing down the barrier she was usually so good at keeping in place.

Ruby smiled across at her. 'My fiancé, actually. I've been waiting to read it since we left London.'

'You've had a letter all this time, burning a hole in your pocket?' May asked, incredulous. 'You silly girl! You could have asked me for a moment in private or read it on our trip here.'

Ruby shook her head. 'I take my job very seriously and . . .'

'How often do you hear from him? Every other month?'

Ruby's shoulders dropped. 'Sometimes. But I've been waiting to hear his thoughts on my joining the ATA, so it's been months, actually, and . . .' Her voice drifted off as she clutched the letter. 'I'm certain that he'll be supportive but there's this little niggle of doubt in my mind, and I almost don't want to read it to find out. His mother was furious with me for even making an application to join you.'

May sat forward, her tiredness momentarily forgotten as she clasped Ruby's hand. 'Loving your fiancé and looking forward to his letters doesn't make you weak, Ruby. The more we have to live for and look forward to after all this, the better we'll be at our jobs. It's what gives us our fighting spirit.' She smiled. 'And I bet your man is incredibly proud of you.'

Ruby's eyes were glistening with unshed tears. 'Thank you.'

'Now read away, and don't you hide another letter for my benefit. You need to embrace your family, and your fiancé, and any contact you get with them.'

The words came easily to her; she just wasn't so good at putting them into practice herself. She quelled her emotions as she remembered her own family. Her mother, who'd always seemed so statuesque with her straight shoulders and bright blue eyes, had been a tiny figure, doubled over, at Johnny's funeral. And she'd been the same when May had left, curled in an armchair, barely even able to look up. Whenever May thought of her now, that was all she could see, and the memory haunted her almost as much as her last conversation with her brother.

Ruby's eyes had already dropped and she held the letter like a precious flower, greedily soaking up its contents as May watched her. But then her face fell, and all colour seemed to drain from her cheeks.

'Everything all right?' May asked, feeling a familiar wave of anxiety. She still remembered reading the letter about Johnny that told her he was gone, and the pain of seeing those words on the page.

Ruby looked up, eyes filled with tears. 'Can I read it to you?' she asked, her voice trembling.

'Of course. Share away.'

Ruby frowned, staring at the paper before reading:

'My darling, you know how much I loved to fly with you, and I am very much looking forward to flying together once more when I return after the war is won. But, sweetheart, you've upset Mother terribly, and I would appreciate it if you could end this little, well, expedition that you're on and return home as soon as possible. I admire your ability, of course, but I agree with her that it's not appropriate for women to be in the air during wartime. What must your own family think? I understand that you might be annoyed to receive this – Mother made it clear that you thought you'd have my support on this matter – but I cannot have you upsetting her or flying with those other women. This is a job for men, and, well, I don't want to discuss the matter further. I expect to hear that you've apologised and mended things with her, because I certainly don't want this to come between us. You're a wonderful pilot, Ruby, when we're flying for fun, but it's a serious business flying during the war, and I cannot condone it.

I am doing well, although dreaming of home-cooked meals, a good bed to sleep in and coming home to you, of course. It's a thrill and honour to be flying such incredible planes, but I'd rather be home.

Yours always, Thomas.'

Ruby looked distraught as she dropped the paper to the seat beside her, and May smiled sadly, seeing what his words had done to her. She wasn't surprised that her fiancé wasn't supportive – far too few men were, despite the assistance the women gave them every day in the air. 'I take it his mother has been in touch with him about her *disapproval*?'

'Disapproval?' Ruby choked, shaking her head. 'I think that would be putting it mildly. Her intention was to write to Tom and insist he call our engagement off. She didn't actually think I'd go through with it, so perhaps she waited and thought I'd change my mind.' She brushed her cheeks with her fingers, then her voice dropped to a whisper. 'I honestly thought he'd support me on this. I thought he'd be so proud, and that he'd tell her to sod off. And he's gone and said exactly what I was worried about – that I'm good at flying for *fun*. I knew he'd think I wasn't good enough without him as my co-pilot.'

'For some reason, men find it incredibly hard to understand the capabilities of women,' May said carefully. 'And your man might come around to it, but right now he's under the influence of his mother, so you either quit and keep them both happy, or you prove to him exactly how capable you are. And don't for a second let me hear you doubting your own abilities, because I will not stand for it. Am I making myself clear?' May would have wrung Tom's scrawny neck if she knew where to find him. 'And it's not just me who needs you, Ruby. Our *country* needs you, because without us? There would be nowhere near enough planes going to the front. There would be no planes coming home from the front to be repaired. Do you hear me? Our boys need us more than they even know.'

'Yes, loud and clear.' Ruby stuck her chin out and May recognised the steely glint in her eye, the change in her demeanour as her words sunk in. 'I won't be quitting.'

She nestled back into her seat, carefully folding the letter and putting it in her pocket. The poor girl should have been able to happily re-read that letter each night to boost her spirits, but instead every time she thought about it she'd remember that her man didn't support her. At times like this, May was pleased she didn't have a sweetheart, for the very reason that she didn't need anyone doubting her abilities or trying to tell her what to do. Dealing with her own mother and everything they'd been through as a family was more than enough for her and, in any case, she had no room left in her heart. It was too broken to let anyone else near.

'Do you have a special someone?' Ruby suddenly asked, breaking into her thoughts.

May tried to make herself more comfortable, wishing they'd stayed the night at the hotel with the Americans instead of trying to make a point and travelling back so late. 'No, I don't.'

'Well, you're lucky then,' Ruby said, still tearful. 'Worrying about them not coming home is the worst.'

May fought not to lose her composure. 'I'm sure it is.'

Sitting silently, keeping her pain to herself, it was as if she'd been punched in the stomach, the wind knocked out of her as somehow the right words came out, words she always said because it was easier than admitting how heartbroken she actually was, how acutely she knew the feeling of waiting for news, only to find out that a loved one had been taken.

They sat quietly then, the rumble and vibration of the train helping May to block out her thoughts. She snuggled deeper into her jacket, drawing it tighter around herself as she gave in to a few stolen moments of the sleep that she needed more than she'd ever needed it before. *Before the nightmares clawed at her and made her too terrified to fall into slumber until the next night, when it started all over again.*

'Benjamin,' May said to her flight mechanic, her hands so cold she could barely wiggle her fingers as she stood in the hangar the next morning at dawn, 'I need you to double- and triple-check everything for me again. I just, I don't know, I have this feeling that we've pushed our luck, that we can't keep on flying without one of the girls . . .'

'Stop,' he said calmly, passing her his mug of coffee. 'Have some of this. How long have you been up? Did you even sleep last night?'

She looked down at the coffee, and when he bumped the mug gently upwards she finally raised it and took a sip. She wasn't about to tell him that sleep was a luxury she could barely afford with the workload and stress that she'd been under lately. Or that she'd merely catnapped the night before on the train ride home.

'Thanks,' she murmured.

'Now come with me. I want to show you this Spitfire.'

May followed. Within minutes her pulse slowed as Ben walked her through every part of his drill, and every important part of the engine.

'When you understand how an engine works and what I do to make sure it's running well, you don't have to fear the unknown,' he said, taking back his coffee and drinking down what was left of it. He led her around the Spitfire to another that was in the same hangar. 'We can do this every day, and I can walk you through what I've done, and triple-check what I've already double-checked, or you can trust that I want to keep our pilots safe, too.'

May stared at him, painfully aware that he was treating her as his equal, just as her brother always had when it came to planes. He'd loved nothing better than to beat her in the sky, but he'd never made her feel that she wasn't every bit as capable as he was.

'Thank you.'

'You're welcome.' He grinned. 'But you do owe me a coffee.'

She nodded. 'Of course. And sorry for being such a pain, making you show me around when you have so much work to do. I'm just so grateful you transferred here to White Waltham with us.'

Ben's laugh was belly-deep. 'You're not a pain, May. You're in command of a squadron of pilots, and you've shown me that nothing is more important to you than keeping them alive.'

She smiled back at him, wanting to be happy, wanting to enjoy his company. But smiles no longer came easily, even when she wanted them to. Not after the trauma of the last few years.

Three hours later, with her head pounding from the rough sleep she'd had on the train home and the multiple cups of coffee she'd already consumed, she walked inside the main office building to a heated argument that made her forget all about Ben for the moment. There were a handful of pilots gathered, standing quietly on one side of the room, and a very angry-looking Elizabeth Dunlop standing in the centre with her hands planted on her hips.

'Absolutely not!' Lizzie exclaimed, her voice loud and her accent unmistakable.

May looked between a furious, red-faced Lizzie with her four pilots standing demurely beside her, and Doc, who appeared as livid as the American.

She fought the urge to collapse onto the nearest chair and massage her temples. It had already been a long morning, and by all accounts it wasn't going to get any easier now that their guests had arrived.

'What's going on in here?' she demanded. When Polly had come running for her, she'd made it sound like a bloody war was about to break out, and she hadn't been wrong.

'This *imbecile* is trying to tell me . . .'

May interrupted her, holding up her hand. 'By *imbecile* I am to presume you're speaking of our good doctor here? The doctor who presides over *all* of White Waltham and is highly respected in his field?'

Face like thunder, Lizzie glared at her, while Doc appeared ready to explode. It wasn't a situation May had ever had to handle before. What was it with this American woman? She seemed to rub everyone, herself included, up the wrong way.

'How dare she speak to me like that!' Doc threw his hands in the air. 'Commander Jones, please tell me you're going to reprimand this, this *heathen* of a woman? I will not stand for it!'

In truth, May had no idea what she was supposed to do, other than get to the bottom of the problem and put an end to the ugly name-calling. The Americans were guests here, not to mention well-trained pilots, but the doctor was equally as important to their operations. A big boom echoed outside and May grimaced, wondering what on earth the mechanics or male pilots were doing. It certainly wouldn't have been one of her girls causing such a noise.

'Doc, Miss Dunlop and her pilots are very important to our squadron, and vital to our relations with the United States,' she said firmly, looking between the two of them as if she were reprimanding naughty children. 'And Elizabeth, Doc here is a very capable and highly respected doctor, and I would like you to treat him as such. Can we keep all of that in mind, please, as we move forward?'

Lizzie gave her a pleasant smile, but May got the feeling that she was like a lion baring its teeth before going in for the kill.

'Tell me then, *good doctor*, why exactly do pilots need to be examined in the buff?' Lizzie asked, her perfectly arched eyebrows making her face look oh-so-innocent. 'Would you like me to take my colleagues straight back home and tell the president exactly what perverted English doctors do to female pilots?'

Doc gaped first at Lizzie and then at May, his mouth starting to move but no sound coming out. May should have spoken up; she knew she should have reprimanded Lizzie, but in truth what could she say? There *was* absolutely no reason for them to be examined naked when he was primarily checking their height, weight, hearing and eyesight, and they'd all been made to feel uncomfortable at their initial medicals. She should have taken a stand herself well before now, but unlike the brash American, she'd been too afraid of women being turned away for being difficult. She lived in constant fear of speaking up in case they were discarded for being – well, for being women. In this case, she was going to let Lizzie get away with her insolence.

'Pick up your stethoscope and get to work, *Doc*,' Lizzie said, impatiently stamping her foot. 'We've got planes to fly and I won't stand for being grounded because of your utter incompetence.'

If this was a sign of things to come, then May was definitely going to have her hands full when the rest of the Americans arrived. But rocking the boat was one thing; she wasn't going to let them capsize the whole bloody vessel. Later, when they were alone, she might have to remind Elizabeth that nothing was more important than assisting the war effort – no person and certainly no policy, no matter how much she might not like it personally. Lizzie needed to lead her women and understand how high the stakes were, because May didn't have time to be a babysitter.

'Jones?' Doc spluttered. 'Are you allowing this?'

'You heard her, Doc. I'm not impressed with the delivery, but she's right. Can we please get their examinations over with, and clothes on, please, unless you can give me a specific reason why they need to be naked?' May said. 'And the fact that it's always been done that way frankly isn't reason enough anymore.'

The door banged open and May looked round. To her surprise Ben stood there, his eyes scanning the room for her.

'What is it?' May asked, as he came straight to her.

'There's been an accident. You need to come with me,' Ben whispered, leaning in close. '*Now*.'

Fear gripped May, slicing through her as she fought to nod and smile at the American women watching her.

'May?' Ben took her hand and tugged it. 'Quickly, there's no time to waste. You're needed outside.'

She forced herself to walk as her mind ran wild. Had their lucky streak ended? Had she lost her first pilot? The second the door was shut, she came face to face with Ruby and Polly.

'What is it? What happened?' May asked, panic rising.

'Fill her in, Ruby,' Ben said. 'I need to see if I can help.'

'It's bad. There was a big crash,' Ruby told her, her voice shaking as they set off.

May's mind was racing. Who was flying right now? Who could have been injured? Were they dead or . . . She breathed deep as the screeching noise of the ATA fire and crash crew pierced the air.

'What crashed? What actually happened?' she demanded, breaking into a run. How had she not heard anything? Then she remembered the big bang, the boom that she'd rolled her eyes at, not thinking it could have been an aircraft landing. 'Ruby, tell me what's going on! Was it one of my girls?'

'A Halifax,' Ruby said, she and Polly running alongside May. 'It came in out of nowhere on the wrong approach, and it tried to land but it didn't go well.'

'Oh hell! Move the planes, then!' May yelled. 'I want every plane parked here taxied away now!'

Why would a four-engine bomber be landing at White Waltham? It must have been an emergency because they didn't have any bombers, let alone a huge Halifax, at their headquarters. At least she knew it wasn't one of her pilots at the controls; none of them had been cleared to fly that type of aircraft yet.

'I'm on it,' Polly hollered back, sprinting off.

May caught Ruby's panicked expression and grabbed her arm. 'Get in the nearest plane and move it. Anyone you pass, scream at them to move one on, too. There could be bombs on board that aircraft!'

May kept running, leaving Ruby behind. Her only priority right now was getting all her planes out of harm's way in case . . . The flames licked upwards as she watched and she hoped to God the fire crew managed to put it out fast. Where the hell had this plane come from, and who was in it?

'Get those planes moving!' she yelled as she passed pilots who'd emerged from a nearby building. 'Get them out of the way!'

They were near a railway line and the last thing they needed was a stray bomb taking out any transport lines or, heaven forbid, any of the planes that were ready and waiting to be delivered. She rushed to the crash site and watched as crew members were pulled out. One of them, a young man of no more than twenty, was so badly burnt that it was almost a relief to see he was unconscious. But five others were taken safely out and she was impressed by how quickly her team had worked, the entire ferry pool jumping into action to help. The Halifax had a full crew of men and they must have ended up off course, or something had gone wrong with the plane. She took a moment to survey the scene, her head pounding. *This could have been Johnny. This could have been him, injured, but with no one around to help, no one to pull him from his burning aircraft and drag him to safety.*

'Commander?' Polly asked, suddenly appearing at her side.

May pulled herself together, tearing her eyes from the young men on stretchers. 'Get that fire out and clear the site,' she ordered, stepping back as the patients were moved. She looked at the planes being taxied away, knowing that she'd probably been overcautious but feeling comfortable with her decision nonetheless.

There was a Spitfire, one of her favourite planes, still too close for her liking, and she took it upon herself to move it rather than ordering anyone else to do so. She broke into a run, feeling clumsy in her big boots. As she reached the aircraft she burst into tears, sobs gasping from her lungs, the pain of seeing the plane engulfed in flames too much when it came to her base and her girls. *And her memories.*

'May? *May?*' Ben was behind her, his forehead creased with worry. 'What do you need me to do?'

She met his gaze and breathed a sigh of relief, wiping her cheeks and taking a big, shuddering breath.

'May?'

'I'm fine. I just . . .'

'You're sure you're all right?' he asked.

She nodded.

'Remember this morning, May. You know this plane is ready to go, and all the others are, too.' He smiled and nudged her forward. 'I've triple-checked every engine myself. You and all your pilots are safe. That wasn't one of your crew back there, and it wasn't a plane I'd cleared.' He held out his hand. 'Here, let me help you.'

She let him guide her up into the cockpit, angry with herself for letting her guard down. She didn't go through all her usual checks or bother strapping herself in, just waved at Ben that she was off and hastily flicked switches, pumping the prop and then pushing the ignition to start the engine. She taxied in the rumbling plane to a safe part of the adjoining field. Her other pilots were climbing out and the planes were all lined up neatly as May forced herself to get out, too. She would have preferred to take off and leave all this behind her and just fly, but for now she needed to focus on being the commander in charge.

'May, will we . . .'

Ruby's question, called out to her as she jumped down onto the grass, faded as she noticed a column of smoke rising into the sky from the crash site. She held up her hand, about to speak, when an explosion boomed around them, like thunder echoing through the air. May watched as the aircraft disintegrated, the explosion taking the entire plane with it.

*Holy heck.* A jagged edge hurtled into the ground at her feet, a piece of the aircraft that had moments earlier landed at her airfield with no warning whatsoever. Thank goodness all the men had been rescued, and that it hadn't been any closer to the railway line! *And I thought the Americans were going to be the most difficult part of my day today.*

'Commander Jones!' May turned to see Polly holding something, her eyes wide and fearful.

'What is it?' May asked, trembling now, the adrenaline that had been pumping through her disappearing and leaving her light-headed.

Polly placed a piece of paper into her shaking hands.

> *Senior Commander Jones,*
> *Your immediate presence is requested at Hamble Airfield. We regret to advise that Commanding Officer Samantha Perry has suffered health complications and is no longer cleared for duty. We also require two more pilots to urgently join Ferry Pool No. 15 to train to ferry four-engine bombers. Ferrying those bombers is now imperative to the greater war effort.*
> *Major Luke Grey*

May stared at the urgent letter. She was so used to being at their civilian headquarters at White Waltham, where the majority of the ATA pilots were based, and she was settled in her role now. But if they needed her to move, then move she would. She knew only too well how few women had their Class V to train to fly those bombers, and if they didn't get those planes to the front, they might never win this bloody war. Which meant she'd have to take Lizzie with her to the more advanced airfield whether she liked it or not. None of her own pilots were as experienced, and she knew Lizzie would pick things up quickly. Part of her wished she'd be training alongside them, but if she was taking over as commanding officer, she'd no doubt be buried in paperwork most of the time.

'Is everything all right?' Ruby asked.

May sighed. 'Nothing's ever all right these days. Gather your things, Ruby, and notify Lizzie that we'll need her to accompany us. I'm transferring to the all-female ferry pool in Hamble, and I need our two best pilots with me.'

'When?' Ruby gasped, not bothering to mask her surprise.

May knew her protégé suffered a serious case of nerves when it came to believing in herself, but she could only hope that throwing her in at the deep end would be exactly what she needed. She folded the telegram and stuck it in her jacket pocket. 'Today. And Polly? I'm going to reassign you. Once you finish training, you'll be taking over Ruby's role here at White Waltham as an executive officer.'

Polly's mouth dropped open and May held out her hand, managing a smile despite the turmoil she felt.

'Thank you,' Polly whispered, as a huge grin crossed her face.

'Congratulations,' said May. 'You certainly deserve the promotion.'

She watched as Polly and Ruby hugged excitedly.

'Sanders, let's get ready to go. And please tell the American for me that she's no longer staying at the Savoy.' May smiled at the idea of knocking Lizzie Dunlop down to size. 'It's time for her to put her money where her mouth is and show us what she's made of.' She was about to head back to her office, but then spun on her heel. 'Oh, and Ruby?' she asked. 'Can you let Benjamin know we're leaving and that I want him to join us, too?'

May wanted a flight mechanic with her that she could trust implicitly, who could anticipate what she needed, and Ben had been good to her from the very beginning. She thought about the way he was always there, as determined to keep them all safe as she was. He was a good man and a good mechanic, and if she'd been able to let down the tiniest section of the wall that she kept so carefully guarded around herself, she might have even admitted he was pleasant company, too. But she wouldn't, not now, and maybe not ever.

'You might be able to tell him yourself,' Ruby murmured as Ben came running over. And not only was he running, he looked completely furious.

'What is it?' May called out. What on earth could have riled him so badly?

'It's the American. She's just taken off without clearance for some sort of air display!'

May's blood boiled as she looked up to see the Spitfire soar like a bullet through the sky above them. *She's taken a plane? Just like that? Without asking for permission?*

'How did she . . .' May stammered.

'She ran out to help move the aircrafts,' Ruby interrupted. 'I told her to put the Spitfire somewhere safe, but I had no idea she'd do this. I'm so sorry.'

The plane flew low, rolling and then diving before being pulled up at the last minute and rocketing into the sky again.

'She's amazing,' Ruby whispered.

Polly laughed beside her, their heads tilted back as they watched the sky. 'Imagine having the balls to fly like that.'

'Even if I wanted to, I wouldn't have the confidence,' May heard Ruby say with a sigh. 'My Tom, he flies like that. I was always going to try those kinds of tricks, but he never seemed to think I was ready.'

May nudged Ruby hard. 'Stop watching her as if she's something special,' she fumed. 'Flying a plane like that might take confidence and ability, but it's also reckless and inappropriate to show off, *especially* given what's just happened here.'

Ben touched her shoulder and she met his gaze. Clearly, he was as angry as she was, but he was shaking his head. She looked at Ruby, at the horror on her face that she'd done something wrong, and realised that she'd projected all her anger at the wrong person.

'I'm sorry,' she muttered. 'It's Lizzie I should be saying all that to. You know perfectly well why we're here and how to be part of a team.' Hearing her protégé speak as if she wasn't as capable, though? It irritated her that Ruby's fiancé, a man who was hundreds of miles from them, could still influence her so deeply.

'Do you, ah, do you want me to get her?' Ruby asked. 'When she lands, I mean?'

'What I want is for you to pull her down a peg,' May fumed as she stormed off. 'And remind her that this isn't some jolly overseas experience, because we're in the middle of a bloody war, in case she hasn't noticed!'

Lizzie might have the fancy training and acrobatics in the air, but Ruby had skill and the quiet respect of the other women. Seeing her watch the American slack-jawed and in awe was more infuriating right now than Lizzie's insubordination.

She'd been asked to take her best two pilots with her to train to fly four-engine bombers, but was she putting her own reputation on the line by taking Lizzie with her? If she couldn't rein her in and she turned out to be a loose cannon, all hell would break loose – not just for her, but for all the women who flew for the ATA. One bad egg could affect the lot of them. But the four-engine bombers were the only planes that women were not cleared to fly outside of training yet, and if she didn't take Lizzie? She gulped. Then she might be signing the personal death warrant of the men who were waiting for them; getting those big bombers to the front was the only way they stood a chance of winning the war, and she knew it.

# PART TWO

# CHAPTER FIVE

## *HAMBLE AIRFIELD, HAMPSHIRE,*

## *JUNE 1942*

## *RUBY*

'Great flying!' May called as Ruby took off her helmet and shook her hair out.

Ruby was breathless, the thrill of training in the big bombers like nothing she'd ever experienced before. She grinned. The rumble and power of the aircraft had stayed with her, still thrumming through her body even now that she had both feet on the ground.

'How did it feel?'

'Amazing!' Ruby answered, walking over. She watched as Lizzie climbed up into the other plane, her shoulders straight, her smile steady as she waved out to them. Ruby waved back, refusing to let Lizzie know how easily she rattled her even though it took every inch of her strength to do it. 'But no doubt she'll show me up. Again.'

'That's enough,' May scolded. 'You're every bit as good as her – you just haven't admitted it to yourself yet.'

Ruby didn't tell her that without Tom's steady, calm voice coaching her, she was as jittery as could be. Lizzie flew like she'd been born in the pilot's seat, with nerves of steel and an unwavering belief in her own ability. It made her easily the best flier among them, and Ruby knew she'd always be chasing her tail in the air *and* on the ground. She was good at her job and she'd mastered the bomber well enough, but Lizzie was something else. From that first time she'd seen her take off in the Spitfire without clearance, Ruby had known she was always going to be in the American's shadow. They had both already surpassed the other pilots on the training programme, but May kept telling them they were still neck and neck in the running to be the first woman to fly a Halifax for the ATA. May's superiors wanted to make a big deal out of it, putting all the pressure on one woman to prove exactly what they were capable of.

As they **stood**, her with her helmet tucked beneath her arm and May with her arms crossed, looking skyward, she admired the way the Halifax hurtled down the runway then lifted high into the sky. It was a big beast to get off the ground, but surprisingly elegant to fly once it was airborne, and she itched to be back behind the controls again, learning to anticipate the power and speed of her new favourite plane.

'She's not better than you,' May said, breaking the silence. 'You do know that I'm serious, don't you?'

Ruby smiled. 'I appreciate your confidence in me, Commander.'

May's words were easy to hear, but actually believing them was something else. Every day, no matter how well she'd done the day before, nerves wracked her, sometimes leaving her bent over the toilet, silently vomiting as she battled with whether or not she was good enough. Working alongside Lizzie was a daily, if not hourly, struggle for her. And Tom's letters weren't exactly helping, reminding her that she'd always had him as her co-pilot whenever she'd tried something new or different. *You need me up there with you. You've never had to make decisions on your own if conditions change or if something doesn't go to plan. What if you see a Luftwaffe plane or your engine stalls?*

'Do you want to be the first to officially fly a four-engine bomber for the ATA?' May asked, turning to face her. 'Do you actually want it, Ruby, or are you just going through the motions?'

'You know I want it,' Ruby said. 'It would be . . .'

'Then start acting like it,' said May abruptly, looking irritated, her tone sharp. 'It's time you started believing in yourself, otherwise everyone supporting you will start to question whether you deserve your place here or not.'

'Yes, ma'am,' Ruby quickly replied.

Had it been so obvious that her confidence had been leaking out of her each day? She swallowed. May was right; she did need to start believing in herself more, without her superior constantly bolstering her. She'd been hand-picked for the conversion programme, and she needed to act like she **wanted** to win if she was going to stay in the race. Ruby kept her thoughts to herself and her eyes on the sky, hoping she wouldn't give May reason to be so short with her again.

Lizzie flew the course perfectly as always, and Ruby watched as she touched down, bringing the big, heavy bird in like it was the easiest thing in the world. If only she could watch herself from where May was standing, maybe she'd be able to see that she did it just as well as her American colleague.

'Have you heard from Tom since you transferred here?' May asked, surprising her.

'Yes, actually,' Ruby replied. 'I received a *lovely* letter from him a few days ago.'

May caught her eye. 'Saying?'

'Something along the lines of how terribly I'd affected his mother's health, that she was furious with me, and he was worried how we'd all get along once the war was over if I didn't end my flying pursuits and hurry back home.' She didn't tell May that he'd also suggested it was ridiculous for her to think herself capable of flying a huge bomber, when half the highly trained male pilots he knew weren't cleared to fly them.

May grimaced. 'So he's still being as supportive as ever?'

'*When the war is over, my darling, I'll encourage you to fly and soar the skies beside me, but you're interfering with the natural division between the sexes. Men are supposed to be away at war and the women at home waiting for them, not flying along with us,*' Ruby quoted, hating that she was struggling not to cry. 'Honestly, sometimes I wonder how I ever fell in love with the man.'

'The best thing you can do is prove him wrong,' May said. 'Prove everyone wrong, his mother included, and one day they'll be able to see the woods for the trees.'

'I just wish he could see me fly,' Ruby said, sighing as she thought about Tom and the flights they'd had together before the war, about how encouraging he'd been of her abilities back then. 'Honestly, I think if he saw me in the air, if he saw the work we're doing here each day, I think he'd understand. But his mother has her claws in deep, and there doesn't seem to be anything I can say.'

'She asked him to call the engagement off, didn't she?'

Ruby felt her cheeks burning. 'Yes.'

'But he hasn't, has he?' observed May. 'So maybe she doesn't have quite as much influence over him as you think. Maybe he's just saying what he thinks he has to say. He'll come around, and if he doesn't, he wasn't good enough for you in the first place.'

'Perhaps.'

Maybe May was right; maybe there was still a chance of making him understand. Ruby certainly didn't want him to end their engagement, but if he threatened it directly? She grimaced.

'You're not still thinking about last week, are you?' May asked, with a quick sideways look. 'Because as far as I'm concerned, it never happened.'

Ruby gulped. 'No, ma'am,' she said, shutting her eyes in embarrassment at the memory of her first time piloting the ginormous Halifax. Lizzie had managed to get into her head; she'd lost all her confidence and buckled under the pressure.

*Don't let her rattle you, don't let her rattle you, Ruby chanted in her head, gripping the controls as she rocketed down the runway and took off.*

*But Lizzie had rattled her. Just as Tom had rattled her, his words playing through her head on autopilot, impossible to shut off. 'You need me, Ruby. You've never flown like this before, and I'm just not sure you have what it takes to fly without me as your co-pilot.'*

*She glanced sideways at the empty seat, wondering if he was right, wondering if she was capable without him sitting beside her, telling her what to do, coaching her if things went wrong. Lizzie didn't need anyone. Lizzie hit every mark without breaking a sweat.*

*Hell! She yanked the controls, pulling the aircraft higher, forcing it up as she narrowly missed another plane coming in; she was flying too low, and wasn't scanning the sky as she'd been taught to do.*

*After landing, having barely completed the course she'd been asked to fly, she had to walk across the tarmac on shaking legs to face May. Her commander's cheeks were as red as she imagined hers to be, but from anger, not embarrassment.*

*'Don't you ever make a rookie mistake like that again, Ruby. You could have had a mid-air crash and killed yourself and the other pilot!'*

*'I'm sorry,' she managed.*

*'You get yourself sorted in here,' May said, tapping her head, 'or go home.'*

She'd vowed then and there not to let Lizzie or Tom get in her head again, but it was proving easier said than done, especially when Lizzie hadn't put a foot wrong. Not once.

'Hello, ladies,' Lizzie called out, bowing dramatically on the runway in front of them as if to rub Ruby's nose in how incredible she was. 'Textbook perfect?' she asked, looking at May.

Ruby struggled not to roll her eyes.

'It was a perfect flight,' May agreed. 'It's a shame our newest American arrival wasn't here to watch you, though.'

'An American? Who?' Lizzie demanded. 'I have full control over every American pilot who joins us here!'

Ruby laughed at the look on Lizzie's face. It was the first time she'd ever seen her rattled and it was impossible not to be amused.

'I thought you might have received word, but no matter.'

Lizzie scowled. 'I don't like surprises, so whoever authorised this will have me to answer to. I don't appreciate being blindsided.' She almost seemed to have steam coming out of her ears. 'Who is she?'

'It's a *he*, not a she, and his name is Captain Montgomery. He's one of your country's top pilots, apparently, but he was injured recently and spent time recuperating nearby. Unfortunately he's still recovering, so he hasn't been able to return to active duty yet,' May said, and Ruby could have sworn she was enjoying herself. 'But he's been sent to assist us on the ground with operations and keep an eye on his fellow American pilots, from what I understand.'

'Brilliant,' Lizzie fumed. 'So I'm to play second fiddle to some cripple just because he's an American?'

'Who exactly are you calling a cripple?' boomed a deep male voice from behind them.

Ruby turned, eyes wide as her gaze fell on an American soldier in full dress uniform, his right arm in a sling. His blond hair was cropped short, his face tanned and his eyes as blue as the sky on a cloudless day. He nodded at both her and May, then fixed his regard on Lizzie and positively glowered at her. Lizzie's nostrils flared, her eyes narrowing as she stared confidently back. Ruby couldn't have been more transfixed if she'd been at the opera.

Lizzie seemed dumbfounded for a moment. 'Well, I see you're still rather capable after all. My mistake,' she finally said, and stepped forward. 'Elizabeth Dunlop. Pleased to meet you.'

'Captain Jackson Montgomery,' he said, clasping her hand.

'And you're here because?' Lizzie asked.

Ruby traded glances with May, trying to hide her smile. This was exactly the little pick-me-up she needed.

'To keep an eye on you, I suppose,' he said. 'I've been told you might need to be brought down a peg or two – is that what you British say?'

'Yes,' Ruby said. 'I think you've got a very good grip on the local terminology *and* the pilot in question, actually.'

Lizzie glared at her, but for once Ruby didn't back down. She already liked this Montgomery fellow.

'Well, I don't know what on earth you think you'll do here with one arm. You'll be as useless as a bull with teats, I suspect, but stay out of my way and I'll stay out of yours.' And with that, Lizzie stomped off.

Ruby stepped forward. 'It's a pleasure to meet you,' she said, extending a hand. 'I'm First Officer Ruby Sanders.'

'The pleasure is all mine,' he said politely, his blue eyes warm now that Lizzie had gone. 'Tell me, is she always like that?'

It was clear from his brief nod to May that they'd already met, and Ruby wondered if May had been waiting all morning to land this bombshell on Lizzie.

'Yes, unfortunately,' Ruby told him. 'But she's one of the best fliers here and she knows it, so I suppose she can behave that way.'

She caught May's frown and turned away slightly.

'Well, she's certainly the most confident,' he said. 'It seems my fellow countrywoman could do with a lesson or two in manners. You know, I was watching both your flights just now. And she might be a show-off, but you're a solid pilot. Good work up there.'

Ruby felt her cheeks turn a tell-tale pink.

'I couldn't agree more,' May said. 'It's nice to hear a second vote of confidence, isn't it, Ruby?'

She nodded. 'Thank you, sir.'

'I've seen this time and again with my men, to be honest. The ones full of bravado aren't always the ones who become our top pilots, so don't let her think she has one up on you. I've heard it's a decision between the two of you to be the first female bomber pilot.' He smiled. 'If you want my advice, it'd be not to discount yourself, no matter how good you think she is. The most important thing is being the one who can be relied on by your entire squadron, no matter what.'

Ruby didn't know what to say, and felt her blush deepen.

'Some of us have to work hard to get anywhere in life,' he said. 'And others have the world at their fingertips and never have to break a sweat.'

'Well, I think you've already read our American friend rather well, Captain,' May told him. 'You're going to have your hands full trying to get a handle on Elizabeth. She's more of a Spitfire than the actual plane over there.'

'She's a bloody pain in the arse,' Ruby muttered, eyes widening as she realised she'd spoken out loud.

'What was that?' Captain Montgomery asked.

'Nothing, sorry,' she said. 'It was a pleasure to meet you, sir.'

Ruby left May talking to the handsome American as she made her way back to the training centre to change. She had reading to do and a session with her flight instructor later in the day before she could return to the lovely little home that she and Lizzie had been assigned to. They were staying with a couple called the Robinsons, and for the most part she didn't mind sharing a room with Lizzie; but when May had mentioned that they were now in direct competition to be the first female bomber pilot, that had thrown a spanner in the works. She doubted Lizzie would let her think for even a moment that she had a chance of being chosen.

'Honestly, can you believe that man?' Lizzie called out as Ruby entered, clearly still seething. 'Waltzing in here and acting all superior to me?'

'He's only doing his job,' Ruby said. 'I wouldn't be so hard on him if I were you.' Heck, she'd have been friendly to *any* Englishman if she'd been on the other side of the world! But Lizzie was Lizzie, and that meant she didn't do anything anyone expected her to. She was as infuriating as she was talented.

She tried to move past, but Lizzie stood in front of her.

'What are your plans for our two days of leave this weekend?' Lizzie asked.

'Ah, I don't have any. Catch up on some sleep and study.' Ruby prayed that Lizzie didn't ask her to do anything off base with her. 'How about you?'

'Oh, I might go and see some of the girls back at White Waltham, check in on how they're faring,' Lizzie said breezily. 'I'm sure they're giving your Brits a run for their money.'

*Or maybe they're more focused on working together for the greater good, to help win the war, instead of being in some stupid competition with their fellow pilots*, Ruby thought, wishing she were brave enough to actually say it.

Lizzie disappeared, pushing the door shut with a loud bang, and Ruby sat down at one of the tables, opening a book about the large aircraft she was soon to be in charge of. But her thoughts drifted, as they so often did, to Tom. Where was he? What was he doing? Was he thinking of her or had he given up on her the moment she'd so brazenly written to him and told him that she respected his thoughts, but at the same time expected him to respect her decision? She fingered the ring hanging from a chain at her neck, remembering the day he'd given it to her, the day she'd truly fallen head over heels in love with the man. How had they gone from being partners in crime to being on opposite sides of the table?

*'Baby, come here,' he said, gesturing to the two-seater plane.*

*Ruby ran over, her long hair pinned up and out of the way, trousers on to make it easier to fly. She caught Tom's hand and twirled closer, leaning in for a kiss, her lips finding his as she sighed into his mouth. Every time, every single time they were together, she wondered how she'd ever managed to find someone who made her heart race as much as it did when she was at the controls of an aircraft.*

*'I don't want you to go,' she said, cupping his cheeks as he stroked fingers through her hair.*

*'Ruby, this war will be over before it even starts,' he said, kissing her lips again, then pulling her close. 'And I'm not going yet. It could be months before I have to leave.'*

*She held him tight, listened to the strong, steady beat of his heart.*

*'Ruby, look at me,' he said, his voice husky.*

*'What is it?'*

*'Fly with me?' he asked, more tender than usual, his hand skimming her arm before gesturing for her to get in the plane.*

*'Since when did you have to ask?'*

*He laughed and followed her up, settled in and started the engine. They taxied down the short runway, then Tom abruptly stopped the plane. She looked over at him, confused, until she saw what he was holding in his open palm.*

*The diamond twinkled in the light, the dainty ring seeming to stare back at her as she froze, then finally raised her eyes to meet Tom's.*

*'Ruby, will you marry me?' he asked.*

*'Yes!' she squealed, holding out her finger as he slipped the ring on and leaned in for a quick kiss, before letting out a whoop and firing up the plane again. They taxied fast down the runway this time, her stomach leaping as they lifted into the air. She laughed as he swooped, showing off, tipping left and then right as they soared.*

In that moment, Tom had been all she'd needed: Tom and the thrill of gliding through the sky as if nothing could ever stand in the way of their happiness. She dropped her head to the table as the memory faded, shutting her eyes and fingering the ring at her neck, still hanging from the little silver chain she'd strung it from to keep Tom near. Was it all worth it? If she lost Tom, would she wish she'd stayed at home and kept on volunteering at the post office instead of running off to ferry planes? Perhaps he was right to want to protect her; perhaps he did know what was best for her.

She squeezed her eyes shut and tried to clear her mind, wishing she could stop the voice in her head and trust her instincts instead.

'I was told I'd find you in here.'

Ruby blinked and sat up. 'Polly!' She stood and threw her arms around her friend. 'What are you doing here? When did you arrive?'

'Oh, you know, I've been ferrying Spitfires. But I was dropped off here on my way home to fly another plane back to base this afternoon.'

'It's so good to see you. Any gossip? What's happening back at White Waltham?'

'Nothing really, but we *are* taking bets on whether it'll be you or Lizzie to be first in the air in a bomber. It's a nice distraction from listening to the wireless and fretting about who's late back. We've been told it's turned into quite the competition!'

Ruby groaned. Of course they all knew about it; gossip spread like wildfire between the pilots. 'It's not going to be me. Seriously, she's so good it's insane. I don't even know why we're competing. Why isn't it enough that *one* of us, a woman from our base, is going to get it? She's turned it into some awful kind of race.'

'Don't be daft,' Polly said. 'First of all, there's nothing wrong with a bit of friendly competition, and second, I didn't place the biggest bet only to lose it. You're a sure thing!'

'Why does everyone else have more confidence in me than I do? And I'd hardly call the competition *friendly*,' Ruby grumbled. 'As soon as May announced that the first flight was between me and Lizzie, it became very serious.'

'Look, just beat her, would you?' Polly asked. 'If it's not me up there in the sky then I want it to be you.'

Ruby stared. 'You wanted to be in the running for it?' she asked, guilt trickling through her as she saw the look on Polly's face. 'I didn't even think. How stupid of me – of course you did!'

'Don't look a gift horse in the mouth, Ruby. You get up there and prove to everyone that you're better than her. I would have loved to be transferred here, but I didn't have enough flying hours to even be considered, so I'm living vicariously through you!'

Ruby took a deep breath. Hearing Polly say that was exactly what she'd needed. She couldn't give up, not now, not when she was so fortunate to be training in a Halifax. 'Did May tell you to come in here and give me a good kick up the backside?'

Polly laughed. 'No, I did that all on my own. Now, can we get a hot cuppa? I'm dying of thirst here.'

Ruby shut her textbook and stood, linking arms with Polly. 'Good idea. And while we're talking about good ideas, do you have any leave this weekend?'

'Yes, why?'

'Because I need a night away. Can you afford a night in London with me?'

'I'll be there with bells on,' Polly said with a big grin. 'It sounds like heaven to me right now.'

They walked arm in arm towards the mess room, Ruby bursting with laughter as she told Polly all about Captain Montgomery and how he'd put Lizzie into a complete tailspin. And just like that, all the stress of flying and being the one to beat Lizzie drifted away as though it had never been there in the first place. It was so good to be with a friend. *Thank God for Polly.*

# CHAPTER SIX

## *HAMBLE AIRFIELD, HAMPSHIRE,*

## *JUNE 1942*

## *MAY*

'I thought I'd find you here.'

May looked up, smiling before she even saw him. Benjamin often sat with her in the early morning, tucked away behind the main hangar for a few stolen moments before the day began, or she'd do his rounds with him and watch as he checked over the engines. He was nursing a mug this morning and she was doing the same, the heat from her tea warming her palms and making it almost bearable to be outside so early.

'Do you have time to sit?' she asked.

'You're the boss, Commander,' he said with a grin. 'Do I?'

May took a sip, the hot tea warming a trail down her throat. 'You need to stop calling me *Commander*, Ben. How many times have I asked you to call me May?'

He shrugged. 'Obviously not enough. Now, how about you tell me why you've got dark circles under your eyes? Aren't you sleeping?'

She absently touched her face, wondering how he'd noticed, but not really surprised. Somehow, her flight mechanic had been the only one to actually see her let her guard down. The women she managed were like family to her – she'd fight for their safety and better training and facilities until she was blue in the face, but she always had her wall up with them. Something about Ben made her relax, as if she didn't have to pretend, at least for the few minutes every day when they sat in the frigid air, drinking tea. Perhaps it was because he checked her engines and those of her girls, promising her hand on heart each time she flew out that he'd been over **every** inch of her aircraft. In a world where she looked after everyone else, he was the only one who looked after her.

She glanced sideways at him, caught his smile as he sat back, ankles crossed, his overalls clean before the day's work.

*Or maybe it's because something about his easy manner and quick smile, the way he just gets on with things and makes everyone around him happy, reminds me of Johnny.* Her darling Johnny who'd been gone almost two long years.

A tear escaped from the corner of her eye and she saw a look pass over Benjamin's face as she quickly brushed it away, but his smile didn't falter. That was another thing she liked about him – no woman could see tears and not make a fuss or ask questions.

'That Halifax, the one that crashed back at White Waltham?' she said. 'I keep seeing it. Now that we're here and my girls are training in them, I keep dreaming about it, only it's one of them being pulled out, all burnt and charred from the fire.'

Ben didn't say anything and she was grateful, but he did reach out and touch her hand, his fingers curling over hers.

'This happening every night?'

She nodded and gulped down more tears. 'Yes. Every night.'

She didn't tell him that some nights that pilot was her brother, or that sometimes she saw him before he crashed, staring at her, his face covered in blood, telling her that it was her fault. That if hadn't been thinking about her, if he'd been able to concentrate, he wouldn't have lost control and crashed in the first place. She knew it was worse because tomorrow would the anniversary of his death, but she wasn't about to tell Ben that, either.

'Did I ever tell you that I have a little sister?' Ben asked as his fingers left hers.

May took a quick gulp of her tea. 'No,' she said, realising how little she actually knew about him. They often sat in silence, or talked about planes or flight conditions; never about his family. *Or hers.* But today he must have thought she needed distracting.

'Look at this,' he said, reaching into his pocket and pulling out a piece of paper folded into a small square.

May set her tea down on the concrete and took it, smiling as she carefully unfolded it. Inside was a picture drawn with pencil, of a big plane and a man standing next to it, and a small child standing **beside** a little house with her mouth drawn in a frown. It was as pretty as it was sad.

'How old is she?' May asked.

'Six,' he replied, grinning as he took it back from her. 'There's four of us. I'm the oldest, and Violet was a bit of a surprise for my parents. She's the youngest by ten years.'

'A nice surprise, then,' May said, imagining Ben as a big-hearted brother. 'She must miss you.'

'There was a letter with that picture begging me to go home on leave. She's not happy that I've been away so long, but I keep telling her that we're fighting to make sure she has a future. So that she can be safe.'

May could see he was missing his sister as much as she was so obviously missing him.

'We're all fighting for the same thing, May – to make sure all the Violets in this world don't have to go through what we're going through,' he said gently. 'I know this is hard on you, but you're doing something you can be proud of, and whether or not one of your pilots crashes one day? That's not on your shoulders. You can't control what happens to them when they're flying, but you can control how well they're trained, and I can control whether their planes are in the best shape they can be. All right?'

She nodded, his words sinking in slowly. 'All right,' she eventually replied.

'Now what about your family? Do you have any brothers or sisters?' Ben asked.

She froze then and tried to hide it, awkwardly reaching for her tea and sloshing half of it over. 'Gosh, look at that, I'd better make another,' she mumbled, looking at her wristwatch. 'And time's run away with me, too.'

Ben stayed still for a moment, looking at her, his deep brown eyes somehow seeing straight through her façade. Usually she was so prepared, quickly deflecting questions about home, but Ben had thrown her off balance.

When he stood, he reached for her mug, his fingers brushing against hers.

'*Are* you all right, May?' he asked, voice so low that it almost broke her, his concern overwhelming and sweet at the same time.

She braved a smile, back straight and chin held high. 'Of course. I'll see you on the tarmac.'

May walked away, refusing to think about the chink in her armour that she'd shown to Ben. *Never again*, she thought. Because if she started thinking about Johnny, if she admitted how long it had been since she'd even written to her family or that she couldn't bear to see them, then she'd be no use to anyone, and certainly not the ATA.

'May!' Lizzie called out to her, her voice booming from the door of the mess room.

May pulled herself together, wondering if talking to Ben about her family would have been easier than dealing with Lizzie first thing in the morning.

'How can I help?' she asked, coming face to face with the immaculately groomed, lipstick-in-place, bright blonde-haired Lizzie Dunlop.

'I want Montgomery off your service,' Lizzie demanded, hands on hips. 'He's overstepping.'

The door was open and May could see through to the other girls, quietly chatting as the wireless chirped in the background about more American soldiers arriving in Europe, painting their nails, knitting, lounging about with steaming mugs in their hands. She wished she could sail straight past Lizzie and collapse into one of the chairs rather than being the one to deal with every crisis, large or small.

'In what way?' she asked, indicating for Lizzie to follow her inside. When Lizzie didn't budge, she realised their conversation was destined to take place in the piercing outdoor air. 'He's been nothing but helpful and courteous to me.'

'He's acting as if he's been sent here to rein me in,' she said. 'He's stifling my abilities.'

'I see.' May hoped she at least appeared genuine in her concern. 'Perhaps we should discuss this with him directly, see what his take is.'

'His *take*?' Lizzie exploded. 'I doubt that he's going to see anything at all wrong with telling me to pull my head in.'

Suddenly Montgomery was in the running for being May's favourite person. 'Lizzie, you need to show him the respect he deserves, not to mention show respect for his rank. He's a talented, clever pilot with hours of experience flying warplanes, which means we're all lucky to have him here.' She sighed, speaking more softly this time. '*You included.*'

'He's so clever that he got shot out of the sky!' Lizzie ranted. 'That doesn't exactly scream *clever* to me.'

May's chest tightened. She clenched her fingers into a ball to stop herself from slapping Lizzie straight across the cheek. Johnny had been one of the best pilots she'd ever seen, and the air force had agreed, but it hadn't stopped him from being gunned down because no pilot knew what the enemy had in store for them. She took a long, careful breath, and considered Lizzie. She had enough to deal with without having to placate the American.

'Elizabeth, are you aware that my country is at war, and has been at war for the past three years?'

Lizzie stared blankly back at her. 'Of course I'm aware. It's why I'm standing here, isn't it?'

'Then perhaps you could show a little respect to not only the men serving our country, but those brave men like Jackson Montgomery who got here before he was even required to be,' May snapped. 'At this base, I expect all my pilots and ground crew to be part of a team, and that team must be built on respect, no matter what. Your insolence is insulting to me and to everyone else here – you're actually here to help the war effort, not run after your own personal ambitions.'

'I don't see myself as being part of a team in the sky,' Lizzie replied, hands on hips. 'And I doubt my father did when *he* was in the sky, fighting for *his* country in the Great War, either. Up there, we only have ourselves to count on. Our own smarts, our own instincts.'

'Really? Well, do you feel part of a team when you see your flight mechanic carefully checking your engine and clearing you for take-off? Do you see yourself as part of a team when you're sent on multiple missions in one day, and people at each base are relying on you? When our men, who wait for us to ferry planes to them, are able to take off within hours of a new aircraft landing, because of the part we play?' May was fuming. 'And I don't care if your father was the best pilot in the sky in the last war. What I care about is your behaviour under my orders. Are we clear?'

'Yes,' Lizzie muttered. 'Perfectly clear.'

'Ah, good morning, Commander Jones. Is this a bad time?'

May spun around to find Montgomery standing a few feet from her, his forehead creased in concern.

'No, this a great time, actually,' she said. 'I've just been talking to Elizabeth about her attitude, and I thought you might like to discuss that further with her.'

'May!' Lizzie protested. 'All I want is to get on with my training instead of being grounded like some incompetent . . .'

'In fact, I think Lizzie could do with some more hands-on training as well as a lesson in respect,' May interrupted. She turned to the Lizzie with a smile. 'We have Tiger Moths that need to be taken back for further repairs, and I think that would be an excellent job for you to do today.'

'Tiger Moths?' Lizzie asked, her voice rising. 'Slow, stinking *Tiger Moths*?'

'When I started with the First Eight, we flew those slow old planes day in, day out, taking them wherever they needed to go, and not *once* did we complain about it, because we knew that we were doing this, selflessly, to help the greater good,' May said. 'And I expect you to take it on the chin, too. How about you, Montgomery?'

He grinned. 'Same here. I flew what I had to fly, kept my head down and worked hard. There ain't no point being part of a squadron if your team have no faith in you.'

'I think we're on the same page then,' May said, her anger slowly subsiding.

'And Ruby? Are you going to make her do the same thing?' Lizzie stuttered.

'No, Ruby is an excellent team player and she can spend the day under my tutelage, training in the Halifax.' May spun on her heel then, leaving poor Jackson to deal with the fallout. But as she turned she caught his eye, and she was certain his amusement was equal to hers.

Wishing Lizzie could see what a decent man he was, she continued on to her desk in the corner of the main room to check the chits and make certain she knew where everyone was for the day. She had girls flying and girls training, and sometimes a combination of both, and she liked to know where they were at all times. It meant she was grounded more than she liked; now that she was running the operation, she did more administration work than actual flying, and she missed it. Ever since she'd arrived at Hamble, she'd had this strange superstitious feeling that they'd gone without a loss for too long, that their luck might dry up soon. It was stupid, but she couldn't shake it. Some of the mechanics joked about their perfect fatality rate, that the girls were able to do what male pilots never could, but even the thought of it, the notion that she might be the one to have to visit a family or write the letter telling them their daughter had died in the air, was like a punch to the stomach. Morbid thoughts like that were sometimes as hard to live with as her memories of Johnny.

'What's going on?' Ruby's soft voice warmed her.

'It's just you in the Halifax today, Ruby.'

'Where's Lizzie?'

'Let's just say that Lizzie has been seconded to Jackson Montgomery's service for the day,' May told her. 'We can all pray that she returns in a more humble frame of mind than when she left.'

Ruby snorted with laughter and May laughed along with her, surprising herself.

'Well, I appreciate the extra training, thank you,' Ruby said. 'But if you'd like me to do any other work today instead, or . . .'

'You want the first solo flight, Ruby?' May asked.

'You know I do.'

'Then don't look a gift horse in the mouth. If Lizzie could get an extra day of hands-on training without you, she'd take it in a heartbeat. In fact, she'd knock you down and trample over you to get it.'

Ruby didn't reply, no doubt because she knew it was true. Lizzie was ruthless, clearly used to getting everything and anything she wanted. It made her an incredible pilot because she was fearless, but it didn't exactly make her an easy ally or friend to have on base.

'The mail's here!' one of the girls squealed, and May saw Ruby's face light up as Polly crossed the room with an envelope in her outstretched hand. She must have just arrived at Hamble on the mail plane, and May was pleased to see her again.

'There's one for you as well,' Polly said, passing it to May.

Her hand shaking, May took the cream envelope, her mother's familiar scrawl across the front. She held it tight, as if doing so would connect them, before opening a drawer and tucking it inside to read later. She sighed as it landed with two others that looked just like it. *Or maybe I won't read it at all.*

Ruby had gone silent, and May looked up to see her rip her letter into tiny little pieces, shredding it until the paper fell all over the floor. Tears rolled down her cheeks.

'He meet someone else?' The American drawl was lazy and loud as Lizzie strolled into the room. 'Don't go getting your knickers in a twist over a man, sugar.'

'Leave her alone, Lizzie!' Polly shouted.

But Ruby didn't even seem to hear them. 'I hate him,' she whispered, her voice low and full of anger. 'He could meet someone else and I wouldn't even care.'

May knew she was only venting; the letter might be in shreds and her heart might feel broken, but Ruby was fingering the ring hanging from her necklace as she spoke, and that told May everything she needed to know.

Lizzie breezed out as quickly as she'd breezed in, her flying hat and goggles tucked under her arm, and May stood, leaning forward.

'Was it him or his mother?' she asked quietly.

Ruby's eyes met hers. 'His mother.'

'And she said?'

'That her delightful son wholeheartedly agreed with her, and that I have four weeks to return home or our engagement will be off.'

Ruby's voice was full of anger, but May wasn't about to go easy on her just because she was hurting. This was the time to push her, to draw on that anger and stop her from holding back.

'Are you going to go home?'

'No.' Ruby's reply was quick, without a beat of hesitation. 'I want to prove them wrong. Why is it fine for him to do his bit, but not me?'

'You're certain?' May asked.

'Part of me wants to give up – there's a little voice telling me that I'm not good enough, that I shouldn't have come in the first place.'

'And the other voice?'

Now Ruby found a smile. 'That voice is telling me that I can do it, that I'm capable of making a difference here, and to hell with what anyone thinks of me.'

'I say we listen to that voice then,' said May, 'because that's the Ruby I want to see on my base flying my planes.'

Ruby was looking down at the paper strewn in tiny pieces all around her feet, and as she bent to collect them, May moved around and squatted down beside her to help.

'If you could fly into his base, once you're cleared to fly a bomber, is that something you'd want to do?' May whispered.

Ruby froze, then looked up, a strength shining through that May hadn't seen before. 'Yes.'

May nodded. 'Then you have my word that I'll try to make that happen, in exchange for you starting to believe in yourself and in your abilities.' She paused. 'Do we have a deal?'

Ruby held out her hand. 'Deal.'

'Then clean this mess up, Sanders, and meet me out front in thirty minutes, ready to show me what you're made of.'

May returned to her desk to study her paperwork. She was always so good at giving advice to her girls, giving them pep talks and helping them to manage their personal and work lives. She glanced at the drawer where her mother's letters were hidden, the pain of her words too much for May to deal with right now. *Pity I'm not better at putting the broken pieces of my own life back together.*

'Did you get any mail yesterday?' Ben's question was friendly, his eyes lighting up as he reached into his pocket and took out a folded piece of paper. It was already smudged with grease. He waved it. 'My little sister again, insisting that I go home to see her when I have leave. She's relentless.'

May sighed. 'You should go. It sounds like she's missing you terribly.'

'It's her birthday in a few months' time, and I was hoping I might be able to save up some leave, head home for a few days?'

May wondered how many men existed like Ben. He worked all day with his hands, bent over engines for so many hours his back must ache by nightfall, but he never complained about it. He complained about the state of the engines plenty, but never about the work he did.

'So, did you get one?' he asked.

'Did I get what?' She was lost in her own thoughts.

'A letter, silly.'

'Oh, ah, yes. From my mother.'

'How is she? Missing her girl?'

May sighed. *Two years*, she thought. It had been two years today since Johnny had been taken from them, and the anniversary was making it even harder than usual to think about her family. Or maybe it was amplifying her guilt at not seeing them or being in touch with them for so long.

'I actually haven't read it yet.'

Ben took a step forward, his gaze fixed on her, so that she couldn't look away.

'One of these days I'm going to ask you about your family, May,' he said. 'And I'm not going to let you walk away without answering.'

She shivered. 'And one of these days I might tell you,' she said, hoping she sounded stronger than she felt. 'Now go and check that engine over one last time and send Ruby up. I want her running rings around Dunlop by tomorrow!'

'Yes, ma'am,' Ben said, grinning as he started to jog backwards.

But then something about her face must have told him that she wasn't strong today, that she wasn't capable of joking around and pretending everything was fine. He stopped and walked back towards her, his smile gone as he reached for her hands.

'That day's today, isn't it?' he said softly. 'It's time I asked you what you're hiding, what happened to your family. What has this war taken from you, May?'

May's lips parted as she fought for the words she was suddenly desperate to share.

'I lost someone,' she murmured. 'I lost someone, two years ago today.'

Ben watched her silently, his fingers tightening around hers.

'Johnny, my brother,' she said, just loud enough for him to hear. 'It's why I don't go home, and it's why I'm so determined to keep these girls safe. I can't lose anyone else, Ben. I just can't.'

She trusted him with her life whenever she went up in the air, and for some reason she trusted him enough with her secret now, too. He opened his arms, pulling her in, holding her as she clung to him. She wanted to cry, to sob, but she sucked it all in, too scared to let go. Instead she shuddered in silence.

'You've kept this to yourself?' he asked. 'All this time?'

May nodded. The relief of admitting the truth to someone was like a pressure valve releasing, letting her breathe again. 'Yes. No one else knows anything about my personal life, but today . . .' Her voice trailed off. 'Today is one of those days that's even harder than all the rest.'

'Your secret's safe with me, May,' he said, stroking her hair as she held him, breathing in the scent of his aftershave mixed with the distinct smell of engine oil. 'You can trust me.'

*I know*, she thought, even though she didn't say it.

He slowly let her go and pulled a flask from his pocket. 'I think your brother would be proud of the work you're doing,' he said, unscrewing the top and passing it to her.

May hesitantly took a tiny sip before giving it back to him, wincing at the burn in her throat.

'To Johnny,' he said, raising the flask to his lips.

'To Johnny,' she whispered back.

Later that day, when the girls were all back and May was seated at her desk again, she studied the room. Some of the pilots had left already; others were milling around, and some, like Ruby, had their heads bent over books. But it was Lizzie who caught her attention, sulking, her bottom lip pushed out as she glared at the open book in front of her.

Resenting Lizzie or disliking her wasn't doing anyone any good, and no matter how annoying she might be, May needed everyone to be part of the team. Taking her off her training wasn't going to help with that, unless it had miraculously humbled her, which May seriously doubted.

'Dunlop,' she called, beckoning for Lizzie to join her.

Lizzie moved slowly, stretching out long like a cat before rising and crossing the room.

'More punishment?' she asked, holding up her hands. 'Because trust me, after the day I had yesterday, I promise to behave. I surrender.'

May tried not to show how pleased she was to hear these words. Maybe her plan hadn't been so bad after all. Besides, it wasn't as if she didn't admire Lizzie's ambition. Lizzie was probably the one woman who understood her desire to establish a squadron and prove what women were capable of; May just struggled with her lack of awareness and team spirit.

'What are you doing this weekend? I'm aware you have two days' leave, the same as Ruby.'

Lizzie shrugged. 'I'll likely head back to White Waltham.'

May saw Ruby watching them and waved her over.

'I don't want to overstep,' May said, looking between them, 'but I heard from Polly the other day that the two of you might be heading to London for a night.'

Ruby nodded, looking confused. 'Is that a problem? I can stay on base if you need me.'

'Of course not. I was only thinking that it's time we put an end to this division or whatever it is going on here,' May said. 'I propose that we all go for a night, away from base, so we can start feeling more of a team. Like friends, even.'

Ruby's cheeks had gone pink; Lizzie looked like she'd just been told someone had died.

'What do you both say? A night in London, the four of us?'

Ruby nodded. 'Of course. I'll send word to Poll.'

'Lizzie?' May asked tentatively.

'Sugar, when have I ever said no to a night out?'

May forced a smile and nodded to dismiss them both, trying not to laugh at the idea of spending an evening out with Lizzie, making friends. But they did all need to get along, and the sooner Lizzie saw that they were all just part of a jigsaw puzzle, one little piece that contributed to the war effort, the better.

# CHAPTER SEVEN

## LONDON, JUNE 1942

### LIZZIE

'We don't have to do this,' Lizzie said as she changed into her dress uniform, careful to untuck her curls from her collar before doing up the buttons on her jacket.

'We're having a fun night out in London, Lizzie. We'll be fine,' Ruby said from the other side of the room. 'Seriously, are we such bad company that you can't even handle one night?'

Lizzie checked herself in the tiny mirror, patting her hair and smacking her lips together. 'If I've upset you it wasn't my intention,' she said, picking up Ruby's jacket from the other single bed and holding it up for her. Ruby looked surprised as she slipped into it. 'I kind of thought we *were* friends anyway, to tell you the truth.'

'Thanks,' Ruby muttered. 'But why are you suddenly being so nice?'

'I *am* nice,' Lizzie said with a laugh. 'I just like winning more than I like making friends.'

'Sounds lonely,' Ruby replied, an eyebrow arched.

They stared at one another and Lizzie wished she'd tried harder with her roommate. Ruby had been nothing but nice to her and she'd treated her like she wasn't her equal – she might not be as good in the air, but she wasn't exactly hard to be around. And it *was* kind of lonely putting all her energy into winning, into being better than anyone else. Had her father felt this way? Had he been friends with his squadron or been isolated as he tried to prove himself? May was always talking about being part of a team, and the other girls were always rolling their eyes at her, but she hadn't come to England to make friends; she'd come to make a name for herself.

'How about we have a few drinks tonight, dance the night away and start over?' Lizzie said, picking up her bag from her bed as a car horn tooted outside.

'You're serious?' Ruby asked.

'You make it sound like I'm so awful I couldn't possibly be nice *or* fun!'

Ruby just laughed as she zipped her bag. 'Fine, we're starting over then. But you can't just say you're going to do it – you actually have to try.'

Lizzie saluted her and opened the door, letting Ruby go first down the narrow little staircase. She looked back at the bedroom, the two beds perfectly made, a small vase of flowers picked by their host sitting on the shared bedside table. The room was sweet but it was also stiflingly small, and she was looking forward to having more space at the Savoy for the one night they were there.

'Hurry up!' Ruby called from downstairs.

Lizzie was about to yell down some smart reply but kept her mouth shut as she raced down the stairs. Maybe Ruby was right – it was going to be hard being nice!

'Goodbye, Mrs Robinson!' she called out to their host, shutting the door behind her. She looked through the open window by the door and caught sight of the older lady, leaning out and waving to Ruby – she was a sweet woman and seemed to love the comings and goings of her two young guests.

Outside, Polly waved from the driver's seat and Ruby climbed in beside her, leaving the back seat for Lizzie. May was meeting them later in the evening, so it was just the three of them heading into London.

'Morning,' she said, smiling at Polly. The pretty blonde had her hair up, her lips painted a bright red to match her nails. 'Thanks for the ride.'

'My pleasure. Now, let's go. We've got a train to catch and I don't want to waste a second of our leave!' Polly said, planting her foot on the accelerator and sending them all flying back into their seats. Lizzie laughed. Maybe the Brits were more fun than she'd given them credit for.

London was nothing like Lizzie had expected. She'd spent time there briefly when they'd first been based at White Waltham, but aside from their scheduled two days of leave every two weeks, there was little time for fun or exploring her new country. But after enduring the newly arrived Captain Montgomery earlier in the week, she was more than happy to escape reality for a night. He was infuriating; the man seemed to enjoy lording his rank and experience over her, and instead of pushing her to do better, he was getting under her skin and driving her mad. She grimaced, wondering if it was actually because he was the first man in a long while to be completely immune to her charms. She'd even fluttered her lashes at him and given him a few sweet-as-pie Southern smiles, but it only seemed to annoy him more.

She stared out the taxi window, nose almost to the glass as she studied the city. Lizzie imagined it would have been beautiful before the war, but the bombs had wreaked havoc: entire blocks were gone, with foundations sticking up haphazardly, reminding her of a graveyard. She also couldn't get used to the barrage balloons that seemed to float so lazily in the sky in an attempt to discourage low-level attacks. Seeing it like this, the reality of war hit her like an unexpected blow. Even though they were flying military planes, she hadn't truly seen the war herself; she hadn't actually lived through it like the local pilots had, and it struck her that her hometown could look like this if war found its way to American shores. Pearl Harbor had already been destroyed, but imagining her own beloved streets bombed, everything she knew and loved being in danger like this, was sobering. She'd found her father's stories glamorous, when in reality war was anything but.

She'd been naive enough to think that London wouldn't be so affected, but between bombed buildings and the blackout, not to mention the wailing siren that echoed to warn of air raids, it was a city struggling. The only thing she'd really noticed where they were based was the food rations, but they still had plenty to eat. Lizzie smiled, thinking about her mother, who'd worried before she left about what food would be available, hands on hips as she'd fretted about how skinny her daughter might be on her return. Once she started flying the four-engine bombers, planes that usually had a crew of more than four men, *skinny* would be the least of her mother's worries.

'Here you are, luv,' the taxi driver said as he pulled over, parked cars blocking him from taking them straight to the door.

Lizzie glanced over at Ruby. 'Come on, let's go.'

But Ruby was still looking out the window, and seemed a million miles away. 'Sorry, I was . . .' Her voice trailed off.

They stepped out and Lizzie linked her arm with Ruby's as they waited for the driver to get their overnight bags, wondering for the first time what her roommate might have lost to the war. 'You're thinking about that man of yours, aren't you?' she whispered.

Ruby laughed, resisting her at first, then leaning in and keeping their arms linked. Then she grabbed hold of Polly so the three of them were lined up in a row. 'So she's not only a better flyer than me – she's a mind reader now, too!'

Lizzie rolled her eyes. She'd been watching Ruby fly, studying her whenever she could, and although she might be more experienced, Lizzie was no longer so confident that she was the best flyer at Hamble.

If Ruby wasn't as good as her yet, she was a close second, and she knew there'd be stiff competition between them to finish top of the class. They all took their bags and walked the short distance to the Savoy.

'So tell me about him. When's this fella going to make an honest woman of you?' Lizzie asked, as they all dodged right around some fallen debris from a building that had recently been hit near their hotel.

'After defying his mother, I'd say we'll be having a quiet ceremony, just the two of us, once the war is over,' Ruby replied. '*If* we get married at all. We'll say our vows and get on with our life, I suppose.'

'Oh Ruby, surely he'll come around. Did the old bat really give you a four-week ultimatum?' Polly asked.

'She certainly did.'

'The whole thing sounds unromantic, if you ask me,' Lizzie said. 'Sorry, but after everything, if you both survive the war and things go back to normal, you deserve a big celebration, don't you think?'

'Lizzie! Leave her alone!' Polly cried.

'Americans,' Ruby muttered. 'They warned us about you, you know? Brash and bold, that's what we were told, and you haven't disappointed.'

Lizzie tipped her head back. 'Well, I wouldn't say *bold* exactly, would you?'

Ruby gave her a look before bursting into laughter with Polly, the two of them leaning their heads together like it was the funniest thing in the world. 'And for the record, I didn't ask for your opinion on our wedding plans! Honestly, you seem to be an expert on everything!'

'Ladies,' said a handsome soldier with his dark hair combed back, holding the door to the hotel wide open for them.

Lizzie gave Ruby a nudge and smiled demurely as he passed by, before they all erupted into laughter again.

'You're the most terrible influence,' Ruby said, still smiling as she wiped the tears from her cheeks. 'Absolutely terrible, Lizzie, you know that?'

'But I've made you want to beat me, haven't I? The only thing you can blame me for is giving you some stiff competition in the sky.'

'Or being a total pain in all our behinds,' Polly moaned.

Ruby gave Lizzie a hard stare. 'We're off duty, Liz. I don't want to talk about who's going to get the first flight, not while we're here. May wanted us to be friends and all get along, so that's exactly what we're going to do.'

'Okay,' Lizzie said, running her finger across her lips as if she were zipping them shut. 'No work talk.'

Lizzie gazed at her surroundings, admiring the beauty of the glamorous, much-loved hotel. This was the one place in London that had surpassed her expectations; even with bomb damage it was still as elegant as ever. For one glorious night they'd be sharing a room here instead of in another family's home. If that meant not talking about who was going to get that first flight, then so be it.

There were already people waiting in a line to check in, so she sat in one of the big chairs and gestured for the other two to do the same.

'You know, the second night I was here the Wailing Willy went off, warning of an air raid, and I had no idea what was going on,' Lizzie told the other two as they sat down. 'I eventually emerged in my dressing gown and was given a good telling off, but I'd decided to just hide under the covers and pray for the bloody best.'

'Ha, listen to you now!' Polly said. 'You sound like a proper Brit, and you haven't been here more than a few months.'

Lizzie supposed she had picked up some of the weird British sayings, like calling the air raid siren a Wailing Willy, but there were other things about being in England that she'd never get the hang of. Like the time she'd asked for the restroom and been taken to a room to *rest* in, with no toilet in sight. Or some of the other unusual sayings that didn't make any sense. But it was the look of things and even the taste of things that she still found particularly foreign. At home she was used to corner drug stores with soda fountains and clean cafes with good food.

And the ice creams? Ugh, she'd tasted one just before their production was banned – they were deemed not to have any food value during wartime – and it was disgusting. More like old dishwater compared to the smooth, silky taste of ice cream back home.

'So where are we going tonight?' Ruby asked. 'What's the plan once we've taken our bags up?'

Lizzie shrugged. 'We're going wherever we can find handsome men, eat a good steak, and dance the night away.'

Ruby shook her head, smiling. 'You haven't forgotten that I'm a promised woman, have you?'

'Doesn't mean you can't have a little fun,' Lizzie said with a wink. 'God knows he will if he gets a night out on the town somewhere, and, Polly, you're single, aren't you?'

'Why, yes I am,' Polly said. 'And it just so happens that I'm dying to meet a fella to take my mind off this war!'

'To hell with it, you're right,' said Ruby. 'I'm an independent woman contributing to the war effort. He'd better not warm anyone else's bed, but we all deserve some fun and he's been an idiot lately anyway. He's lucky *I* haven't called off the engagement!'

Lizzie could see how hard Ruby was trying to be brave; she'd heard the other girls talking about how difficult her fiancé had been. 'He's lucky to have you, Ruby,' she said. 'Honestly, he is.'

Ruby looked amazed for a second, before slowly smiling. 'Thanks, Liz. That actually means a lot.'

'Come on, let's check in and get our party frocks on,' Lizzie said, not wanting Ruby to think she'd gone all soft on her. She only had one dress, but after months of wearing her uniform day in, day out, it felt like she was about to put on the most special dress in the world – not to mention her beautiful brown silk stockings that she was so careful with. 'All I can think about is what we're going to be eating tonight, and it had better not include cabbage or Brussels sprouts!'

'I need a big juicy piece of meat. And some jolly good gravy to go with it.' Polly sighed. 'Heaven on a plate.'

'Don't forget the gin,' Lizzie added. 'I'd go for one of your British gin and tonics right about now.'

'May said she'd be here by early evening at the latest,' Ruby told them. 'I actually think she might be impressed by how well we've been getting along so far.'

'I wouldn't go getting too ahead of yourself,' Polly teased.

Lizzie flashed Polly a smile, liking the smart-mouthed Australian.

'Have you been elsewhere in London during an air raid?' Ruby asked as they approached the reception desk. 'When you first arrived, I mean?'

'No, just that once. I probably didn't take it seriously enough.'

'Most of London is squashed into the underground during a raid, on cold damp floors, but the crowd here gets pampered even when we're being bombed.' Ruby shook her head. 'Liz, it's scary when the sirens go off, if you've been here when a bomb has actually hit. When you've got to race for cover, when you're not staying somewhere fancy like this, it's terrifying. It makes it all so real, that we're only one bomb away from being a casualty.'

Lizzie squeezed Ruby's hand. 'I'm sorry, I was just trying to make light of it. You know me.'

Ruby's smile was sad, and Lizzie wondered if she'd pushed too far.

'Just don't forget that this war is real,' Ruby reminded her. 'And we've all lost someone or something. It's not a game to us.'

'I promise you, it's not a game to me either,' Lizzie assured her.

'Well, we'd better not have a bloody air raid tonight. I want to party for hours then sleep for longer than I've slept in months,' Polly moaned, as Ruby laughed and gave their names to the front desk clerk.

Lizzie couldn't agree more. 'Let's go to our room, take a nap, then get ourselves all dolled up so we're ready when May gets here.'

'I thought I'd find you ladies in here.'

'May!' Ruby and Polly chimed at the same time, as their commander walked into the bar.

'When it started to get dark we thought you weren't going to make it.' Lizzie beckoned the waiter over as May settled into the seat next to her. 'But you're just in time. We've only had two drinks.'

'I was called into a late meeting, but I wouldn't have missed this for the world,' May said.

'What can I get you to drink, ma'am?'

Lizzie studied May as she ordered champagne, watching the confident way she held herself and the commanding way she spoke. Since they'd been transferred, Lizzie had noticed the change in her commander, the way she'd seemed to grow into her role and was more comfortable being in charge with every passing day. But it was clearly taking its toll on her – the lines around her eyes were more pronounced, the tiredness impossible not to notice. Also, she had the distinct feeling that May was holding back, that with her new-found confidence she was also somehow distancing herself from the others.

'So what have I missed?' May asked.

'Lizzie's had me looking for handsome fellas for her,' Ruby said. 'Haven't seen one yet that's she's interested in, though.'

Lizzie laughed. 'I think our young friend is a virgin, she's so shy.'

'Lizzie!' Ruby gasped, swatting at her.

'We can't all be as experienced as you, Miss Dunlop,' Polly quipped, taking a slow sip of her drink and winking, which sent them all into raucous laughter again.

'But she's not such bad company after a drink!' Ruby said with a grin.

'How dare you even *think* that I'm some sort of a hussy!' exclaimed Lizzie, in mock horror. It wasn't like she'd bedded more men than she could count, but she was no innocent and she wasn't about to pretend otherwise. 'But we're not quite so prim and proper as you Brits back home in the US of A.'

'Ladies,' said a deep, welcoming voice from behind them.

Lizzie turned to see three men dressed in air force uniform. 'Well, look what the cat dragged in,' she drawled.

'And just like that, bees to honey,' May whispered under her breath, making Lizzie laugh.

'Don't come near me – I'm engaged,' Ruby announced.

Lizzie rolled her eyes at her, then noticed May busying herself with her champagne. Polly was the only one looking interested.

'Boys, can't a girl have a drink without being approached?' she asked.

'Oh, you're American,' said the first man, as one of his buddies gave him an obvious nudge.

'As American as can be,' she said, then gestured towards her glass. 'If you gentlemen are going to join us . . .'

'Get the girls more champagne,' he said, giving her a grin that made her want to laugh. He looked like she'd just invited him to join her in bed. 'I'm James, *Officer* James Caldwell.'

'Well, fancy that, ladies,' Lizzie said. 'We were just about to head to the Officer's Club, weren't we?'

'Could you not just stay here for a drink first?' he asked. 'We're . . . well, I'll let Danny tell you all about it.'

Lizzie swapped glances with Polly. She couldn't wait to hear the pick-up lines that were about to be deployed.

'You see, we're pilots and . . .' The flyboy she now knew to be Danny gave a sorrowful look that she was certain was well-practised as he leaned closer and lowered his voice. 'Well we're going to be in the sky facing the enemy, wrangling with machines you couldn't even imagine.'

'Is that so?' May said, finishing her drink and gratefully accepting another from the third man. She winked over at Lizzie.

'Sorry darling, I didn't catch your name,' Lizzie said to the man carrying the drinks.

'Oh, I'm Patrick,' he said, passing champagne to Polly.

Lizzie saw James kick him, and bit her tongue in amusement.

'*Officer* Patrick Todd,' he quickly added.

'Ah, so you're a pilot, too.'

May pulled her chair closer and gave Lizzie a wide-eyed look. 'Do tell us more. What are you boys up against?'

'Well, you see, ladies,' James said, 'we're in dangerous situations every single day.'

'Uh-huh,' May said, nodding.

When Danny took Lizzie's hand, she smiled sweetly and let him hold it.

'Honey,' he said, 'my engine could quit on me, any time, any day. You have no idea what kind of big planes I'm in charge of.'

At that moment Ruby came to life and burst out laughing. 'Oh, but we do!' she said gleefully.

Lizzie hid her smile and watched as May coughed, her eyes dancing. These poor boys were going to be mortified when they realised they were all pilots, and that May was technically superior to them. She'd never realised her commander could be so much fun!

'Honey, trust me,' Patrick said. 'There's no way you could understand what we go through every day. It's tough work, but someone has to be brave and do it.'

'But . . .' Ruby started.

May interrupted by holding up her hand and reaching into her bag. She pulled out a newspaper and unfolded it.

'There was another reason I was late tonight,' she said, as Danny reached for the paper. 'I wanted to be the one to show it to you so it didn't come as a surprise, and I was waiting to receive a copy.'

'Oh my Lord, it's me!' Ruby squealed and leapt off her chair, snatching the paper from Danny and waving it at them all.

Lizzie swallowed, forcing a smile as she digested the picture splashed across the front page of the *Picture Post*. Ruby was smiling as she ran her fingers through her long dark hair, dressed in her flying suit and striding away from her plane. A bomber. A *huge* bomber. As if she were a world-class movie star staring down the lens of the camera. And just like that, all thoughts she'd had about being friends with the other girls disappeared, and instead her desire to be the first female pilot in a Halifax lit up again, like a flame. She wasn't going to admit to her father that a woman with half the flying hours could beat her. Failure was not in her vocabulary, and it should have been her on the cover!

But it was the headline that riled her the most. She would have done anything to send a cutting like that to her daddy!

*Beauty and the Bomber. Will this pin-up pilot be the first to fly a big-boy bomber over London?*

'I thought you'd want to see it,' May said, one hand on Ruby's shoulder. 'You should be proud that they put this on the front cover. It's validation for all of us.'

Lizzie sucked up her pride and kept her smile firmly in place, not about to let on that it had rattled her to see that image of Ruby's beautiful face. Why was she jealous? This stupid picture didn't mean anything. But she knew it wasn't her beauty that bothered her; it was that Ruby had been publicly earmarked by the papers as the first female to ferry a four-engine bomber, and it was an accolade that she'd wanted to secure ahead of every other woman she trained with. *She* wanted to be the one recognised by everyone, on both sides of the pond, as the best female flier to ever pilot a bomber, and she wasn't going to let this stop her from getting there.

'Congratulations,' she said through gritted teeth, trying to sound warm. 'It's a gorgeous picture.'

Ruby passed the paper back to May. 'The picture looks all glamorous, but I'm not going to be the one flying the first bomber and we both know it.'

Lizzie shrugged and held up her glass, looking at the men, who were all standing with their mouths hanging open. She knew it wasn't sporting to think so, but the more Ruby doubted herself, the more chance she had of beating her.

'Sorry, that's you in the picture, right?' Danny asked. 'The, ah, pilot?'

'Of course it's her, you idiot,' James cursed, cuffing him around the ears.

'Senior Commander May Jones,' May said, sitting back in her chair. 'And these three women here happen to be among my most talented pilots. First Officer Lizzie Dunlop,' she indicated, 'and First Officer Ruby Sanders, from Ferry Pool No. 15 at Hamble, as well as our very talented Executive Officer Polly Simmons, who is based at White Waltham.'

Patrick's gulp was visible. 'I'm sorry, I . . .'

'At ease, my boy,' May said. 'Now, how about you tell us more about these *extraordinary* big planes you're in charge of?'

All three men went beetroot red, their cheeks on fire as first Danny stumbled a few steps back, followed by the others. They muttered their excuses and headed for the bar.

May and Polly laughed and so did Lizzie, but Ruby was staring at the paper again, clearly in shock.

'Put that rag away and let's go,' said Lizzie abruptly, not wanting to even glimpse the headline again.

May gave her a sharp look, but Lizzie ignored her, not about to be drawn in to any conversation about who would or wouldn't be flying the first bomber. She had something to prove, both here and at home, and if the decision hadn't been made yet, then she still had time when they got back to Hamble – front page news or not.

'Where are we going?' Ruby asked, appearing more sober now.

'To Hyde Park to dance,' Lizzie said, finishing her drink and putting her bag over her shoulder. 'I've heard the Lansdowne is the place for great music. And in the morning, before we leave, we're going to the Red Cross Club for the best darn milkshakes around.'

Ruby shook her head. 'How about something to eat here and then I can sneak off to bed?'

Lizzie glared at her. 'Not a chance. This is our one night of fun and I'm not letting you sleep through it.'

'I second that!' Polly said.

Ruby groaned, but held up her hands in defeat. 'Fine, but at least let me go to the toilet before you drag me all over London.'

Polly went with her, and the moment they disappeared May touched Lizzie's arm.

'I didn't mean the article to upset you,' she said. 'But I thought it was better for you to see it now, rather than splashed across all the papers in the morning.'

Lizzie shrugged and waved her hand as if it were the least of her worries. 'I'm happy for her, truly,' she said, lying through her teeth. 'She's a great girl and she's a talented flier.'

'But you still think you're better,' May said quietly, her words a statement rather than a question.

'I know you Brits don't like bragging, but, yes, I do think I'm better than her. I thought that much was obvious?' She furiously blinked as tears pricked her eyes; she mustn't let anyone see how upset she was. 'I'm going to win, no matter what some stupid paper says.'

May's brows shot up. 'Stop calling us *you Brits*. It's getting on my nerves and you're as good as one of us now. That's what this whole night was supposed to be about,' she snapped. 'And this isn't a race between anyone, Lizzie. The first woman chosen will be representing all the women of the ATA, to show what we're capable of, to pave the way for all the rest of us. It's not about one woman winning, it's about the right woman taking the lead on the first flight, and the only reason I have you training against one another is to push you both to be the best pilots you can be.'

Lizzie took a deep breath. 'That's it, isn't it? You can't have an American take the honours of first flight, can you? Am I even in the running? Or do you already have this whole thing stitched up while pretending it's an even contest?'

May looked fierce, and folded her arms across her chest. 'The first woman pilot to take command of a four-engine bomber will be chosen on merit, not nationality, and that decision will be made by myself and at least two of my superiors,' she said firmly. 'And Lizzie, you *are* a better pilot under normal circumstances and in a lighter aircraft, but in a big bomber? You and Ruby are neck and neck. You've logged the same number of training hours, and the only difference right now is that you're more confident than her.'

'Neck and neck about what?' Ruby asked, from behind them.

Lizzie spun around. 'Nothing. Now let's get out of here.'

'I can't believe you're taking me out dancing,' Ruby murmured as they moved through the crowd of beautifully dressed men and women.

'Well, believe it,' Lizzie said, wishing she was in the air proving May wrong rather than walking arm in arm with her British friends towards the door. 'This is going to be a night to remember.'

But just as they stepped outside, the unmistakable noise of the air raid siren cut through the air.

'Oh, sod off, Wailing Willy!' Lizzie muttered. 'My one night. My *one* night away from base!'

Ruby sighed as people around them began to hurry for shelter. 'Looks like I'm heading for my nice hotel bed after all.'

# CHAPTER EIGHT

*HAMBLE AIRFIELD, HAMPSHIRE,*

*JUNE 1942*

*RUBY*

Ruby looked up when she heard the click of heels across the concrete floor. She'd been knitting, something she had never been good at and didn't seem to be getting any better at, but it was an easy way to pass the time as she listened to the wireless and tried not to worry about what was happening at the front or whether her engagement was over. In light of everything that was happening to their country, it seemed so stupid that she and Tom were at odds, that they were arguing about anything at all. But it had certainly been heartening to hear that the Allies were successfully bombing parts of industrial Germany; it gave her hope that they were making progress, and it wasn't all for nothing.

It was May crossing the room, wearing a grim expression as she marched towards the flight board, which told Ruby exactly what was about to happen. She'd barely seen her commander since they'd returned from their night at the Savoy; they'd been ferrying multiple planes on every shift. The other women were lounging at tables, chatting and knitting too, with Lizzie reading rather than taking up the 'sock-knitting for soldiers' crusade the rest of them were on, but they all stopped what they were doing now.

Who was missing? Who hadn't returned? May strode past them all without so much as a good morning. Did it mean they'd lost someone? Had they had their first fatality?

Lizzie caught her eye, looking serious for once, and Ruby gulped as May stopped, reached for a cloth and rubbed out a name from the board. When she turned to face them, tears shone in her eyes, but she never said a word; just stood there, silent, as they all watched her.

Ruby had heard that if anyone died, if they didn't return, their name would simply be erased from the board as though it had never existed, and she was afraid that it would be one of the girls she'd made friends with.

'Susan?' one of the other pilots gasped.

Ruby dropped her knitting and reached for Betty's hand, holding it tight as tears ran silently down the other woman's cheeks. A sob lodged in her own throat, but she stifled it, checking her emotion.

'How?' Lizzie asked, her voice like a rasp.

'Girls, let me make it clear that Susan isn't dead, but she won't be rejoining us. She parachuted out in bad visibility to avoid going down with her plane,' May responded, her reply sounding rehearsed and wooden. 'Polly was flying the same course and has reported that the cloud cover was like a thick blanket, so she trusted her gut and dropped down to 600 feet. She was able to land, but Suzy followed protocol and stayed high, electing to parachute out when things went bad.' May smiled tightly. 'Somehow she ended up miles off course over the Thames Estuary, and an extremely gallant officer leapt from a nearby naval vessel and dived in to search for her. She was rescued and hauled onto the boat, before being taken to the closest hospital, where she's suffering from hypothermia and damage to her lungs. We're told she should make a full recovery, but she'll be returning home to recuperate following her discharge.'

Relief washed over Ruby, but it was quickly replaced with anger. Susan could easily have been their first fatality, and it was only luck that it had been a near miss. She hated that all they had up there in the sky were their instincts!

'If we were trained with instruments and allowed to use our bloody radios in emergencies at least, this sort of thing wouldn't be happening,' she said, her cheeks flooding with heat as she stared defiantly at May. 'You know it and I know it, yet for some reason we're treated as second-class pilots. Are they waiting for one of us to end up in a coffin? Will *protocol* change then?'

'I agree,' Lizzie echoed. 'You can bet your bottom dollar that when I'm leading a squadron, I won't stand for it. It's ridiculous that we're treated this way!'

Ruby was shocked that Lizzie had sided with her, but the girls had all swung from horror to annoyance that they weren't trained with instruments.

May stood immobile. 'The lack of radio is for our own good and for the safety of everyone, and I'm not going to officially comment on the instrument status, other than to state that, well . . . we're all experienced pilots, and smart women at that. We all know the difference instruments and a radio would make. But orders are orders, and each and every one of us knows what we signed up for and what the hazards are. Nothing has changed.'

'What was she flying?' Lizzie asked.

'A Spitfire,' May replied.

'You know what Suzy used to say about them?' Lizzie asked, a smile playing across her lips. '*She's a lady up in the air and a bloody bitch on the ground.*' Her faux-English accent was worse than terrible, and made everyone laugh.

'But when she flies, *oh baby* does she fly!' Ruby finished for her.

They all laughed again, and when Ruby looked across at May she mouthed, 'Sorry' – and meant it. She shouldn't have stepped out of line and challenged her; as senior commander, May had the authority to reprimand her for disrespecting their rules. She hoped a private apology later would smooth things over.

May addressed them all again. 'The Anson taxi has arrived, ladies, and you'll be heading directly to the factory. From there you will transport the new aircrafts to Thorney Island Airfield before returning assorted damaged planes for repair at various airfields. I trust you'll all use your best judgement on your return flights. Please refer to your chits to see where and what you're flying. Stay strong, and don't question your instincts.'

Ruby gathered her tangled knitting from the floor and began to follow the others to the toilet, knowing it could be some time before she'd be able to use one again. Unlike their male counterparts who were able to relieve themselves with their special tubes *and* pilot their aircraft, women didn't have the same luxury.

'Ruby,' May called. 'Lizzie, you too.'

Ruby turned and caught Lizzie's eye as they both walked back to May. There had been some tension between them since the *Picture Post* article, and Ruby had no idea how to tackle the ever-present rivalry between them; though Lizzie had also been preoccupied with ruffling the feathers of Captain Montgomery, which had helped somewhat.

May regarded them calmly as they reached her.

'What is it?' asked Lizzie.

'Tomorrow is the day,' May said quietly. 'The weather isn't looking ideal, but we're to decide tomorrow which woman will be taking the first official solo flight in a Halifax.'

Ruby's stomach felt like it had dropped a hundred feet. Her mouth went dry. 'Tomorrow?'

'Tomorrow?' Lizzie echoed.

May nodded. 'Be prepared – it's going to be stiff competition and no decision has been made as yet. I'll most likely be joined by Major Grey, Captain Montgomery and perhaps even MacMillan. The powers that be have a lot riding on a successful first flight, so the more decision-makers we have, the better.' Ruby was surprised when May gave her a quick hug, and then did the same to Lizzie. 'You both be careful out there today.'

'Always,' Ruby replied, squeezing May's arm.

Ruby felt a tremor through her body as she followed Lizzie in silence to their ride. Tomorrow she'd know which of them had won, and for the first time she felt a shiver of anticipation that she could actually do it. The title could be hers for the taking, and if she did get it she'd prove to Tom and her demanding future mother-in-law that she was most definitely talented and capable enough to be in the sky.

She hadn't heard from Tom since her face had been plastered across the *Picture Post*, and she was terrified by what his mother might have said about it. At least her own mother had loved it, and that was all she was letting herself focus on. The war was bigger than their relationship, what she was doing was bigger than their relationship, so she had to press on regardless and believe that, somehow, it would all work out.

'I can't believe it's tomorrow,' Lizzie whispered, as Ruby took her seat next to her in the Anson plane.

'I know.' She didn't want to talk about it. Her stomach was doing cartwheels just thinking about it.

'You know, I have this strange feeling our superiors have already chosen you. In fact, I've known it from the moment I saw the *Picture Post*,' Lizzie said matter-of-factly. 'The powers that be know the importance of good propaganda, and choosing the perfect English rose is a logical decision.'

Ruby's cheeks flamed. Lizzie might be one of the best fliers, but sometimes she was just downright rude! 'I'll have you know that I'm a darn good pilot, Lizzie!' she hissed. 'How dare you belittle me as if I'm somehow second-grade!'

Lizzie shrugged. 'I don't mean to ruffle your feathers. I'm just saying I can understand why they wouldn't want an American to be the first. I can be the first at home. My time will come, so I'm happy for you.'

Ruby snorted. 'You're bloody unbelievable sometimes, Lizzie. But you're wrong. You heard May. They're deciding tomorrow – the best pilot will be chosen, and that's that.' She actually wanted it more than anything now, wanted to stick it to Lizzie and to Tom, show them that she was capable. But even thinking like that made her feel shallow. *Thinking like that makes me as bad as Lizzie, acting like our personal competition is even important, given the state of the country right now.*

As they prepared for take-off, the girls all shuffled forward, helping the twin-engine aircraft by transferring their weight. It easily took up to twelve passengers, but they'd learned fast to move up the front to help with weight distribution.

Ruby ignored Lizzie as the plane finally lifted, glancing across at June, who was holding a hot water bottle to her stomach. She felt sorry for her. They all resorted to them when they had their period; at least being in an all-female ferry pool they had nothing to hide from one another.

'I'm sorry,' Lizzie finally said, reaching out her hand to Ruby's. 'I know we're supposed to be trying to get along, and you're right, you're a good pilot and I need to learn to shut my mouth.'

'You're only sorry because you've realised you haven't lost yet,' Ruby huffed. She had a mind to slap Lizzie's hand away, but she didn't have it in her to be rude.

'Not true!' protested Lizzie. But she withdrew her hand and busied herself with her ferry notebook. When she looked up, she changed the subject. 'What's on your chit today?'

'I'm to fly an Oxford on the first leg of my return,' Ruby replied. 'Then a Hurricane back to White Waltham.'

Lizzie gave her a surprised look. 'Me too. Well, not the first one, but I'm heading back to White Waltham at the end of the day as well.'

Ruby didn't think anything of it until she opened her notebook to read up on the Hurricane she'd be bringing back, wanting to use her time wisely. She'd flown them before, but she still remembered having less than an hour to prepare for her first ever flight in one. It had always amused her that they were given these perfect little 4x6 cards bound on two rings that supposedly contained everything they needed to know about an aircraft, from flying speeds to cruising, landing and stalling speeds. The men who flew them had direct training in each aircraft, but they seemed to think a quick read on the way to collect a plane was enough for the ferry pilots.

'Oh,' she said, puzzled as a note fell out.

> *There will be a car waiting to take you to London to attend an event tonight. I need both you and Lizzie there with me. I'll tell you more when I see you. Your uniforms will be waiting in your room at the Savoy. Fly safe. MJ*

'I just . . .' Ruby started, as Lizzie held up an identical note.

'Seems our commander has been keeping secrets from us, but I'm not about to complain about another night out in London.'

'Me neither.' Ruby touched her small bag, pleased she always took her powder and lipstick with her on every flight. The last thing she wanted was to spend all day flying and then look dowdy come nightfall. 'Especially if we get to stay the night in a comfortable bed with a feather pillow ahead of our big flight tomorrow.'

# CHAPTER NINE

*LONDON, JUNE 1942*

*MAY*

May took a deep breath as she surveyed the crowd she was about to plunge into. Compared to flying, it was akin to navigating a minefield.

She straightened her shoulders and self-consciously touched her hair. It had been a long time since she'd had to worry about her appearance – usually brushing her hair and teeth and ensuring her uniform was immaculate were all she had to be concerned about. But today she was wearing make-up, her pink lipstick applied with a shaky hand as she'd wondered who the woman in the mirror really was. She'd started out with the ATA feeling so young and so terribly inexperienced, but the face looking back at her had a maturity far beyond what she felt. She *looked* capable of being a senior commander now. Inside, she yearned to turn back the clock, to be her old self again: the fun, inquisitive, ready-for-anything girl. Sometimes she wondered if that version of herself was even in there any longer.

*I also wonder what that girl would think about trying to impress a roomful of dignitaries, politicians and wealthy Londoners.*

On paper she could convey anything she needed to get across, and on base, she never doubted herself or her decisions. But the room she was standing in made her feel way out of her depth. And her brother was lurking in her mind today, perhaps as a result of the letter she'd received from her mother. She could have made the hour-long drive to see her, or she could even have told her to come to London to meet her; but just imagining the sadness in her mother's gaze was enough to stop her. She couldn't deal with that, or going home knowing she was never going to see Johnny there again, that she'd never laugh with him and share a meal at their kitchen table, or tease him about one of his many girlfriends.

'I didn't think I was going to make it, but here I am.'

May turned and found herself staring at Ben. Her jaw dropped as she took in his black suit and bow tie, his freshly shaved cheeks and his hair brushed back from his face.

'Benjamin!' she exclaimed, laughing as he took her hand and leaned in for a kiss. 'Oh my gosh!'

'Is this what I'm supposed to do? Kiss your cheek and tell you how great you look?' he teased.

'That's exactly what you're supposed to do.' She was so used to seeing him in his overalls, grease smeared over his fingers and his hair all haphazard, that for a moment she didn't realise how quickly she'd laughed, like she hadn't in years. There was definitely something about Ben that was good for her soul. 'You scrub up rather well.'

Now it was him laughing. 'Don't go giving me a big head.'

She'd asked him to partner her, mostly so that she had someone with her before the others arrived, and she was pleased she had. She looked skyward, wondering if Johnny was laughing down at her, seeing how rattled she was. She felt so comfortable around Ben, but seeing him in a tuxedo made her realise he wasn't necessarily the brother figure she'd always viewed him as.

'Should I get you a drink?' Ben asked. 'Or do you want me to stay here with you?'

She smiled at him. 'Stay with me,' she said. 'I'm as confident as can be in the sky, but put me in a room full of strangers and I go back to being a nervous little girl.'

He held out his arm and she looped hers through it. It was Ben, and no matter how he might look, he was still the same flight mechanic that he'd always been. And there was something about him that allowed a flicker of her old self to come to the surface.

'I won't leave you,' he said, his eyes meeting hers.

'Good evening, Commander.' The warm, rich American accent caught her attention and May turned to see Jackson Montgomery. He stepped forward to kiss her cheek.

'Jackson! Look at you, dashing as can be in that tuxedo!'

'I'll take the compliment,' Jackson said with a grin. 'Thank you.'

'Champagne?' Ben asked, taking glasses from a passing waiter.

May gratefully accepted hers and took a small sip.

'It's nice to see you here tonight, Ben,' Jackson said. 'Nothing beats a night off base, huh?'

Jackson held up his glass to first May and then Benjamin, and she clinked it, hoping neither man had noticed her flushed cheeks.

'May, I've been wanting to have a quiet word with you about something, although it's not something I should be sharing,' Jackson said in a low voice. 'It's about the pay disparity between male and female pilots.'

She exchanged glances with Ben. 'Pay disparity?' she repeated. 'Are we not paid the same?'

'I'm afraid not,' he said, moving closer and glancing over his shoulder. 'This didn't come from me, though – they'd have my head on a block if they found out I'd told you.'

May almost choked on her drink, the bubbles catching in her throat. 'How have they got away with this?'

'There she is! The one and only Commander Jones!'

May turned at the sound of her name, the room seeming to fall quiet just as she locked eyes with the deputy prime minister. She'd been told Winston Churchill himself would be attending, but now that she was faced with his second in command, Clement Attlee, she guessed that might no longer be the case.

'Thank you so much for inviting me tonight,' she said, not telling him that he'd missed the *senior* part of her title, something she was certain any male commander would have pointed out immediately. 'It's an honour.'

'The honour is entirely ours,' he said, looking slightly awkward. 'Now, do tell me, will there be other pilots joining us tonight? We'd like to wait until they are here to thank you all at the ATA for your service.'

To say she was surprised was an understatement. For so long they'd been merely tolerated, and now they were being celebrated? Perhaps it was to do with them taking over the Class V bombers, which were so essential to the war – it might have helped change opinions. With four-engine bombers being delivered as fast as they were made available, their boys had more firepower at their fingertips than ever before.

'Yes, sir, there will be more joining me, but they've been flying and ferrying aircraft all day, so they may be a little late. I actually have one of our guests from the United States joining us as well as another top pilot. Both of them are in consideration for our first female bomber pilot, sir.'

'Well, I'll look forward to becoming acquainted with them both,' he enthused, as he stepped away.

'Sir, before you go, I wanted to ask you . . .'

'Commander Jones, excuse me a moment,' Atlee said, touching her arm and frowning as if he didn't really want to go. 'Please accept my apologies, but I promise we'll have time to talk later.'

May opened and shut her mouth, wishing she'd taken the opportunity when she had it, but Atlee had gone and was already talking to someone no doubt more important and more influential than her. She moved to stand with the men again, frowning as she interrupted them.

'Jackson, you're absolutely certain we're paid less?' she asked.

'I probably shouldn't have said anything,' he apologised. 'Honestly, it wasn't my information to share, but I've seen how hard you all work, and you're all doing the same job, so the double standard is disappointing.'

She was seething, but not at him. She didn't like being taken for a fool, and she could just imagine a tableful of men sitting pleased with themselves for getting women to do the same job as men, but for so much less. Why had she never thought to investigate this before now?

Jackson grimaced. 'You're paid twenty per cent less, May. It's grossly unfair,' he murmured. 'But that information hasn't come from me.'

Her mouth went dry. *A whole* 20 *per cent less? For the same job?*

'You needed to know so you could work out costings in the event your country allows women to fly. That's why, isn't it?' May asked, everything falling into place. 'Please don't tell me the United States government will try to do the same thing if they establish a flying squadron?' She felt foolish, stumbling over things she hadn't even processed properly. She suddenly wished Lizzie was with her to hear all this, and she scanned the room to see if she'd arrived – Lizzie was being paid the same as the rest of them as an ATA pilot, but she'd be interested to hear about the disparity and that the same might happen in the US. 'I'm sorry, I shouldn't have said that. Please don't feel you have to answer.'

Jackson nodded and looked between her and Ben. 'You'll be discreet?'

May nodded, finally spotting Lizzie and waving her over. 'Of course. But I intend to ask for equal compensation.'

He held up his glass again. 'And so you should.'

'Jackson?' Lizzie said as she joined them, looking Jackson slowly up and down.

'Nice to see you too, *Elizabeth*,' Jackson said. 'Don't you look stunning tonight in your dress uniform!'

'Well, I . . .' Lizzie started, her cheeks turning pink. May wasn't surprised she was stuck for words; Jackson did look awfully handsome all dressed up in his tux with his hair slicked back. She wished she'd worn a dress, but it had seemed more appropriate for them all to wear the uniforms they were so proud of.

'You might not have recognised my dashing date. Seems Ben scrubs up rather well too, don't you think?' May said.

Lizzie raised a brow at Ben, still speechless, before turning back to Jackson.

'Where's Ruby?' May asked.

'She's just powdering her nose. I said we'd meet her over there, where it's not too busy.'

'Let's head over now,' Jackson said. 'Hopefully we'll pass a waiter with drinks.'

Lizzie seemed to regain her composure, clutching her purse as she nodded and strode off ahead of him. May stifled a laugh as the crowd parted instantly.

'Would you like my advice?' Ben asked, leaning in so close that she could smell the woody scent of his cologne. 'Because I can tell you're chewing over that nugget of information like a dog worrying a bone.'

May nodded, wishing she weren't so transparent. Or perhaps it was only because he knew her so well. 'Of course.'

'Just ask for it outright. Go for it – ask for what you deserve and don't hold back.' He caught her hand. 'You deserve to be paid the same, May, because we can't win this war without your pilots delivering those planes.'

May took a deep breath. 'Thank you,' she said. She felt lighter than she had in a long time. 'I . . . I hope you know how refreshing it is to have a man like you around.'

'So you'll ask for it?'

'I promise I will. I'm not going to take this on the chin, that's for sure.'

Ben tugged on her hand. 'Come on, we need to get another drink before Churchill finally arrives and wants to talk your ear off for the rest of the evening with a bunch of boring old farts. I need to enjoy your company while I can!'

May burst out laughing, and realised she hadn't laughed so hard since sitting around her parents' table with Johnny and his friends before the war. The memory was sobering but she tried to push past it, clinging tighter to Ben's arm as she fought to stay in the moment, to actually let herself have fun.

'Thank you, Ben,' she whispered. 'I needed you here with me tonight.'

She couldn't breathe when Ben's eyes met hers, his body close as his gaze dipped to her lips then moved up again.

'It's nothing,' he said, but she heard a huskiness in his voice that hadn't been there before. 'We're friends, right? That's what friends do for one another.'

May bit down on the inside of her mouth, relieved when he started walking again. 'Yes,' she murmured. 'Friends.'

'Is that *Ben*?' May turned at Ruby's shriek, and saw that her friend had joined Lizzie and Jackson. 'Well I never!'

'He's mine,' May quipped, clutching his arm. She meant it as a joke, but it came out sounding oddly serious and she wondered who she thought she was kidding.

Then Jackson gathered them all together in a conspiratorial sort of way. 'Ladies and gents, I can't speak on behalf of my president, but I have a little secret that you might be interested in,' he said.

They all crowded around.

'Tell us immediately,' Lizzie demanded.

Ben exchanged glances with May. Jackson certainly was a fountain of information tonight!

'The first lady is planning a visit, and after meeting with the prime minister's wife, they'll be coming to tour White Waltham,' he said. 'I expect you'll all want to be there on the day.'

May watched as Lizzie gulped down her champagne.

'It seems she wants to see exactly what women are doing here in Britain,' Jackson carried on. 'From the Women's Land Army to the ATA and the women ferry pilots and everything in between.'

'Captain Montgomery!' Lizzie demanded, looking furious. 'Exactly how long have you known this information? You shouldn't be keeping secrets like that from me about our own country!'

Jackson raised an eyebrow. 'Perhaps I should have shared this with your British sisters only? They seem far more grateful for confidential information I pass to them.'

'Honestly, Montgomery, you're such a bore sometimes.'

May followed the exchange, feeling sorry for Jackson. His behaviour tonight had shown that he was firmly on their side; what's more, he had freely shared his knowledge of flying large aircraft and she respected him for that.

'Perhaps I didn't want to share classified information with the biggest loudmouth around?' he said. 'You haven't exactly given me reason to confide in you, Elizabeth.'

'The fact that Eleanor Roosevelt is coming here and no one told me about it until now is criminal!' Lizzie hissed. 'And I'm not a *loudmouth*!'

'Perhaps if you were more of a team player you'd have been given that information before now,' he replied, clearly unconcerned by how riled up she was.

May could see where this was going. She was about to intervene when Lizzie stepped right up to the captain, her chest puffed out.

'There is no team to rely on when I'm in the sky, only me. So don't go telling me that I need to be a team player! It's getting tiresome, all of you!'

May watched as Jackson stopped a waiter and took a champagne bottle from him, then attentively topped up everyone's glass except for Lizzie's. He placed it back on the waiter's silver tray and held his glass up before taking a slow sip and winking at Lizzie, and May had to bite her lip to stop herself smiling.

'*Lovely* to see you all, but I have a colleague I'd like to speak with. I trust you'll all have a wonderful night.'

And with that he spun around and walked away, leaving Lizzie visibly seething. Ruby put a hand to her shoulder, only to be shrugged away as Lizzie muttered under her breath.

Then May was distracted by a light touch to her back. When she turned and came face to face with Winston Churchill, a sense of calm settled over her that she'd never experienced before.

'Prime Minister Churchill, what an honour to be here tonight in such esteemed company,' she said quickly.

'Senior Commander Jones, the pleasure is all mine,' he said. May was used to hearing his voice on the wireless, and in person he was as authoritative and appealing as he sounded there. 'We are immensely proud of all you're doing for the war effort. The assistance has been well received and greatly appreciated.'

'Thank you, sir.'

'If there's anything we can do to assist you further . . .'

'Well, actually, sir, there is one thing,' May said, lowering her voice.

'Yes?' he asked, a frown puckering his forehead. She was certain he'd expected her to merely nod and not ask for anything.

'I'm rather appalled to learn that we're being paid twenty per cent less than our male colleagues, and it's something I'd like to see remedied immediately,' she told him. She'd missed one opportunity, and she was darn sure she wasn't going to miss another; she saw no point in waiting until the morning, when the decision-maker himself was standing in front of her. '*Obviously* I'll go down the appropriate channels to ensure this is fixed, but with my pilots on the cusp of ferrying much-needed four-engine bombers to our boys at the front . . .' She purposely left her sentence dangling, glancing down at her drink for a moment before looking up again and smiling. 'In fact, our first and best bomber pilots are here with me tonight.'

Churchill's stare was impossible to decipher.

'It was lovely to make your acquaintance, Senior Commander,' he said, abruptly ending their conversation. 'Thank you for your service, and I trust you'll enjoy a rare evening off.'

May nodded and watched him go, her heart beating wildly. Then a hand touched her shoulder, and she looked straight into the eyes of Ben.

'Have this,' he whispered, passing her a fresh glass of champagne. 'I think you deserve it. *Bravo*.'

Her hand was shaking as she reached for it, but when Ruby and Lizzie started to clap, a slow smile spread across her lips as she realised they'd overheard the conversation. Ben joined in, doing a dainty little clap and making her laugh. She still couldn't get over how clean his hands were.

'First of all, let me say that your little speech there has made me actually appreciate the concept of teamwork,' Lizzie said, slinging an arm around her. 'And second of all, we're getting *twenty per cent less pay*?'

May blew out a breath. 'Yes, Lizzie, we are. I just found out tonight.'

'Well then, bravo, *Commander*. We'll know who to thank if we get a pay rise.'

Ruby cleared her throat and pointed to the front of the room as Churchill appeared, ready to address the crowd. 'Here goes.'

May glanced sideways at Ben, and her heart raced as his eyes met hers again. Churchill should have been the most interesting man in the room, but it was Ben who claimed her full attention. *He's a friend,* she reminded herself. *A friend and nothing more.* She couldn't survive another broken heart, that was for sure. After tonight, he was just her flight mechanic, nothing more, nothing less.

She looked around at the packed room and wondered what would happen if an air-raid siren echoed out, how frantic the stampede of people would be. Before, she'd have never looked for an exit, never considered London to be dangerous, but the reminders of war were everywhere – in her mind, in every bang that made her jump, in every building reduced to rubble. And she wondered if she'd ever stop waiting for a bomb to land, for one of her girls not to make it back from a flight, or ever lose that trembling fear that their city, their country, could be overrun with Germans at any moment.

Ben slipped his arm around her, and suddenly she couldn't fight her desire to be closer to him. It was only one night, and, for some reason, when she was with him the world didn't seem quite such a terrifying place.

# CHAPTER TEN

## *HAMBLE AIRFIELD, HAMPSHIRE, ENGLAND,*

## *JUNE 1942*

### *LIZZIE*

Lizzie strode past the gathered group and grinned at Ruby, who was standing a few steps away, already waiting. They were both dressed in their flying suits and she gave her rival a wink.

'May the best woman win,' she whispered.

Ruby had a bead of sweat shining above her top lip and all she did was nod, not saying a word, as if paralysed with fear. It was the only reason Lizzie knew she'd be able to beat her – Ruby's nerves were definitely going to get the better of her in the air, and the Halifax required nerves of steel.

There was a large crowd watching: other pilots, engineers and of course May and the two men who were making the decision with her. Lizzie stared at the back of Captain Montgomery, hating that an American superior to her was on base throwing his weight around. Thankfully he was still recuperating so wasn't there all the time, but he was most definitely getting in her way. And she wished her daddy was watching her; she couldn't wait to write him and tell him blow by blow what had happened. He'd always been proud of her, but everything she did, she did to show him that she was a chip off the old block.

'Ladies, we have a Halifax waiting for each of you. Please prepare yourselves for take-off,' May instructed, standing to attention before them. May's own superior flanked her on one side, while Captain Montgomery in full dress uniform stood on the other. 'First Officer Sanders, you will be flying first and we'd like you to perform your usual training drill, which will be timed and studied by all three of us.'

'Yes, ma'am,' Ruby replied.

'First Officer Dunlop, you're to wait on the runway until Ruby is safely grounded, and you're pre-cleared for immediate take-off after that. You will perform the same drill.'

'Looking forward to it,' Lizzie said.

'Commander Jones, am I to remain in my aircraft until Lizzie has landed?' Ruby asked.

'Once the runway is clear you may exit. Thank you for asking,' May replied. 'And ladies, we're expecting to make a unanimous decision. However, if one cannot be reached, we will decide by a majority vote. I want to remind you that this is not a personal competition. The purpose of narrowing the process down to our two most highly trained pilots, and then to one of you, is to prove what we can do in the air, what *women pilots* can do, so we can step up our assistance to our fighter pilots and help win this war once and for all! The woman chosen will represent the entire women's division of the ATA on that first official flight.'

Lizzie headed for the magnificent airplanes waiting for them, signalling to Ruby that she was going to take the one on the right. This might be for the war effort, but she couldn't see why there was anything wrong with wanting to take it personally.

'Good luck up there,' Ruby called out.

'Honey, luck has *nothing* to do with it,' Lizzie called back.

She knew Ruby would be rolling her eyes – heck, she knew *everyone* would be rolling their eyes at her. But she wasn't going to go around pretending like she wasn't going to win, because she always got what she wanted. And when it came to flying, it was the one thing she never had to bluff. *You'll be proud of your little girl, Daddy*, she thought. He'd always been the one to believe in her, and she wasn't ever going to let him down.

She climbed up with Ben's help, calmly sitting behind the controls and waiting, watching through the windscreen for Ruby. Five full minutes later, the roar of the other Halifax was unmistakable and slowly Ruby taxied away, rolling down the runway before taking off. It was a textbook take-off and Lizzie squinted as the plane ascended higher before beginning the short cross-country flight they'd been assigned. She listened to her own breath as she waited for it to reappear, the long minutes ticking past. Ruby would circle first, and then eventually come in to land.

*There she was.*

'Contact!' Lizzie yelled, ready to get her engine started. Within minutes she saw the plane coming down, watched as Ruby neared her, descending slowly.

*Go!* she thought, grinning as she took off just before Ruby's wheels had hit the runway, pushing the aircraft hard and rocketing down the tarmac before pulling up and getting it into the air. She flew low and did an extra circle, showing off, before ascending to the correct altitude and following her cross-country course. She relaxed and enjoyed the flight, but she didn't slow down, wanting to go faster and beat Ruby's time; they'd be watching the clock. *When you have a chance to prove yourself to your superiors, you seize it, Lizzie. Give it everything you have.* Her father's words echoed through her as she finally headed back down. She'd waited all this time, and she'd finally had the chance she'd been waiting for.

Lizzie decided to show the crowd below exactly what she was made of one last time, doing a slow roll in the ginormous Halifax before bringing it down and coming to a halt close to where she'd started. It might be a beast, but it was a beast she had full control over.

She'd done it! The flight had been perfect, and she'd even shown them that she could outmanoeuvre the enemy if she needed to with her perfect roll. Ruby had played by the book, but *she'd* shown them exactly how versatile she could be.

Lizzie climbed down, laughing as Ben helped her, taking off her flying helmet and running her fingers through her hair.

'What did you think?' she asked him, used to his ready smile and words of encouragement. 'Was that a perfect run, or what?'

Ben said nothing, only pointed towards May and mumbled something she couldn't decipher. Lizzie shrugged, unconcerned, and sauntered off, surprised to see Ruby staring at her feet and May looking furious. Where were Major Grey and Captain MacMillan?

'So how did we do?' Lizzie asked as Ruby slowly met her gaze.

'How did you do?' May asked, her face reddening as she lifted her chin and glared back. '*How* did you do?'

'I wasn't aware it was a loaded question,' Lizzie teased, wondering why May looked so angry. 'What's going on?'

'You embarrassed not only your commander, who has so generously hosted you here, but your country, Lizzie. Not to mention that Grey and MacMillan both stormed off in disgust before you even landed,' Montgomery snapped, stepping forward. 'It was a very easy decision to concur with them and tell Senior Commander Jones that I don't believe you're deserving of the first bomber flight for the ATA, and she wholeheartedly agreed with me.'

Lizzie baulked, and heard Ruby gasp.

'Excuse me? Did you not see me up there?' she asked, looking between them. 'Is this a joke?'

'No, Lizzie, this is no joke,' May said, shaking her head, her eyes filled with such obvious disappointment that Lizzie stepped closer, only to be rebuffed as May stepped quickly backwards. 'You took off before it was safe to do so and then attempted to entertain us with theatrics that had no place in your test, or in a Halifax, full stop. Flying recklessly like that could put an end to women being cleared to fly four-engine bombers at all! It's as if you missed the entire point of this exercise and what we've been training for.'

'May, please . . .' Lizzie blinked away tears. Had she been so reckless? Had May truly believed in her so much, in her ability, and she'd thrown that respect away?

'The decision has been made, and that's final,' Montgomery interrupted. 'Rivalry is one thing; it helps to push pilots to their limits and encourages them to do their best. But you went too far.'

'Too far?' She lifted her chin, not about to let them treat her like this, even if she was struggling not to cry. 'With or without your support, I know I'm the best pilot here. I'm going to make a name for myself in the sky just like my father did, and neither of you can stop me!'

'You're excused, Elizabeth,' Jackson said.

'*Excused?*'

'Excused,' he repeated. 'And you're nothing like your father. He would have been ashamed of you today.'

His words were a blow, but she refused to back down. 'My father would have been proud to watch me fly like that! How dare you talk about him as if you know him!'

Montgomery walked closer, so close she could feel his breath on her face. 'Our fathers were in the same squadron,' he said, so low she doubted anyone else could hear. 'And I know that your daddy flew for the team, for his squadron, and if they hadn't been there supporting him, protecting him from enemy fire, he never could have had his victories.'

She stared back at him. 'I don't believe you.'

'Ask him yourself, then,' he said, backing away. 'But your father wasn't always the big gun out the front. He supported his crew and they supported him. There's no point being the best out front if there's no one on your tail or to your side to back you up.'

'Congratulations, Ruby. You flew a perfect, textbook flight today, and you are a talented, *respectful* pilot who deserves to represent the ATA by being the first woman to ferry a four-engine bomber,' May said in a loud voice, her back turned to Lizzie now. 'We are all so proud of you.'

Ruby's cheeks were flushed, and Lizzie couldn't stop her mouth from falling open. Shivers raced down her spine as she stared at the people in front of her, unable to comprehend what had just happened. And how dare Montgomery act as if he knew anything about her father's victories!

'You know she's not as good as me!' Lizzie fumed, anger lashing through her body in waves.

'I was speaking honestly in London, Lizzie. You were neck and neck until today, and I supported you both equally all the way, but the decision was simple in the end,' May said bluntly, giving her no more than a cursory glance. 'The best pilot has been given the honours, and that's final. Depending on the success of Ruby's first flight and your own conduct, you'll be cleared to ferry four-engine bombers within the month, too.'

'You spineless bastard!' Lizzie screamed at Montgomery. 'How could you not support me? How can you not see how capable I am?'

Montgomery stepped closer again, unblinking. He took her by the elbow and steered her away from the others. 'You're out of control, Lizzie. Rein it in.'

'Don't speak to me like that!'

'You're easily the best pilot here, I'll give you that,' he muttered. 'But there's no use in being the best if your leader can't rely on you to follow orders. It's time you looked at the bigger picture, Lizzie.'

Lizzie stood in stunned silence as May and Ruby disappeared, and then Montgomery walked off too. She realised then that the entire crowd had gone, and she had no idea how much any of them had heard. Now it was just her, standing alone in a field, horrified by her public outburst.

Tears slid down her cheeks then, fast and furious. Lizzie wiped at them before giving up, falling forward and crying, fists clenched as she sobbed.

What had she done? Was Montgomery right – *was* she out of control? How had she become this person? Or had she always been her?

Suddenly her clever tricks and fast take-off seemed immature, everything she'd thought so incredibly clever actually so terribly, terribly wrong. She'd lost the flight, the one thing she wanted more than anything, and she had no damn idea what to do about it.

Suddenly black boots appeared on the ground in front of her and she looked up through tear-blurred eyes.

'Get up.'

A hand extended towards her and Lizzie blinked, taking it and looking up at Jackson Montgomery. Why had he come back?

'What have I done?' she whispered. 'How did this all go so horribly wrong?' Her daddy would be waiting for the mail, eager to hear news of whether she'd been awarded the first flight, and now she was going to have to tell him that she'd lost it.

'You behaved like a princess,' he said, letting go of her hand. 'And if you can't see that then I can't see how I can help you.'

She gulped. 'I think I can see that now.'

'Good,' he replied. 'So brush away those tears, pull yourself together and go tell your fellow pilot how proud of her you are, and that she deserved the first flight.'

Lizzie was hollow inside, and she sucked back a breath. 'I can't.'

'You can and you will. And then you're going to start following orders and proving that you're not only the best, but that you're also reliable and capable of being part of a team. We're not all born with a silver spoon in our mouths, Elizabeth, and even those who are still need to work hard. Some of us have had to work for every step up the ladder, and I want to see the same attitude from you. Do you think I could have pulled stunts like that and got away with it?'

She listened, unable to take her eyes off his face. His expression had softened; he was no longer barking orders but coaching her like he actually wanted her to succeed.

'No,' she said honestly. 'Of course not.'

'You can't expect to lead your own squadron back home if you can't get your act together here,' he continued. 'So stop acting so entitled. No one likes a show-off, especially one who doesn't seem to take the war seriously.'

He started walking and she scrambled to keep up. Just like that, he'd managed to give her the kick up the backside she'd needed. If someone else was given command of a squadron back home, if she missed *that* job? Then life truly wouldn't be worth living. If this was her second chance, then she was taking it with open arms.

'Thank you,' she said, in a low, husky voice.

'I'm sorry, what was that?'

Lizzie groaned. 'I said thank you!'

'Now that's more like it.'

She still hated him, but for the moment at least, she respected him, and that was something.

'Do you really know my daddy?' she asked.

'I've heard a lot about him from my own father,' Jackson said. 'Perhaps it's time you wrote to him and asked him for some advice.'

And for once, Lizzie had to admit that Captain Montgomery might just be right.

# CHAPTER ELEVEN

## *HAMBLE AIRFIELD, HAMPSHIRE, ENGLAND,*

## *JULY 1942*

### *RUBY*

The cloud cover had been thick all morning. 'Like pea soup,' May had muttered, storming back to her desk. Ruby knew there was as much pressure on her commander as there was riding on her today, but if they had to call the entire thing off due to weather conditions for a third day in a row it would be infuriating.

She sat outside, waiting. She was going to stare at the sky for as long as it took, because she *was* flying that four-engine bomber today, and nothing was going to stop her. She still couldn't believe she'd won against Lizzie, and she still couldn't help but wonder if she *was* actually the better pilot. If Lizzie hadn't shown off, she would have won; she'd heard what Montgomery was saying. But Lizzie hadn't won, and that meant that Ruby needed to believe in herself. If Tom's letter, his words of *discouragement*, hadn't been sowing seeds of doubt in her mind, she might not have found it so hard.

Ruby's stomach lurched at the thought of being the first, of the pressure of flying pitch-perfect. There would be hell to pay and she'd become the most hated pilot in the ATA if she failed in any way – as well as being plastered over every newspaper as the girl who'd thought she was good enough to fly a bomber made for men. She shuddered. It wasn't worth thinking about. But if she mucked this opportunity up, women might not be permitted to fly four-engine aircraft after all.

'Are you going up today?' Lizzie asked, dropping down to sit beside her.

'I think so. Well, actually I don't know,' Ruby replied. 'I suppose I'm holding out hope that it'll clear.'

'Just remember that it's your call. You're the pilot. Don't let anyone pressure you into it,' Lizzie said, clasping Ruby's hand. 'The visibility will be terrible all day and you know it. It's not your fault the weather's been awful all week and the last thing I want is something happening to you up there.'

Ruby nodded. 'It'll clear,' she said optimistically. 'Thanks for your support though.'

Unlike the male RAF pilots, they got to make their own decisions about whether to fly or not. It was their risk and their decision. Some of the girls thought it made them more important, but Ruby wasn't so naïve. It meant the authorities didn't care so much if they lost them; though they'd be more than annoyed to lose a plane, she was certain.

'Have this,' Lizzie said, holding out her other hand. 'This is me saying in the only way I know how, well, how incredibly sorry I am for my behaviour. The best pilot is taking to the skies today, and I want you to know it.'

Lizzie dropped something into her palm, and Ruby saw it was chocolate. 'Ohhh,' she murmured, salivating at the perfect dark square. 'I suppose I can't be angry with you now, can I?'

Lizzie grinned, and Ruby laughed when she produced a smaller piece of chocolate from her pocket. 'I've saved a little piece for myself.'

Ruby popped the square into her mouth at the same time as Lizzie, rolling it around, and savouring the bittersweet taste.

'You know, I'm really proud that you're representing us all today, Ruby. I honestly thought I deserved it, that it was supposed to be me, but I was wrong.'

Ruby shook her head. 'I think you *were* supposed to be the first.'

'No,' Lizzie said, her smile kind. 'I wasn't. Because we're both just as good up there in a Halifax, we've both put in the hours and we're both excellent pilots. But I was wanting the first flight for me, and that's not what it was all about.'

Lizzie brushed away tears and Ruby realised just how much losing the flight, and being called out by her superiors, had affected her.

'I believe in you, Ruby,' Lizzie carried on. 'You're the one to pave the way, to show there's so much more women can do to help, and you're going to do us all proud.'

'Thank you, Liz. It means a lot.'

Lizzie gave her an awkward hug and they both laughed. 'This friend thing is kind of difficult,' she teased. 'But I could probably get used to it, if I *had* to.'

'Don't go making too much of an effort for my sake,' Ruby quipped straight back.

Lizzie grinned, and then her smile faded. 'You know, the powers that be really want you in the sky today,' she said.

'How do you know what the *powers that be* want from me?'

'May's inside right now with Chief Instructor Captain MacMillan, and he looked like he was about to have kittens.'

Ruby gulped and almost swallowed the chocolate. 'What? They're talking now?'

'Uh-huh. And I don't think they want to delay this flight, from what I heard. They desperately need that Halifax delivered, and everyone's on edge about the whole thing.'

'Anything else?' Ruby asked, wiping her hands on her trouser leg to dry her sweaty palms.

'They want the rest of us up and flying them by the end of the month, but they need the good publicity from you first, and then higher up needs to sign off on it.' Lizzie grimaced. 'And I hate to say it, but everything hinges on whether you're a success or not. I heard them say that every inch of your journey from take-off to landing is going to be scrutinised.'

*Hmmm*, Ruby thought sarcastically: she just needed to fly perfectly and not get lost in cloud cover, crash into a mountain or muck up her landing. All despite the fact she had no instruments, no radio and no crew as back up – all things a male pilot would have at his disposal.

She looked up again and saw that the cloud wasn't as thick; or maybe it was her imagination. And then it started to rain.

'Bloody hell!' she cursed under her breath. 'Could today get any worse?'

'First Officer!'

Ruby turned her head to see May standing on the step of the main building with the captain beside her. She had a feeling it was time to fly, weather be damned.

'Good luck,' Lizzie whispered, squeezing her shoulder. 'Not that you need it.'

Ruby's heart was pounding all over again as she marched back over.

'How are you feeling?' May asked, as they all walked to her desk.

'Aside from furious about the weather?' Ruby joked, not wanting anyone to see how nervous she actually was. 'How can we have so many dismal days at this time of year?'

'Well, by all accounts it should clear soon,' Captain MacMillan said, his voice less gruff than usual. 'It's your decision as pilot to go up or not, but . . .'

'Let's prepare regardless,' Ruby said, surprised by how confident she sounded. 'The cloud cover is clearing, and a little bit of rain isn't going to put me off.'

MacMillan nodded and so did May, and Ruby went to find some water, deciding to have a small glass now. It was always a balancing act, trying to stay hydrated for the flight, but knowing it would be a long time before she could relieve herself.

She heard them talking but tuned it out, not wanting to eavesdrop. She could do this. She touched her chest, feeling the weight of her engagement ring hanging there. There was another reason she wanted to go today – a reason she hadn't shared with anyone else. *Tom might be there.* May had whispered to her that it might pan out well; a week earlier, Ruby had heard that he was stationed at Elvington, Yorkshire, but he hadn't known how long for. At the time she hadn't thought anything of it – but she hadn't received her ferry chit at that point. Now she realised that if he was still there, if he wasn't flying, if the stars aligned, perhaps she'd be able to see him. It had been so long – over a year now – since she'd actually held him in her arms and gazed up into those beautiful hazel-brown eyes.

When she shut her eyes she could feel his hands gliding up her arms, she could imagine the softness of his lips as they brushed against hers. And part of her kept thinking that if she could only see him, if he could only see her and how capable she was, then all the animosity over her decision to fly would disappear. But at the same time, she was ready to scream bloody murder at him and tell him to sod off with his mother's four-week deadline to return home. She had almost reached that deadline now, and she had no intention of packing her bags.

'Sanders?'

She said a silent prayer before turning back to her superiors.

'It's starting to clear.'

Ruby nodded. 'Wheels-up as soon as we can, sir.'

'You know, I have every confidence in you,' MacMillan said, surprising her; his praise was as rare as a rooster that laid eggs. 'I was in the control tower the day you landed after your first solo training session in a Halifax, and the group captain nearly fell off his chair when he was told a woman was bringing the beast in to land. I think his jaw hit the ground when he watched how well you'd mastered it, although he wasn't impressed to see a woman land a plane that his men moan about trying to bring down.'

His praise did precisely what he'd no doubt intended. A weight immediately lifted from Ruby's shoulders and she smiled, knowing how badly he wanted her to succeed. And how much he believed in her.

Much to her amazement, or perhaps because of the constant litany of prayers she was sending skyward, the clouds slowly began to lift. The light patter of rain didn't disappear, but Ruby wasn't scared of a little rain.

'I can do this,' she whispered under her breath as she strode toward the monstrous plane. She nodded to Ben, pleased that he'd been the one to clear her for take-off.

When she entered the giant aircraft, she groaned and realised she'd forgotten to check there was a cushion for her. She was tiny – it was no great secret that she was technically too small to be flying, given the ATA guidelines – and she had no hope of a successful flight if she was so far from the controls.

'Excuse me,' she called out, 'I need someone to get me a cushion.'

Ben had already disappeared, but Ruby heard the laughter from the ground crew below and tried to stay calm as blood rushed to her face and anger pulsed through every inch of her.

'Not comfy enough in there for you, luv?' one of the guys called back.

She took a deep breath and prepared to climb out. 'I'll have you know . . .' she started, then realised it didn't matter. No one was interested in helping a stupid little woman, and no one was ever going to go back to the mess room for her, even for the first woman to pilot a bomber.

'Fine, I'll get one myself!' she fumed. She could have tried rolling up her jacket or putting her bag behind her, but it was an important flight and she needed to be comfortable and safe. She clambered back out of the cockpit, but as she did so a figure appeared, running along the tarmac.

'You looking for this?' Lizzie called out, waving a cushion.

Ruby grinned in relief. 'How did you know?'

'I knew those *arseholes* wouldn't get it for you,' responded Lizzie with an almost faultless British twang. 'And I wanted to wish you luck one last time.' She gave Ruby a big, warm hug. 'You're going to be amazing, Ruby. I can't wait to hear all about the first flight.'

'Thanks, Liz,' Ruby murmured, hugging her back. Then, with Lizzie's help, she climbed back up into her seat.

'Go show them what girls can do!' Lizzie hollered, then turned to the men gathered around. 'And next time get the woman a damn cushion when she needs one. You're acting as if you've never seen a woman fly a bomber before!'

With the cushion underneath her and her heart starting to thud, Ruby prepared the plane, flicking switches and checking the controls.

'Contact!' she yelled, before turning on the big engine.

The noise of the huge plane rumbled through her. As she taxied down the long runway, she whispered a prayer and felt her heart leap the moment the wheels left the ground. And just like that, she was flying, the first woman ever to ferry a four-engine bomber – a Halifax with a 98-foot wingspan at that!

'I did it!' she squealed. 'I did it,' she whispered this time, and settled in for the cross-country flight to Yorkshire. She knew her route, had maps to consult as she needed them, and the weather was still clearing. All she had to hope for were no rogue German planes, increasing visibility and a decent landing at the other end – although the Halifax was fully loaded, and she knew exactly which button to push if she needed to unleash her fury on a plane marked with a black swastika on its fuselage.

She was the first four-engine female bomber, and for the first time since she'd started flying she didn't need to glance at the co-pilot seat beside her. She didn't need Tom, she didn't need an instructor to back her up, she just needed to trust in herself and her ability to get the job done. She listened to the blissful silence inside her own head. All this time, Tom's voice had been in there, telling her what to do, talking her through every step. But now the only voice she could hear was her own.

# CHAPTER TWELVE

## HAMBLE AIRFIELD, HAMPSHIRE, ENGLAND, JULY 1942

### LIZZIE

'Lizzie?'

Lizzie sniffed and quickly wiped her cheeks. She didn't need May to see her like this, or anyone else for that matter.

'What's wrong? Do you need a moment?' May asked.

She shook her head. 'No, I'm fine, I just . . .'

May frowned and touched her shoulder. 'Liz, what's going on?'

Lizzie tried to speak, but her words choked in her throat and all that came out was a big sob.

'Oh dear, Lizzie,' May said, presenting her with a handkerchief and patting her shoulder.

'I'm sorry, I just . . . I can't seem to get my head straight today.'

'I know how hard it must have been for you to accept my decision,' said May, her voice soft.

'It's not that. I mean it is,' Lizzie managed to say. 'I'm actually happy for Ruby, honestly. She deserves that flight, and you and Montgomery were right about me. I was acting like the only thing that mattered was my personal success, instead of realising that everything we do is for the war effort. You've all lost so much, and it's easy for me to pretend like this is just a big adventure.'

May smiled. 'I can't tell you how good it is to hear you say that, Lizzie. And I overheard some of what you said to Ruby earlier. I'm proud of you.'

'All I ever wanted was to show my daddy that I was the son he never had, that I was as good as any man, that I could achieve what he'd achieved in the Great War,' Lizzie shared. 'It sounds shallow now, but it's true.'

'It's all in the past, Lizzie,' May said. 'I'll be proud to have you second up after Ruby if all goes well today. Heaven knows we have more Halifaxes to ferry than we have pilots.'

Lizzie exhaled in relief. When Jackson had dismissed her, she truly hadn't known if she'd been dismissed from training altogether.

'Anything you want me to do, I'm here for you,' she said honestly. 'And feel free to give me a good kick up the backside if I go back to the old version of me, okay?'

May laughed. 'Roger that.' She paused. 'I actually came to tell you that I received word from the US ambassador today.'

'What did he have to say?'

'Exactly what Jackson told us. The First Lady's visit is confirmed, and we're to meet with her at White Waltham.'

'That's great,' Lizzie said, although she was feeling nervous. She'd hoped to be telling Eleanor that she was the first bomber girl, and she hated to think she might have disappointed her. 'I still can't believe Montgomery didn't tell me earlier, though.'

May said nothing for a second. 'Lizzie . . . There's something else you weren't told, too.' She met Lizzie's eyes, her expression pained.

'What? What is it?' Lizzie demanded.

May cleared her throat. 'The ambassador also said that . . .' She hesitated. 'That a women's flying squadron has been established in your absence.'

Lizzie opened her mouth to reply, but nothing come out. Her skin went cold, her throat dry. It couldn't be true. There must have been a mistake.

'He said it was a plane-delivery service, but I don't know any other details.'

'The bastards,' Lizzie swore, standing up and kicking at her chair. 'The bloody bastards!'

She'd come here, she'd done what they'd asked of her, she'd brought her best pilots with her, and they'd gone and established a women's flying squadron without consulting her or asking her to head it? Was this to punish her for something? Was *Montgomery* involved? Had he said she wasn't capable? She began to shake. She could cope with Ruby getting the first flight; she could live with that. But this? It was unimaginable!

'Can I offer you some words of advice before you do something impulsive?' said May, reaching for her hands.

Lizzie just stared back, seething.

'Use this information wisely, and demand to take over as head of the programme. Lord only knows you deserve it, and you've more than proven yourself to me now,' May said. 'But show them the Lizzie we all know you can be, the Lizzie I've just seen today. Don't make contact with anyone in a state of anger or shock. I want you to carefully think this through. I want you to be the leader and pilot that I believe you can be.'

Lizzie could hardly breathe. Had she done this to herself? Had she been so caught up in her own ambitions that she'd lost the role that was supposed to be hers? 'They've forgotten about me. They've actually forgotten all about me, haven't they? And here I was thinking I was proving myself and waiting patiently to be called back.' She gulped. 'Either that or I've blown it.'

May folded her arms across her chest. 'Well, remind them exactly who you are then, but do it the right way. They won't forget you a second time. But watch your words.'

Lizzie clenched her hands into fists to stop them shaking. 'Oh, I will, don't you worry.'

'Going back to the task at hand, though, I'll need you to take a temporary back seat on the four-engine bombers over the next week or so – all of you, actually,' May said. 'It's a logistical nightmare, but we're in a hurry to get as many Spitfires as we can to Malta, and I'll need all hands on deck.'

'Including you?'

May nodded. 'Including me. I'm actually looking forward to flying instead of being permanently buried in paperwork and training. This could be a game-changer for the war, and that means they need us to deliver every plane possible with every pilot at our disposal.'

'Whatever you need, May, I'm here. You can count on me.'

'Good,' May replied. 'We should fly out soon after the First Lady's visit, depending on when the planes are ready.'

Lizzie looked down at her hands and fisted them when she still couldn't stop them from shaking. 'May, do you mind me asking how you got along with the pay disparity dispute?' she asked, to take her mind off it. 'Or will you be fighting that until you're blue in the face?'

A slow, proud smile lit up May's face. 'Would you believe that I got it? They crumbled the moment I kicked up a fuss. It seems they weren't prepared to face an angry woman with a female squadron behind her.'

'Already? You got it *already*?' Lizzie knew how efficient her English boss was, but this was impressive, all the same.

'So long as they don't go back on their word, yes.'

Lizzie stepped forward and gave her a big hug. 'I hope you're proud of yourself. You've achieved so much for so many women.' May had gone into battle for every single female ATA pilot, to ensure they were paid fairly for the sacrifice and contribution they were making for their country, and she hoped they all knew how far she was willing to go for them.

'It's nothing,' May said with a shrug. 'Anyone else in my position would do the same.'

Lizzie shook her head, not surprised that May didn't want a fuss. 'Since I don't have any flights today, would you mind if I took the next few hours off? I need to go to the post office to send a telegram.'

'Of course. That's fine,' said May. 'But promise me you'll take some time before sending anything back home about the flying squadron?'

Lizzie grinned. 'I'll walk there, so it'll give me time to think.'

'Go then, and don't be too hard on Montgomery when you see him. Perhaps he knows nothing about all this.'

Lizzie raised a brow. 'I'm certain he does.'

Lizzie said goodbye to May and started to walk, pleased the sun was shining so she could wander and figure out exactly what she was going to say to General Hap Arnold about the flying squadron.

Lizzie looked skyward and sent up a prayer that Ruby was delivering the bomber safely. She put her head down and walked fast, grasping for words other than, '*What the hell were you thinking, doing this without me?*' She doubted Hap would have a welcome party for her if she started out her telegram like that.

'Lizzie!'

She turned to see Jackson Montgomery's familiar outline jogging towards her from the administration building.

'In case you're wondering, I've made my apologies,' she said, expecting him to launch straight into a lecture about her on-base behaviour. 'Ruby knows that she has my full support, and so does May. They're great women, it just took me a little longer to see that.'

'It's not that,' he said. He looked different somehow; his eyes were soft, troubled even, and Lizzie folded her arms. Was he going to admit what was going on back home, or was he going to pretend he didn't know anything? Right now she didn't trust him as far as she could kick him, even if he had passed useful information to May.

'Spit it out then,' she said impatiently.

'Elizabeth, I needed to see you before I leave base,' he said, his brows furrowed. 'And I need to talk to you about something.'

'Leave base?' she asked. Now she was furious – he *had* to have something to do with it!

He nodded. 'I've been called home and I have a few days' leave before I fly back.'

She frowned, still pretending she knew nothing. 'Home? I thought you'd be kept here until you could fly again?' Was he not returning to active duty?

'Lizzie, I do hope we cross paths again, despite everything. I think under different circumstances we might have gotten along better.'

Lizzie gasped. 'You're going home to join this other woman pilot, aren't you? I can't believe it! Are you going to be running the programme with her?'

'Lizzie, please, I . . .'

She turned away, wanting to scream that he was a spineless bastard, but managing to hold herself back.

'Yes, I've been asked to go back and take over a training position, mainly of our new male pilots, but I could be overseeing the women's flying detachment training too. I'm not going to lie to you.'

'Just go, Jackson. Go!' she snapped.

'Lizzie, stop,' he ordered. 'You need to listen to me.'

She ignored him, and began to walk on. 'I've heard enough!' she called back.

But a heavy hand soon fell on her shoulder.

'Get your hands off me!' she exclaimed.

But Jackson's hold stayed firm. 'Lizzie, I was going to tell you about the new squadron. It's one of the reasons I was looking for you, but it's more than that. I need . . .'

'What?' she snapped. 'What do you need?'

'It's your father,' Jackson said. 'I'm so sorry that I'm the one to break this news to you, Liz, but I wanted it to be me.'

Lizzie's heart started to pound. 'My father?' What on earth did Jackson know about her father? 'What are you talking about?'

'He's had a heart attack, Lizzie. I'm so sorry.' He reached for her hand. 'I was in the office when an urgent message came through for you from head office, and I wanted to be the one to break the news to you.'

Lizzie's breath stuttered from her lungs. She felt her knees buckle as she stared back at Jackson, whose hand found her arm, this time holding her up. 'Is he alive? How do you know? What . . .'

'He's alive. He's in hospital. I'm so sorry – I know how much he means to you.'

Lizzie was struggling to take it in. He'd always seemed so strong, so invincible to her . . . but . . . a heart attack?

'Thank you. For telling me,' she managed.

'Your father . . .' he started.

'You let me worry about my father,' she said briskly. She raised a hand and took a step back. 'Until our paths cross again.'

He nodded, a look passing over his face, an expression she couldn't fathom. 'Goodbye, Lizzie. And good luck.'

She watched him as he started to back away, wondering what was going on in his head. She waited, barely breathing, until he was out of sight, before collapsing to the concrete and sobbing like a child. She couldn't lose her daddy, she couldn't lose him while she was on the other side of the world! She needed him, she needed to show him what she'd done, how much she'd grown, what she was capable of. And more than anything, she wanted to be the one to care for him and nurse him back to health.

'Don't you die on me, daddy,' she whispered. 'Don't you dare go and leave me.'

---

Lizzie marched into the post office, breathing heavily after walking so far. But she'd had time to clear her head, and she knew exactly what she needed to say. She quickly composed a telegram to her mother, telling her she'd been informed of her father's condition and would be coming home as soon as she could. And then she took a deep breath and composed the words she'd been reciting for the last half-mile of her walk, wanting to make sure the entire army knew she was ready and capable of stepping up to lead a team.

> GENERAL HENRY ARNOLD.
> I'VE BEEN INFORMED A WOMEN'S FERRY SERVICE HAS BEEN ESTABLISHED IN MY ABSENCE. I TRUST THAT I'M STILL EXPECTED TO HEAD ANY WOMEN'S SQUADRON TO ASSIST WITH THE WAR EFFORT. I AM READY TO TAKE ON A LEADERSHIP ROLE AND DO WHATEVER IS NEEDED OF ME. INFORMATION REQUESTED IMMEDIATELY ON WHEN I SHOULD RETURN. ENDS.

*I'm coming, Daddy*, she thought, sending a silent prayer skywards as she stepped out of the post office. *Don't you go dying without letting me say goodbye. I've got way too much to tell you before you go.*

# CHAPTER THIRTEEN

## *RAF ELVINGTON AIRFIELD, YORKSHIRE,*

## *JULY 1942*

## *RUBY*

Ruby pulled out her compact and quickly powdered her nose, wanting to look fresh on her arrival. She might want to be taken seriously as a pilot, but she was still a girl and she liked to look like one – and if Tom was there, she wanted to knock his socks off.

Next she took out her lipstick and reapplied it, pleased there were no other planes flying in formation with her or looking to her for guidance. She laughed to herself, thinking about the first time she'd led the way; she was known for her knack with maps and landmarks. One of the other pilots had flown up beside her, worried about all her zigzagging, only to see her applying her powder. Ruby had almost dropped it in fright, and all she'd been able to think of was how ridiculous she'd have looked if it had ended up all over the cockpit.

With her make-up done and her mid-air acrobatics over, she glanced at her markers, knowing she was close. In another fifteen minutes, she was looking down on the aerodrome, her heart pounding as she realised she'd actually made it. The weather had been terrible at times, but the visibility had proven to be sufficient and if she was successful in her landing . . . She pushed the thought of failure out of her mind. This wasn't just for herself, but the rest of the squadron and the other women pilots who'd managed to get their Class V conversion. She could do it.

She was grateful that she hadn't had any bored ack-ack units mistaking her for the enemy in the big bomber, and for the fact she hadn't seen any stray Luftwaffe pilots who wanted to shoot her out of the skies. And she'd been able to make textbook decisions throughout the flight. By all accounts it had already been a success. She eased back and listened to the change in the engine; the more she flew the Halifax, the more she was becoming familiar with it.

Ruby circled and prepared for landing, calmly checking her speed and mentally running through what she had to do. There was no room for error, despite the fact that she had no training in using the landing instruments, and she found herself holding her breath as she approached the runway and successfully touched down.

As she finally cut the engine and sat for a moment, Ruby fought the urge to burst out laughing. She'd actually done it! She'd landed the damn thing as perfectly as could be, and she'd had a perfect flight too. Every worry, every little niggle of doubt, had disappeared. She'd been chosen to be the first pilot, to prove what women could do, and she'd jolly well done it!

She started to climb out, smiling to a mechanic wearing overalls who held out a hand. She took off her hat and ran her fingers through her hair, shaking out her dark curls and hoping they weren't too flat.

'Where's the pilot?' he asked, looking concerned as he hurriedly climbed up.

'Excuse me?' she said. Surely they'd been told what a big day it was, that she was the first woman to deliver a Halifax? She'd half-expected a line-up of people waiting for her, applauding what she'd just achieved. Did this flight mechanic honestly not know?

'Where is he? What's going on?' He appeared again, head poking out, and then disappeared, presumably to search the cockpit for the mystery pilot. When he re-emerged, the man's face was a mixture of horror and humour; she couldn't decide which.

'*I'm* the pilot,' she said, dusting off her flying suit. 'I don't dress like this for the fun of it.'

He was holding her cushion, as if perhaps he'd expected to find a six-foot male beneath it. Did he think she'd somehow abducted the true pilot and made away with his Halifax?

'What's this then?'

She stifled a laugh. 'Well, the rudder pedals are a little hard to reach. I used the cushion to give me a bit more height, although the G force made it jolly hard to stay put in the seat at take-off!'

The look he gave was hilarious – as if she was most definitely trying to pull the wool over his eyes. 'Have you seen the size of this plane? No disrespect, ma'am, but you're the size of a grasshopper and this is a beast.'

Ruby went to open her mouth when she heard a low whistle and spun around to see a group of pilots gathered behind her. Perhaps the poor mechanic thought one of them was playing a joke on him.

'This waif of a girl here is trying to tell me she's the pilot!' he exclaimed.

'Do you see anyone else in there?' she seethed. 'Feel free to call Captain MacMillan or, actually, I met Churchill himself the other night. You may send him a telegram to confirm my credentials, if you must.' She glared at him. 'Why is it that men think a pilot needs to be two hundred pounds or more to handle a big plane?'

'I don't believe you,' he spluttered.

A voice from the group of men made her limbs turn to jelly. 'Are you calling my fiancée a liar?'

'Tom?' she gasped, scanning the pilots' faces. With all the fuss she'd almost forgotten that he could be standing watching. But there he was: just behind the others.

'Hello, Ruby,' he said, shaking his head as he walked forward, a smile faintly playing across his lips.

She moved a few steps closer, studying his face, resisting the urge to run and throw her arms around his neck. She wasn't going to be that girl, not after all the letters he'd sent insisting she return home and give up on her dreams. She clenched her fingers and considered whether a short, sharp slap across the cheek might be more appropriate.

'You know her?' the mechanic asked. 'This woman who claims to be the pilot?'

'I'm engaged to be married to her, actually,' Tom said, his eyes never for a second leaving her face. 'But for some reason she's become very independent in my absence and has taken to flying these monstrosities rather than returning home.'

'You're my fiancé, not my keeper,' she said, her heart beating wildly as she remembered exactly why she'd fallen for him in the first place. His eyes were intoxicating, the way they made her feel like she was the only person in the world. The way his lips kicked up at one side in a smile, and the dark mop of hair that he was constantly having to push back from his forehead. And she loved the way he stood, always confident, always commanding. Only now, she wasn't in awe of that; she admired it still, of course, but right then and there, on the runway with her Halifax at her heel, she knew she could hold her own. The flight had defined her; it had proven to her exactly what she was capable of. It was the first time she'd truly felt the joy of confidence.

'So we're equal now, are we?' he asked, folding his arms.

She mimicked his stance. 'We are. And while we're at it, I'm not putting up with your mother trying to tell me what I can and can't do.' She chuckled. 'As for returning home by my deadline? You can forget it.'

The guys nearby, clearly listening to every word, clapped and hooted, and she broke into a smile. It was impossible to keep a straight face, and she was actually pleased there was an audience to help her embarrass Tom.

'So what exactly do we do about this, er, *situation*, Ruby?'

'We behave like equals,' she said, taking another step closer, and then another, so close to Tom, so impossibly close that she could smell his scent, knew exactly what it would feel like to press hard into him. 'I expect you to celebrate with the rest of England that your fiancée is the country's finest female bomber pilot,' she whispered, just loudly enough for him to hear now. 'And then I expect a proper bloody welcome.'

'Well, maybe you should have asked for that proper *bloody* welcome first,' he said.

He caught her around the waist, his mouth finding hers, and she kissed him back. It had been a year and three months since she'd seen the man she was supposed to marry, and if that wasn't an excuse for a public display of affection, then she wasn't sure what was. Whistles echoed out behind them, but she didn't care – this was her man, and she'd just flown a giant plane and landed it like she'd been doing it all her life. She pulled back to look at him, his face between her palms now, before kissing him all over again.

'I can't believe my girl landed this beast,' he whispered in her ear, holding her tight.

'Well, believe it,' she whispered back.

'I suppose I'll have to,' he said with a laugh. 'Actually, half the men in my squadron cut out your photo in the *Picture Post* and have it beside their beds! I'm reminded on a daily basis that not only are you beautiful, but you might actually be a better pilot than me now!'

She giggled, cheeks warm as she tucked tight against him, not caring about being reprimanded or what anyone might think. Besides, he was the one in the RAF, not her, and she doubted the ATA were going to care about a woman embracing her fiancé after delivering a much-needed plane.

'I am proud of you,' he murmured, lips to her hair. 'I didn't like it in the beginning. Heck, I didn't even like it last week, but seeing you fly in here today . . .'

She looked up at him. 'I knew if you saw me it'd help to change your mind,' she said smugly.

'It's made me realise how talented you are. I was just worried about you, and I was having to deal with letters from my mother every other week . . .'

Ruby groaned. 'Please can we not talk about your mother?'

He grinned. 'Roger that. And I'm sorry, I should never have gone along with her giving you a timeframe to return home.'

They joined the other pilots walking back to the base. 'We didn't think you'd be coming, what with the visibility the way it's been,' one commented.

'It was touch and go, but the decision was mine,' Ruby told him boldly.

'What do you mean, *yours*?' Tom asked.

She felt her pride swell as he looked at her curiously. 'It's different for us. We're charged with deciding whether to go up in fog, rain or even snow. It depends how badly someone needs the plane we're delivering. Flying without instruments and radio is difficult at the best of times, and when the weather is touchy . . .'

'Without instruments or radio?' Tom interrupted, eyebrows knitted. 'That's actually true? We thought it was a joke.'

'It's just the way it is for us,' she said, trying to make light of something that put the fear of God into her every time she flew. 'Now, where will my debrief be? And is there any chance of a hot cup of tea and some sandwiches?'

Tom pointed ahead to a nondescript building and gave her a quick salute. 'Yes ma'am,' he teased, bending to give her a quick kiss. 'The captain awaits you over there.' He saluted again before breaking into a jog and heading towards another building nearby.

'How are you getting back?' another pilot asked, holding out a cigarette to her. She shook her head and he lit it for himself instead.

'Ah, I believe there is a Hurricane that I need to limp home in,' she replied. 'The flights away from base are always good ones, and the ones back usually involve planes that have seen better days.'

'Well, I'd put those plans on hold,' he said as he puffed. 'The weather's getting worse, and no matter who's making the decisions, you'd have to have a death wish to head back out with the wind and rain coming up like that.'

Ruby looked up and saw the clouds closing in; a big plop of rain landed on her nose. Being stuck here wasn't exactly the worst thing that could happen to her, given that she'd found Tom.

She entered the building and saw the captain waiting for her. 'I hope you've got quarters for women,' she told him by way of greeting, 'because it looks like you're stuck with me for the night.'

He stood and held out a hand, beaming. She shook it and stood back, liking the older man with the big bushy moustache immediately.

'First Officer Sanders, I've heard an awful lot about you.'

'I hope only good things, Captain,' she replied.

'My dear, do you have time to talk to some of my men while you're here?' he said, pouring himself a nip of whisky and holding up a glass to her. Ruby shook her head. What she needed more than anything right now was a toilet, not more liquid. 'Those idiots out there keep telling me what *bastards* Halifax aircrafts are to land, but you just showed a textbook perfect touchdown without seeming to break a sweat. Bravo.'

She bit down on the inside of her mouth, trying not to smile at his praise.

'I don't mean to offend, but you're hardly larger than a child, my dear. Clearly it's not a matter of brute strength, but skill, wouldn't you say?'

160

'Yes, sir,' she agreed. 'They're not exactly Spitfires, but with half a brain and a dollop of good old determination, I'd say there's nothing to it.'

The captain let out a hearty laugh just as Tom burst through the door, running his hands through hair that looked more haphazard than she'd ever seen it before.

'I see you've met my fiancée, sir,' Tom said as he crossed the room, mug in hand, and passed her the steaming brew of tea. She instantly regretted asking for it, given that she hadn't found a toilet yet.

'She's quite the woman, I have to say.'

'My Ruby is most definitely one of a kind,' Tom said with a wink in her direction.

'Well, let's get your wonderful fiancée to the mess room and see if we can't rustle her up a nice dinner. What do you say?' the captain asked.

'Sounds brilliant,' she said honestly, clasping her fingers around the mug.

'You can use the unoccupied quarters of the group captain in his absence. It'll be basic, but it'll suffice, and you'll have your privacy,' he continued. 'Tom, see that First Officer Sanders is well looked after for as long as she needs to be here.'

Tom placed a hand on the small of her back and Ruby leaned into him, her arm snaking around his waist.

'Anything I can get you?' he asked.

Ruby looked up into his eyes. She'd braced herself for arguments; she'd even been prepared to tell him that it was over between them if he wouldn't support her. But this . . . this was nice. This was everything she'd been hoping for.

'A toilet,' she told him honestly. 'I think I'm actually in danger of bursting.'

Tom's laugh was deep as he took her hand and hurried her towards the next building. 'I'm going to apologise now for all the pictures of scantily clad women on the walls,' he said. 'And the picture of you.'

Ruby might have cared before, but given that they had only hours together, that she hadn't seen him in so long, and now she knew what it was like to be part of a squadron . . . She grinned, and shrugged. Scantily clad women were the least of her problems, so long as they were only in pictures and he hadn't touched any in real life. But the pictures of *her*? She doubted she'd ever get used to that.

Hours later, Ruby waited in her room for Tom. She wondered if he would come, if he'd be able to sneak away without being seen or reprimanded; maybe she was hoping for the impossible. She shivered as she waited, more from anticipation than from cold.

She went to the small window and rubbed away the condensation that had clouded the glass. Rain was falling hard on the concrete now. She doubted she'd be stuck for long, but if she was going to be marooned anywhere, it couldn't get any better than being on base with Tom. In fact, if it had been any of the other airfields, she'd probably have just insisted on flying back. But she was exhausted. Her eyelids were drooping and her body was lethargic, probably because she'd hardly slept the night before, tossing and turning as she'd worried about her big day. She leaned into the window with a blanket around her shoulders, listening to the pitter-patter on the tin roof. She shut her eyes.

Tap, tap, tap.

Her eyes popped open.

A loud knock echoed through the room and Ruby ran to the door. Tom's hair was wet – droplets of rain were even caught in his eyelashes – and she grinned back at him as he gave her a big, wide smile.

'Tom!' she said, hauling him in and quickly pushing the door shut. 'Get in here.'

He stood there, his grin slowly fading. 'I can't believe you're actually here,' he said, shaking his head and sending water flying. 'I can't believe, after everything, that we're standing here together.'

Ruby lifted one hand and touched his jaw, tracing along it as she stared up at him. She suddenly didn't feel tired anymore. And she didn't want to talk anymore, either.

He slipped his arms around her, circling her waist. 'The guys are still talking about you. You'd think they'd just seen an elephant land a plane.'

'You're comparing me to an elephant?'

Tom chuckled. 'Oh, I just mean they're acting like, well, as if it's so unusual . . .'

'Stop talking and kiss me,' she muttered, standing on tiptoe and wrapping her arms around his neck.

Tom's lips met hers, softly at first, brushing like silk back and forth. Ruby shut her eyes and bathed in the warmth of him, his embrace, the way he deepened their kiss and left her gasping.

'We only have one night,' he said. 'All this time I've been imagining our first night together, wondering when I was ever going to see you again, and then you just drop from the sky like an angel.'

She touched her forehead to his chest and listened to his steady heartbeat, loving the feel of his body against hers. 'I still can't believe I was the first one.'

'To fly a four-engine bomber?' he asked, tucking his fingers beneath her chin to raise her head.

'Yes,' she said softly. 'Lizzie thought it was going to be her, but they chose me. Imagine what your poor mother would say. I mean, how *unladylike!*'

Tom kissed her forehead before pulling her tight to him again. 'I thought we weren't talking about my mother tonight.'

'No. You're right.'

'Although I will tell you that in her last letter she said you were small enough to be mistaken for a child, and she was going to demand to know how a woman of such petite stature was able to rise through the ATA ranks so fast.'

'She didn't!' Ruby gasped, looking up at him.

Tom was laughing, but she could tell from the guilty look on his face that he wasn't joking.

'It's the truth,' he said. 'But you'll be pleased to know that I'm going to reply.' He kissed her again, his fingers tracing her face. 'And this time I'm going to tell her that if she says another bad word against you, either to me personally or to anyone else, I won't be returning home after the war.'

'You're serious?' Ruby asked, holding his hand as she moved them both closer to the little stove. 'After all this time, you're going to do that?'

'I am.' He smiled. 'Listening to those guys out there, seeing you with my own eyes – it's like being smacked across the face. I've had some sense knocked into me, and to hell with her stupid deadline.'

Ruby gazed up at him, trying not to laugh. 'Well it's about time, *Thomas*,' she teased.

'Easy,' Tom said, grabbing her wrist and giving her a wicked smile. 'Now let's get this bedding beside the fire and you can tell me all about your training and what it's like at Hamble.'

Ruby reached for the blankets and laid them down. It was amazing how they'd been parted for so long, but had picked up like it had only been weeks or months instead of well over a year. At home, when they'd flown together, they'd become friends before it had developed into something more and Tom had asked permission to take her out, and she wondered if that was why she felt so comfortable with him. And why she'd almost forgotten what a state of turmoil she'd been in for months over his lack of support. At any other time, she'd have given him the silent treatment and made him grovel for her, but this was war – there was no time to go off in a huff and make up a few days later. They had to take every minute together they could.

'Come here,' she said, a nervous flutter in her belly.

'Are you all right?' he asked.

She smiled and lowered herself down, tugging him with her. 'I don't want to waste time talking about training,' she said. 'We have one night, Tom, and I want to make the most of being right here with you.'

He ran a hand through her hair, gently stroking and then undoing her hairpins so that it fell around her shoulders. His smile was kind as he leaned closer, lips finding hers again and sending shudders through her body when his fingers skimmed down her side, settling on her hips. His mouth was warm and his touch was light, and she bravely reached out to him, feeling the curve of his muscles, loving how hard and strong he felt.

When he pulled back, his mouth leaving hers, her fingers travelled upwards to the base of his head. 'What?' she asked.

'I never thought I'd be taking *trousers* off you,' he joked, looking down at her flying gear, the only clothes she had with her.

Ruby burst out laughing as she yanked him forwards, pulling him down on top of her. As he rained kisses down her neck and across her collarbone, she arched up to him, wanting more, craving his touch.

'Are you sure you don't want to wait until our wedding night?' he murmured.

'I thought we might not be *having* a wedding night, given how stubborn you've been about me flying,' she teased.

He kissed the tip of her nose. 'I'll apologise a hundred times over if I have to,' he whispered, 'but there will definitely be a wedding night.'

'We could be shot out of the sky or crash our planes any day, Tom,' she whispered back, not teasing now. 'I love you and I don't want to wait. Do you?'

His kiss was softer this time, and he propped himself up on one elbow, looking down at her. 'I love you, Ruby. I'm so proud of you and I love you so much.'

Tears pricked her eyes, but she blinked them away as she reached for him, stroking his cheek and brushing his hair back. 'I love you, too.'

It was bittersweet being with Tom, but she wouldn't have traded this one night with him for anything in the world. One night, in a little cabin belonging to someone else, stranded at an aerodrome after landing a Halifax. It would go down as one of the best nights of her life.

'Kiss me,' Tom said, his lips so close she could feel them move as he spoke.

Ruby didn't need to be asked twice, and she stroked her arms down his back as her lips met his again, her exhaustion long forgotten.

Knock, knock, knock.

Ruby opened her eyes and looked around, wrapping the blanket tighter around her bare shoulders as she shivered. Where was she? She turned and blinked, smiling when she saw Tom, his eyes still shut, dark lashes almost brushing his cheekbones. The night before flooded back and she buried herself deeper into the blanket, snuggling into Tom.

Knock, knock, knock.

Oh no! She leapt up and grabbed her undergarments, hastily pulling them on and reaching for her flying uniform. 'Tom!' she hissed, giving him a kick. 'Wake up!'

She kicked him again and frantically pulled her trousers on, wriggling into the darn things and then reaching for her jacket. When Tom looked up, perplexed, she groaned and piled the blankets on top of him before sprinting for the door.

Knock, knock . . .

Ruby swung the door open, almost yanking the handle off.

'Here's your tea, sir,' a cheery young voice sang on the wind.

She watched his cheeks turn beet red at the realisation that she wasn't a sir.

'Thank you,' she said.

He stuttered and passed her the tea, looking like a rabbit caught in headlights, his hands shaking.

'I'm sorry *ma'am*, I . . .'

'Thank you for the tea,' she said politely before swinging the door shut again.

She breathed a sigh of relief and pressed her back against the wall, taking a quick gulp of tea as Tom emerged from the nest of blankets.

'That was close,' she muttered.

'Ah, I think my absence may already have been noticed,' Tom said, looking guilty. 'I . . .'

'Urghhhh,' Ruby groaned. 'I don't want them thinking I'm some kind of, of . . .'

'Hussy?' he asked, standing up and crossing the room. 'Lady of the night?' He chuckled, seeming to enjoy how mortified she was. 'Raunchy pilot?'

She darted away from him, embarrassed at his nakedness. 'Tom!' she scolded.

'You were practically begging me to take my clothes *off* last night – now you want me to put them on?'

When he dodged towards her she laughed and held up her tea to stop it from spilling, but he swiftly took it off her and took a big slurp. He was grinning as she looked on, trying not to drop her gaze and get an eyeful of his nakedness.

'Come here,' Tom said, catching her wrist, still holding the cup in the other hand.

Ruby's breath started to come in fast pants, her pulse thumping as Tom slowly bent to kiss her.

'We're starting over,' he murmured. 'Good morning.'

She touched his bare chest and traced a circle where she imagined his heart to be. 'Good morning,' she whispered back.

'Thomas!' a deep voice boomed from outside. 'Get your backside out here right now!'

Ruby froze. *Oh my goodness.* They'd been caught red-handed and instead of trying to sneak Tom out, she'd ended up back in his arms again.

'Dammit,' he cursed, leaping away from her and scrambling for his shorts. She watched him pull them on, followed by his undershirt, then open and shut the door and disappear.

She leaned against the door and tried to listen. She cringed. It wasn't exactly hard to hear his superior's booming voice.

'I'm sorry sir!' Tom apologised. 'I won't disobey a direct order again, sir.'

'Put some clothes on, boy, and then report for duty immediately,' he was told. 'And don't expect this to go without punishment.'

'Yes, sir,' Tom replied.

There was a pause and Ruby wished she could see what was happening.

'And tell our guest that there has been a change of plan,' the other man instructed. 'I want her to take back a Typhoon that needs repairs and return as soon as practicable with a brand-new Halifax that we're waiting for.'

'Yes, sir, I will.'

Ruby jumped back as Tom opened the door again. He kicked it shut and wrapped his arms around her. She held on tight, not knowing when they'd have a moment alone together again. This time when he kissed her, it was full of love and tenderness, a goodbye kind of kiss, and tears welled in her eyes.

'Goodbye, Ruby,' he whispered, kissing a tear from her cheek.

'Not goodbye,' she said, her voice cracking as she tried to be brave. 'Until next time.'

'Yeah, until next time, beautiful,' he said, stepping back and stroking down her arm until he caught her fingers. He held them up and kissed them. 'And I'm so sorry. For everything. I acted like an idiot – some of the things I said to you, I'm just . . .' He ducked his head lower and looked straight into her eyes. 'I'm sorry and I love you.'

She smiled through her tears. 'I love you, too.'

He kissed her, long and slow, one last time.

'Will I see you when I come back with the Halifax?' she asked, wiping her cheeks with the back of her knuckles. 'Or will you be gone by then?'

His smile faded. 'If the cloud has cleared, I'll be gone. This was just one hell of a coincidence, us ending up on base together.'

She watched him dress, stepping closer to hold up his jacket for him to shrug into. Suddenly she didn't care that all the men on base knew what had happened, that he'd snuck in and spent the night with her. They'd been engaged to be married since before the war, and as soon as it was over they'd be husband and wife. Either of them could go down in a plane before then, and she didn't want to live with regrets. He might have been an idiot these past months when she'd been wanting his support, but he'd more than made up for it now.

The door shut with a bang and she swallowed a sob as she gathered her things and dressed properly, powdering her nose and using the little mirror in her compact to apply her lipstick. Her stomach growled, but she ignored it.

She had a plane to fly, and it was time to go. There wasn't time for tears; there was only time to do her job.

# CHAPTER FOURTEEN

*White Waltham Airfield, Berkshire,*

*August 1942*

*May*

Over the past few years, May had experienced so many firsts she could hardly keep up with them. But waiting to meet the first lady of the United States? Her head was spinning just at the thought of it. What was she supposed to say? How was she supposed to behave like a normal person without talking too fast or . . . ? She glanced up, noting anxiously that black clouds were gathering ominously overhead. She was sitting outside around the back of her old hangar at White Waltham; in less than an hour she would be meeting Eleanor Roosevelt, holding out her hand to greet her and welcome her on base.

It had been a momentous few days. What with Ruby's overwhelming success on her first solo bomber flight and preparing for the official visit, she'd hardly stopped to breathe.

'No tea today?'

She looked up at Ben, standing over her, his overalls cleaner than usual and one hand tucked behind his back.

'Did you send those home for your mother to wash?' she asked. 'You almost look respectable for once.'

'Very funny. Now do you want something to ease those nerves or not?'

He revealed a small silver hip flask and held it out to her. 'I was thinking this would be better than bringing you a cup of tea,' he said. 'Although any more teasing about the state of my overalls and I won't be sharing.'

She unscrewed the top and took a tiny sip. When she coughed he laughed and sat down beside her, patting her back, then taking it from her hand.

'Why are you so nice to me?' she asked, studying his face, realising how much she'd hoped he'd find her. She'd invited Ben to join them on this trip, as a way of saying thank you for all his help since they'd transferred to Hamble, and she was looking forward to spending some time with him.

'Well, you're kind of my boss, so I have to be nice to you. I didn't know I had a choice.'

'Ben!' she remonstrated. 'Seriously, why? Why do you even bother with me?'

He stared at her, tucking the flask into a pocket before raising his other hand to her cheek. May's heart started to race as he slowly bent forward, his lips grazing hers, brushing her mouth so gently that she wondered if she'd imagined it before pulling back.

'That's why,' he said, his voice low. 'Why else do you think I volunteered to work on my day off?'

'I . . . I . . .' she stuttered.

Ben leaned in again, hovering as if waiting for her to push him away, before his lips touched hers, firmer now as he kissed her. His lips were warm, his face freshly razored and so, so soft as she reached her hand up and touched her fingers to his cheek.

'I can't do this, Ben,' she whispered, pressing her forehead to his as she tried to catch her breath. 'I can't lose anyone else.'

'You're not going to lose me, May.'

'You don't know that.'

He wrapped an arm around her and she tucked into him despite her protestations, holding him, breathing in the scent of him and wishing she could stay in his arms forever. How had her feelings for Ben snuck up on her like that? How had she not realised what had slowly been developing between them? And why was she giving in and letting him hold her instead of running away?

'Tell me about him. Your brother,' Ben said, his mouth moving against her hair as he spoke.

She squeezed her eyes shut tight and slowly let the words escape her lips. 'Johnny was a pilot,' she told him. 'I loved him so much. He was my best friend as well as my brother, and then he left to fly for the air force.'

She cried then, the tears raining down her cheeks as she buried her face in Ben's chest, sobbing as she finally let herself remember Johnny. She could see his smile, the glint in his eye when he thought he was going to beat her at something, the stupid way he'd danced with her around the kitchen when he'd told her she needed lessons if she ever wanted to meet a husband. And she saw him in her dreams, distracted, not concentrating because he was thinking about the way he'd left things between them, the things she'd said. She turned to Ben and, in a few stuttering words, described what had happened on that awful day when he left home.

'I've always wondered if I'm somehow responsible, if I upset him so much that he wasn't concentrating,' she whispered. 'Maybe I put him off somehow?'

Ben shook his head and held her closer. 'Those are dark thoughts, May. You can't blame yourself, because no matter what happened between the two of you, his death does not rest on your shoulders.'

She nodded as tears started to fall again. The truth was, her fear that she'd been responsible for Johnny's death was worse than the constant, gnawing realisation that their country was only ever a battle away from being overrun by Germans.

Ben held her, his palm warm on her back as he rubbed in big circles, just like her mother had done when she was a child.

'I'm sorry,' she gasped, sitting up and pushing away from him, embarrassed. 'I shouldn't have let go like that.'

'You've been needing to do that for a long time, May,' Ben said, stroking her hair from her face and pushing it back. 'You should know you don't have to hide from me. And I'm not going anywhere.'

She blinked away the last of her tears and brushed under her eyes with her fingertips, knowing what a mess she must look. 'Thank you,' she whispered.

Ben laughed and looked down, gesturing at his overalls. 'I didn't even get an hour with these bloody things clean!'

May laughed at the make-up smudges all over his front, then stood, holding on to him to draw one last burst of strength.

'I need to go and get cleaned up,' she said.

'Even tear-stained, you're beautiful,' he said. 'And there's nothing wrong with having a good cry over your brother.'

'I don't want anyone to see my weakness,' she admitted. 'I'm their leader. I've held myself together for so long, and they can't see me fall to pieces, can they? I just live in fear every single day of losing one of them. I want this war over with, so we can stop losing good people for nothing.'

'It's normal to be scared. And you can always confide in me,' Ben said, stepping in and cupping her face in his hands, pressing one more warm, slow kiss to her lips. 'You don't need to be brave for me, May Jones.'

May smiled up at him. She should have been terrified of the way she was feeling, of how vulnerable she'd been opening up to him like that; but for the first time since she'd started with the ATA, she actually felt like herself. And instead of being afraid, she liked it.

An hour later, May stood with her other pilots waiting for their guest. And trying not to think about what had happened between her and Benjamin.

*Darn you*, she cursed as she looked up. *Can't you at least give us a cloudless day once in a while?* The cloud cover was her biggest enemy, but she'd hoped they could at least tour White Waltham with Mrs Roosevelt without the heavens opening and pelting them with rain. The chance of that was no longer looking likely.

'She's coming,' Lizzie said, standing beside her. 'The cars are on their way.'

May smiled through her nerves. 'How are you doing?' she asked, knowing how badly Lizzie had taken the news about her father. 'Have you heard anything else?'

Lizzie bit her lip. 'He's stable, and they're hoping to have him home by the end of the week.'

May wondered how she could have slowly become almost fond of someone so difficult. She was certain Lizzie had caused her at least a handful of grey hairs over the months they'd spent together.

'If he's half as strong as you, he'll be fine,' May said. 'I'm so pleased you're here for the visit.' She realised now how much she was going to miss Lizzie when she was gone.

'Me too. I'm pleased I'm still here,' Lizzie said. Was her accent no longer as pronounced, May wondered, or was it just that she'd got used to it? 'You want to know something ridiculous?'

May raised an eyebrow. 'Do I *want* to hear what you're going to say?'

Lizzie grinned. 'I actually thought about staying, and not going back at all. I actually wondered if I'm more help here – if I'm better being on the front line and ferrying planes for the ATA.'

'But you changed your mind?' May almost hoped she would stay, after everything. Lizzie was finally starting to show them a nicer side.

'I miss my family so much,' Lizzie admitted, and May saw that the arrogant smile and the sharply raised eyebrow had gone. This Lizzie seemed more open, more emotional. 'If my daddy dies while I'm on the other side of the world, I'll never forgive myself. And I can see that, after being here, I can share that knowledge with our women pilots back home.'

May took her hand and squeezed it tight. 'I'd have given the world to see my brother again, just one last time, if I'd had the chance. So you get yourself back home as quickly as you can.'

'But your brother – you said he was a flying ace? That first night . . .'

May inhaled and slowly let the breath go before forcing the words out. 'My brother *was* an amazing pilot, but he died in the air, Liz. And I miss him so badly every single day.'

Lizzie's eyes flooded with tears and May had to swallow hard to stifle her own.

'Honey, I'm so sorry,' Lizzie whispered. 'I had no idea. I would never have said all that if I'd known.'

'Just go back and see your father, Liz. Promise me you'll go straight to him before it's too late.'

At that moment, a murmur rippled through the group, and they both turned to see what the commotion was about.

'Ah, here she is, our shining star!' Lizzie cooed as Ruby walked towards them in her striking dark-blue uniform, her cheeks pink.

'Stop it!' Ruby hissed, coming up to them. 'You know I don't like a fuss.'

But Lizzie started to clap, and soon everyone gathered was clapping, too – the other pilots, the ground crew and even Captain MacMillan.

'We're so proud of you, Ruby,' May said to her, breaking from formality and giving her a big hug. 'I was talking to Captain MacMillan earlier, and we both agree that you deserve every accolade. Congratulations on your success flying the Halifax.' She glanced at Lizzie, expecting to see her bristle, but she was smiling instead.

'I don't want to brag about knowing a celebrity, but . . .' Lizzie started to say, dramatically pulling a newspaper cutting from her pocket and unfolding it. She held it out and Ruby let out an audible moan.

### Britain's Four-Engine Bomber Girl – Ain't She Grand?

There was a grainy photo of Ruby beneath the bold, black headline, shaking her long, dark hair out as if she were advertising a special brand of shampoo. Her flying suit was unzipped a tiny bit at the neck, as if she was trying to show a hint of cleavage, and she was wearing a huge smile.

May glanced at Ruby, who looked utterly mortified.

'Put it away,' May scolded.

Lizzie grinned as she folded and tucked the paper away. Then they all craned their necks as the sound of vehicles drifted across the base.

'In position, everyone. They're here,' said May, her heart beating faster as a cavalcade of black cars came into sight, driving slowly towards them. The vehicles came to a halt in front of the gathered group, and security men leapt out to attend to the doors.

May held what she hoped was a calm expression as the first guest emerged. Then she almost gasped as out stepped . . . Jackson!

'Captain Montgomery, what a pleasure to see you again!' she said, holding out a hand and smiling when he kissed her cheek instead. She'd thought he'd left the country already, but clearly he'd stayed behind to escort the first lady on this outing.

'The pleasure is mine,' he said, before turning back to the vehicle and helping an elegantly dressed woman from the car. 'Senior

Commander Jones, it is also my great pleasure to introduce you to the first lady of the United States of America, Mrs Roosevelt.'

May tried not to gape at the woman who emerged, her smile fixed perfectly in place as their eyes met.

'Welcome, Mrs Roosevelt. It's our absolute honour to have you here,' she gushed.

'Why thank you, Senior Commander. I can't tell you what . . .'

Before she could finish her sentence, rain started to pelt them, falling in huge, angry drops from the sky.

*Why now? Honestly! Why were they having so much awful weather?* May leapt to take the first lady's arm and usher her out of the wet, but a man approached and bustled her out of the way, proffering his arm and an umbrella.

'Elizabeth, look at you!' Mrs Roosevelt said, catching sight of Lizzie. 'Looking every inch the bomber girl, I have to say.'

May listened to Lizzie chat and laugh with the first lady as they huddled beneath the roof of the hangar, but she caught sight of Ruby, standing slightly away from the others beneath the giant wing of a Handley Page Halifax. May could see she was unsure what to do; perhaps she was feeling distanced from the others now that she was flying a different type of aircraft, or maybe she was nervous about meeting their guest.

May held up a hand and received a little wave back.

'Is that her?' she heard Mrs Roosevelt ask.

'Ruby? I mean First Officer Sanders, yes,' Lizzie replied. 'The one and only.'

'She's the girl whose face I've seen plastered on every inch of newspaper since I arrived,' the first lady exclaimed. 'What an achievement!'

Without warning she took an umbrella from one of her bodyguards and strode into the rain, taking shelter with Ruby beneath the wing. The pair were like chalk and cheese: Ruby petite and dressed in her sturdy shoes and uniform, the first lady in a greatcoat with a fox fur draped around her neck, every inch the wealthy president's wife. But as

May crossed to join them with Lizzie, she saw that her smile was genuine and her words of praise warm, and she couldn't help but like her.

'So, how does it feel to be the first woman to fly a four-engine bomber?' Mrs Roosevelt asked, over the pelting rain.

'It feels spectacular, actually,' Ruby replied, her voice more assured than usual. 'I'm so proud of all we've accomplished here.'

'Well, you deserve every accolade.'

'Thank you,' Ruby said, her chin pointed up slightly. May smiled, knowing how hard it was for Ruby to accept praise, but she'd seen a change in her since that first flight.

'It's even better that you're so tiny,' Mrs Roosevelt said jovially. 'Shows the men that brute strength is nothing compared to brains and determination!'

They all laughed.

'Now tell me about Elizabeth here. I hope her competitive spirit hasn't got in the way at all?'

May saw Lizzie's cheeks flare in embarrassment.

'She's a livewire, that's for sure,' Ruby said with a grin. 'Elizabeth is an accomplished pilot and we certainly had a boisterous rivalry to become the first bomber pilot. It was neck and neck all the way and, if anything, she helped me to be the pilot I am today.'

May looked between the two women, watching Ruby's easy smile and Lizzie's shocked one.

'Is that so? Well, it's good to hear she's been behaving.'

'We're going to miss her terribly,' Ruby continued. 'But she'll be an asset to whatever squadron she leads when she returns home.'

'Thank you, Ruby,' Lizzie said. 'But I can honestly say, hand on heart, that the best pilot paved the way for all of us. We all have Ruby to thank for our new ferrying role.'

'Mrs Roosevelt, we'd like to invite you in for lunch now,' May said, taking charge. 'Perhaps it would be a good idea to get out of this rain and tour the airfield when it clears instead?'

'Of course,' the first lady replied. 'Elizabeth, would you go and find Captain Montgomery, please? He's such a gorgeous man, and I insisted that you both sit with me today. I'm sure the two of you get along marvellously, am I right?'

'Ah, yes,' Lizzie said, raising a brow at May and Ruby. 'In fact, I'd love nothing more than to sit with him for lunch. How delightful that he managed to stay in the country for your visit. I thought he'd be home by now.'

May stifled her laugh and escorted Mrs Roosevelt towards the big hangar, which was set with huge tables and a feast for them all. She realised that not even the rain could ruin their day. Almost all of Lizzie's pilots from America were in attendance, waiting to meet their guest, and they had enough food and champagne to feed and water an army.

Today, she was going to relax and enjoy a rare moment of fun. Tomorrow she'd be taking to the skies for the first time in months, to deliver much-needed Spitfires to Colerne so they could be transported immediately to Port Glasgow and then on to Malta by the RAF – and after that? She doubted there'd be any time at all for *fun* or anything remotely resembling it. She decided to go and find Ben to walk together for lunch in the hangar. She had a feeling things were going to be on the up for the Allies now – from what she'd been told, the number of four-engine bombers they could now ferry to key bases and the delivery of the Spitfires to Malta could have a huge influence.

# CHAPTER FIFTEEN

## *HAMBLE AIRFIELD, HAMPSHIRE,*

## *AUGUST 1942*

### *LIZZIE*

Lizzie hadn't expected to be so emotional about leaving England. When she'd arrived she'd thought it was a gloomy, unexciting place, but since then everything had changed. She'd explored London, ferried all types of planes and made the most amazing friends despite the constant fears and trepidation about being in a country at war. She blinked away tears as she thought of Ruby and May – on first meeting she'd found them as boring and uptight as a pair of old nuns, but that couldn't have been further from the truth. In reality, it had been her who'd needed the personality adjustment, and when she thought back to how she'd behaved, it was impossible not to cringe.

But she had to leave – her country needed her. *And so did her father*. She needed to get home to see him, to sit with him and tell him how proud she was of him, before going off to lead her squadron.

'We're going to miss you terribly,' said Mrs Robinson, enveloping her in a big hug.

'Thank you. For everything,' Lizzie said, hoping they knew how grateful she truly was.

'I only wish it was before the war,' Mrs Robinson replied, dabbing her eyes. 'I would have been making light fluffy cakes and scones with jam for you. Oh, and the stews! Without all this rationing I'm quite the cook, you know.'

Lizzie laughed through her tears, surprised by how hard it was to say goodbye. 'I'm sure you are. And you cooked us wonderful, hearty meals, so there's nothing to be worried about.' In all honesty, she'd eaten enough Brussels sprouts and Woolton pies for a lifetime. 'Did I tell you that Mrs Roosevelt knew all about the rationing here? She told me over dinner that even the Queen has to use a ration book, so there was nothing fancy for the first lady when she stayed at Buckingham Palace.'

'Honestly? I thought it was all nonsense that the royal family was on rations.'

'Not at all. And even the hot water for Mrs Roosevelt's bath had to be rationed. I'm sure it was quite an experience for her.'

'Well I never,' Mrs Robinson clucked. 'I thought it was all propaganda to make us feel better, and that they were probably still living a life of luxury.'

'Lizzie!' Ruby exclaimed, as she burst down the stairs. 'Were you going to leave just like that?'

'Don't be daft, we were only letting you sleep in a bit,' their hostess said.

'I'd never leave without saying goodbye,' Lizzie told her. 'In fact, why don't you travel in with me to base? May is coming to get me herself.'

Ruby nodded. 'Give me a minute, will you?'

'You need breakfast first!' Mrs Robinson insisted, dashing off to the kitchen. Lizzie grinned, wondering if the older woman actually liked looking after them. She certainly seemed to enjoy keeping them well fed, and both she and her husband enjoyed listening to their stories;

she would bet that they loved bragging to their friends about the two female pilots living with them.

A car horn sounded outside, and Lizzie turned to embrace Mr Robinson, who'd been standing quietly in the corner.

'Thank you for being so gracious,' Lizzie said honestly. 'I'll never forget your kindness.'

He was gruff as she kissed his cheek, then picked up her single suitcase and stepped out of the front door. Mrs Robinson came rushing up behind her and pressed something into her hand, and when she looked down and saw the cookies wrapped in paper, she didn't know what to say.

'I've been saving up my sugar and butter in case I needed to make a special cake, but I decided to bake some proper biscuits for your journey instead.'

Tears started to trickle down Lizzie's cheeks then. Suddenly all she wanted was to get home to her own father, to hold him and kiss his cheek.

'Thank you,' she said.

May was out of the car and had the back door open, and Lizzie got in as Ruby came leaping down the steps with a piece of bread in her hand. As her friend scrambled in beside her, Lizzie leaned back and stared at the house she was leaving behind. Every bone in her body was ready to go home, but it didn't make leaving any easier. She waved one last time to her English family as May pulled away.

'A telegram arrived for you this morning,' May said, as they headed down the road, passing it back to her. 'I offered to bring it directly to you.'

Lizzie reached for it, hand trembling as she pressed her thumbnail beneath the envelope flap and then unfolded the letter inside, hoping it wasn't bad news about her father. When she saw General Hap's name she breathed a sigh of relief.

FEMALE SQUADRON IS COMMENCING AS PLANNED. YOU WILL ESTABLISH THE WOMEN'S FLYING DETACHMENT ON YOUR RETURN AND TRAIN WOMEN PILOTS FOR FERRYING MILITARY PLANES. NANCY LOVE WILL CONTINUE TO HEAD HER OWN SQUADRON. CAPTAIN JACKSON MONTGOMERY WILL BE ON BASE WITH YOU TO ESTABLISH YOUR OPERATIONS. RETURN DIRECTLY TO WASHINGTON AFTER YOUR VISIT HOME TO MEET ME IN PERSON. GENERAL ARNOLD.

She was actually getting it! She was going to be leading her own squadron! The only disappointing part was that she was going to have to put up with *Jackson Montgomery* back home. Why hadn't he been redeployed? She carefully folded the telegram and took a deep, shuddering breath.

But Jackson was the least of her worries. She had no idea who this Nancy Love person was, who'd somehow managed to establish an entire flying division without her being notified. She gripped her seat, reminding herself that she was part of a bigger picture, that she needed to think of everyone as a team. If it helped win the war, there was nothing wrong with her and Love having a squadron each.

'Everything all right?' May asked.

Lizzie met her gaze in the rear-view mirror. 'I'm bloody amazing,' she replied.

And then they all burst out laughing, because finally, after months on British soil, she'd actually managed to sound like an Englishwoman without even trying.

'Come on, what is it?' Ruby asked, curiosity written all over her face.

'I'm going to be leading my own squadron,' she said, hardly believing the words.

'Congratulations, Lizzie!' Ruby exclaimed.

'Thank you,' she said, letting excitement wash over her. It was actually, *finally*, happening!

'Well deserved,' May said. 'I'm so proud of you, Liz.'

'Would you believe that Jackson Montgomery is going to be my sidekick though?' she told them. 'Or perhaps *I'm* supposed to be *his* sidekick. Either way I'll just have to deal with it, because nothing is taking the shine off my new job!'

'He wasn't exactly hard on the eye,' Ruby murmured. 'You have to admit.'

'He was a pain in the backside, that's what he was,' Lizzie grumbled. 'And no, I absolutely do *not* have to admit that!'

'Sweetheart,' May chipped in, 'if you thought he was a pain in the backside, you clearly have no idea what you were like to work with sometimes!'

Lizzie had to laugh. She wasn't going to argue with May there.

'I can't believe this is it,' Ruby said, as she flung her arms around Lizzie less than two hours later.

Lizzie hugged her back, then turned to her commander. 'May, I hope that I can be half the leader you are one day,' she said. 'And I'm sorry I'm not here to help with the Spitfire deliveries. I'd have stayed if I could.'

'Elizabeth Dunlop, was that a compliment?' May asked, exchanging glances with Ruby. 'And don't worry about the Spitfires, we've got them under control.'

'Ha ha, very funny. I suppose you have Jackson to thank for my new-found humbleness.'

'Oh, we thank him every day,' Ruby teased. 'He's the only thing that made you bearable.'

'Oh, stop it,' Lizzie said, giving May a hug. 'Can't a girl have a decent send-off?'

May held her tight and kissed her cheek. 'I thought you were going to be a thorn in my side when you arrived, Lizzie, and you certainly were. But I'm actually going to miss you.'

'Me? A thorn?' Lizzie laughed. 'Never!'

She took one last look around the airfield where she'd been stationed for so long; the all-women ferry pool at Hamble had been incredible, and she was going to miss everything about it.

'I'm sorry ladies, but it's time.' A Daimler was waiting, much like the one she'd driven when she'd first arrived in London, although this time she wouldn't be driving it herself.

'Goodbye,' Lizzie said, bending to pick up her bag. 'And thank you, for putting up with me and showing me what it truly means to be part of a team. I'll never forget my time here with you.'

'It was nothing,' Ruby said, tears in her eyes.

Lizzie took a step towards the car. 'With women on both sides of the pond ferrying planes, I think we can actually work together to win this damn war, don't you?'

Ruby laughed, but May just nodded. 'I'm sure of it.'

'And May,' Lizzie added, 'please, one of these days, admit to yourself that you're head over heels in love with that gorgeous flight mechanic of yours, would you?' She grinned. 'You're not fooling anyone.'

'May and *Benjamin*?' Ruby gasped. 'Are you joking?'

May positively glowered, but her flushed cheeks gave her true feelings away. 'Ben is a lovely man, but . . .'

'This is war, May. It's life or death every day, and that means there's not a day to miss. If you want him,' said Lizzie, 'go and get him. Because you deserve to be happy and he's a good man.'

May just shook her head, not saying a thing, while Ruby still stood gaping. Lizzie got in the car, still laughing at May's mortified expression, then turned to stare at the two women who'd become like sisters to her in the short time she'd known them.

'Ready to go?' the driver asked.

'Yes,' she said, holding up a hand as the car moved away and her friends became smaller and smaller until they finally disappeared. A Halifax appeared in the sky and she watched as it circled, preparing to land. They'd come a long way in so little time.

'It's going to be no different back home,' she muttered to herself.

'Sorry luv, what was that?' the driver asked.

She smiled and shook her head. 'Oh nothing, just talking to myself.'

# CHAPTER SIXTEEN

## *CHATTIS HILL AIRFIELD, HAMPSHIRE,*

## *SEPTEMBER 1942*

## *RUBY*

'It's strange not having Lizzie here with us, isn't it?' Ruby said to May as they sat passing the time. There were no ferry notes to swat up on this time – they were all piloting Spitfires and they knew the aircrafts like the back of their hands. They'd flown in that morning to Chattis Hill to collect the brand-new planes, which were all lined up and waiting for them on the runway.

'To start with she was like an exotic creature, completely foreign in every way, but in the end she was just like us,' May replied.

'Just like us?' Ruby queried. 'Well, I don't know if either of us is as glamorous *or* outspoken.'

'Speak for yourself!' May grinned, and Ruby laughed, enjoying how much more jovial May had been lately.

She thought back to all the times they'd shared with Lizzie. She was a real character – she'd helped to liven things up and she'd been a heck of a pilot. Perhaps that was why Ruby had been so determined to fly the Halifax: without the competition, perhaps she never would have pushed herself so hard to succeed. If women were going to keep making a difference, maybe they had to be forced to see how capable they were.

'Do you think she's seen her father yet?' Ruby asked. 'It must have been hard for her being so far away, and she always spoke fondly of him.'

May shook her head. 'I haven't had word from her.'

She stood as someone called her over, and Ruby waited to hear the news. May was soon back, a nervous flicker crossing her face that made Ruby wonder what they were in for.

'Ladies, we'll be wheels-up within the next half-hour, so I suggest you use the toilet and do anything else you need to do.' She paused. 'We're all travelling to Colerne, as you know, to ferry the new Spitfires. They need to get there yesterday, to be frank, because they'll be sailing on the USS *Wasp* to Malta as soon as can be.'

'How many of them?' Ruby asked.

'Forty-seven in total, but not all from here,' May replied. 'Any questions, come and see me, otherwise prepare yourselves for a fast flight, ladies. Getting these planes to Malta could change the course of the war, and this is a Priority 1 Wait if we can't all take off on schedule. These planes *will* be delivered today.'

Ruby had listened to the wireless and talked it through with her host, Mr Robinson, the night before. Securing Malta was critical to British control of the Mediterranean. Without these Spitfires? They'd be bombed to oblivion. The last thing they needed was for Malta to fall, which was why Roosevelt had loaned the British an aircraft carrier, the USS *Wasp*, for the single trip to get the planes where they needed to go. It was all hands on deck, and everyone was relying on them to get the Spitfires to Colerne.

'I want you first up behind me, Ruby. Let's go.'

'You'd better watch out – I wobble all over the place when I'm putting my lipstick on before landing,' Ruby joked.

Ruby loved the Spitfires – they were the aircraft she'd miss most when the war ended; *if* it ever ended. The big bombers were amazing, especially the Halifax, which was so enormous it had room for a crew of six, but she felt most alive, most in charge, flying the smaller, more elegant Spitfire.

She paused as May spoke to Benjamin, grinning as she watched Ben pull May close for a second before she quickly walked away.

'I thought you said you didn't have a sweetheart?' she teased.

'I didn't and I don't,' May said, her cheeks a little red. 'Now focus on flying, would you?'

'Ben and May: it has a nice ring to it, don't you think?'

'Shoo,' May scolded. 'I'm your commander and I insist you go to your plane!'

Ruby blew her a kiss and jogged to her aircraft, still laughing. Good old Lizzie, for spotting what was going on!

Surprisingly the weather was clear enough, with only small pockets of cloud cover, and soon she was sitting in the cockpit, rubbing her hands together to warm them.

'Contact!' she yelled, before switching on the magnetos and starting up the engine, the propellers pulling through and kick-starting it to life.

After wrestling the little beast of a plane into the air, it was smooth sailing. She'd followed May up, and she was flying just behind her, keeping an eye on her tail and scanning constantly around her. For weeks she'd had this sinking feeling, a recurring nightmare: she was flying through cloud cover only to happen upon a plane flying towards her with a huge black cross on the fuselage and a swastika on its tail. Today that feeling was thrumming through her tenfold. There were so many of them in the air that they made an excellent target; what if the Germans took out a handful of female ATAs? She shuddered. It wasn't worth thinking about.

And she had something else to be mindful of. She thought of the warmth within her, wondering if she was right. She'd missed her monthly cycle, and after that magical night with Tom she was almost certain she was pregnant. The very idea should have alarmed her when they weren't even married, but she loved her Tom and she had no doubt he loved her just as much. Only she wasn't telling him or anyone her news, not until she had to. The last thing she wanted was to be forced to stop flying, not when she was one of only three British women to get their Class V conversion. Pregnant or not, she wasn't about to give up flying bombers, or any kind of plane that might be needed – not when she finally believed that she was capable of doing it.

*Tom.* Just thinking about him made her smile. After so long, she'd almost convinced herself that he would be a let-down when she was finally with him again, *if they even got that far.* But the look on his face, the genuine joy she'd seen when he'd watched her take off her helmet beside the Halifax and insist she was the pilot, had told her everything she'd needed to know. All the doubts she'd been having, all the anger she'd felt over his letters, had disappeared when they'd finally laid eyes on one another again.

And they were getting married on her next two days of leave. How he'd managed to secure the same two days she had no idea, but he'd written to her to check before insisting they marry at once. Her mother was going to be heartbroken, but she'd forgive her. At least this way *his* nosey, interfering mother would have nothing to do with it, and it might stop her from sending malicious letters – once they were married they were married, and that would be that. She wondered if he'd even tell her, or wait until after the war.

She scanned the sky again, wondering why she had such an unusual sense of foreboding. Perhaps it was that Lizzie had gone, or that May was flying with her when she was usually grounded and busy organising everyone else; or simply that there were so many of them travelling in the same direction, on the same flight path at the same time.

Whatever the case, once they landed she was going to take to ask May and Polly if they could be there on her wedding day. She would have asked Lizzie too, if she was still here.

She settled in for the flight, scanning the sky again and regularly checking her gauges. Her bottom already felt numb and she cursed the fact that she'd forgotten to bring a cushion to make the flight a bit more comfortable.

The mechanics waiting for them at Colerne hadn't been able to hide their excitement at the Spitfires arriving through the mist, and Ruby loved the pride she always felt at accomplishing something that so many people were counting on. She'd half-expected the feeling to pass once she'd been in the role for a while, but the gratitude they received from the pilots and ground crew at various airfields now was something she'd never tire of.

'Did you see that?'

Ruby turned and looked to where May was pointing. They'd all been sitting outside despite the cold, nursing hot cups of tea as they waited for notification to leave, and the last of the pilots were landing in dribs and drabs. They hadn't all come from the same base, and there were still a handful of ATAs expected within the next few hours.

'What?' she asked, not sure what May was so fixated on.

'It looked like that plane was making an uphill final approach.'

Ruby peered into the sky. Maybe May was right; it seemed unlikely, but the cloud cover was dense after a lovely morning when they'd first taken off, and some pilots might turn back rather than attempt to make their final push toward Colerne.

'There's nothing more frightening than knowing you've made the choice to fly, and then hurtling through the sky wondering why in God's name you decided to be the brave one,' May muttered.

'You think that's what happened there?'

May was standing now, one hand raised as she studied the sky. She stayed silent and then started to pace.

'Here she comes,' May muttered, as a figure appeared in the distance, walking towards them. 'Polly!'

Ruby leapt up and followed, wondering why May was so worried.

'Polly, what was all that about? We watched your approach,' May asked.

The other girl looked past May and gave Ruby a strange look. The colour had drained from her face, leaving her ashen. She was usually so fun, so full of life, but today she was nothing like her usual self.

'Go and get her a hot cuppa, would you?' May asked, frowning as she held out a hand to Polly.

But something made Ruby pause. The way Polly kept looking at her was unsettling, her eyes darting back and forth. What was going on?

'Visibility was bad?' May asked.

'Terrible. I only took off because I'd memorised the sequence of landmarks to get here. I had to fly so low just to mark off each road and railway line.'

'You could have turned back, or not taken off at all.'

Polly made a strange spluttering noise and gave Ruby a furtive glance again. 'That wasn't an option. Visibility increased, and I flew as slowly as possible, but I had to fly the last mile along a lane, which was uphill to here.'

'And the others?' Ruby asked.

May turned around, as if she was surprised to still see Ruby standing there.

'I think they turned around, but I can't be sure.'

'Why didn't you?' Ruby asked, staring back at Polly. 'Turn back, I mean? What's actually going on here?'

Polly burst into tears.

'Get the tea,' May murmured. 'Or something stronger.'

192

Ruby froze, her feet rooted to the ground. 'Why did you persist?' she asked again, suddenly needing to know.

'We had word, a call came in, I . . .'

Ruby breathed deep, wrapping her arms around herself. Was it their base? Had something happened to the other pilots? She watched as May stroked Polly's arm, and then her friend slowly raised her eyes to Ruby's.

'I don't know how to tell you this, Ruby, but . . .'

Ruby went ice-cold, and a shudder descended her spine. Was it her family? What in God's name was going on?

'Spit it out!' May ordered. 'What message do you have?'

'There was a call for you, Ruby. It's your fiancé,' Polly stuttered. 'Your Tom is missing in action, presumed dead. I'm so sorry.'

Ruby opened her mouth, but no sound came out. She went from ice-cold to burning hot and back to freezing again as she gaped at Polly.

'*My Tom?*' she managed to choke out, his handsome, strong face swimming in front of her eyes. She inhaled and could smell the musky, masculine scent of him, could feel his fingers as they traced against her skin. Her hand fell to her stomach.

'What happened? Did they give any information?'

Polly, wide-eyed, shook her head. 'They only said that he was struck by enemy fire. A Luftwaffe fighter appeared from nowhere and three aircraft were in enemy sights. They all engaged, but Tom took a direct hit and parachuted out.'

Ruby felt herself nodding, as if she were trying to reassure Polly that she understood what she was saying. 'The enemy aircraft? What happened to it?'

'Obliterated,' Polly whispered back. 'That's all I know.'

'So there's a chance, I mean, if he was seen exiting in his parachute, if . . .'

May's arms closed around her as she babbled, trying to convince herself that he might be all right. Why couldn't he survive that? Was it so crazy to believe that he could be alive still?

'This was almost two days ago, and he hasn't been heard of or seen since.'

Ruby gasped, a sob catching in her throat. So her Tom was dead. All this time, all these months and years of holding on to what her life would be like post-war, the snapshot image in her mind of them in a little home of their own, with children, happy and having fun again: all gone. And for the past forty-eight hours, she'd been dreaming of their little baby, of how to tell him, of marrying the man on their scheduled leave. And he was already gone.

Her legs buckled beneath her and suddenly May was on one side of her and Polly on the other. She should have thanked her friend for telling her the news, for risking life and limb to get to her in person, but she couldn't.

*Tom was gone.*

The words repeated over and over in her mind, as she walked, as she listened to May demand a stiff drink for her and as a hush fell over the mess room when May quietly told the others what had happened.

Ruby looked up and saw so many faces, so many women whom she loved and respected, and it hurt. They'd all lost someone to this war; they'd all had their share of heartache, but until now, she hadn't. Polly held her, rubbing her back, stroking her face as she sat there, crumpled inside.

*And now she'd lost the one person in the world she'd been living for.* She touched her stomach again, but refused to look down, shutting her eyes instead.

*Please, Tom, please come home to me*, she thought.

'Just breathe, Ruby. Just breathe.'

She heard May's voice, but she couldn't breathe. Tom was gone, and he was never, ever coming back.

'No!' she finally wailed, lurching forward as the noise broke free, the pain too much as it tore through every inch of her.

'Shhhhh,' May cooed, as if she were cradling a baby. 'Shhh now.'

Ruby wanted to run, she wanted to bolt away and never look back, never admit what she'd heard, never truly digest it. But she curled into a ball instead, sobbing in May's arms, tears streaming down her cheeks as she squeezed them shut and tried to block it all out.

*'I love you, baby,' Tom crooned, stroking her hair from her face.*

*'I love you, too,' she whispered. 'I swore I wouldn't fall into your arms, that I'd make you work for it after all those awful letters, but you're the one, Tom, you always have been.'*

*'I fell in love with you the day you arrived for your first flight,' Tom murmured, his lips brushing her hair. 'That big smile, your eyes twinkling as you looked from me to the plane and back again – I thought, that's the girl I'm going to marry.'*

*'You didn't,' she scolded. 'If you thought that, why did you take so long to ask me out?'*

*He laughed and pulled her closer. 'Because I wanted to take things slow.'*

*'I can't believe we have all night together,' she whispered, tucking even closer to him, cocooned in his arms in front of the fire.*

*'Ruby, once this war is over, we'll have every night together for the rest of our lives.' He laughed. 'Before we know it, we'll have a big house of our own and four children to fill it.'*

*'Four?' she asked. 'How about two?'*

Ruby wailed, one hand on her stomach as she tried to shut down the memories that kept crashing back, of their one night together on base. *One,* she thought, squeezing her eyes shut. *We only had one child, Tom. And now this little baby is going to be born without a daddy.*

# CHAPTER SEVENTEEN

*HOUSTON MUNICIPAL AIRPORT, TEXAS,*

*SEPTEMBER 1942*

*LIZZIE*

'You're very badly needed, every single one of you,' Lizzie said, beaming as she looked at her first ever class of pilots. Jackson, seated beside her, had arrived on base with General Hap that morning, and she'd tried her best to ignore him so far. They'd barely spoken since their final encounter back in England, and she was still angry that he'd kept information from her. But Hap had insisted they work together, and she didn't see that she had much choice in the matter. 'What you have signed up for, what you are preparing to do, I am certain will be admired in years to come. My time in Britain flying for the ATA with the most talented women pilots showed me how a female ferry division can work, and I have no doubt we can be equally as successful as our British sisters.'

The women all looked back, hopeful and buzzing with an excitement that she could feel. She gestured to the man at her side.

'I'd like to introduce you all to Captain Jackson Montgomery, who will be the army captain in charge of our training centre here,' she said.

'He is a very accomplished pilot and instructor, and was invaluable in Britain while I was there. I'd like you all to give him a warm welcome.'

The women put their hands together and started to clap, but Jackson held up a hand, frowning as if he didn't approve of the fanfare. Lizzie wasn't used to seeing him without one arm in a sling, and there was something different about him now that he wasn't recuperating; perhaps it was because he was no longer in an informal position, as he had been in England. She knew May had liked him and respected his opinion, but she'd expected to be running the show when she was finally given command of her own squadron, and with Jackson here it felt like she'd been sent a babysitter. Perhaps if he'd been honest with her about what was going on in the US when they were both still at Hamble, she'd trust him more. But he hadn't.

'I'm sorry, ladies, it seems our captain is used to salutes, not applause,' she joked. This was her programme, and she wasn't going to feel intimidated by him or anyone else.

'You are here to learn to fly the way the army flies, and no exceptions will be made,' he said, his voice deep and full of authority. 'If you've come here thinking you're hot pilots, then make no mistake, you'll be out on your ear. You have a lot to learn, and no one here knows how to fly an army plane like an army pilot yet.'

Lizzie cleared her throat. She'd be having words with him about that later.

'You will be treated as army recruits,' Jackson continued, 'and make no mistake about it. You misbehave or don't obey army rules, you wash out. You flunk out on your classwork or fail one test flight too many, you wash out. And trust me, you do not want to wash out.'

He gave Lizzie a long, hard look, and she wondered what he was thinking. Did he not think they were up to the task? Did he not think *she* was up to the task? Or was he simply not impressed by having to train women to fly military aircraft? Now that they were back on home soil there was something very different about the man – he was being tough as nails. At Hamble he'd been very much in a secondary role, but she could see he was taking this new leadership position very seriously.

'You will receive the same level of military training as our male cadets, with the exception of learning combat skills,' Jackson told them. 'You will rise at 0600 hours and be ready for training at 0700 hours. We will commence with ground school, including navigation and weather, and then move on to flying. Dinner will be at 1900 hours, followed by homework and lights out at 2200 hours. Are we clear?'

Lizzie looked around the room, expecting to see worried faces, but every single woman appeared full of anticipation. She smiled to herself; she'd clearly chosen well.

'Do I hear a *yes, sir*?' he asked.

'Yes, sir!' most of them called back, receiving a sigh from their new captain. Lizzie hoped they could muster a louder response next time.

When Jackson gestured for her to speak again, she gave him a tight smile and faced the crowd. 'Ladies, I'm afraid to say that you will still be staying in the motels for now, but I'm working as hard as I can on a new location for us. I only had weeks to establish this training facility, and the lack of barracks isn't ideal.' In truth the location in Houston was terrible, especially with the thick fog that continually rolled in from the Gulf of Mexico. 'Today will be as much an initiation as anything. We want you to familiarise yourself with the airfield and each other. Please report to your classroom after lunch for your first instruction. Class dismissed.'

As the women began to talk among themselves, Lizzie stood, but soon found herself face to face with Jackson. She wished she hadn't left it so long to talk to him, because it had made the situation even more awkward.

'I thought you might have focused more on uplifting our new recruits rather than trying to scare them into leaving,' she said dryly, raising her chin. Jackson was at least a foot taller than her and his uniform fitted his broad shoulders like a glove. Unlike hers, she thought, which was a terrible fit. Thank goodness she'd been able to cinch the waist in with a belt and take the arms and legs up herself, or she'd have been swimming in it. 'I can see you were going easy on us in England.'

'I'm interested in training pilots, and I care little for the feelings of your bunch of recruits,' he said. 'I want them to understand the realities of their new job, and train them accordingly.'

'Oh, I see. So you have a problem with training *women*, is that it, Captain?'

He had the gall to laugh, and she glared back at him. 'No. A pilot is a pilot. Makes no difference to me.' He shook his head. 'Honestly, Lizzie, I thought you at least knew me that well.'

'Then do you have a problem with me?' she asked, keeping her voice low to stop the other women from hearing. 'Is it because of what happened that day, over the Halifax? Because I'm not that woman anymore. I've come a long way since then and you need to believe it. I just don't understand why you're being so hard on these recruits instead of filling them with positivity!'

He shook his head. 'Lizzie, I'm sorry if I offended you. I've been asked to train these recruits with military precision, and that's exactly what I'm doing.'

When he turned and walked away from her, heat flooded her cheeks. What was it about him that rattled her so badly? They were always at odds, no matter what roles they were in!

Lizzie started to compose a letter in her head to May and Ruby, desperate to tell them what she was going on. If only they were here to talk to now.

'Dunlop!'

She cringed to hear her name called so crudely. Surely she should have a title, given that she was running the show?

Jackson had spun back around to face her. 'Anyone taught your ladies how to march?'

Lizzie rolled her eyes dramatically, more to annoy him than anything. 'They've just arrived, Montgomery,' she said. 'Give them a goddamn break.'

'That's *Captain* Montgomery to you,' he replied. 'And I expect them to march everywhere like real soldiers. We're not in Britain now, Dunlop!'

'I thought we weren't real soldiers?' she asked, perplexed. 'And I'm well aware what side of the pond we're on, *Captain*.'

'If you're under my command, you'll be treated like a soldier,' he barked, making every young woman within earshot stop and stare. 'When you're training in a PT-19 you will be treated like a soldier, and if you're issued with more than seventy demerit points, you *will* be treated like a soldier and sent home.'

Lizzie gulped, wondering if this was a routine part of his show to scare new recruits into submission, or whether he was deadly serious. She'd certainly never seen this side of him before.

# CHAPTER EIGHTEEN

### *LONDON, SEPTEMBER 1942*

### *RUBY*

Ruby brought the plane in to land and went through the motions, careful to check everything twice before stepping out of the cockpit. She gratefully took the mechanic's hand, probably holding it too hard as she clung to him on her way down.

She headed straight for the mess room, trying not to shake, trying not to think, trying to stay numb. Her body felt like a prison, keeping the real her, the *feeling* her, locked away, stifling how she truly felt and how she wanted to act. It took all her willpower not to fall apart.

*He could still be alive.* Those five words kept echoing through her head, as they had every single minute, every hour, every day since she'd heard the news. *He could still be alive.* Was she stupid to hold out hope? Was this what every wife, daughter, mother thought when they received similar news, or was she just naïve?

'Ruby!' May's call rang out across the field. Her commander came running over and placed her arm protectively around Ruby's shoulder. 'You're certain you don't want to take some time off? You can have all the time you need until . . .'

'No,' Ruby croaked. 'Please, no.'

She needed to fly, because if she couldn't do her job then all she'd have were her thoughts, and they terrified her. And the last thing she wanted was to go home and have to deal with his mother; she needed to stay strong and keep Tom in her prayers and thoughts, believing that the news might be wrong.

'Do you believe Tom could be alive?' she whispered, clutching May's hand. 'Am I so stupid to believe he might have made it?'

'It's unlikely,' May answered, 'but not impossible. We both know the odds. But there's always a chance.'

'But what do you think, really? I need to know what you honestly believe.'

May looked at her long and hard, and Ruby knew. 'Ruby, listen to me,' she said gently. 'I don't want you to give up hope, but believing that someone could still be alive when everything is suggesting otherwise – it's a cruel trick of the mind.'

Ruby gulped down tears. 'So you think I'm being silly, holding out hope?'

May took her hand, and Ruby saw her tears reflected in her commander's gaze. 'I lost my brother, Ruby, and I loved him more than anything in the world,' May whispered. 'But when his plane went down, my mother clung to that hope, believing there was a way he could have survived, and she drove herself crazy holding on to that. Refusing to believe he'd been taken from us.'

May had lost her brother? Why hadn't she ever said anything before now? Ruby was lost for words. 'I had no idea. I mean, I knew your brother was a pilot, but . . .'

May nodded. 'He was. And a mighty fine one at that. But we lost him early in the war and I don't think I'll ever stop grieving for him.'

'I can't believe I didn't know,' Ruby said. 'I'm so sorry for your loss, May. Truly. I wish I could think of the right words to say.'

May took a big breath. 'He's the reason I work such long hours, and the reason I'm so determined to keep you all safe,' she said. 'And it's the same reason I never go home, even when I'm on leave in London. I just can't deal with going back there – it seems harder than anything else I've faced.' She looked stricken. 'But hope can be a false friend, so I want you to be mindful of that.'

Ruby nodded, not about to pass judgement. If May couldn't face going home because of her loss, then that was her business. She shuddered at the thought of having to come face to face with Tom's mother, and a fresh wave of tears engulfed her. 'How do you keep going?' she asked. 'How do you get yourself out of bed each day and face it all over again?'

May's eyes shut for a moment before she answered. 'Some days I don't know the answer to that question, but mostly I think about my pilots here, and how I need to be strong for them. It gets me out of bed in the morning and keeps me going through the day. I hate the risks we take sometimes, but I do everything I can to keep my girls safe.' She paused. 'Come on now, let's get you inside.'

Ruby walked in and was pleased to find only Polly there; the others were all out flying, but her friend must have delivered a plane and stayed to see her. She would make sure she was gone before the rest returned, still not ready to face anyone and to have to stay strong through their questions and sympathies.

'You look like a girl who needs a good strong drink,' Polly said, trading glances with May.

Ruby flopped into a chair, wrapping her arms tightly around herself; the cold seemed to seep into her bones. Polly curled up beside her, finding her hand and not letting go.

'When do you leave?' she heard May ask.

'I'm taking the first lot of girls back later this afternoon with me,' Polly replied.

'Where are you going?' Ruby mumbled.

'Just back to White Waltham,' Polly said with a yawn.

Ruby nodded as the two women chatted and laughed beside her, perhaps aware that she was craving normality so long as she didn't have to be part of it.

*He could still be alive*, she said to herself, repeating the words over and over in her mind. No matter what May had said, she wasn't about to give up hope, not yet. *Please, God, please let Tom still be alive.*

# CHAPTER NINETEEN

## TEXAS, SEPTEMBER 1942

### LIZZIE

'Hey Daddy!' Lizzie squealed, and threw her arms around her father, holding on to him tight.

'Elizabeth! You'll give the poor man another heart attack carrying on like that!'

Lizzie laughed at her mother, swatting her away with one hand as she held on to her father with the other. No matter what anyone said, she wasn't letting go of him.

'How's things?' she asked him.

'Well, I'm feeling better about the fact that our forces are progressing through Europe. It's about time we threw our weight around and helped the Allies win the war!'

Lizzie smiled. 'I meant *you*. How are things with you?' she said. 'I'm happy about the progress the Allies are making too, but right now I'm more interested in how your heart's doing!'

He sat down and reached for his pipe, but Lizzie pushed it away.

'Don't you arrive home and go getting all bossy with me,' he said.

'Daddy, did the doctor say you could smoke?'

'No, he didn't,' said her mother quietly, sitting down beside Lizzie.

Lizzie reached for her hand and then leaned in to kiss her cheek. 'It's so good to be home again,' she whispered. 'I miss you both so much whenever I'm away.'

Her mama kissed her back, then got up again. 'I'll get us all something to drink. You must be exhausted, Liz.'

Lizzie sat back and studied her father, hating how much he'd aged since she'd left. Before England, he'd seemed young and vibrant still, but now he was older, vulnerable even, and it was hard to accept.

'Sweetheart, you've never told me about that first bomber flight. I want blow by blow details of how it all went down.'

Lizzie had been dreading this question, knowing it would come up eventually. On her other visits he hadn't been well enough to sit and chat, but now he seemed more like his old self. 'Well, I wasn't the first, Daddy. Another highly capable pilot beat me to it, but it was a fair race.'

'Good to hear. Did you get the next flight?'

'Yes,' she said. 'It was a great learning experience, actually.'

'Well, good. Nothing worse than a cocky pilot, Liz.' He patted her hand. 'You seem more grown-up, more level-headed. Don't get me wrong, I loved you just fine the way you were, but England did you good. I'm so proud of you.'

Lizzie blinked away tears and leaned into him. All she'd ever wanted was for him to be proud of her, and hearing him say it was the best thing in the world.

She sat with him all afternoon, talking, but when her mother called them for dinner, she realised she hadn't asked him something she'd been holding on to for some time.

'Daddy, I met a pilot in London. He told me that his father was on your squadron.'

'His name?'

'Montgomery,' she said.

'Ah, yes. What a coincidence.' She watched as he reached for his pipe again and this time she didn't stop him. 'He was always to my right. I couldn't have flown without him.'

She swallowed hard. 'I always imagined you flying solo, and taking down the enemy all on your own.'

He laughed and then coughed, spluttering on his first inhale. 'Darling, there's no such thing as a solo assault. We always flew in formation, and we had each other's backs.'

She nodded. 'I know that now.' The fact that Jackson had known more about her father's flying escapades than she did cut deep, but she could see how wrong she'd been.

'I wasn't a hero, Lizzie. I might have been the one to receive the medal and make my targets, but I was never doing it for myself. All of us,' her father coughed again and cleared his throat, 'we all did what we had to do for our country.'

Lizzie curled up beside him, inhaling the aroma from his smoking pipe and placing her head on his shoulder. She might only have forty-eight hours leave, but it had been worth every second to come home and see her daddy.

'Was that Montgomery a pain in the backside?' she asked.

Her father chuckled. 'Not at all. Why?'

'Because this one is,' she muttered, trying not to grin.

Her daddy started to laugh. 'I have a funny feeling *you're* usually the pain in everyone's backside, Liz.'

She glared at him, but couldn't keep a straight face. Her daddy was probably right.

# CHAPTER TWENTY

## *HAMBLE AIRFIELD, HAMPSHIRE,*

## *OCTOBER 1942*

## *MAY*

May crossed the tarmac and looked for Ben, wanting to see how much longer he'd need to finish checking the two Spitfires she was waiting to send up. Ever since they'd heard about Tom going missing, she'd avoided him, no longer sitting in her spot for tea. Thinking about what Ruby was going through had brought every vivid memory back to her, making her relive how Johnny had died all over again. Only the night before she'd been up, pacing, wondering for the millionth time if she'd somehow caused him to crash, and then panicking that one of her girls might be next. But now, with all the girls off flying and hardly anyone on base, it was time to seek Ben out again.

'Benjamin?' she called, walking into the hangar. 'Ben, are you here?'

She heard the familiar sound of a tool falling to the concrete and waited for him to appear.

'Hi stranger,' he called out from somewhere beneath a plane.

When Ben finally emerged, rubbing his hands on a cloth, her heart skipped a beat. This was why she'd avoided him. Because the warmth she felt whenever she saw him, it scared her. Feelings like that were too easy to lose, to disappear in one stroke of fate.

'I've missed you,' she said, the words flying from her mouth before she could stop them.

He stopped a few feet away, his dark brown eyes searching hers out. 'No tea for me *again*?' he joked, looking at her empty hands.

She shook her head, about to say no, but ran the distance between them instead, throwing her arms around his neck and kissing him like it was the last kiss of her life. She held his face to hers, stopping only when his hands skimmed down her back to rest on her hips.

'I think I'll forgive you for forgetting the tea,' he murmured.

She pulled him closer, not wanting to stop. 'I don't want to be scared anymore,' she said, her voice shaking. 'I want to live. I *need* to live again.'

He frowned, studying her face and stroking her hair. 'What are you scared of?'

'I was so scared of losing you, of letting anyone close and losing them, but the worst thing would be not having anyone in the first place, don't you think? After seeing Ruby lose Tom, feeling her pain, I just want to be happy again.'

He kissed her forehead, holding her close. 'You're not going to lose me,' he said. 'I promised you that already. I'm not going anywhere if I can help it.'

She held on to him, her face pressed to his chest, listening to the sound of his heart thumping away against her ear. She believed him. Even though they were in the middle of a war, Ben was grounded, Ben was as safe a bet as she could have.

'Senior Commander!'

She jumped back, smoothing her hair and clearing her throat.

'Yes!' she barked, spinning around.

'Telegram for you, ma'am. It's on your desk.'

The pilot disappeared, red-cheeked, as May turned back around to Ben.

'Do you think she saw?' she asked, horrified.

Ben laughed and rubbed her cheek with his cloth. 'I think the grease on your face was probably impossible to miss.'

She swatted at him, but missed; he caught her wrist and tugged her in close again, his mouth inches from hers. 'Don't go MIA on me again, May,' he murmured.

She groaned and kissed him, forgetting all about the Spitfires, before turning on her heel and racing to her desk. Sure enough, a telegram was sitting there. She opened it, swallowing away the lump in her throat, nervous about the fate of her girls, hoping it wasn't about one of them. But then she clamped a hand across her mouth. She read it again, slowly this time, barely able to believe the words. She wasn't sure why the telegram had been sent to her as commander rather than to Ruby, but regardless, she couldn't wait to tell her the news.

PLEASE INFORM FIRST OFFICER RUBY SANDERS THAT HER FIANCE, FLIGHT LIEUTENANT THOMAS FRANCES, IS ALIVE. SURVIVED IMPOSSIBLE CONDITIONS AFTER DEPLOYING PARACHUTE. INJURIES INCLUDE BROKEN ARM, CRACKED RIBS, LEG TRAUMA AND BLEEDING FROM HEAD. FULL RECOVERY EXPECTED.

She breathed out a sob of relief. Tom was alive! Ruby was going to be beside herself – it had been a long wait for more information, and May hadn't been hopeful that there would be any news, good or otherwise. How on earth had he survived being shot down near Cologne, the only pilot not to make it back from the night-time bombing there, and a parachute jump from his plane? And how had he managed to stay alive all this time? She blinked away tears, knowing exactly how incredible this piece of news would feel to her friend.

*'May, he could still be alive. If no one saw his body, if no one . . .'*

*'Stop it!' she screamed. 'Just stop it! John's dead, Mum, he's dead!'*

*Her mother doubled over like she'd punched her, her heart-wrenching, guttural sobs too much to bear.*

*'I'm sorry,' May whispered, 'but he's gone. He's never coming back and we have to accept it. Our Johnny's gone.'*

*Her father stepped in then, wrapping his arms around her mother, his eyes filled with unshed tears. And she ran out of the door and kept on going, feeling she couldn't bear to be in that suffocating house that reminded her every second of every day that she had to live the rest of her life without Johnny.*

'Ma'am, there's another urgent telegram for you.'

May looked up and met the gaze of one of her administration staff. 'Thank you,' she said, and opened the new telegram at once.

COMMANDER MAY JONES. SPITFIRES AND MORE SPITFIRES NEEDED! IMMEDIATE ASSISTANCE REQUIRED. ALL AVAILABLE PILOTS ON STANDBY FOR FERRY MISSION TO COLERNE.

What on earth? They needed *more* than the forty-seven planes they'd already delivered?

'Jones!' May recognised her captain's call as he burst into the building, red-faced and short of breath. 'You received word?' he asked.

'About the new aircraft needed? What . . .'

'Bloody German bombers hit the Spitfires! They survived the sailing from Port Glasgow and they were launched at Gibraltar with three cruisers and eight destroyers as an escort, but the damn pilots decided to take a lunch break when they landed in Malta, and they were bombed when they were lined up on the ground! Only six Spitfires survived.'

*Six?* May could barely comprehend that almost every single Spitfire they'd so diligently delivered had been bombed. They'd risked life and limb to get there!

'So what can we do? Are there even enough new aircraft to deliver?' she asked.

'Roosevelt has given permission for the USS *Wasp* to make a second trip. We need all your available pilots ready to fly as soon as we have enough planes. If we don't do this?' He shook his head. 'We could lose this war, Jones. It could be curtains for the Allies.'

'One would hope they won't stop for lunch and leave the planes lined up as sitting ducks this time,' May said dryly. She doubted female pilots would have been so foolish.

'Not a mistake I expect will happen again.'

The unmistakable roar of an engine alerted May that she had an aircraft safely back home, and she stood to excuse herself. Ruby was due back in a Lancaster, and she was looking forward to debriefing her and sharing the good news.

'Keep me posted,' she told Captain MacMillan. 'You know my girls will be ready to fly when you need us.'

She strode out towards the plane, standing back as she waited for the engine to stop, hand held high to shield her eyes from the glare above. For once it was sunny and there was no cloud cover to send her into a panic about her pilots. Today was an ideal day for flying, and there was something hopeful about the sun shining on her shoulders, not to mention the miracle she'd just been told of.

Ruby finally appeared, with Ben helping her down from the cockpit, but May could see something was wrong at once: Ruby was walking rigidly, as if every step was causing her pain. Over the past week she'd seen Ruby doubled over from grief and shaking from fatigue, but this was different. She was bent forward slightly, one hand to her stomach as Ben held her arm, and May's first thought was that she must be sick.

'Ruby!' she called out, hurrying towards her. 'What's wrong?'

Ruby always looked tiny, but when you spoke to her or watched her take command of a plane, there was no mistaking her for anything other than a highly competent pilot – but now she looked so weak and frail.

'What happened?' May asked, taking her other arm.

Tears pooled in Ruby's eyes. 'I . . . I . . .' she started.

'Ruby, I have wonderful news! I just . . .'

May looked down as Ruby flopped against her, and saw the stain on her flying suit, the unmistakable darkness of blood. Ben backed away, his gaze telling her that he'd let her deal with this.

'Oh, you poor thing, getting your monthly on a long flight like that,' she whispered. May held her tight, wondering if Ruby was just embarrassed or if something else was upsetting her. 'Ruby, I . . .'

Ruby let out a heart-wrenching sob and May held her tighter, hurrying her back to the mess room, where Ruby fainted just outside and sagged to the floor. May struggled with her, dragging her a little and then flopping down beside her.

'Ruby? Ruby, wake up!' she hissed. Ruby's eyes fluttered open and May breathed a sigh of relief.

Ruby gasped and reached for her hand. 'I think I'm losing my baby.'

May froze. Her mind reeled. Ruby was *pregnant*? She quickly took control and got them both up on their feet. 'Come on, there's hardly anybody else here. Everything's going to be fine. It might just be some, ah, unrelated bleeding.'

She walked her through the mess room, quickly passing a couple of other pilots, June and Evangeline; they were laughing and chatting, and barely looked up. May avoided eye contact with them as she took Ruby into the bathroom.

'How long have you known you were pregnant?' May whispered, shutting the door. She reached for a towel, not sure what to do. 'Poor

Ruby, alone with this – I would have kept your secret.' But even as she said it, she knew she would have had to put an end to her friend's flying, which was probably the one reason she had kept it to herself.

'I don't know, I . . .' Ruby struggled with her trousers, and May reached to help her. 'We've only been together the once, and I . . .'

May could see she was in shock. 'Ruby, how long have you been bleeding?' she asked calmly. 'Do you want me to call for a doctor?'

Ruby shook her head, looking terrified. 'No. Please don't. I wasn't that far along. I don't want anyone knowing.'

May nodded and brushed the hair from her forehead, noticing how clammy she was. 'You've flown a huge plane home at the same time as experiencing a trauma, Ruby. I can't imagine what you're going through, but I'm going to look after you. Everything is going to be fine.' She gave her a big hug. 'I promise you, I'm here for you. And, Ruby, I have wonderful news, about Tom.'

'Tom?' Ruby whispered. 'What about Tom?'

A memory sliced across May's mind.

*'Mum, I'm so sorry. But they've found his body,' May whispered. 'He's not coming home, Mum. He's gone.'*

*'No,' her mother sobbed. 'No!'*

'He's alive, Ruby!' she said, wishing someone could still say those words to her, that her brother had made it, too. 'I only received word moments before you landed. It's why I was running out to see you. He's alive, Ruby. It's true.'

'Tom's *alive*?' Ruby's words were barely audible, and May caught her hand, hoping her friend wasn't about to faint again. 'But how?'

'I don't know all the details, but somehow he survived and made his way back to safety,' May told her. 'He has injuries but nothing life-threatening. It'll be amazing hearing his story in his own words.'

'Tom's alive,' Ruby repeated again, the light coming back into her eyes as she burst out laughing. 'He's actually alive!' Her laughter quickly turned to gut-wrenching sobs and May caught her as she fell, slipping to the floor.

'He's alive, Ruby,' she whispered. 'Your Tom's alive. I promise you it's true.'

She could only imagine the emotions, the guilt of losing one thing and gaining another, the fear of loss and the euphoria of knowing something that you thought was gone had been returned to you. May shushed her and held her tight, cradling her like a child, until the sobs slowly turned to gasps. Poor Ruby had been through so much. May shut her eyes as she pushed out the grief that threatened to take hold of her, the hope she'd held on to for so long, the thoughts that were trying so hard to come back into her head. Ruby's Tom was alive, and that was all she was going to let herself think about.

She helped Ruby to undress, her heart breaking as her friend silently stood there with tears running down her cheeks, grieving the baby she'd lost as she came to terms with having a fiancé again. When Ruby was down to her undergarments, May excused herself and took the soiled flying suit with her, bundling it up to be washed. She'd wash it herself to avoid Ruby any further embarrassment. Then she went to Lizzie's locker, hoping she might not have cleared it out entirely.

'What are you looking for?' June asked.

May fixed a smile. 'Ruby's monthly came while she was flying,' she said in a low voice. 'I was hoping to find Lizzie's old flying suit or something else she could wear.'

'The poor thing. Happened to me last month too.' June opened her own locker and took a folded suit out. 'This is Lizzie's suit – I was going to start wearing it because mine needs mending, but it's no problem.'

'I have some spare undergarments if she needs them,' Evangeline added, rummaging through her locker. 'Give her these, and these rags. Do you want us to get a hot water bottle or anything?'

'Thanks, but I've got that under control. She's just a little embarrassed.'

'Happens to all of us,' Evangeline said. 'God's gift to women, eh?'

May disappeared back into the bathroom and found Ruby with a towel around herself, her cheeks pinker now, as if the lifeblood had started to flow back.

'You're going to be fine,' she whispered, helping her to change.

She knew that Ruby was struggling with her grief and her joy, and the only thing she could do was sit with her and help her to keep putting one foot in front of the other.

# CHAPTER TWENTY-ONE

## YORKSHIRE ARMY HOSPITAL, YORKSHIRE,

## OCTOBER 1942

## RUBY

'I can't believe you're alive.' Ruby leaned over Tom, cradling him as best she could. He was lying on the bed with only one pillow behind him to help prop him up. 'Let me get you more pillows – you look terribly uncomfortable.'

'No, don't,' he said, groaning as he tried to shift his weight.

'Tom, for goodness' sake, let me pamper you a little,' she joked, kissing his forehead and standing.

'Stop,' he said, fingers curling around her wrist. Ruby was about to tell him off when she saw the pained expression on his face.

'Please, I'm fine, Ruby,' he said. 'I don't need anything more than you sitting beside me. Don't fuss.'

Something in his gaze made her stop and she slowly lowered herself again to sit on the edge of the bed. 'I was only trying to . . .'

'I shouldn't be alive,' Tom said, holding her hand now, fingers intertwining with hers. 'There are men here that've lost limbs, or they're so badly burnt or . . .'

Her heart broke as he sucked back a breath. The pain within him was palpable, and she knew no words could change the way he felt. Just like no words could change the pain inside her when she thought of the little baby she'd lost, the baby she'd been so excited about.

'I'm so lucky, I have you and I'm going to be fine. That's all I need,' Tom said.

She nodded, holding his hand tight. It must be a strange thing, surviving a near-death experience, and she couldn't imagine what he'd been through.

'Something's wrong with you, too,' he said, rubbing her hand with his thumb. 'Are you all right?'

She froze. She'd been so careful, so certain that he wouldn't detect anything different about her. 'I'm just exhausted from getting here and from worrying about you,' she told him. She wasn't lying: both were true. 'I still can't believe you're alive.'

'Thinking about you, about getting back to you, was all that kept me going, Ruby. I had to walk for so long until I reached Belgium. I was shot flying back after we bombed Cologne, and I just kept seeing your face. I hate to think what state I was in when the Resistance found me, but they're running quite the operation saving Allied airmen,' he said, the huskiness of his voice pulling her closer, making her want to hold him and look after him and never let him go. 'We have them to thank for getting me home, that's for sure. Without them I'd have never made it back.'

She bent and touched her forehead to his, eyes shut as she took a deep, shuddering breath.

'Now tell me what's wrong, because I know you're keeping something from me.'

'I was pregnant,' she whispered, not even sure that she wanted to tell him. But the words just spilled out, and relief washed over her. Holding the knowledge to her heart and keeping it a secret had felt wrong.

She felt Tom go still, before he finally whispered back, '*Were?*'

Ruby ducked her head to his chest, fighting tears. She'd been wracked with guilt from the moment she'd found out he was alive, and now she was going to have to tell Tom why. Her hand instinctively went to her stomach, something she'd done a lot when he'd been missing and she had felt such a strong connection to the baby, but now she quickly pulled her hand away. She had to keep reminding herself that there was nothing there.

'When I found out you were missing, I had this horrible thought,' she confessed. 'I'd been so excited about my little secret and I'd been planning how to tell you . . .' Ruby gulped. 'But then . . . all I could think was that I'd rather have you than the baby. I didn't truly mean it, but I kept thinking it and . . .' Her voice trailed off.

Tom didn't say anything, but when she looked up, finally braving his gaze, she didn't see the disappointment she'd expected. 'Sweetheart, I'd pray to have you back, too. You don't have anything to feel guilty about.'

'But to bargain for you over our baby?' she asked. 'Doesn't that make me a horrible person?'

He stroked her face gently. 'No, it makes you human,' he said. 'I love you, and if I had to choose you over a baby that wasn't born yet? It'd be you every time, Ruby, I promise.'

Relief pulsed through her and she fought the urge to cry. The past two days had been overwhelming; what with hours of flying, then losing the baby, finding out about Tom and travelling to be with him, she doubted she'd had more than a few hours' sleep.

'If our baby had been born, if you'd held the child in your arms, you'd never have had to bargain me over him or her, Ruby,' he whispered

219

as she shut her eyes, tears escaping and wetting his shirt. 'I promise you, we'll get pregnant again. What you did hasn't changed whether or not we'll have a family, and your thoughts aren't that powerful, sweetheart. It's not your fault that you lost the baby. Some things just aren't meant to be, no matter how cruel that sounds.'

Tom's arms soothed her, but when he groaned, she realised she was leaning on his chest.

'Am I hurting you?' she asked.

'Ah, a little,' he said, grimacing. 'Tuck in here with me until we get caught.'

Ruby brushed her tears away and did her best to lie beside him, his good arm around her as she snuggled close.

'How much leave do you have?' Tom asked.

'Only three days,' she said. 'Less if we have to make our second trip back to Colerne before then, for the second lot of Spitfires to be sent to Malta.' It was the first time she'd resented work; all she wanted was for her and Tom to cocoon themselves away together until she knew he was going to be all right. Until she was convinced that *she* was going to be all right.

'Then let's get married before you go back,' he whispered.

She hiccupped a noise that didn't even sound like it belonged to her. 'Here?' she managed.

'I don't care where. All I know is that I want to marry you,' Tom said. 'I should be dead, Ruby, but I've been given a second chance. This war, it's changed things, and after almost dying out there? Marrying you is the only thing I'm sure about.'

She breathed deeply. 'Yes. But . . .'

'No buts,' he said. 'I don't care if I'm lying in this bed during our ceremony – I want to be married to you.'

Ruby felt a quiet thrill of joy. Their circumstances might have completely changed, but they were going to carry out their plan. She would marry her Tom after all.

'Just because I'm your wife, you can't tell me to give up flying,' she murmured, hating that it was the first thing that came to mind, but needing to say it anyway. 'You can't go back to being all bossy about my choices as a pilot, Tom.'

'I wouldn't dream of it,' he said.

'Oh, but *I* dream,' she confessed. 'I dream of us both walking away and finding a little house somewhere, being safe and just raising a family together. I think of it all the time. Even when I thought you were gone, I couldn't stop imagining it.'

'We all do that, Ruby. We need that dream to help us do what we do, to know that we're fighting for the freedom to build that life. To survive this bloody never-ending war.'

Ruby shut her eyes again, imagining they were there already. There was an emptiness inside of her, knowing that she'd been growing a little life that had been extinguished so fast; it was almost as if it had never been there at all. But it had, and she wasn't going to give up on that dream of having a baby and creating a home with Tom.

'Do you think this war will ever end?' she asked him. 'Will we win it?'

'If it doesn't end, all of this, everything we've lost, will be for nothing, and I can't accept that.'

She wanted to ask him how he'd survived, wanted every little detail so she could piece together what had happened, but something was holding her back. Tom was clinging on to her like his lifeline, and just as she didn't want to relive the moment she'd miscarried, she doubted he'd want to revisit the excruciating moments he'd endured in order to live.

'Can I have my senior commander as witness, if she can make it?' Ruby asked. 'And my friend Polly?'

'Of course.'

Two days later, Ruby glanced at May and Polly standing beside her, proud to have them by her side. They didn't have long – May had come to get her en route to collecting the second batch of Spitfires and Polly was having to pick up a large aircraft to ferry a group of them back from Colerne – but it was long enough.

'You look beautiful,' May whispered to her.

Ruby looked down at her uniform, something she was so proud to wear, but wished that today she'd had a dress; that she could have been the radiant bride wearing lace and silk.

'You do, Ruby. You're absolutely radiant,' Polly said.

'Thank you,' she said honestly, knowing how special it was to be wearing the uniform at all.

'She's right, you do look beautiful,' Tom added, as a man approached them. 'And here's our ticket to wedded bliss.'

The captain who was marrying them hurried over, a big smile on his face as he arrived, slightly out of breath. Ruby fought a childish giggle as he smoothed two fingers across his thick moustache before speaking.

'Ah, our lovely couple. What an honour it is to marry two such accomplished pilots.'

Ruby beamed, so proud of what they'd both achieved. It would be weeks if not months before Tom was able to fly again, but fly he would, and soon they'd both be back in the sky.

May and Polly both stood to her side in the garden as she held hands with Tom, and they spoke their vows. Within minutes he was carefully circling his arms around her as she gently held him back. She slipped her hands around his waist as he tipped her back, and she kissed him through laughter as enormous drops of rain started to pelt them, striking her face and slowly soaking her hair as they stayed wrapped in one another's arms.

'No!' she moaned. 'Not today!'

Tom grabbed her hand, and she leaned in to him one more time, kissing him full on the lips with everything she had. 'I love you,' she murmured against his mouth. 'I love you so much, Tom, with all my heart.'

The poor man was still limping, and she knew how much it must hurt him to even attempt to run, but they moved as fast as they could back towards the makeshift hospital that was to be his convalescing home for the coming weeks. It was a house that had been requisitioned in Yorkshire, and the wide verandas provided the perfect shelter from the mid-morning storm.

Once they were in the dry, she touched her hair, dismayed that the beautiful up-do had been ruined in the space of minutes. But then Tom held her tight and she soaked up the feel of his warm body, the light in his eyes as he stared down at her, and the musky, male scent of him.

'I'm sorry to interrupt, lovebirds,' May started, clearing her throat from behind them. 'But it's time to go.'

'Already?' Tom groaned. 'Can't I have her for another few minutes?'

'Sorry, Romeo, you'll have to consummate your marriage another day,' Polly said with a giggle.

All four of them laughed, until Tom slipped a hand around Ruby's neck and leaned in for a last kiss.

'You keep her safe,' he murmured, his gaze fixed on May.

May shook her head. 'You know that's a promise I can't keep, but your girl is one hell of a pilot.'

Ruby hugged him and committed every inch of her new husband to memory. Her love for him and her love of flying threatened to tear her in two, but she had a job to do.

'I'll see you soon,' she said. 'Stay safe.'

Tom held up a hand as she backed away then ran through the rain after May and Polly. It was her wedding day, and instead of a blissful afternoon with her husband, she was going to be flying a Spitfire.

# CHAPTER TWENTY-TWO

## SWEETWATER AIRFIELD, TEXAS,

## OCTOBER 1942

## LIZZIE

'Dunlop.'

She looked up and saw Captain Montgomery striding towards her. Trust him to be the first person she laid eyes on as she walked outside for fresh air. Lizzie held up a hand to shield her face from the sun, irritated by his presence.

'Good to have you back,' he said briskly.

'I much prefer Texas to Washington,' she replied. 'Four days of meetings there and I'm pleased to be back.' She'd been visiting her family before that, too, so it had been a week since she'd been on base.

He made a sort of grunting noise. 'Well, we're pleased to have you. You're good for morale.'

She stifled a laugh. *Good for morale?* She certainly hoped she was good for more than just that!

'We're going to be sending our best graduates to specialised training centres from here,' she told him. 'I've received confirmation from

General Arnold that they want our WASPs to be able to deliver as many planes as possible. It looks like we're going to be kept busy – they're preparing for the Europe invasion.'

Montgomery nodded. 'Good call. They'll be delivering planes to every port and base in the country, so it makes sense. And it's great news that women are now permitted to fly in military planes with men. I'm thinking your time in Washington might have given rise to this new decision?'

Lizzie gave a wry smile. 'It seems women aren't such a terrible distraction after all.' She couldn't help the sarcasm; the rule had been ridiculous and she was pleased it had finally been scrapped.

'Oh, I'm sure they all think you females are a terrible distraction, but it makes sense for women to catch a ride when they can. But don't think they were trying to placate you – I'd say it's simply someone higher up trying to save time and money on buses, trains and commercial aircraft to get women back to base.'

Lizzie had to agree. Honestly, she wanted to shake the men making the decisions in the army most of the time!

'Walk with me?' she asked the captain, hoping she wouldn't regret it; he seemed to rub her up the wrong way at every step. But something about him kept drawing her back, and she had to remind herself that it had been Jackson who'd picked her up and pulled her through her darkest hours after losing the bomber flight, and him once again who'd broken the news of her father's heart attack. Perhaps she'd been too hard on him when she'd first arrived home, and not given him enough credit.

'How is the new intake coming along?' she asked as they passed the Link Trainer, which was a faux-type plane that never left the ground. 'Has their instrument training progressed well this week?'

He nodded. 'Yes, they're all doing well, although it does take some of them time to get used to listening for instructions through the headpiece rather than looking through the cockpit window.'

She nodded. 'It's a useful skill. The women I flew with in England would pass with flying colours.'

'I don't know how they haven't lost any women over there,' he said. 'Flying without instruments and radio is unheard of.'

'And terrifying!' she replied. 'They have their instincts to follow in bad conditions and nothing else. I can't believe May didn't push harder for something to be done, but whenever she tried they just reminded her of her excellent wastage rate.'

'It's an awful term, *wastage rate*,' he said. 'But they were an incredible bunch of women.'

She smiled, not sure whether he was including her in that praise. 'They most certainly were.'

They passed a classroom, windows open, so they could hear the instructor talking inside. Lizzie was so proud of their training facilities, and she only wished she could somehow show May and Ruby how everything looked and what was going on. There was only so much she could convey in letters.

'Are you happy with the training schedule or are there any changes you'd like to make?' she asked.

He frowned. 'The programme you've designed for them is solid. The only thing I'd like to do more of is stalling mid-air. It's one thing to know what to do in a controlled environment, and another altogether in an emergency.'

She nodded. 'Done. So they'll start with emergency landings and lazy-eights, slow rolls and so forth, and then we'll go straight into stalling mid-air and spins. It'll scare them silly to begin with, but if they do it every day for a couple of weeks, spinning toward the ground and then having to get out of it without crashing, they'll be prepared for anything and it'll become second nature.'

Jackson nodded, then laughed.

'What is it?' she asked.

'See the well there?' he asked.

She looked over, and could hardly miss the stone wall. 'What about it?'

'The girls have taken to throwing one another in after their first solo flight. Apparently it's a way to cool off a *hot* pilot.'

She coughed. 'They what?'

His smile gave her a hint of the man beneath, and for the first time she didn't feel quite such dislike towards him. 'I tried to punish them, but they couldn't stop giggling and I ended up leaving them to it. Honestly.' He chuckled. 'The short sheeting tricks on their beds I reprimanded them for, but they've all adapted so well, I let them have one little win.'

'I wholeheartedly approve then, and I'm a little surprised at how soft you've become,' she said, teasing. She turned back towards her office. 'I'll see you this afternoon, Captain. I have admin to do before I get back to training my girls.'

'Or you could show the girls exactly why you're so respected as a pilot,' he said quietly. 'I think they need to see what they could be capable of one day.'

She turned and met his gaze. 'Did I hear you correctly? You actually *want* me to show off?'

He laughed. 'Yes.'

'Fine. Have a plane ready for me after lunch.' She turned sharply on her heel. 'And make it something decent!'

Lizzie chuckled to herself. Jackson was right; it would be good to give the girls an air show. She just hadn't expected him to suggest it.

At noon, Lizzie strode up to Jackson, walking tall with a hum of excitement surging through her body that she hadn't felt in months. When she'd taken over the controls of the Halifax for the first time, becoming the *second* girl in England to be given leave to fly one, the thrill had been enormous. And, right now, she had the same kind of feeling.

'Jackson, what do you say we skip lunch and hit the sky together instead?' she asked.

There was no one else around, just the two of them, and she was tired of being grounded when all she wanted to do was fly. She was going to do the flight he'd suggested to show their recruits what the planes were capable of after lunch, but right now she wanted to have some fun.

He folded his arms across his chest and smiled. 'You're joking,' he said.

'Come on, you can still remember how to fly, can't you, Captain?' she asked sweetly, trying not to laugh. 'Weren't you some whizz in the air before you were stationed here to babysit me?'

'You're challenging me to some sort of flying duel?' he asked. 'Or are we just going to run through some training drills?'

'We're just going to have fun,' she replied. 'Don't you miss the actual flying part of our jobs? I thought we could fly together, just this once, as a reward for all our hard work.' Lizzie grinned. 'This isn't about me proving I'm better than you, in case that's what you're worried about.'

'I know you *think* you're the best pilot this side of the Atlantic, Dunlop, but it sure as hell doesn't mean you're better than me.'

She laughed. 'Come on, what do you say?'

'This is just for fun?'

She beckoned towards the runway. 'Yes. Just you, me and the sky.'

As much as she wanted to show him she was the better pilot, she'd grown a lot since her time in England, and this was as much about flexing her flying muscles as it was showing Jackson that they could get along well. They both loved the same thing, and she was itching to get back behind the controls.

She headed to the closest aircraft, pleased to see that there were two AT-6 Texans, silver with a single white star, available. They would be perfectly matched in identical aircraft, and the 600-horsepower plane would be more than adequate.

She climbed in, waited for Montgomery to do the same, and then fired up the engine. The trainees would be flying these sleek aircraft eventually, so it was good for her to fly one before she resumed teaching later that afternoon. It had been a while since she'd flown anything similar herself.

The flight engineer waved her off and she signalled to Montgomery before taxiing towards the runway. She hurtled down the tarmac, her stomach leaping as it always did when she was wheels-up and away. Lizzie circled and gave her rival plenty of space to take off and join her, and soon he'd fallen in beside her. She wondered what it would feel like to be flying in formation with him, preparing for war and going into combat, knowing that he was protecting her and she him. She waved at him before putting some space between them and doing a slow roll. She looked over and saw him repeat the same trick, only he followed it up with a lazy-eight.

Lizzie laughed. This was definitely fun. Her body hummed, her mind quiet and content as she followed her instincts and glided through the sky.

She crossed over and fell into the space to Montgomery's left; he deftly dropped lower and put himself back on the left-hand side, as if he were trying to prove that she wasn't the boss. Lizzie wasn't going to have him out-play her, so she forced her plane into a spin well away from him, her heart thudding as she worked the controls fast to get the plane on course again. She barrelled lower through the air and her engine stalled, but she quickly righted herself and got it going again, soaring back up and taking her place to his left.

Lizzie saw the look on his face through his cockpit window, and knew he was having as much fun as she was. Soon they were both doing rolls and then racing; her cheeks hurt from smiling so hard, loving every minute of their silly antics.

When they finally came in to land, Lizzie was breathless and high on adrenaline. She leapt out of the cockpit and strode towards the captain as he climbed down from his Texan. She didn't remember ever feeling so alive!

'Truce?' she said, extending her hand. 'I think it's easy to argue and forget that we're firmly on the same side.'

'Truce,' he agreed, clasping her palm, his smile as wide as hers.

'That was the most fun I've had in months,' she declared. 'I actually think we're perfect sparring partners. We should do that again some time, if you're up for it? We need to keep our own flying hours up.'

He nodded, running his fingers through his blond hair. 'I'd actually forgotten what it was like to just fly like that,' he admitted. 'Whenever you want to take to the sky, I'll be ready. No more barbs, Lizzie. Let's just agree we're both damn good at what we do and enjoy the flights we get.'

Lizzie grinned in response and strode over to find her trainees, ready to empower them, to tell them how exhilarating it was to take command like that and know in your heart that anything was possible. She couldn't wait to fly for them that afternoon, to see their faces and understand how exciting it was to watch someone and believe that you could do it too. She'd felt the same when standing as a little girl with her father, hand up to block out the bright sun, her stomach leaping cartwheels with every trick in the air: the day she'd proudly told her daddy that she was going to be a pilot herself.

She looked over at Montgomery and his blue eyes twinkled back at her with what she hoped might be admiration. Maybe he wasn't quite the villain that she'd thought. Maybe she'd been far too hard on him when he was only trying to do his job; maybe he was actually a teddy bear beneath his fierce, commanding exterior. She laughed. Maybe he wasn't so different to her, after all.

# CHAPTER TWENTY-THREE

*COLERNE, WILTSHIRE,*

*OCTOBER 1942*

*MAY*

May couldn't help but smile as she followed Ruby in the air. Only hours earlier they'd been standing together in Yorkshire as Ruby and Tom were married, and now she was following her newly wedded friend in a Spitfire, watching her zigzag all over the place as they headed for Colerne. If only they had radios, May would frighten the life out of her by barking at her to fly straight. Ruby was notorious for powdering her face and putting on her lipstick before landing, and her beauty was probably half the reason she'd received so much press coverage as a pilot.

It was hard to believe they were ferrying Spitfires for the second time, and that the first shipment had been almost entirely obliterated. And to have to risk all her pilots again for the same mission . . . It was horrifying, especially given how tense she was feeling about their perfect fatality rate. Just the other day she'd heard two of the women laughing about the mechanics teasing them for being a statistical anomaly. She shuddered. The fact they hadn't lost a pilot yet wasn't a joking matter;

their luck couldn't keep holding forever. And it brought her mother's words back to her as she sobbed that she didn't want to lose another child, that she couldn't be left with no one.

*'I miss him as much as you do,' May said, holding on to the door jamb, her fingers digging into the wood. It took all her strength not to run, to force herself to stay and listen to her mother.*

*'I've never held you back, May, I've never wanted to tell you that you couldn't do something, but to think about losing you, as well as our Johnny . . .'*

*May wanted to go to her, to hold her and hug her tight, but since losing Johnny she'd been unable to do anything that involved letting her guard down. She didn't want to cry, she didn't want to feel.*

*'I want to make sure every single plane that needs to be delivered can be,' she said instead. 'The faster we win this war, the faster everyone else's sons, husbands and fathers get home safe.'*

*'I'm so proud of you,' her mother sobbed. 'I want to keep you here, but I'm so proud of you, May. Johnny would be so proud, too.'*

*May nodded and left the room, collected her bag and walked out the door. She looked up at the window she'd been standing in when Johnny left. And part of her wondered if her mother would have been so proud if she'd known how cruel she'd been to him, how cutting her words had been when she should have been hugging him and telling him how much she'd miss him.*

The plane in front of her straightened up, and May stayed focused, scanning the air for enemy planes, any incoming targets and of course the planes flying in formation with her. It was unheard of to have so many in the air together and she was nervous about how exposed they were. She'd talked to Ben before flying out, confessing her fears, and she had seen the look on his face, knew that she wasn't overreacting because her fears were mirrored in his eyes. *Ben.* She shook her head just thinking about him. She'd been so determined to shield herself from any man, but somehow he'd taken her by surprise and slowly got under her skin. It wasn't that she didn't like it, because she did. The thought of seeing him each day, of being caught in his warm gaze or exchanging smiles with him – it was nice, but it didn't stop her from worrying about how she'd manage to survive loss a second time.

It was time to prepare for landing; she double-checked the conditions and brought her plane in just after Ruby, taxiing down the runway and coming to a stop beside her. The Spitfires were going to look stunning all lined up together. And for once the weather hadn't hindered their flight or their landing.

'Looking good,' she said to Ruby as they walked to the base together, shaking out their hair.

'A girl has to do her lipstick,' Ruby said with a grin.

'Especially a girl on her wedding day!'

They both laughed as Polly ran up behind them. 'Happy wedding day, gorgeous! The girls all got together to buy you something, but you'll have to wait till we're back.'

'Oh, you're so sweet!' Ruby said, hugging Polly. 'Thank you.'

There was no mistaking the happiness radiating from Ruby. May had been worried about her; after losing the baby, she'd seen a pain within her friend that she'd secretly worried might never leave her. She'd worried about putting her back in the air again so soon, but clearly her instincts had been wrong this time.

'Anyone else dying to use the toilet?' Ruby asked.

'About as much as I'm dying for a cuppa,' May replied. 'Think we'll have time before we taxi back?'

'I don't care if they say we have time or not, I'm having a cup of something hot and putting my feet up,' Ruby insisted.

'I'm taking you back, ladies, and there's *definitely* time for a cuppa,' Polly said.

'Oh dear, incoming,' May said, as a swarm of officers appeared from nowhere: seeing a bunch of women on the tarmac had obviously caught their interest.

'They watched Ruby shake out those gorgeous long locks,' Polly teased. 'She's got them all excited!'

Ruby flushed and May linked arms with her, both holding their heads high.

'Ladies,' said one of the officers as they walked by.

'Cup of tea, anyone?' another called out.

'Married,' Ruby stated, holding her newly minted ring finger in the air.

'A cuppa sounds glorious,' May said, stifling a laugh. 'Is it this way, fellas?'

'Right this way,' another overly helpful man volunteered.

By the time they reached the bathroom through the officers' quarters, she and Polly were in peals of laughter, imitating Ruby's gesture as they waited their turn. Others from their squadron started to file in slowly, and they all turned their backs to the pin-up girl posters fixed to the walls. It was almost impossible to land at an airfield and find a clean bathroom to use, let alone one that wasn't so obviously male.

Ruby always got the lion's share of attention whenever they were around men, and today was no different, despite her announcing to everyone that she was married. All May could do was sit back with the others and laugh. But with a hot cup of tea in her hand and a biscuit in the other, she felt comfortable enough; it was nice to be flying again rather than buried in paperwork and trying to recruit ever more pilots.

'Oh, I forgot to tell you that a letter arrived!' Polly said, plucking out an envelope from inside her flying suit. 'It's from Lizzie, and it's addressed to us all.'

May took it eagerly. 'Shall I read it out aloud?'

'Yes,' Ruby urged, as all the other women nodded and clustered closer.

May cleared her throat in anticipation; she'd been dying to hear from Lizzie for weeks.

'To my girls,

I can't believe it's been so long since I was with you. The past weeks have flown by in a whirlwind, and I'm so pleased to tell you all that my father has made a full recovery. On base, it's been a mixture of recruiting, training and being a babysitter and mother figure to all these young women. Me, a mother figure, can you imagine? I feel like den mother, only I'm far too young and to be honest I wonder sometimes if I even know what I'm doing. Except when I'm flying, of course – that's the only moment I feel in control. I only hope one day I'm not found out for the fraud I am, as responsible as a teenager and as reckless as one, too!

I hope she's not reading this, because I have to confess I now have a much greater appreciation for everything May does, so please go easy on her.'

May looked up, smiling and raising her eyebrows. 'Hear that? She wants you to go easy on me, ladies.' Giggles followed as she returned to the letter.

'The rest of my time seems to be wasted butting heads with Captain Montgomery, who, unlike your kind and understanding Captain MacMillan, is an absolute tyrant. I mean, this man literally makes me want to explode more now than he did in England! I fantasize sometimes about giving him a jolly good punch on the nose, just to get a reaction from him, but instead I grit my teeth and try to get along with him. He treats my girls like army slaves, despite the fact that we get no such recognition here, and I'm sick to death of having to face him every day. Sometimes I think it'd be easier to go to war than deal with him, but hopefully by the time this letter reaches you, he'll have realized how capable I am and left me to train my girls without his constant interfering. We had a fun day flying the other day and I thought we'd found common ground, but he's back to his bossy, demanding self again already.

I miss you all terribly, and I wish I was still there, if I'm honest. I was so desperate to get home, but in truth it was much more enjoyable being in England. I take back everything I said about England being gloomy and uneventful, and Brits being a bunch of old bores!

Hugs to you all, and next time pray that I'll be writing you from a new headquarters. Another few months here and it'll likely kill me.

With all my love,

Lizzie'

The room was silent when she finished. Lizzie's personality had jumped from the page, making May miss her presence all the more.

'You know, when I first met Lizzie, all I could think was what a pain in the rear end she was going to be,' May confessed, folding the letter.

'Trust me, she *was* a pain in the backside,' Ruby added, making everyone laugh.

'Oh, I know she was, but I still miss her.'

'Excuse me, ladies,' an officer called, smiling and catching their eyes, 'I'm looking for Senior Commander Jones.'

May held up one hand. 'That'd be me.'

'It's time to leave. The weather is starting to close in and we want to get you up in the air.'

There were more pilots due to land throughout the day, and May wondered if they'd all make it in. The worry was always there, always niggling at her, reminding her that there was no way she could keep every single one of her pilots safe for the entire duration of the war.

'The cloud's rolling in?' she asked.

He nodded. 'It is.'

She stepped out into the damp, cold late-afternoon air, wondering where Polly had disappeared to. She'd been so worried about them being shot out of the sky, and now it was the bloody cloud that was more likely to be their undoing. *Again.* She felt better that it was Polly flying them back, though; she was a solid pilot and she knew she could trust her.

She found Polly standing by the large dark-green wing of the Avro Anson they'd be flying back, and tried to put aside her feelings of unease.

'Let's get you back, Commander Jones,' Polly said, giving her a mock salute.

'How do you feel about the conditions?' May asked.

'Well, I wouldn't say ideal, but then when are they?' Polly said with a casual shrug. 'I'd like to move as soon as possible, so I'm not about to ground us if that's what you're concerned about.'

'Mind if I co-pilot with you, Polly?' May asked.

'You don't trust me?' Polly asked, frowning. 'I've had that a fair few times from men, but I thought . . .'

'Stop right there,' May said, touching her shoulder. 'I'm feeling anxious and I need to be able to see, that's all. I have girls in the air still, and I'd rather pass the time up front. This has nothing – *nothing* – to do with your abilities as a pilot.'

'You're certain?'

'Absolutely. Now let's board this plane and get going.'

'Yes ma'am.'

May climbed up after Polly and buckled herself in. They waited as the other women loaded in, and for the ground crew to signal approval, then she sat back and relaxed as Polly completed the perfect take-off into the air. The Anson was different to the kind of aircraft she was used to, sturdy and solid but without much speed, and it was an interesting experience being in the cockpit without having any control.

The cloud was making visibility more difficult by the moment, but Polly was flying well, and May knew she was trusting her gut when she rose higher to avoid it. So many of their pilots had been lost making that decision, whether to go high or low, but May knew that some of them had better instincts than others. She had always had that instinct, and Ruby and Lizzie were the same, which is why they had all cleared their Class V conversion without any fuss. Once they landed, she'd tell Polly that she'd be transferring her to the Hamble training programme to fly the four-engine bombers. The promotion was well overdue.

After almost thirty minutes, May finally sat back. The cloud was worrying, but it wasn't as bad as she'd expected, and the closer they got to base the more confident she felt. She'd flown in much worse, and Polly was more than capable.

And then her stomach lurched. 'No,' she gasped.

She wished she was in control, that she was in charge of her own destiny as her eyes widened.

The Luftwaffe aircraft was unmistakable, the swastika symbol alone making May's mouth go dry. Where had he come from, and what was going to happen to them? It wasn't like they could engage; even if they wanted to, the Anson didn't have any ammunition to fire!

May gripped her seat as Polly expertly dropped them into the cloud, and May prayed they weren't going to fly into anything. Without instruments, it was impossible to know where they were in such conditions. She didn't even glance at Polly, but simply kept her jaw clenched and her fingernails digging hard into the leather, trusting her pilot. *Dear God, please don't let us die*, she thought. *Please spare us.*

After more than a few minutes, she felt Polly's eyes on her and quickly looked around and back, trying to make out the sinister figure in the air. If he'd seen them, like sitting ducks in the sky, he'd have taken out twelve of the ATA's best female pilots. This exact moment had been her fear for months, if not years, and somehow it had happened and they'd survived it – unless he was a better pilot than Polly was giving him credit for and was about to appear on their tail and blast them to oblivion.

She reached for Polly's hand, holding her tight over the controls, feeling the tremble echoing through her. May shut her eyes and thanked whoever it was that was keeping her girls safe. Somehow, against all odds, their fatality rate was still zero.

'Thank you,' May said when they eventually landed, pulling Polly in and holding her tight in a long hug. 'You handled that exceptionally well. I'm so proud of you.'

'I had precious cargo to protect,' Polly said stoically, and May saw herself in the young woman.

'You're an amazing young pilot, Polly,' she said honestly. 'And I'd already made this decision before you saved my life, in case you were wondering, but would you like to be considered for conversion to fly the four-engine bombers? You're more than capable of being charged with a Halifax flight now.'

Polly looked like she was going to faint. Either that or she was going to scream. 'Yes! I would love to do that.'

'Consider your application approved then. You'll receive your orders as soon as I have all the paperwork completed.'

Polly's smile said it all, and May prepared to exit the aircraft. But then she had a thought. 'Can I ask how you knew to fly high and when to drop through that cloud? I don't know if you just have incredible instincts or whether there was something else at play.'

'I'm used to navigating that particular airspace, and I suppose I'm good at trusting myself.'

'Well, you were great out there, Polly. I couldn't have flown better myself.'

When they stepped out and the rest of the women joined them, May whistled for everyone's attention. 'Ladies, listen, please!'

Their chatter turned to murmurs and then silence.

'I'd like you all to give our pilot a round of applause.' May began to clap, and the others all joined in. 'While you lovely ladies were back there snoozing and knitting, Polly here was navigating our plane away from an enemy aircraft. We're all very lucky to be alive.'

The clapping stopped, and every single woman stared in stunned silence.

'It was my worst nightmare come true, and then some,' Polly said. 'Sorry for dropping the plane so suddenly back there.'

'Are you crazy?' exclaimed Ruby. 'You saved us all!'

Polly smiled, a little bashful. 'I'll be flying straight back in the morning, as soon as visibility is better. And then I'll bring anyone back who needs a lift from Colerne.'

May left them all to talk and headed back towards her desk. After almost thirty-six hours away from base, there would be a lot for her to attend to, even though what she really longed to do was find Ben and throw her arms around him. After that near miss, she craved his reassuring touch; for a moment there she'd thought her poor mother was going to lose her other child, too.

She stopped as one of the administration staff raced towards her.

'Commander, we've received bad news.' Andrea, one of their few office workers, was wringing her hands together.

May wasn't sure she could cope with anything else today; already, she was fearing the worst.

'What is it?' she asked, trying to keep her voice steady.

'Only one more pilot reached Colerne after you left.'

May swallowed. 'The rest are essentially missing then?'

Andrea nodded. 'Yes, ma'am.'

Missing didn't mean dead. Missing meant they simply weren't accounted for at this exact moment. May started to shake and clasped her hands tight. 'Thank you. Please update me the moment we hear more.'

She shouldn't have ignored her gut. She was never wrong when she had that feeling. 'Andrea,' she called out, and the young woman turned. 'Please keep this on a need-to-know basis. I don't want any of the other pilots worrying without cause.'

It was going to be a long wait. May went inside and consulted the board, made a calculation of how many pilots she had in the air and cross-checked the pilot allocations. They'd all flown from different bases due to the new Spitfires being in different locations this time, so some of the girls had flown out directly from Hamble. She sat down to write a letter to Lizzie, not able to concentrate on anything more pressing.

Dear Lizzie,

Your letter was a welcome morale boost for us all today, and I read it aloud as we all sat waiting to fly back to base. It's hard to explain our role to an outsider, and now that you're in charge of so many women, you'll realise that your life becomes an exercise in 'what if'. As I write this I'm waiting for news, and all I can think is that I'm the one who put those women in the air, who decided when and what they were going to fly. Logically I know that the war is out of my control, as is the work that comes in from Ferry Control each night, but the feeling never goes. I sometimes wonder if the captain or commander who sent my brother into the sky felt the same degree of guilt when he never returned.

On a lighter note, I have a feeling that your next letter might paint your Captain Montgomery in a different light? Sometimes the men who infuriate us most are the ones we are most drawn to, and I could sense a spark of something between you both here, even though it probably felt like nothing more than anger and butting heads to you! He's a good man, Lizzie, truly he is. You know, you were right about me and Ben. He's a good man too, and I'm finally ready to admit how much I need him.

Tell me more about your logistics if you're permitted to. I'd certainly like to hear what obstacles you're up against and whether you need any advice on navigating such a difficult transition. The acceptance of women pilots is, for some reason, not something that comes easily.

Yours truly and with all my love,

May

She set her pen down as Ruby burst through the door, breathless.

'What is it?'

'Sandy just landed,' Ruby told her. 'She turned around as soon as she realised the weather was making a safe landing impossible. She said the conditions were challenging.'

'Just her?' May asked, standing and holding the edge of her desk.

'Yes.'

May breathed deep as hope filled her heart. 'There could well be more. I'm coming – we have to keep an eye out for them, Ruby.'

She headed back outside. If Sandy had returned, then more of them may well do so, too. *Unless they encountered the same enemy aircraft, but weren't so lucky.* She saw the young pilot further down the runway and ran over to give her a big hug. 'I'm so glad to see you.'

Sandy hugged her back, visibly shaken. 'Me too. The visibility made it impossible. I couldn't see anything, and I had to turn around while I could.' Her face was pale, and May held on to her, hoping she wasn't about to faint on the spot.

'Did you see anything else?'

'No, but I was scared. The clouds were so dense and . . .'

'Shh, we can debrief later,' May said. 'Now get yourself into the mess room. You can warm up and we'll talk soon.'

Sandy left her, and May stared at the sky, relief coursing through her as an engine roar caught her ear, followed soon after by a Spitfire emerging out of the clouds. They had a little longer until dusk, and she'd keep standing there until she saw every one of her women land. Some might have carried on, but others would come back to the place they knew how to find in the cloud. There was no protocol for turning back, but she was confident they'd all make the best decision they could.

'What's up?' A hand brushed her shoulder and she recognised Ben's voice. She leaned back into him, needing him, not caring who saw. He put his arms around her from behind, warming her as his lips brushed her hair. 'What are you doing out here?'

'Something doesn't feel right. I just . . .' Her voice trailed off. 'Who was I kidding, thinking I could keep them all safe with no radios? With no instrument training? Why didn't I push back harder on this instead of being told what to do? I think I may have lost some of my pilots, Ben. I think our luck has run out.'

Ben pulled her even closer, as she blinked away tears. They stood together, teeth chattering in the cold, staring at the darkening sky.

'You don't have to wait with me,' she said.

'Yes,' Ben said, like a warm blanket cocooning her close. 'Yes, I do.'

As the sun finally started to rise, May didn't care that her body was so cold it felt like her bones had turned to ice. She was not giving up her position until she saw her girls with her own eyes; the only thing she cared about was her list of pilots and trying to account for each and every one of them.

'May,' Ben said gently, pulling up the blanket that had slipped from around her shoulders. She'd been awake all night, staring into the sky, then pacing, then checking her list and starting the process over again. Nothing would still her mind as she waited, although she was grateful that Ben had been by her side through the long hours. 'May, you're needed.'

She turned and saw Captain MacMillan approaching, his smile sending relief through her.

'They're alive, May,' he said. 'Anyone unaccounted for turned around and landed at a closer airfield, and a couple even made it safely to Colerne, except for one pilot who landed in a field and spent the night with a farmer.'

May laughed, throwing her arms around Ben. 'They're alive! Oh my goodness, oh my goodness! This is wonderful news!'

Ben kissed her and took a step back as other pilots came closer, some still yawning from a late night and an early start. May had ended up telling everyone on base what had happened before sending them off to rest the night before, unable to lie to her team when she was asked why more pilots hadn't returned.

'Great news, ladies! We've heard that no pilots were lost. Everyone has officially been accounted for!' She grinned as the women all squealed and laughed in relief. 'But those additional Spitfires we have here still need to get to Colerne,' she said, smiling up at the clear day as the sun rose around them. 'There's no rest for the wicked, I'm afraid.'

'Would you like me to assign flights today?' Ruby asked. 'You must be exhausted.'

'I only need to put the allocations out,' she said, pulling the blanket from around her shoulders. 'But thank you. I appreciate the offer.'

May didn't want anyone to see her fall apart, but the relief that her girls were all alive, that she didn't have to wipe any names from the board, that she didn't have to tell anyone's mother or father that they weren't going to make it home, threatened to cut her off at the knees.

She made it to the bathroom and shut the door, pressing her back to it as a sob erupted from deep within her, choking her as it made its way through her throat. She slid to the ground, tears streaking down her cheeks as she gasped for air, silently crying as she remembered her brother, as she wished that she could see him just one more time. Then, hands shaking, she wiped her cheeks, gulping back air as she tried to pull herself together.

'I can do this,' she whispered. 'I *can* do this.' She'd pulled herself together when she'd stepped up as commander, and she was going to darn well pull herself together again this time. No one had been lost. They'd survived. But the long night of waiting had rattled every emotion inside her.

She pushed herself up to her feet and folded the blanket she was still clutching, holding it tight against her for a moment. She breathed deeply, ready to go into the mess room and deal with the flights for the day.

'May?' Ruby's voice echoed out from the other side of the door.

'Coming,' she called

She hurried out to find Ruby standing there, ashen, as if she'd seen a ghost.

'What is it?' she asked, her heart starting to race.

'I'm so sorry, May, but Evangeline just arrived in on the first flight back from those other airfields, and she said there was a plane behaving erratically, and then she saw it drop suddenly, far too low.'

'And you think it was one of ours?'

'We don't know, but we're sending out an ambulance responder now, even though it must be at least an hour's drive away, if not further.'

May thought quickly. 'I'm sure it's not one of ours,' she said. 'I don't even think anyone was cleared to fly out yet.' She walked to collect her chits from her desk, trying to stop her hands from trembling. 'I need to put these out. We have plenty of planes to ferry today and we're already behind schedule.'

Ruby followed her. 'Should I go with the ambulance, in case they need assistance?'

May frowned. 'Why would you go?'

Ruby looked uncomfortable. 'I have a bad feeling that it might have been . . .'

May stared at her. 'Might have been who? Who flew out?'

Who could have been given clearance to leave so early, before the chits were even put out? Her friend shook her head, as though trying to convince herself she'd got something wrong.

'*Polly*,' May suddenly gasped. 'Oh my gosh, it's Polly, isn't it? She left for Colerne to bring the other pilots back here. I cleared her last night to leave early!' May felt herself break into a cold sweat. 'Find Ben for me!' she said. 'Tell him to stop whatever he's doing and to come and find me.'

Then she stepped forward from around her desk to address the girls in the mess room. 'We've had a rough night,' she said in a low voice, 'but the show must go on, and we need to thank our lucky stars that someone up there was looking down on us all. Now, here are your cards – please take your ferry notebooks as required.'

May's bottom lip started to quiver. She dug her fingernails deep into her palms, and quickly left the room. Ruby was waiting in a car when she emerged back out into the brisk morning air, and she saw Ben in the driver's seat.

'Do you have clearance to take this?' May asked, climbing in.

Ben didn't respond. He simply put his foot down and they sped off after the ambulance, which May could just make out in the distance.

May went back in her mind. She could remember the rumble of the departing plane now: she'd known Polly was leaving and she hadn't thought anything of it. But that didn't mean this was her. It could be a male pilot, or someone from another airfield.

'It doesn't have to be Polly,' she muttered.

'No. But something keeps telling me it's her,' Ruby said.

May didn't question her; she just nodded and stared straight ahead. If Polly was injured or worse . . . She swallowed and chewed the inside of her lip, refusing to think about that yet.

They drove for well over an hour before the ambulance ahead of them slowed. May was surprised at the pockets of fog that still lingered, and hadn't been present back at Hamble. She knew first-hand how tough it was to navigate through conditions like this without instruments, and without clearance to fly higher. May's mouth ran dry as she stared into the field at the base of a hill. She saw the plane – or what was left of it. The entire aircraft was smouldering, and the moment Ben stopped she pushed her door open and started to run.

'Here, over here!' a woman yelled, waving her hands frantically.

May forgot her fatigue and ran as fast as she could, arms pumping as she saw something on the ground, a farmer bent over a body while the woman beside him cried.

As she neared, everything seemed to go in slow motion. She saw the legs, saw the burn marks, the skin black, charred, like food cooked on an open burner. She saw one arm, unmistakably a woman's slender arm, and then she saw the desperate look on the farmer's face. His mouth opened but she couldn't hear the noise; all she could see were tears dripping past his lips.

May stopped moving as medics pushed past her. She stumbled and then righted herself, watching as they dropped to their knees, as they shouted and then stopped. No one did anything. Ruby moved past her, saying something, her mouth opening and closing, eyes wide, hands moving fast.

But May still couldn't hear, she could only see, and when Ben's arms closed around her she fought against him, silently fighting to get closer, to do something. To do *anything*.

The farmer's hands now covered his face, his wife standing over him. The medics were shaking their heads. May looked at the plane and started to walk towards it, but Ben grabbed her hand, tugging her hard, refusing to let her take another step.

*Polly was dead.* That was *Polly's* body back there. Polly, who'd flown them home safely, and shown such aptitude in the cockpit. Polly who was so bright and cheerful, who she was just about to put forward for conversion to fly four-engine bombers at Hamble. Polly who'd obviously had to drop too low to try to see, with no instruments to guide her. Polly who'd smashed straight into a hill, taking a risk that had cost her her life.

May looked up and the sun blinded her at the same time as the bright sky started to spin. She reached out a hand to break her fall, and as Ben's arms caught her, everything went black.

# CHAPTER TWENTY-FOUR

## *AVENGER FIELD, SWEETWATER, TEXAS,*

## *NOVEMBER, 1942*

## *LIZZIE*

Lizzie stood before her squadron of women to give a speech she'd given many times before, but today she felt stuck for words. She conjured an image of May in her mind, imagining how she was coping, how she was still managing to keep commanding her squadron after such a loss. May had always been an exemplary leader, and Lizzie hoped to inject as much enthusiasm and self-belief into the women she'd just finished training. But after receiving the news about Polly, she wished she had her commander and friend by her side. It had come as a blow out of nowhere and she'd cried into her pillow all night, imagining the terror her beautiful friend must have experienced, and hoping upon hope that her death had come fast. Speaking to her squadron seemed impossible, but she knew they were counting on her. She had to pull herself together.

They'd been at their location at Avenger Field in Sweetwater, Texas for a couple of months now, and it was so much easier to run her operation from the bigger, more suitable airfield; she was so much closer to her father, too. The difference was that now it wasn't just in theory: they actually had women in the air ferrying planes, and the realities of what her female pilots were up against had hit her hard. The news of Polly's death, a death that could have been avoided, had filled her with sadness at first, then made her angry – angry that women could be treated so unfairly, as if their lives somehow weren't as important.

She cleared her throat, glancing at Captain Montgomery, who was standing out to the side, and two officers who'd been instrumental in training her pilots. She had to begin.

'Ladies, I'm so proud of every single one of you,' she said, annoyed by the croak in her throat. She cleared it and tried again. 'As of today, you have all passed your training and become WASPs. Well done!' She clapped, and they all joined in. She studied their faces, knowing that it was her job to fill them with confidence. 'It's time for you all to go on and make me proud. I hand-picked every one of you, sat through hours of interviews and reviewed so many candidates – you are the women I chose to fly our mighty warplanes. You will be ferrying planes over our great country, which will allow our men to fight, and to succeed in winning this war.'

*Polly was gone.* She swallowed hard, refusing to let the thoughts creep in. She held her head high and jutted out her chin. She'd under-estimated how difficult it would be to deal with the turmoil in her head, but she wasn't about to ruin the day by failing to deliver her speech – not with so many women graduating.

'We are all making history here, paving the way for women to not only fly, but also to defy the gender roles that we are so often defined by. Women can make a difference, and we are showing that against all odds, and despite having to fight to be heard and fight to be here flying, we deserve our title of pilot. The army may not recognise us as such, but that does not take away from the incredible role each and every one of you will play.'

A single tear plopped down her cheek and she steeled herself, waiting for the moment to pass. Her breath shuddered as she thought again of Polly, imagining her terror as her plane smashed into the hillside. She opened her mouth, but this time, not a sound came out.

Captain Montgomery was at her side then, standing close to her, almost shoulder to shoulder. Then he stepped forward to take over, as if he could feel her pain and wanted to spare her, and she was both stunned and grateful. They would have all heard a pin drop as he began to speak.

'I have treated you like I would any soldier, and you women, every single one of you, have proven me wrong,' he said, his voice low and deep. Everything about the man oozed authority, and Lizzie admired the strength in his stance and the breadth of his shoulders as he stood on the small makeshift stage. 'You are all courageous and fiercely talented, and I applaud you as you graduate here today and take the next step in your careers.' He paused and held out a hand to Lizzie. 'You have this very special woman to thank for your new positions, because without her determination to see women in the air, you wouldn't be sitting here today.'

Everyone in the room clapped and Lizzie smiled, trying to be brave.

As Captain Montgomery saluted the crowd and stepped from the stage, Lizzie tracked him with her eyes. He was the perfect example of a leader in the way he held himself and the way he commanded, but she'd also found him to be overly exacting and demanding of her pilots. Yet today she'd seen a different side of him, and she was shocked to find respect replacing her disdain for him.

As she moved through the crowd and congratulated each woman individually, fixing their wing pins to their jackets, Lizzie decided it was time to thank him; it was stupid to continue with their rivalry and unfriendliness.

'Congratulations, girls. You will find out later today which bases you will be sent to. Please enjoy the afternoon,' Lizzie announced, before seeking Montgomery out.

'That was quite a speech,' she said, hoping to break the ice.

'I could say the same,' he replied, one eyebrow arched. 'You've done well today.'

She touched her hair, her fingers absently smoothing strands that were already perfectly in place. 'I don't often admit to being wrong, but I think we not only started off on the wrong foot, we've stayed there.'

He smiled, and for the first time she saw how handsome he was; a dimple flared in his right cheek and humour shone from his bright blue eyes. It was quite a combination, such blond hair and golden skin, and eyes that matched the sky on a perfectly cloudless day.

'Come with me,' he ordered.

Lizzie opened her mouth to rebuff him, but quickly closed it. They didn't have to butt heads all the time – for once she could follow his orders. They started to walk, and Lizzie was soon struggling to keep up. He didn't even look like he was moving quickly, but his long, determined stride was almost impossible to keep pace with.

'Where are we going?' she demanded.

'Dunlop, who the hell ever had the patience to be your flying instructor?' he asked.

She stopped walking and gaped at him. 'Excuse me?'

'You heard me.'

'I could say the same to you,' she shot back. 'Who on earth could put up with your arrogance and single-minded bloody . . .'

'*Bloody*?' he chuckled. 'I think you spent too much time with the Brits.'

'Ugh!' She threw her hands up in the air.

'Come on, sweetheart,' he said. 'I was only wanting to offer you a drink.'

*Sweetheart?* How dare he! 'I'm not your *sweetheart*,' she snapped. 'Some respect would be appreciated, and I'd actually have liked to stay on the right foot instead of landing on the wrong one all over again!'

He was smiling. The idiot was smiling at her like he found all this *funny!*

'I've two minds not to have a drink with you at all,' she fumed.

'Fine, but I thought it was about time we cleared the air between us,' he said. 'Now you can either huff off back to your quarters, or we can sit down and open a bottle of good whiskey.' He held out a hand to his office door. 'It's up to you, but I know I could use one, and I think you could, too.'

Reluctantly, Lizzie entered his office and looked around. She'd been in there many times, but usually she was storming in to demand answers about something. Today she was here as his guest, and it felt different somehow; or perhaps she'd finally glimpsed the real him.

'Tell me,' he said, pouring dark brown liquor into two short glasses. 'Did the army provide those wings you pinned on today?'

She laughed and arched an eyebrow. 'What do you think?'

'I think it's about time the army stepped up. There's no good reason for you to be buying silver wings for those women.'

She raised a brow at him. 'You think they shouldn't have wings, then?'

He passed her a glass, holding on to it even though her fingers had curled around it already. 'Don't twist my words. Those women will be flying aircraft for the military, and they damn well deserve their wings and every accolade they get. I just don't think your pocket should be the one in debt.'

Lizzie knew she'd picked an argument over nothing, but she was so used to constant arguments flaring up for no good reason. 'I'm sorry.'

He smiled at her over his glass. 'I'm not sure I heard you correctly?'

Lizzie took a slow sip of whiskey, trying desperately not to splutter. It was like liquid fire sluicing down her throat, and a cough burst from her.

'Actually, your pain is enough – I won't force you to repeat it,' he said.

So she hadn't fooled him, then. 'I'm not exactly an experienced drinker of straight liquor, Captain Montgomery. I prefer cocktails and champagne.'

He looked amused as he sat and stretched out his long legs. 'You do know you can call me Jackson, don't you? Or Jack – whatever comes easiest.'

Lizzie had been so caught up in trying to prove him wrong and push his buttons, but now she couldn't help studying him, wondering if perhaps she had never taken the time to see the real him. His blond hair was short at the sides and slightly longer on top, and his skin reflected the hours he spent outside, and his hands . . . She sighed. His hands were big and calloused, like those of a man used to real work. She averted her gaze and attempted another tiny sip of whisky. Those hands were strong and capable, and certainly didn't look like they should be pushing papers in an office.

'Jackson, then,' she said.

'Well, now that's sorted, why don't we have dinner and do some work on staying on the right foot, so to speak?'

She struggled not to choke on her drink again, more from being flustered this time. 'And how many of my pilots have you asked for dinner already?' she asked. 'It's an instant dismissal for dating an instructor!'

Jackson held up his glass and drained it, then made eye contact again. 'First of all, I'm not your instructor, or theirs, and I haven't asked anyone else for dinner,' he said. 'Christ, what is it with you, being so defensive all the time?'

She didn't have an answer to that.

'It's because you're used to being the one calling all the shots, personally and professionally,' he muttered. 'Honestly, you're hard to please, Dunlop.' She smirked. So she was back to being *Dunlop* already. 'It's only a *date* if you want it to be a date. Otherwise it's dinner between two colleagues, nothing more, nothing less,' he said firmly. 'Does everything with you have to be so hard?'

Lizzie hated the way she was behaving, but she just couldn't seem to help herself. 'Fine. Dinner it is.'

'Tonight?' he asked.

She shrugged as if it were no big deal. 'Sure, why not? It'd be nice to celebrate graduation day.'

Jackson stared at her and then shook his head, chuckling. 'Shall I pick you up from the Avengerette Club?'

Lizzie braved his gaze. 'Yes.'

The Club was a special place for all her girls. It was a room above a fabric store that they'd been given by the town of Sweetwater, and all the girls loved going there. The WASPs could play records, chat and dance; there was little else to do.

'Oh, and Lizzie?' he said, his eyes softening. 'I am truly sorry about Polly. She was a great girl and it's not fair what happened to her.'

'Thanks,' she said, holding back tears. 'She was.'

'Until tonight then,' he said, holding up his glass. 'To Polly.'

Lizzie gulped. 'To Polly,' she agreed, feeling guilty all of a sudden for flirting and joking around when her friend wasn't even with them any longer. 'She died bravely in the air, and she'll be missed.'

'Wow.'

Lizzie had decided to wait outside for Jackson, not wanting to make a fuss about their dinner. She could have told the girls it was work-related, but given the fact she'd put on a dress and heels, not to mention done her hair and applied more make-up than they'd probably ever seen her wear, she knew she wouldn't be fooling anyone.

Jackson was dressed in his uniform and looking as handsome as ever, and she smiled when he opened the car door for her.

'Where are we heading?' she asked, as he slipped back into the driver's seat.

'Not where you're expecting.'

She frowned and sat quietly, desperate to ask questions but knowing it would only amuse him.

'Lizzie, before we have dinner, I want to ask you how you're holding up? I know you were close to Polly, and I wasn't sure if you had anyone to talk to about it.'

Lizzie shook her head at the mention of Polly's name. 'Some days are better than others, but I know she'd be furious with me if I gave up now and collapsed into a heap.'

Jackson touched her hand. 'You ask for my help if you need to, okay?'

She nodded. 'Thanks.'

'I also wanted to say something about what we discussed earlier. About starting over,' he said. 'I want you to know that I'm not the bad guy here, and I never have been. You painted me as the villain from the start, when all I was interested in doing was offering your pilots the highest level of military training. I'm sorry if I gave you the wrong impression.'

Lizzie smiled. 'Seems like it's a night for opening up to each other, huh?' She settled back into her seat as he drove, still wondering where they were going. When they pulled in, it seemed they were at the back of a restaurant, not the front.

He touched her hand, their skin connecting for the briefest of moments, before getting out and then ducking his head back in.

'Sit tight. I won't be a moment.'

Lizzie sat, curiously waiting for him to return. When he came back, he was carrying large paper bags, and she tried to see what was in them as he placed them on the back seat. There was a bottle of champagne, two glasses, and some blankets . . . She spun back around as he got back into the driving seat. Were they going on a picnic?

'Aren't we dining here?' she asked.

'No.' He gave her a wink. 'I'm friends with the chef, and he made us up some food. I thought it would be nicer to breathe in some fresh air and enjoy the outdoors.'

Lizzie burst out laughing and stared at him. He couldn't have surprised her more if he'd tried!

'Why are you being so nice to me?' she asked. 'Is this because of Polly?'

His smile was hard to read, his eyes leaving the road for a moment to meet hers. 'Lizzie, I've always been on your side. How can you not have seen that?'

She sat deeper back into her seat and looked out the window. Had she been the one pushing him away and making him into the villain? Was *she* the hostile one?

'I was only ever doing my job,' he said. 'It always amazed me that you were so prickly about it.'

'But you were so, so . . .' She trailed off.

'So hard on your recruits? So demanding?'

'Well, yes,' she replied.

'Would you have wanted me to treat them like ladies instead of pilots? Did you want me to reinforce the gender stereotype that they couldn't cope with being treated like any other recruit?' It was him laughing now. 'I thought you wanted women who could hold their heads high and know they were every bit as well trained and capable as their male counterparts? I wanted to prepare them for the worst, to instil them with a sense of honour and commitment.'

She nodded. 'And you did exactly that.'

His smile was almost crooked this time as he gave her a quick sideways look. 'Can we agree that I'm on your side, then?'

She smiled back, feeling a welcome shudder of warmth. 'Yes.'

'And can we please agree that we're off the clock now, and we won't talk work again?'

'Is that champagne back there for us?' she asked, feeling lighter, more relaxed than she had in a very long time.

'Absolutely.'

'Then *absolutely yes*, we can be off the clock. It's about time I had a night off and forgot about everything.'

Lizzie turned slightly, facing Jackson now, studying his profile and wondering what he was really like beneath that uniform. Glimpsing this softer side of him had thrown everything she'd previously thought about him off balance. And he was right: she'd made him out to be the villain when really he was just an exceptional captain who tolerated nothing less than excellence and expected those under his leadership to follow his orders to the letter. After all, wasn't that what she'd wanted for her pilots?

'What are you thinking?' he asked.

'I'm wondering where you're taking me,' she replied, not about to admit that she'd been admiring his smooth jaw and perfect cheekbones, and the way his broad shoulders took up the entire seat. 'And I'm so pleased that I decided to come home.'

'Well, you don't have to wait to find out. We're here.'

She looked around as the car slowed and they bumped along off-road. She wasn't sure where they were, but the beautiful lake that glistened in the near distance gave her some clues.

'Is this where the girls come when they're off duty? I've heard about a swimming hole,' she said.

'It certainly is.'

He stopped the car and jumped out, opening her door for her. Lizzie inhaled the fresh, earthy air and let out a sigh. It was perfect. She'd been working what seemed like a hundred hours a week, falling into bed each night and always waking somehow more tired than she'd been the day before.

'This is magical,' she said, honestly.

'Neither of us gets a lot of time off, so I figured we'd be better spending an evening here than sitting in a restaurant.'

He couldn't have been more right. 'It's lovely.'

She waited for Jackson to gather their things, offering to take the wine and glasses for him while he carried everything else. She followed as he found a nice spot near the lake and spread out the blankets.

'Take a seat,' he said, gesturing and waiting for her to sit before joining her on the rug.

'I thought this would be, I don't know, more of a work dinner,' Lizzie admitted, not sure exactly what was going on. *Were* they on a date, or was this simply a friendly dinner between colleagues?

Jackson shrugged. 'Champagne?' he asked, holding up the bottle, then popping the cork.

Lizzie wrapped herself in one of the blankets, then sat back and watched as he poured a glass, the bubbles extending all the way to the top and then slowly settling back down. She hadn't sipped champagne since . . . She smiled as she remembered that night in London, when he'd not poured her a glass. How times had changed.

'To good friends,' she said, taking the glass and inhaling the sweet smell. 'Lost but not forgotten.'

'To good friends,' Jackson repeated, holding up his glass and gently clinking it to hers. They sat in silence for a moment, and Lizzie shut her eyes, imagining Polly looking down on them.

'Tell me about yourself,' Lizzie said, suddenly wanting to know everything about him. 'How did you end up as a captain?'

'Well, I'd say we have similar stories there,' he said. 'I listened to so many tales of my old man flying up a storm during the war that when the opportunity came up to volunteer, I was one of the first to hit the sky.'

Lizzie grinned. 'Sounds familiar.'

He nodded. 'But I haven't brought you here to talk about me.'

'Why, are you secretly married and don't want me to know about your wife?'

He cleared his throat. 'I did have a wife. Well, a fiancée that I was about to marry, actually,' he said. 'She was killed aboard the USS *Solace* when Pearl Harbor was bombed.'

Lizzie's heart hit the ground. Why had she said that? 'I'm so sorry, I didn't, I was . . .'

'It's fine. It's taken me a long time to be able to talk about it, but we're all starting to lose someone to this war now, aren't we?'

'What was she like?' Lizzie asked, tucking her legs up beneath herself and sipping her champagne, which was making her feel warm and happy inside.

'Maria was wonderful,' he said, smiling. 'She was charming and intelligent, and she loved helping others. But she was also determined and pig-headed, so we had some huge arguments about all sorts of things at times.'

'She doesn't sound so different to me then,' Lizzie joked. 'Well, the pig-headed part. I think it's the only way I ended up in this role.'

'I was stationed at Pearl Harbor, too. I was there on that day and I saw her body, and since then I feel like I've been ignoring what happened and putting everything into my work instead. I found out I was good at what I did, and it stopped me from having time for anything else, including thinking about her.' He smiled, but it didn't reach his eyes. 'I understand what it's like to lose someone, Lizzie.'

She held out her glass for a refill, not ready to say anything yet. His eyes shone as he stared into the distance, but she watched him instead of following his gaze. There was a lovely, very real man beneath his uniform, and she couldn't believe it had taken her so long to realise it. He pulled a blanket around his shoulders as she watched him.

'Thank you, for telling me about her,' she said, shuffling a little closer to him.

'I wanted you to know. It's nice to keep her memory alive.' He reached into the paper bag and pulled out food and plates. 'Now, tell me about you, Lizzie. What makes Elizabeth Dunlop tick?'

She could sense he didn't want to talk about Maria anymore, so she took over, filling in the void as he dished up the food. 'Well, in the beginning, my mother was horrified with me when I first announced my ambitions, but my father always indulged me. I think I was the only girl with a father telling her she could do anything and be anything she wanted to be.'

'He sounds like a good man.' He laughed. 'Although I've heard plenty about what a great man he was from my father, so it doesn't exactly surprise me.'

She smiled as she pictured him, seated beside her in her little plane. 'Yeah, he is.' She paused as Jackson watched her, wondering what about him made her feel so vulnerable. She was usually the forward one with men, the one who was first to joke and flirt and have fun. She set down her food and rose to her knees. *She was either about to make a horrible mistake, or the best decision of her life.*

'Kiss me,' she said, bending towards him.

Jackson's hand lifted and caught the back of her head, drawing her in as her mouth gently brushed his. She slowly moved her lips, drinking in the taste of him, loving the feel of his skin, of their mouths meeting.

When she pulled back, he ran his hand gently down her back.

'I thought you didn't like me,' he whispered.

'That's what I thought too,' she replied. 'Maybe I won't like you again tomorrow, but I very much like you right now.'

They both laughed and went back to eating their food, occasionally making eye contact and sitting in companionable silence.

Then Jackson stood. 'Come with me,' he said, and led her by the hand to the water's edge. They stood and stared at the water, and Jackson slowly moved around behind her, encircling her in his arms. She leaned back against him, not entirely sure what they were doing but not caring.

It felt nice, being in his big, strong arms, imagining what it would feel like to spin in his embrace and kiss him again.

'The others come here all the time on Sundays,' he said, his voice low as he spoke into her ear. 'When the weather was warmer they swam and sunbathed, but I think they just enjoy walking or having a picnic on sunny days.'

'They don't have to work like we do,' she groaned.

'Promise me we'll come here again. We deserve to have some playtime, too. I'm tired of being the workaholic who never takes leave.'

Lizzie did spin in his arms then, turning slowly and linking her hands behind his neck. 'Forgive me if I'm a total cow to you tomorrow. It's not in my nature to ever say *yes, sir* to a man.'

His laughter was deep and throaty. 'I don't ever, ever expect you to say *yes, sir* to me, Lizzie. I'd think you were unwell if you didn't argue with me every step of the way.'

She leaned into him, indulging in him one last time before clasping her fingers around his. Then they went back to their picnic and collected their things; he bundled the blanket under his arm and gathered everything else into the large paper bags, while Lizzie picked up the champagne bottle and glasses.

It was funny how things could change, although she expected that once they were back in their usual roles, on base again, he'd return to scowling at her and she'd be calling him out over every order and fuming at his superiority.

She smiled to herself as he opened the door for her. *Or maybe she'd act like a grown-up and stop giving the poor man such a hard time.*

# CHAPTER TWENTY-FIVE

## ENGLAND, CHRISTMAS 1942

## MAY

'I thought I'd find you here,' Ben said, sitting down in the chair on the other side of her desk.

May looked up, papers spread around her, her head a jumble of thoughts. She'd been working long hours and staying clear of Ben, hiding from him and her grief at the same time, but seeing him now, it hurt. She'd missed him so much and all she wanted to do was collapse into his arms and let him pick up the pieces. But she couldn't.

'Sorry, I've had so much to do and . . .'

'I'm not one of your pilots, May,' he said, shuffling the chair closer. 'I can see your lies a mile off.'

She was about to tell him she wasn't lying, but his look told her he wouldn't believe her for a second.

'I thought you were going home for Christmas?' she asked. 'Don't you need to leave soon?'

'I am and I do,' he said. 'So unless you want me to disappoint my little sister, you'd better hurry and get your bag packed.'

She stared back at him. 'Excuse me?'

'You heard me. You're coming with me. And before you tell me you don't have leave, it's already arranged. Captain MacMillan agrees that you need time off after what happened, and my family would love you to join us.'

Her face flushed and she shook her head. 'No, absolutely not. And how dare you go behind my back and—'

Ben rose, palms planted on her desk. 'Don't *you* dare pull rank with me or order me around,' he said. 'Polly died on your watch, May, and it wasn't fair, but it also wasn't your fault. Now get your things together, and I'll either take you home to your family, or home with me to mine. Your choice.'

*No.* There was no way she could go home, to her mother waiting for her, to her father's sad gaze as he contemplated Christmas without his son. She took a deep, shuddering breath. 'Why are you doing this to me?' she asked, fighting tears.

Ben came around to her, dropping to his knees beside her chair and looking straight into her eyes, his fingers curling beneath her chin. 'Because I love you, May,' he whispered. 'And because you're hurting. You need someone to look after you.'

May crumbled then, the façade she'd been so carefully holding in place falling away. She clung on to Ben, sobbing, wishing that she were stronger, that she could have pushed him away, but she couldn't. She was broken and he could see it.

'You're certain I can come?' she asked, suddenly not wanting to be left alone.

'I am,' he said, dropping a kiss on her hair. 'Tidy up whatever you're working on, and we'll leave in an hour.'

He left her to it, and May sat, dead still, trying to breathe. And when the door shut behind him, she slowly reached for her top right drawer, pulling it open. She placed a hand inside, touching the unopened letters from her mother, imagining what they said, knowing how badly her mother must be missing her and how cruel she'd been to block her out for so long.

May took the top one from the pile and stared at her mother's familiar handwriting, the deep curve of the letters taking her back to when she'd sat beside her at her desk, years ago, trying desperately to make her writing look as elegant.

*I wish I could come home*, she sobbed silently, bravely sliding her nail along the seal and taking the letter out, reading her mother's words for the first time in more than a year.

> Darling May,
>
> Father and I are so proud of you. It would have been Johnny's birthday today, and not a day goes by that we don't miss him. Please, come home. We need to see you, we need to know that you don't somehow blame yourself.
>
> We love you, May.

She threw the letter back in the drawer and slammed it shut, sliding her hand in an angry sweep across her desk and sending her paperwork flying. Why? Why did she have to lose Johnny? Why did she have to lose Polly? Why had they both been taken, and for what?

May wiped her eyes and stood, running from her desk and heading for her quarters to get her things. Ben was right, she needed to get away, and she needed him to look after her.

'Ben!' she screamed, frantically searching for him. 'Ben!'

There was hardly anyone left on base; some women were flying, some were home on leave, and others were already at their billeted homes.

Her head felt ready to explode as arms finally encircled her, holding her tight. Ben eased her around to face him, never letting her go, and she cried against him, soaking his jacket.

'Take me home with you,' she sobbed. 'Please, just get me out of here.'

Ben's arm scooped her close, holding her upright as he walked her away. Away from the one place where she'd thought she could hide from her pain.

May sat at the table hours later, her face freshly scrubbed and her hair washed. Ben's mother had taken one look at her and shooed her upstairs to their little bathroom, washing her hair for her over the basin, laying fresh clothes out on a little bed in the attic and telling her to take a nice long nap before supper. The combination of sleep and feeling so clean, with the smell of lavender in her hair, was exactly what she'd needed.

Ben smiled at her as his mother ladled food onto their plates. He'd known to bring her home, known that it would pull her back from the darkness, and he'd been right. Since Polly's death, she'd spent her days arguing with anyone who'd listen about their lack of control in the air, the fact that their pilots should be trained with instruments and be able to use radios in emergencies, but it had fallen on deaf ears and left her even more disillusioned, more heartbroken, with each passing hour.

'Does she actually *fly* the planes, not just work on the engines?'

May grinned as Ben's littlest sister appeared at the table, her hair pulled up into two pigtails, a sprinkle of freckles across her nose; she was as cute as a button.

'That's right,' May said, gesturing her to come sit beside her.

'You don't have to indulge her,' Ben's mother said. 'My other girls would never have asked so many questions when they were her age.'

From the way she had treated May, taking her into her arms and knowing exactly what she needed, it was obvious she was the mother of daughters, and May had all the time in the world for her little girl.

'Your brother does all the work to make sure the planes are safe and running properly, and then I fly them to where they need to go. We make a good team.'

Violet looked confused. 'But you're a girl.'

May laughed. 'I am. Girls can do anything, you know. Even fly huge warplanes.'

May thanked Ben's mother for a beautiful meal, then they all joined hands as they bent their heads in prayer. Violet's hand was tiny and warm in May's, and she sighed as she inhaled the smell of chicken and vegetables in front of her.

'Thank you, Lord, for the food in front of us. Thank you for bringing us together, and for the time to rest. And most of all, thank you for those we love.'

As Ben slowly released his grip, May caught his eye, keeping hold for a second longer.

'Thank you,' she whispered, blinking away tears. She'd needed this more than she could ever have realised.

'Benny, are you in love with her?' Violet blurted. 'She's so pretty and you're looking at her all funny.'

'That's enough, young lady!' his mother scolded.

May looked around at Violet giggling at her brother, at Ben's mother reprimanding her daughter, at his father eating his food, and smiled. She only wished Ben's other sisters had been there so she could have met them.

'You'd be a brilliant pilot when you grow up, you know,' May said, nudging Violet and receiving an excited grin in return. 'We need plucky girls like you who aren't afraid to stand up to big boys like Ben.'

Violet stuck her little chest out. 'When can I start flying then?'

That made them all laugh, but Ben's mother wagged her finger. 'Not until you've finished your dinner, young lady!'

It wasn't until later that night, after helping his mother clean up and standing side by side washing dishes with her in the kitchen, that

May had any time alone with Ben. She was sitting on the end of her bed when he came in, just as the dark thoughts were starting to creep back into her head, as she wondered how she'd sleep without falling into the nightmares that plagued her every single time she shut her eyes.

'Afraid of going to sleep?' he asked.

She nodded, and he reached down to hold the covers back, gesturing for her to climb under. Ben tucked her up and then lay behind her, on top of the covers, his big body warm against her as he spooned her.

'You can't stay in here. What if you mother sees? Or Violet?' she whispered.

Ben held her even tighter. 'The door's open, we have nothing to hide. There's nothing wrong with me holding you like this, May, nothing at all.'

'Your family is so lovely,' she said, her voice cracking.

Ben was silent, his breath warm against the back of her neck.

'Ben, being here tonight, seeing your parents, I . . .' Her voice was no more than a whisper now. 'I need you to take me home.'

He kissed her hair. 'I thought you were never going to ask.'

The next day, May waved goodbye to Violet from the car, grinning at the little girl jumping up and down on the veranda.

'She's going to hate me for taking you away so quickly,' she said.

'Hate you? She's already told me that she wants to be just like you when she grows up.'

May laughed, the darkness that had plagued her for so long making way for something warmer and lighter.

'When we get there, I want you to just go,' she told him. 'Come back to Violet and your family and leave me.'

'You're certain?'

She nodded. 'This is something I need to do alone.' All this time, pushing away her feelings, ignoring her mother and trying to stay in her own cocoon and protect herself from hurt and love, meant it was something she needed to find her own way through. All the same, without Ben's strength, she'd have been lost. She leaned over and kissed his cheek. 'Thank you.'

They travelled in silence for the hour-long drive. When they pulled up outside, her house looked the same but different; and as she stepped out and stared at their wooden house and the little garden out front, a flutter of snow touched her cheek.

She turned to see Ben standing behind her and she opened her arms, standing on tiptoe to kiss him.

'Go home before the snow settles,' she said. 'I'll see you back at base in a few days' time.'

Ben held her and kissed her one more time before finally letting her go. May turned to face the house, taking a deep breath and starting to walk, then run.

'Mama!' she called, as she pushed the front door open. 'Mama!' she sobbed, suddenly needing her mother like she hadn't since she was a child. '*Mama!*'

'May?' came a voice, and her mother appeared in the hallway, a tea towel in her hand as she stood, open mouthed, staring at her daughter.

'Mama!' May ran, colliding with her, wrapping her arms around her mother. The smell of her perfume, the food that had been cooked already, the fire crackling . . . She was home. She was finally home.

'Gerald!' her mother yelled. 'Gerald, our May is home!'

May stood back and held her mother's hand, gazing at her face, seeing the lines etched into her skin; the years since the war had started had aged her more than she could have imagined.

Her father appeared, his glasses perched on his nose. He opened his arms and May buried herself in his chest, crying as she held him, wishing she could stay hidden against him forever.

'I'm sorry,' she cried. 'I'm so sorry I never came home, that I never wrote, I . . .'

'You're home now,' her mother said. 'That's all that matters. Now let me get you something to eat. How did you get here?'

'Ben,' she said, squeezing her mother's hand. 'My Ben brought me home.'

'Well, how about you come and tell me all about this Ben,' she said with a chuckle. 'I think I like him already.'

*And so do I, very much so.* 'I need a minute, Mama. Can I go upstairs?'

Her mother nodded, and May walked past them both, needing to go up, to stand in the room where she'd said goodbye to Johnny. She climbed the staircase slowly, inhaling the familiar smell of home as she bravely nudged open her bedroom door. May hesitated for a moment in the doorway before crossing to the window and looking down.

'*Goodbye, Johnny,*' she whispered, touching the glass with her fingertips. 'I love you.' But as she said the words to Johnny, it was Ben she saw. He hadn't left; he was still standing by the car in the lightly falling snow. She waved to him and he waved back, and she watched as he finally climbed back into the car, no doubt almost frozen to the bone, and drove away.

Ben had saved her. Ben had brought her home and made her face her demons. Ben had made her remember. And no amount of *thank yous* could ever tell him how truly grateful she was that he'd somehow stumbled into her life.

# CHAPTER TWENTY-SIX

## ENGLAND, EARLY 1943

## RUBY

'You were right,' Ruby said, waving the letter at May as they sat in the mess room. 'I can't believe it.'

With their ferry chits allocated and their day mapped out, they were all waiting for the milk run plane to collect them. May had come to sit with them, and it was a nice mixture of women sprawled out, reading books and knitting mostly.

'What does she have to say for herself?' May asked.

Ruby was still worried about her friend after they'd lost Polly. They had both struggled, but as Ruby had slowly managed to push away the awful images, May had seemed no better; although her time away with Ben had seemed to help. She hoped this news from Lizzie might at least make her smile. 'It seems she's developing a soft spot for a certain captain.'

'I had a funny feeling about the two of them,' May said, and Ruby was relieved to see her lips twitch.

She sat back and held the letter up, reading aloud.

'Dear May & Ruby,

Well, it turns out that Captain Montgomery isn't the ogre I thought he was. Would you believe he's taken me out for two romantic picnics now? I still can't believe it, but the man absolutely took me by surprise and charmed the socks off me! Well, don't go thinking he charmed anything OFF me so to speak, because I'm certainly not going to be ending my career with a baby on the way!'

Ruby started to laugh, imagining Lizzie telling poor Jackson exactly that, and May chuckled beside her. 'She's brutally honest, isn't she?' she said. 'I mean, who else would say those things?'

'I think Lizzie says whatever's in Lizzie's head, whereas most of us have a special filter that tells us when to say things out loud or not.'

They both laughed again, and Ruby wished she could thank Lizzie then and there for putting a smile back on May's face.

'I know it's early to be talking marriage, but I keep making it very clear to him that I'm not the marrying type, because I don't want him getting any fancy ideas that he can be the one to make me settle down. My darling mother would adore him, but honestly, I can't imagine anything worse than being tied to a man for the rest of my life. Imagine him trying to tell me what to do! It would be preposterous. Anyhow, things are going mighty well here, aside from Jackson still trying to throw his authority around and making my girls march everywhere like little tin soldiers.

Keep those chins up, girls. We'll never forget who we lost, but she would want us to be happy, right?'

Ruby lowered the letter. 'I miss Polly so much,' she said. 'I still can't believe she's gone.'

'Me too.' May said. 'I don't think I'll ever get past it, that pain of knowing she's gone and we're still here.'

Ruby hesitated, then decided not to hold her tongue any longer. 'I know,' she said in a low voice. 'And after everything, I mean . . .' She sighed. 'You're always here for us, May. But who's here for you? If you need someone to talk to, about what happened, I want you to know that I'm here.'

May nodded and smiled, but Ruby could see the tears glistening in her eyes. 'We've all been through a lot,' she said, 'but I'm fine. Ben was— Well, he's been there for me. I actually feel better than I have in a long time.'

Ruby let out a breath. 'I'm happy to hear that. He's a good man, and he's good for you, May.'

May squeezed her hand and headed back to her desk. Ruby folded Lizzie's letter and tucked it into her pocket. She also had a letter from Tom squirrelled away that she'd read at least three times already; it didn't look like they were leaving anytime soon, so she unfolded it again and stared at his familiar handwriting.

> Dear Ruby,
>
> I'm in some sort of hell. Honestly, I know hospital was bad, but I'd do anything to be back there and not under the same roof as my mother. I've tried, honestly I've tried so hard, but sometimes she's insufferable. My poor father! Please promise me that we'll never be like this with our children? I don't know how I ever listened to her about you. Please accept my apologies a hundred times over!
>
> She is most upset that I'm at home convalescing and you're still away flying, despite me trying

to explain to her that you're not exactly gallivanting around having fun instead of caring for me! I honestly don't know why she's still bleating on about your decision to fly. Remember that I will stand by your side no matter what, even if it means constantly telling my mother that she doesn't know what she's talking about and needs to show you more respect.

The one nice thing has been getting to know your parents better, although I can tell it must be hard for your delightful mother being with me when she's so worried about you. But the look on her face when she talks about you, or when she tells someone that her daughter and son-in-law are pilots, is something to behold. She's a wonderful woman, and I can see that the apple doesn't fall far from the tree. Your father is fantastic – we had a whisky or three the other night and toasted our marriage, and my father came along too.

Stay safe in the air, my darling. I'll be back on base again within the week I expect, and perhaps then you can arrange leave to visit me? Or even just figure out a way to fly into my base so I can make all the other officers jealous again.

Tom

Ruby read the letter one more time before carefully folding it into a small square and slipping it back into her pocket. She fingered the ring she still wore on a chain around her neck, smiling as she thought about Tom, and imagining a time when the war was over and they were back flying together. She wanted to perform acrobatics in the sky and challenge him to races, or fly in a two-seater and just enjoy being in the air for fun.

Her pulse raced as she thought about him getting back in the sky again, knowing how much more dangerous his role was than hers. He was engaging in air attacks, whereas her biggest enemy was the cloud.

'Time to go, ladies!'

Ruby picked up her small bag and stretched out her back; these days she felt so stiff and achy all the time. It was going to be a long day with a Spitfire to fly to the first base, then a Halifax further afield, and if the weather held long enough she'd be bringing back a Lancaster before having to make her way by train to Hamble, with her bag, parachute and maps in tow. Central Operations at Andover had a horrendous job, trying to shuffle planes and ferry pilots all over the British Isles, and she seemed to be regularly logging three flights instead of two each day as more planes were needed.

'Oh, listen!' one of the other girls called out, turning up the volume on the wireless. 'Our boys bombed Berlin last night! Twice!'

Ruby gasped and swelled with pride, wondering if the four-engine bomber she'd delivered the day before had been the one to do it.

# CHAPTER TWENTY-SEVEN

### TEXAS, EARLY 1943

### LIZZIE

'Captain!' Lizzie called out, seeing Jackson walk past her office. His head appeared in her open doorway and she beckoned him in.

'Well, don't you look like the cat that got the cream,' he said, eyebrows raised. 'What is it?'

'I've just received a letter from General Arnold,' she told him, still clutching the paper like a lifeline.

'And what exactly did your good friend Hap have to say today?'

Lizzie rolled her eyes at him. 'You make it sound like I've brainwashed the poor man into being my best friend.'

Jackson laughed. 'Well, I've heard worse things said about how you managed to convince a burly general to let women climb into planes and fly them all around the country.'

'Who's saying these things?' she asked, horrified. 'I would never do that!'

He was clearly enjoying this, and she hated how much he'd managed to rile her. She knew people would gossip and say all sorts of things about her, but the only thing she was guilty of was believing in women and wanting to serve her country.

'Do you want to hear what he has to say or not?' she asked.

He shrugged. 'Just get on with it. I've got work to do.'

'Congress is considering a bill that would finally make the WASPs part of the Army Air Forces!' she said excitedly. 'Can you believe it? After all this time, they're starting to realise what assets we are.'

'And it took women being stationed at one hundred and twenty bases around the country before they did,' Jackson said. 'What a bunch of idiots. They should have done this from the very beginning.'

'I know there are some women who don't want to be part of the army, but most will be thrilled.'

'What's the reluctance? Won't they finally be paid properly?' he asked.

She nodded, dropping the letter to her desk. She'd campaigned so long for them to be fairly recognised, it was almost hard to believe it was going to happen at last. 'Our pilots will be paid the same as any male pilot. They'll be supplied with proper uniforms at all times, and they'll be covered by army insurance. It's incredible.'

Jackson smiled. 'I hope they all remember to thank you.'

'I'm going to start as many WASPs as possible in the army's four-week officer training course. We have around four hundred who'll be interested.'

If Jackson was surprised, he didn't show it. 'Good.' He paused. 'Is there something you'd like to say to me?'

'Why, is there something I've forgotten? It's not your birthday today, is it?'

'I thought you might want to thank me, actually,' he said. 'Your girls have pretty much already been through army training, so they'll find officer training a walk in the park.'

Lizzie grabbed a ball of paper and threw it at him, laughing when he dodged it and jumped out of the doorway. She still found it hard to believe that someone who'd annoyed her for so long had come to mean so much to her. Even if he did still drive her crazy most of the time.

Jackson popped his head back around the door, and his eyes met hers. 'Any chance you want to go see that new movie, the one based on you girls? Some of the others are attending the first screening tonight, I'm told.'

'Will you take me to dinner first?' she asked, not letting on that she'd already planned to go to the first screening. They were all so excited about the film.

'Will you come with me to the movie if I say no?'

She folded her arms across her chest. 'No.'

'Dinner it is, then.'

Lizzie shooed him away, laughing, and picked up the letter again. It was actually happening. Women were on the cusp of being fully accepted by the army. She couldn't wait for the day it was announced, so she could see the looks on the faces of every single WASP. They were all going to feel so proud. She only hoped this new movie, *Ladies Courageous*, was as good as they all expected it to be.

They'd endured so much, and the fact they were women hadn't had any impact on their flying skills. They'd flown through painful periods and cramps, endured hours without being able to go to the bathroom, and despite all the negativity thrown in their direction. *And still they'd succeeded*. Nothing was going to stand in their way now. Nothing.

Later than night, she followed Jackson into the little theatre.

'I'm nervous,' she said, keeping a respectable distance from him as they sat side by side.

The theatre was full of WASPs and some locals who'd always been huge supporters of theirs; there was a low hum of chatter, and she dug her fingers into her knees, wishing she could reach for Jackson's hand. In truth, she could have; who was going to care if she made it plain that there was something between them? But she didn't want to cross that line. Both she and Jackson were highly respected by the recruits, and she didn't want anything to jeopardise that.

'It's going to be great,' he said.

'I just . . .' she groaned. 'I hope they give us the respect we deserve. I'm quietly terrified.'

'I've heard a rumour that there's a group of men causing a bit of a fuss over you girls at the moment, especially given the publicity you're getting over this film,' Jackson whispered. 'I wasn't going to say anything, but the army has closed some flight schools where these men were flight instructors. They've lost their jobs, which is why they're so upset.'

Lizzie felt her eyes widen. 'What do you mean? What sort of a fuss?' she whispered back. 'What does that have to do with us?'

'Well, they want your head on a stick to start with,' he muttered.

Lizzie blanched at the thought, but she knew full well how many men she'd riled with the very existence of the WASPs. But how was this her fault? She hadn't even known about the closures.

'Apparently, they've trained all the new pilots they need, which is great on the one hand because we haven't had as many pilots killed in battle as expected. But with your WASPs taking over so many non-combat roles here, well . . .'

'What are you trying to say?' she hissed.

'Most of those men, the flying instructors, they were civilians. They were excused from joining the army only because they were training our pilots, but now with those flight schools being closed, they might well end up as foot soldiers.' His hand covered her knee and she didn't bother reprimanding him. 'I thought you'd want to know.'

'So they want our jobs?' she asked. 'Is that it?' She'd been so excited about the bill in front of Congress, so certain everything was working in her favour, and then to be told this?

The screen crackled to life and she shuddered, suddenly seeing everything falling to pieces around her. How could this be happening when they were so close to being recognised by the army? Would this little group of men, jumping up and down in protest, derail all the progress they'd made?

'These instructors have been teaching beginner pilots. It would take them forever to train well enough to handle advanced aircrafts,' Jackson said. 'So let's hope it's nothing more than a bump in the road.'

She looked back at him, wondering if he was just saying that to make her feel better. She had the feeling he was keeping something from her still; she could tell from the tight lock of his jaw, the way he wasn't meeting her gaze.

'There's more, isn't there?' she asked sadly, tucking her fingers around his. 'Tell me. I need to know, otherwise they'll blindside me when I'm least expecting it.'

'They've started a campaign to discredit you,' he whispered. 'They've already got wind of this bill before Congress, and they've started a deliberate attempt to get rid of the WASPs entirely. The first story ran today in a small paper, but I can see that it'll be picked up everywhere soon. It's why I knew I couldn't keep it from you.'

'How bad was it?' she asked in a low voice, as the black-and-white images crackled over the screen.

'They're saying that women have stolen men's jobs, that you have a terrible accident rate, and that it costs a fortune to train a woman to fly a military plane.'

Lizzie gulped and sat silently as a tear ran down her cheek, then another and another. She held tight to Jackson's hand, not needing to tell him how wrong it was; he knew it as well as she did.

They officially had a lower accident rate than men flying the same missions. There was no difference at all in the cost to train them; in fact, they cost less, as they didn't even receive the same quality uniforms. But no one was going to care about that. All they'd see were the headlines screaming 'Women Stealing Men's Jobs' or something equally obscene. The women pilots would be told to go back to homemaking and knitting, instead of being lauded for the serious contribution they'd made to the war effort.

She would fight every slanderous word until her last breath, but for the first time she wondered if this was one fight she didn't have a hope of winning. The only thing she could do was ensure the bill received support, and to do that she'd need to exercise an extremely bold bluff.

'I'm going to tell Hap that if the WASPs can't be in the Army Air Forces, like every other army pilot, then the WASP programme will come to an end,' she murmured.

Jackson nodded, and she knew she had his support. The only problem would be if her gamble failed, but she had to believe they were too important to the army for them to risk losing her or her programme. And if they didn't think that, then the demise of the WASPs would be on her head. She couldn't see any other way forward through this mess.

She stared at the screen and wished she hadn't. *What on earth?*

Lizzie looked around her and saw the horrified faces of her pilots as they watched the film. They'd come to see a movie about their incredible work, about women flying enormous military planes and taking on roles that should have impressed anyone, and instead they were being portrayed as silly girls more interested in flirting with officers and gossiping. She groaned at the immature actress on screen giggling and making love-eyes at a man in uniform, wishing she'd just stayed on base for the evening.

She'd never been so embarrassed in her life.

'This is ridiculous,' Jackson said, loud enough for everyone around them to hear.

Lizzie shut her eyes and blocked it all out. It was like the world was conspiring against her, and she wasn't going to stand for it: just as she'd refused to take no for an answer before she was sent to England. This was not going to signal the end for the WASPs, and she was not going to let this ridiculous film make a mockery of their work.

'Let's go,' she said to Jackson, standing.

He looked surprised, but he stood.

'We don't need to sit and watch this nonsense,' she said in a loud voice to the women around her. 'Stay for a laugh if you like, by all means, but remember that this is fiction and does not for a moment reflect the incredible work of the WASPs.'

And with that she walked out, holding her head high. She'd collapse and cry in her own bed later, but now she needed to set an example to her girls.

'Elizabeth?'

She was surprised to see one of her office assistants standing outside the venue, holding a sheet of paper in her hand. The paper was trembling.

'Gina, what is it?' Lizzie asked.

But when the other woman just handed the envelope to her, her face ashen, Lizzie felt all colour drain from her own.

She unfolded the page quickly, scanning the words fast. It only took her a few seconds before she was reading the words again. And again. And again. Until Jackson took the paper from her and wrapped her in his arms, holding her as her legs gave way beneath her.

ELIZABETH. YOUR FATHER HAS HAD ANOTHER HEART ATTACK. NOT EXPECTED TO MAKE IT THROUGH THE NIGHT. PLEASE COME HOME.

'No,' she whispered. 'No, Daddy, you can't die on me.'

Jackson swung her up into his arms, carrying her as she clung to him like a child. 'Gina, report to base and get a telegram to General Arnold. Tell him I will be taking over duties for Elizabeth for the next few days,' she heard him say.

*Stay alive for me, Daddy. Please, just hold on.*

'I'm taking you home, Lizzie,' Jackson murmured into her ear, striding across the road and somehow getting her into the passenger seat as she numbly let him move her, incapable of saying a word.

*I still have so much to prove to you, Daddy*, she thought as she stared out of the window, her forehead pressed to the glass.

The past few hours had felt like a blur. Lizzie knew she'd sat in the car with Jackson, pointed out her parents' home to him, held her mother in her arms and then let Jackson hold her, kissing her forehead. But the only moment that felt real was right now, lowering herself to the chair beside her father and staring at him lying there, his eyes shut, his breathing raspy.

'Hey, Daddy,' she said, trying to sound bright even though every part of her was cracking apart. 'Daddy, it's me, I'm here.'

She wanted to scream at someone to call an ambulance and get him to hospital, to do *something*, anything to help him. But she knew it was too late. Her mother had made the decision to keep him at home, where he wanted to be, rather than spend his last days or hours or minutes hooked up to machines in a hospital, surrounded by strangers.

The nurse had told her it was a miracle he was still alive, and she wanted to believe that he'd waited for her, that he wanted to be with her one last time before he passed.

'Daddy?' she whispered.

His eyes opened, and she smiled at him, blinking through her tears. Her father was a big, strong man, but now he looked a shell of his former self.

'Lizzie,' he rasped, barely audible.

'I'm here,' she said. 'Don't think you can leave without saying good-bye to me.'

Then Jackson leaned forward. 'Sir, I just want to say what an hon-our it is to meet you,' he said, as her father's eyes seemed to search his. 'I want you to know that I'll always look after your Elizabeth. She's a wonderful woman and I will *always* be there for her.'

Lizzie sobbed as her father slowly blinked, as if acknowledging Jackson's words.

'I'll be sure to tell my own father, Lieutenant David Montgomery, that I had the great fortune to meet you, sir. I know he holds you in very high regard.' He cleared his throat and dropped a kiss onto Lizzie's hair before moving quietly away.

Her mother came forward then and placed something in her father's hands, and Lizzie watched as he slowly pushed it towards her.

'For,' he murmured, 'you.'

Lizzie glanced at her mother.

'He wanted you to have it. He made me promise to give it to you, and tell you he was so proud of you,' her mother said, coming to sit with her and placing an arm around her shoulders. 'We're both so proud of what you've achieved.'

Lizzie reached for his hand, opening his palm and sobbing when she saw his Distinguished Service Cross. She traced her fingertips over it, touching the eagle in the centre and then the two words.

'*For Valour,*' she whispered.

'He was in the middle of writing to you when the pain started in his chest,' her mother continued, handing her a letter. 'I'll leave you both for a moment so you can read it.'

Lizzie put the medal on the bed beside her father and unfolded the paper, glancing at her daddy, seeing that his eyes were still open, searching for her still.

She cleared her throat and quietly started to read aloud.

'To my darling Elizabeth,
I'm so very proud of everything you've achieved. I can hardly believe that my little girl is commanding an entire squadron of pilots, and women at that!'

She smiled, reaching for his hand.

'You always believed in yourself, and without that confidence we may never have seen women in the sky during this war. When I was a pilot, we would have laughed at the idea that women could help us the way you're helping us now. But look at you, doing this for the war, being the leader of a team, just as I was. We're nothing without our squadron, and . . .'

The words abruptly stopped, and Lizzie looked up, wanting to know what else he was going to say.

'Daddy?' she said, bending forward. His eyes were open, a faint smile on his lips. 'Daddy?'

She shook his hand, but received no response. Then she gently squeezed his shoulder as a cold sensation passed through her.

'Fly high, Daddy,' she whispered through her tears, the letter slipping from her fingers as she dropped over him and gave him one last hug. 'Fly high.'

# PART THREE

# CHAPTER TWENTY-EIGHT

## TEXAS, 1944

### LIZZIE

'No!' Lizzie screamed, anger thumping through her as she hastily read the letter from Hap. Her hands shook as she balled it up and threw it across the room.

She ran out of her office and into the open, gulping in breaths of warm air as she tried to come to terms with what she'd just read. It couldn't be true, could it? Could this really be the end? The sun was beating down, sending her temperature soaring. First her daddy and now this?

She saw her pilots, some milling about in groups, some walking on their own. She saw planes lined up, looked skyward and saw aircraft in the sky.

'Liz?' Jackson's big, warm hand covered her shoulder.

'It's over,' she choked. 'We're done.'

'What do you mean, *we're done*?' he asked.

She pointed towards her office, not wanting to go back in there. She didn't want to read it again, didn't want to acknowledge that her threat had led to the end of the WASPs. Maybe Hap was simply too busy to worry about a group of women; he was directing the war in the air over Europe, after all. But without them, without the WASPs, they wouldn't have had the necessary support at home, they wouldn't have . . . She pushed her thoughts away and walked down to the barracks, taking in the pilots sunning themselves, wooden chairs tipped upside down so they could lean back and sunbathe.

When she finally returned to her office, she found Jackson sitting in her chair, holding the crumpled paper in one hand. He looked up when she entered, but his gaze said it all. She marched over and took the letter from his hands, needing to see it again to make sure she hadn't dreamt it up; but it was very much reality.

'*I am proud of you young women*,' Lizzie read, clearing her throat and skipping down a bit further. '*When we needed you, you came through and have served most commendably under very difficult circumstances.*'

Jackson came to stand beside her, tucked his arm around her. '*You have freed male pilots for other work, but now the situation has changed and your volunteered services are no longer needed*,' he continued for her. '*My sincerest thanks and Happy Landings, as always.*'

They stood side by side in silence as rage built within Lizzie.

'The bastard!' she swore. 'How could he do this to us?'

Jackson let the letter drop to the floor and wrapped her tightly in his arms as she cried into his chest. Lizzie never cried; she never let anyone see her vulnerabilities, but in Jackson's arms she cried and cried and cried until she couldn't cry any longer. First over her father, and now this.

'We can fight this,' he muttered. '*You* can fight this.'

'No.' She shook her head. 'No, we can't. It's over, Jackson.' She shut her eyes, knowing she needed to pull herself together before she bravely faced her girls. They would all be receiving the letter the following day, and she needed to be there for them, to be strong and reassure them what an incredible role they'd played in this war. Her daddy's passing had almost crushed her, but she'd refused to give up, returning to base within a week of his death. He'd made it clear to her that his squadron was everything to him, and hers was to her now, too.

'It's one thing for men to let women fly, but it's another thing entirely when they start to think you're replacing them,' Jackson said. 'The idiots can't even see why we need you so much.'

She placed a hand to his chest, standing on tiptoe to press a kiss to his lips. Jackson's hands slipped to her waist and he kissed her back, his lips so gentle as he comforted her. He'd been there for her when she'd truly needed him, and it was about time she showed him how much that meant to her.

'Thank you,' she whispered, as he gently wiped her tears, his thumb drying her wet cheek.

'For what?'

'For being here when I needed someone. For everything.'

She looked over her shoulder at the letter on the floor. They had a few more months before they were discarded like dirty laundry, that's what he'd said. Those still training could finish up and graduate, but they'd all be home by Christmas. Everything she'd worked so hard for was going to be gone like a puff of smoke, as if it had never existed.

'Want me to come with you when you announce the news?' he asked.

Lizzie shook her head. 'No. I need to do this on my own.'

She'd been the one to tell them all when they'd been accepted into the programme, and she'd be the one to tell them it was over.

Jackson dropped a kiss on to her hair and turned to go. As she watched him, she knew that letting him walk away from her once the programme was disbanded was something she couldn't bear to think of. She might lose her job, but she had Jackson, and that was worth more than she could have imagined. *One step at a time*, she told herself. First she'd deal with this, and then she'd make sure she didn't lose Jackson *and* the WASPs. She'd had enough loss these past few months to last her a lifetime.

# CHAPTER TWENTY-NINE

## ENGLAND, 1944

## MAY

'I can't believe it's been more than a year since we lost her,' Ben said, as May placed flowers on the grass.

May straightened up. 'It feels like a lifetime,' she agreed, reliving the day she'd seen Polly lying there and wishing the memory had faded more. 'And it was for nothing – we're still flying blind.'

Ben's arm slipped around her shoulders. 'You've done everything you can do, May. It's not your fault if no one will listen.'

She knew that, but it still drove her mad that there was nothing more she could do to keep her girls safe. The only consolation was that things were finally turning in favour of the Allies, which meant that everything they'd done, every sacrifice they'd made, had been worth it.

'Have you heard from Violet this week?' she asked, as they headed back to their borrowed car.

'Yes, actually, I have,' Ben said. 'In fact, she wanted to know when I was going to ask you to marry me.'

May's heart started to race. 'And what did you say to that?' she asked, trying to keep her voice steady.

Ben took both of her hands in his and dropped to one knee, kissing her knuckles as he looked up at her. 'I said I'd ask you and see what you said.'

May's mouth opened, but no sound came out. 'What?' she whispered.

'May, when this war is over, will you marry me?'

She dropped to her knees with him and kissed him, her hands planted on his cheeks. 'Yes!' she gasped. 'Yes, Ben, I'll marry you.'

He took her hand then and held something out, and she smiled when she saw it was a piece of metal welded into a small circle.

'I promise I'll give you a proper ring when the war is over,' he said, pushing it onto her finger. 'But for now, this is from the damaged engine of a Spitfire. I pulled that engine apart and rebuilt it to keep your pilots safe, so I thought it was the perfect keepsake for you. I made it myself.'

She looked down at her finger. 'It's perfect, Ben. Honestly, it is.'

Ben pulled her to her feet and swung her up into his arms, then carried her to the car. She nestled into his neck, nuzzling against him, wondering how on earth a girl so determined not to get close to anyone had somehow ended up head over heels in love.

'Can this be our little secret?' she whispered.

'Yeah,' he said, kissing her forehead. 'It can. For now.'

'Did you hear from Lizzie again?' May asked the next day, pleased to be catching up with Ruby. They were sitting outside the large hangar at Hamble, after flying back from delivering bombers to Yorkshire, catching the late morning sun. When May had found out that Ruby would have a few hours off before her next flight, she'd cleared her schedule so that she could spend some time with her before she flew out again. Part of her wanted to tell her about Ben, but the other part of her was almost too scared to admit to her happiness. They were both always so busy that they didn't often get time to sit and talk together, just the two of them.

'She's heartbroken about the whole thing,' Ruby said. 'Honestly, I can't believe she lost support for the WASPs. Surely they still need them? She's had a rough year, hasn't she?'

May nodded, fingering the ring Ben had given her. She'd put it on her necklace to keep it close. 'You know how men get when they think women are stealing their jobs,' she said dryly. 'It's easy to discard us when they're no longer desperate for our help.'

'Do you think the same will happen here?' Ruby asked. 'After everything we've done? After everyone we've lost and . . .' Her voice trailed off.

'We'd be naïve to think any differently,' May replied. 'But for now I think we're safe. They need us too much and there's no one to replace us – it's not like it is for the Americans. We're still a required commodity, as crude as that might sound.' She sighed. 'But part of me thinks we're getting close, that it actually could be over soon. The Normandy landings were a huge success, we've taken Italy . . . It's all looking like the Allies might win this darn thing once and for all.' There was still a long way to go, but compared to the previous year when it had felt like the Allies were losing, things seemed to be changing; even the broadcasts from the BBC were sounding more positive. 'How's Tom?' May asked. 'Settled back into flying again?'

'As well as can be expected. I think we're both focusing on what we have to look forward to if the war ever ends, but he's happy to be back with his squadron for now.'

May could understand that; she'd been doing the same when it came to Ben. She could still see the look on her mother's face, feel the happiness of being reunited, and then the recognition that it was Ben who'd taken her there. Ben who'd been brave enough to stand up to her and make her go home.

'Will you keep flying if you can? After the war, I mean?' May asked. 'Hearing that Lizzie's wartime flying career is almost over, it's made me start thinking about what it'll be like for us. Trying to live normal lives is going to be weird.'

'It'll be downright boring, that's what it'll be!' Ruby moaned. 'It'll be like learning to live without a limb if I can't fly anymore.'

'I know. Trouble is, we'll have to fund our own flying again, and who among us will be able to afford it?'

'Would you give it all up? To have a family or get married?' Ruby asked, looking a little tearful. 'When all this is over, I mean?'

'After all we've done, I expect it won't be so unusual for us to want to continue flying to some degree *and* be wives and mothers.' Maybe she was hoping for too much, but Ben didn't seem in the least bit concerned by her love of flying. 'Surely Tom will understand that, being a pilot himself? I just don't know if we can be expected to become home-makers and give up our role as fliers.'

'I know, I feel the same, and I hope Tom does understand,' Ruby said quickly. 'But will our men still think like that when our lives go back to normal, or will they start to forget how much we've done? Will they just go back to their old expectations and expect us to change again, too?'

'And be influenced by their mothers or other family members?' May asked gently. 'Is that what you're worried about?'

Ruby's face flushed. 'Yes.'

May knew how much her friend struggled with her mother-in-law; it wasn't an easy position to be in, although there must be many older women who held her old-fashioned views. Maybe it was simply because they couldn't comprehend what women could do, or hadn't been given the same opportunities.

Meanwhile, their futures rested in the hands of men, and May wasn't certain it would come down to keeping the best for the job. More like the best man for the job. 'I'd like to think that women will be able to apply for other aviation jobs once the war is over, like piloting commercial aircraft.'

'And do you think that will happen?' Ruby asked.

'I'm hopeful, but not certain,' May raised her eyes as an aircraft approached, watching the ungainly beast as it slowly hit the ground and taxied down the runway. 'Perhaps, after all we've achieved here, I'm starting to let my dreams run away with me.'

'Well, I hope you're bloody right,' Ruby muttered.

'One thing's for sure,' May said with a grin. 'Our mothers and sweethearts are going to be shocked to hear us swearing and carrying on like a bunch of men when we return home!'

They burst out laughing and May thought of her own mother. She'd never said a curse word in front of her children in her lifetime, and she'd never been further than an hour's drive from their home; whereas May had seen the length and breadth of their country from the air.

She smiled at Ruby. It was strange how much life had evolved, but she wouldn't have changed hers for the world. And for the first time in years, she couldn't wait to go home again, but this time with Ben proudly by her side.

# CHAPTER THIRTY

## TEXAS, 1944

## LIZZIE

Lizzie had never struggled so much to keep her emotions in check, but as she stood on the stage to address the WASPs seated in front of her, she could barely contain herself. This was her final graduation. No more women would ever complete her programme. She'd lost the fight; they'd only have a week or so of actual flying as fully fledged WASPs, and all she could do was give these incredible women the send-off they deserved.

'This is a very special day for all of us, not least the incredible pilots who are graduating today,' Lizzie said, staring straight ahead despite the tears that threatened to fall. She refused to give in to them, holding her head high. 'What we have done, the great service the WASPs have given our country, is something that we must all be incredibly proud of. You, all of you, are my greatest achievement by far, and nothing I've done before, or will ever do in the future, will come close to this. I may have been the starting point for this programme, but I am a very small part of what we have become.' She glanced over at Jackson, resplendent in his full uni-form. He was watching her so intently that it only made her all the more emotional. She took a deep, shaky breath. 'As you know, this programme also couldn't have happened without the support of General Arnold, the commander of the Army Air Forces, who has made the effort to be here with us today.' She looked at Hap and smiled, pleased to have him with her on this final day. He had shown unwavering support for women pilots since the beginning, and she couldn't blame him for Congress voting against them or their programme being shut down. There was, after all, only so much one man could be expected to do. 'But before I step aside for my good friend and mentor, I would like to share some statistics with you. As we all know, there has been much said about us that is untrue and downright mortifying, and I want to set the record straight.'

Lizzie looked down at the notes in her hand. Until now she'd been speaking from the heart, but she wanted to get these facts and figures correct. There was a journalist in attendance to witness the last ceremony, and her hope was that he would at least report correctly when he wrote his story.

'Since the women's pilot programme began, we have had an astonishing twenty-five thousand applicants. As you know, the acceptance process was tough, and as such we accepted fewer than two thousand women. We have had one thousand one hundred and two women serving as WASPs, including the twenty-eight women fliers in Nancy Love's original WAFs squadron.' Lizzie looked at the strong, beautiful faces staring back at her and bravely continued. 'Thirty-eight women pilots died while serving our country, and I would like to take a moment to remember those incredible women. They died in the line of duty, and I know they will never, ever be forgotten.' She placed her hand on her heart and shut her eyes for a moment, hoping the others would do the same. When she opened them and saw every single head bowed, a single tear slipped from the corner of her eye. She'd started out to set the sky ablaze with women pilots, and somehow, through the grace of God, she'd done it, which was why today was so heartbreakingly painful for her.

'Women ferry pilots have flown seventy-seven kinds of planes and flown some sixty million miles, and one thing it has shown me is that women truly can do anything they set their minds to.' She raised her voice, wanting this to be the part they remembered. 'We are told as little girls what our expectations should be, and it's made abundantly clear what our limitations are, but I'm standing here today to tell you that there are no limitations for women, or at least not in the sky. You don't need to be a burly six-foot man to fly an enormous four-engine bomber, but you do need a brain and single-minded determination. It's no wonder men feel threatened by us, instead of seeing us as their sisters in arms.' She paused again. 'But we *are* different from our male counterparts, and we should be proud of our differences. As women, we feel deep compassion and gratitude, and we know how important our role is. I for one know that I first embarked on this challenge to prove to myself and to my dear father exactly what I was capable of, but I quickly discovered that what I was doing was so much bigger than that.' She smiled. 'I've heard stories of many women writing notes and leaving them in the aircrafts as they deliver them, wishing the intended combat pilot good luck. I've had male pilots report back that seeing us arrive, ferrying planes to them, has given them hope. Many of them love us, although they didn't necessarily in the beginning, and they scribble images of our little "Fifi" icon as they wait to fly. As women, we should never doubt the impact we've had on our great country.'

The women all clapped, some stamping their feet, and Lizzie beamed back, unable to suppress the huge smile any more than she'd been able prevent tears earlier. She held her daddy's medal in her palm as she spoke, drawing on his strength, remembering him as she stood before the gathered crowd.

'I present General Arnold to you all. Ladies, thank you.'

The clapping continued, and Lizzie held out her hand to Hap, clasping it and then stepping forward to kiss his cheek. His embrace was full of warmth, and she happily stood back as he addressed her graduates.

'To all you wonderful women pilots, I would like to say thank you. Not so long ago, I stood and testified before Congress, detailing the most excellent performance record of the WASPs, and every word I spoke was the plain truth,' he said. 'It is with great sadness that I come to witness the final graduation ceremony, but it is also a great honour.' Hap laughed and leaned forward, like he was about to let them in on a secret. 'Frankly, I didn't know in 1941 whether a slip of a young girl could fight the controls of a B-17.' He grinned. 'Well, now, in 1944, we can only come to one conclusion. The entire operation has been a success. It is on the record that women can fly as well as men. You have worked hard, incredibly hard, and you have buckled down to the monotonous, routine jobs that are not much desired by our hot-shot young men headed toward combat. In some of your jobs, I think the commanders like you better than the men, to be honest.' He paused. 'Every WASP has filled a vital and necessary place in the jigsaw pattern of victory.'

Hap clapped his hands together loudly and then gestured to Lizzie, his smile infectious. She had known how much the programme meant to him, but the pride in his words today truly confirmed it. She clapped along with him before taking Hap's arm and walking from the stage.

'If I could have made any other decision,' Hap started, shaking his head as he murmured words for her ears only.

'Stop,' Lizzie said, taking his hand and holding tight. 'You don't have to explain.' And she meant it; she'd been so angry when that letter had first arrived, but his hands had been tied. She understood that now. She'd commanded a successful squadron at a time when women had been desperately needed to serve; she'd managed to contribute to the war effort, and make her father proud.

'Well, at least you don't have to suffer Captain Montgomery any longer,' he joked, glancing at Jackson, who was just approaching.

Lizzie groaned. Jackson had one brow raised; he'd clearly overheard. 'She actually said she had to *suffer* my presence?' he demanded.

Hap laughed. 'There was worse, but I'll spare you the rest of it, Captain.'

Lizzie's cheeks were burning. 'I'm sorry, I . . .'

'Well, she was pretty damn insufferable herself most of the time,' Jackson said, before putting an arm around her shoulders. 'But what I can say is that she eventually grew on me.'

Now it was Hap's eyebrows shooting skyward. 'You two? Well, I never would have guessed.'

Lizzie gave Jackson a playful shove, laughing at the apologetic look he gave her. 'Come on, enough talk about us. We have a party to attend and you're the guest of honour.'

Jackson proffered his elbow, his grin infectious. What the heck, she thought, accepting it and smiling up at him as they walked towards the empty hangar, where the party was already underway. She'd been a stickler for protocol all this time, but Jackson was part of her life now, and it was about time she came to terms with it. Despite everything that had been taken from her, Jackson had become a pillar of strength, the one and only thing she'd always be able to count on.

She looked nostalgically at the planes lined up on the runway, knowing that, within two weeks, she was going to walk away from them and never see another woman seated at the controls. Would she ever have the opportunity to fly a military plane again?

'You okay?' Jackson asked, his voice barely audible.

She leaned her head against his shoulder for a moment. 'Not really,' she admitted. 'But I'll be fine.'

'He'd be proud of you, Liz,' Jackson said.

She imagined her daddy looking down on her, smiling at everything she'd achieved. 'I know.'

It was over. The WASPs were about to be decommissioned, but no one could take her memories from her. They couldn't change the fact that she'd been instrumental in putting women pilots in the air, or that she'd flown aircraft that no one would have ever believed a woman was capable of piloting. And that was something that she would hold close to her heart for the rest of her life.

# CHAPTER THIRTY-ONE

## ENGLAND, 1945

## MAY

May stared out at the horizon. It was a curious thing, knowing that she only had days left at White Waltham. Part of her was relieved, after dedicating such a huge part of her life to the ferry programme; another part of her felt like she was grieving the death of a loved one. But orders were orders, and they were no longer needed. When she and Ruby had talked about it, it hadn't seemed possible; the war ending had seemed more like a fantasy after almost five years of turmoil and tragedy. Now the few of them that were left were based at their original headquarters, so they'd come full circle in a way.

When Ruby appeared, May opened her arms and enveloped her in a big hug. Things were about to change forever, and she didn't know if their paths would ever cross again, or what her future held. But she did know what might be in her dear friend's future. And she did know that not one of her pilots was going to be lost to the skies again, that the women still under her command had made it. The relief that she'd lost so few, that they'd been so lucky despite everything, was almost painful.

'So now you're not only the girl who flew a Halifax, you're the girl who flew a Meteor jet,' May said. 'And to Berlin, no less!'

Ruby was grinning from ear to ear, her excitement palpable after her amazing ground-breaking flight. 'It was pretty incredible,' she said. 'I've never known anything like it.'

May smiled. 'Can you believe this war is almost over? That the Allies have actually done it?'

Ruby reached for her and they embraced for a silent, surreal moment. 'We've survived,' she whispered. 'My Tom survived, we've survived. I just can't believe we did it.'

May stepped back, wiping her eyes. 'When you're in the thick of it, working so tirelessly day after day, it's almost impossible to imagine that it could ever actually end.'

'You can say that again.'

May pointed down the runway. 'Can we walk?'

'Of course.'

They fell into step, walking side by side in comfortable silence. It was a warm summer evening, and May was sick of being at her desk, completing all the final paperwork and cross-checking all the logbooks, so it was nice to feel the warm breeze on her skin.

'I have some exciting news for you,' she said.

'More exciting than the war ending or flying a Meteor jet?' Ruby joked. 'Actually, as surreal as the end might be, I don't think anything can beat flying at two hundred and seventy miles per hour today. It was like being a bullet!'

May gave her a wink. 'This might be even better.'

Ruby stopped walking and stared at her. 'What is it? Tell me!'

'As you know, most of us are being released from our jobs. There's a huge surplus of pilots now, and even the best of us can't be seen to be taking jobs from men.'

Ruby groaned. 'I'm so sick of hearing people say that! They used us when they needed us, and now they want to pretend we're the inferior sex all over again.'

May couldn't have agreed more, but now wasn't a time to debate the great gender divide. They only had their base at White Waltham left now; all but six pilots had gone, she knew it would soon be as if they'd never even existed. She had no idea how any of the ATA were going to find work, when new jobs were harder to find than butter; and with their pay soon to be stopped, times were going to be harder in peace than war.

'Ruby, now the war is as good as over, you've been seconded to the RAF.'

'What?' Ruby gasped, all colour draining from her face.

'It seems you impressed someone with your flying skills. They want you to join them to fly the Meteor jets.'

Ruby squealed and hugged May, jumping up and down. 'Are you serious?'

May laughed. 'Yes, Ruby, I'm very serious. You've been shoulder-tapped from very high up in the RAF – it seems you have some fans there.'

'Gosh, I wonder what Tom will say,' she said. 'I'm going to have to ask him . . .'

'Don't ask him for permission, Ruby. His blessing, perhaps. But this is your decision and no one else's,' May said firmly, hoping she wasn't speaking out of turn. 'You learnt from the beginning to trust your own instincts, and this shouldn't be any different. Tom fell in love with you all over again despite the choice you made, remember?'

Ruby nodded. 'I know.'

'And I know for a fact that he will be kept on with the RAF, so you might find it all works out perfectly after all.'

They started to walk again, this time with their arms looped, like the two young women they'd been before the war rather than two highly trained pilots.

'What about you?' Ruby asked.

'Well, actually, Ben and I are going to get married. As soon as we're both home.'

Ruby beamed at her. 'May, that's wonderful news! I'm so happy for you. When did he ask you?'

'It was actually some time ago, but we decided to keep it secret for a while. Now that my duties are over though, I'll be shouting it from the rooftops,' May said with a grin. 'He's a good man, Ruby. I have no idea how I was so lucky to find him, but I needed to keep him just for me. I had this fear that if I told anyone, I'd lose him, too.'

'Will you keep flying, do you think?' Ruby asked.

'I'm so proud of what we did here, and I'll always want to fly, but this isn't me. I mean . . .' What did she mean? She'd loved her role with the ATA; even when she'd been desperately tired and sometimes didn't know how she'd face another day, it had been her life and she wouldn't have had it any other way. She'd been running from her past, from her pain, and it was finally time to stop and take a moment to just breathe. 'What I'm trying to say is that I always imagined a traditional life for myself in many respects, but one where I continued flying whenever I wanted to. Although I don't know exactly how I'll make that happen.'

Ruby nodded. 'I know the feeling. In my heart I adore Tom and I want more than anything to be his wife, but that's not enough for me anymore. I need to fly, too, and I don't think I could be with him if he didn't understand that.'

'I have such a jumble of thoughts in my head – it's nice to be able to talk it through with you,' May confessed. 'I doubt anyone in my family would understand, and it's going to be hard going back to normality after this.'

'Pretending like we're just regular women, when in fact we achieved the unachievable?' Ruby added.

'Exactly. Only if you take this position, you'll be the one *still* achieving the unachievable. I'm so proud of you.' May thought back to the day she met Ruby, the tiniest woman who'd applied to ferry planes for the ATA, but the one who showed the most potential. If she hadn't demanded that the doctor ignore her height, Ruby might never have taken to the air and become their poster girl. Ruby had, without a doubt, been her biggest personal achievement within the ATA.

May wondered whether anyone would ever know what so many English women had done during the war, how truly courageous and dedicated they'd been to ferry every plane the military had to wherever it was needed. She looked across at Ruby. It didn't matter. Even if no one else understood what they'd done, they would know.

'Have you heard from Lizzie?' she asked.

Ruby laughed. 'Yes, and she's being typical Lizzie. Still demanding that women pilots be allowed to fly for the military and commercial aircrafts too. That woman will never give up – she's permanently wired to not take no for an answer.'

May smiled. The world needed more women like Lizzie to keep rattling chains. 'If anyone can do the impossible, it's her. I pity poor Jackson though. Do you think he has any idea what he's in for?'

'He deserves a medal,' Ruby replied. 'I doubt it'll be easy trying to make her settle down, but at least he's seen her at her worst.'

They both laughed, silenced only by the low roar of a plane approaching.

'What do you say we all go out tonight?' May asked. 'Let our hair down and celebrate surviving this bloody war?'

Ruby clasped her hand. 'Sounds like a marvellous idea to me, so long as Ben isn't waiting for you?'

'Ben can come too, if he's brave enough,' May replied, laughing as she watched her last pilot disembark the Spitfire. 'Tonight I want to be with my sisters in arms.'

'Can I confess something to you?' Ruby asked, her cheeks flooding with colour.

May looked at her suspiciously. 'What have you done?'

'I *may* have engraved my initials into the last Spitfire I piloted.'

May swatted at Ruby, who deftly ducked out of her way. 'Ruby! You've vandalised air force property!'

'After everything we've done for them, I think it's the least they could let me get away with.'

'Says the only woman asked to join the air force!'

They both guffawed, and May knew in that moment that she'd miss her days with the ATA for the rest of her life. Nothing would ever come close to the work they'd done or the friends they'd made, and she would cherish that for as long as she lived.

'You ladies waiting for me?' Sarah, the pilot, called out, shaking her shoulder-length hair out of her helmet.

'We're going out to celebrate,' May called back. 'You with us?'

Sarah grinned. 'I've never heard such a grand idea in my life!'

# CHAPTER THIRTY-TWO

## TEXAS, 1945

## LIZZIE

'Honey, I'm home!' Jackson called out playfully and Lizzie panicked, desperately trying to pick up the pieces of a letter she'd just shredded all over the carpet.

He popped his head into her office and she quickly stuffed the bits into her rubbish bin, but they fell like snowflakes and Jackson noticed at once.

'Lizzie?' he said. 'What are you trying to hide from me?'

'I finally received a reply from American Airlines,' she said nonchalantly.

'I'm guessing it wasn't the response you expected?' Jackson sat down in the big leather sofa that faced her desk.

'Well, they had the nerve to completely ignore my pilot application and invite me to be a *stewardess* with them.' She choked on the word. 'A *stewardess*, Jackson. I'm one of the country's most experienced and highly trained pilots and they asked me to serve cups of coffee!'

'Come here,' he said, patting the spot beside him.

'Is it so wrong that I want to keep flying?'

'No,' he said firmly. 'It's not.'

She sighed and went to him, falling into the spot beside him on the sofa. Jackson's arm drew her in, and she relaxed against him as he kissed the top of her head.

'They're fools,' he said, 'but then so was the army, and look what you managed to achieve. Keep writing. Keep making your voice heard.'

'Really?' she asked, looking up into blue eyes that still managed to mesmerise her.

'Really,' he insisted, kissing her. 'There is nothing, *nothing* that can stop you.'

She groaned and buried her face in his chest. 'Actually, there is,' she mumbled.

Jackson pushed her back a little, tilting her face up with his thumb. 'Lizzie Montgomery, tell me what it is,' he said sternly.

'Well, let me begin by saying that I kept meticulous records of all the WASPs. Well, actually, I made the doctor at the training centre keep them, to ensure we had records of when the women had their periods to track their performance and health.' Jackson shifted uncomfortably, but she continued, not caring if it made him feel squeamish. 'What I'm trying to say is that the doctor found that women flew as well at that time of the month as any other – in fact we had *less* time off, despite having to deal with the discomfort of our periods. At most, some of the women would use a hot-water bottle during a flight to help with their cramps.'

Jackson was frowning now. 'I'm not sure I'm following. Why are you telling me all this about women's monthly cycles?'

She averted her gaze. 'I'm only trying to say that regardless of whether a woman might have her monthly courses or be *pregnant* even, it has no impact on her flying abilities.' Lizzie held her breath and forced herself to look at Jackson, her heart thumping.

'*Pregnant?*'

She blew out a breath that made wisps of her hair fly up. 'Yes, pregnant,' she confirmed.

'Hold on, that entire speech was you trying to tell me that you intended to take a flying job while you were *pregnant*? With my child?'

She laughed. 'I suppose it was, yes.'

'Over my dead body!' he growled, leaning in and holding her close.

'I'll be deciding what to do with my own body, thank you very much,' she muttered.

'We're actually having a baby?' He had tears in his eyes. 'Oh, Lizzie. This is incredible news.'

'Try to stop me flying and I'll divorce you immediately,' she said.

'I'll tell you right now that you won't be flying dangerous aircraft with my baby on board,' he told her. 'This is not a negotiation, Liz, this is me firmly putting my foot down!'

'Just try stopping me.' Lizzie stood, hands on hips as she glared back at him.

'Fine, then you can't fly without me in the cockpit beside you.'

He stood too, and a flicker or excitement ran through her. This was what it had been like working together, the fire between the two of them always flaring, and she'd missed it.

'I'll think about it,' she replied with a shrug, knowing that it was probably the best compromise she was going to get.

'You'll be doing more than thinking about it.'

'I haven't told Mama yet, but I've asked her around for dinner,' she said, ignoring his words. 'I thought I'd cook for a change instead of her having us over. I actually can't wait to tell her.'

He groaned. 'Can't your mother do the cooking? You know I'm only going to have to go buy ready-made food after you set the oven on fire.'

She swatted at him, but he just laughed at her.

'Come here,' he said, grabbing her and pulling her in, kissing her fiercely as she clung on to him. He was one in a million, her Jackson, and there wasn't another man who'd ever have managed to get her to marry him, let alone have his child.

'I love you,' she whispered into his ear.

'My crazy flygirl,' he whispered back. 'I love you too.'

# CHAPTER THIRTY-THREE

## LONDON, ENGLAND, 1946

## MAY

'What is it that could be such a big secret?' May asked grumpily as Ben led her into their sitting room. 'I don't see why you can't just tell me!'

Ben gave her a long, hard stare. 'Can't a man do something nice without being interrogated?'

May was about to apologise when there was a knock at the door. She rose, but Ben's hand on her shoulder firmly pushed her back down.

'Just sit, woman. Would you please follow orders for once?'

May swallowed her smile. 'Yes, sir,' she said obediently, saluting. What on earth was going on?

He disappeared and seconds later Ruby burst into the room, looking as frustrated as May felt.

'Ruby!' May said, standing to hug her. 'What are you doing here?'

'I honestly have no idea,' Ruby said, hugging her back. 'It's lovely to see you, but I don't know what's got into Tom. He wouldn't tell me where we were going and . . .'

'Benjamin!' May called out. 'Will you please explain all this?'

She traded glances with Ruby as they both sat down.

'They're up to something,' Ruby said. 'Why all the secrecy? Why didn't he just tell me we were coming to your house?'

'I hope you're sitting down,' Ben said, appearing in the doorway. 'Because this is the best kept secret in the history of—'

'Lizzie!' Ruby screamed, her voice piercing through May as she leapt off the chair.

'Surprise, ladies!' Lizzie drawled, holding one arm up in the air dramatically, the other cradling a bouncing baby girl on her hip, who frantically flapped her arms in response.

'Lizzie,' May whispered, waiting for Ruby to stop squealing and hugging their friend. 'How are you . . . ?'

Ben came up beside her and kissed her cheek. 'Enjoy your reunion, my love. We're off to the pub with Jackson.'

She barely heard Ben's words. She crossed the room and wrapped an arm around Lizzie as a wave of emotion washed over her. Then she opened her arms for the little girl, who was holding out a fist to her.

'She's beautiful, Lizzie,' May laughed, kissing and cuddling her. 'Look at her! She's just perfect.'

All of them were transfixed by the smiling, babbling child, who with her halo of blonde hair and bright blue eyes was the spitting image of her mother.

'I could hardly make you two little Polly's godmothers and not have you meet her, could I?' Lizzie asked, her voice cracking.

'Little Polly,' May cooed, passing her to Ruby, who looked desperate to get her hands on her. 'It's lovely that you named her after our Polly. It means so much to all of us.' It was true; it allowed Polly to live on in a way, and kept the memory of her alive.

As Ruby held little Polly, stroking her hair and soaking up every inch of her, May took Lizzie's arm. 'Come on, let's go into the garden. Polly can crawl around on the grass and we can sit and talk. How long do we have you for?'

'A month. So you'll be well and truly sick of me by the time I leave,' Lizzie teased.

May pushed the doors wide open, sunshine greeting them as they stepped out. Once she'd wished for Lizzie to go home and never come back, but that seemed like a lifetime ago. Now, she'd relish every moment with her until the very last second.

'You look good with her,' Lizzie told Ruby. 'It's the best thing, having a little one. Who would imagine me, all clucky over a child?'

May laughed. 'Not me, that's for sure.'

'I, we . . .' Ruby stuttered, kissing Polly's little hand. 'I've lost two, pregnancies I mean. We're trying.'

Lizzie embraced her, so much softer than she'd once been, so much more open and understanding. May stood for a moment, not able to take her eyes off her friends as they sat on her lawn under the shade of the oak tree. Suddenly everything in the world felt right. They were a country at peace after six years of devastation; they were safe, they weren't going to lose any more soldiers or pilots or civilians. And now the two women who meant the most to her in the world were sitting in her garden.

She went to make them tea, listening to the laughter and baby talk, imagining a day when she and Ben might have a brood of their own playing out there. After half a decade of everything feeling so painful, of not being able to see the light, suddenly she felt as if she were bathed in it.

'You didn't die for nothing,' she whispered, as she looked skyward. They'd lost so many men, but they were free now. And without all that sacrifice, there would only have ever been darkness.

# EPILOGUE

## *White Waltham Airfield, England,*

## *August 2008*

## *Ruby*

Ruby held on to her grandson's arm as they walked out towards the airfield at White Waltham on the sixty-fourth anniversary of V-J Day. She smiled over at May, Ben, Lizzie and Jackson as she stepped onto the grass, remembering the first time she'd eyed up a Spitfire, ready to prove her flying skills, and the moment she'd stood beside May, her commanding officer, and received news that she was to transfer to Hamble and fly four-engine bombers. It was a lifetime ago; a time that her grandson would never be able to comprehend, no matter how many times he asked her about the planes she flew and the near misses she'd had in the sky. He was an impeccable young pilot himself; she was hardly able to believe that she was old enough to have a grandson dressed in a Royal Air Force uniform, serving his country as she'd done at the same age.

'You okay, Grandma?' he asked, patting her hand.

She smiled up at him. 'I might be old, but an itty-bitty Spitfire isn't enough to scare me,' she said. The truth was, she wondered if she still had the nerves to go up in the aircraft at all, but at almost ninety years of age, she wasn't about to turn down the opportunity to fly one last time. She could imagine confessing her fears to Lizzie afterwards and the old biddy telling her to toughen up, and the thought only made her more determined to climb into the cockpit.

'You don't have to be brave for me, Grandma,' Lewis said with a grin.

He reminded her of the men she'd met when she'd been flying, except that her grandson had grown up seeing women doing anything and everything, and back then they'd been the first of their kind. She'd never forgotten the look on most of the male pilots' faces on seeing her climb out of a plane, especially a Wellington or a Walrus. They'd almost tripped over their jaws.

Ruby looked back at the gathered crowd and wished her husband were there to see her. He'd been her biggest advocate, her Tom, even when his mother had refused to attend the christening of their first child in protest at her daughter-in-law's flying for the RAF; he would have been so happy to see her in a Spitfire once again. *You've made me the proudest husband, Ruby.* She could still hear his words: he'd said the same thing to her every year when they'd quietly toasted the anniversary of V-J Day. *How many men can say their wives actually helped to win the war from the sky?*

'You know, these were my favourite planes, even though I did like being in charge of those big bombers,' she said.

Lewis laughed. 'I know, Grandma,' he said, and she realised she'd probably told him a hundred times. 'I'm embarrassed that you've flown more planes than I ever will.'

'The perfect ladies' plane, that's what they used to call the Spitfire. Although I doubt they were ever designed with women in mind.' She stood beside it now, a wave of nostalgia hitting her harder than she'd expected. She took a deep, shaky breath as memories flooded back from her flying days. Sometimes it only felt like yesterday – the adrenaline rush of flying high, the dread of seeing a pilot's name erased from the board in their mess room or the stomach-curling feeling of limping back to base in a plane that was no longer airworthy. Seeing the wreckage of the plane that had killed her friend Polly. They'd done things that even now seemed impossible.

'Grandma, we looked for this plane for a very long time,' Lewis started, his smile as wicked as his granddad's had always been. 'I think you might have flown her before. Does she look familiar?'

Ruby's eyes were wide as she looked it over. 'Help me up,' she said, knees creaking as she pulled herself up and into the cockpit. She bent and squinted, studying the cockpit, looking for the letters she'd scrawled there all those years ago.

'Well, I'll be damned,' she said, laughing and sitting down in the seat, shifting back and recalling the hours she'd sat there.

'If we scribbled our signature in a plane now, we'd be fired on the spot,' he told her, looking pleased with himself for surprising her. 'Now, what do you say we get this old lady up in the air?'

'Don't go calling me an old lady,' she retorted.

'Grandma, I was talking about the plane,' he said with a laugh.

The truth was, they were both old ladies now, and she knew this would be her last flight in a fighter plane, the very last time she'd ever take to the skies unless in a commercial jet liner. Her only wish was that Tom were beside her, so she could smile across at him as they took to the sky side by side.

Ruby shut her eyes for a moment, remembering every step, knowing the plane as well as she knew her little car. She settled into her place and Lewis helped her with her straps, securing her just as their mechanics had always done. Ground crew appeared, and she noticed them assisting, but her eyes couldn't leave the interior of the beautiful old warplane, taking her back in time, her memories coming to life. Once upon a time, this was all she'd lived for.

Lewis took control and started her up, the engine kicking into life, the noise even louder than she remembered. Or maybe it was the way it rattled her old bones that intensified the noise and vibrations, her legs somehow even shorter in her seat than they'd been back then.

'Ready, Grandma?' he shouted.

She nodded, blinking away tears as she tightened the knot in her scarf and thanked the heavens that she'd worn warm clothes. But even if she got frostbite, it would be worth it to be back in the air. She'd survived colder temperatures for hours all those years ago, she'd been almost frozen into her seat, so she'd survive this.

Her stomach flipped the way it always had at take-off, and when they finally started to taxi down the airfield she felt a sense of relief. The plane lifted, the nose pointing skyward as they slowly rose, higher and higher, settling just below the cloud cover as they'd always been instructed to do.

The sky was blue and bright, and Ruby watched her capable grandson, remembering a time when it had been her husband teaching her and showing her the ropes. Lewis had turned to smile back at her and was gesturing at the controls. He couldn't be serious, could he? But his thumbs-up suggested he was.

*He wanted her to take over.* She was certain the RAF wouldn't be so happy to know an old pilot who was about to celebrate her ninetieth birthday was flying one of their best and most well-preserved aircraft, but the opportunity was too good to miss. She'd never been one to look a gift horse in the mouth, and she wasn't about to start now, no matter how terrifying the prospect might be.

She nodded and took a deep breath before taking over on the dual controls. It all came back to her, as natural as breathing; suddenly it was as if she were in her twenties again, settling in for a long flight to deliver a plane. *You don't need me as your co-pilot anymore. You've turned into more of a Spitfire than those planes you love so much. You can do this without me, my little bird. Don't be afraid.* Tom's words were comforting as she soared through the sky.

'You're a beautiful old girl, that's for sure,' she muttered to herself. She decided to fly along the railway line that had been so fiercely protected during the war before turning in a perfect arc and heading back towards the airfield and doing a sneaky barrel roll. She laughed along with her grandson, feeling as lightheaded as a girl on her first ever flight. The scenery was familiar, yet different at the same time; she vividly recalled her first cross-country trip, proving to herself and to her commander that she understood geography and could find her way wherever she needed to go. Once she'd completed a large circle she signalled for Lewis to take over again, her hands unsteady and shaking the moment she relinquished control.

Years ago, before landing, she'd have giggled to herself as her plane zigzagged while she fixed her lipstick and quickly powdered her nose. She'd have been in the plane for hours and desperate for a toilet stop, but nothing stood in the way of her doing her face before she landed.

She shut her eyes as they made their descent, loving the shudder through her bones as the plane changed, the vibrations different now that they were heading back in, the noise of the engine spluttering more slowly. She felt like that young pilot again, that young, brave girl flying her favourite plane as Lizzie and May watched on below.

'Well, someone's a show-off!' Lizzie called out as Ruby climbed out of the cockpit, her grandson's hands guiding her safely on to the grass again. 'Don't think I didn't see that roll!'

Ruby grinned at her friends, not noticing their grey hair or the way Lizzie's hands were gnarled and knotted. Instead she saw her bright eyes and remembered her the way she'd been, with her sweep of lipstick and her perfect curls.

'We did our country proud, didn't we?' May said, wiping her eyes.

'We sure did,' she whispered back, and they all embraced, holding each other tight.

'You do know I received a medal from President Obama, don't you?' Lizzie said. 'That outranks your little stunt in the air.'

May laughed. 'She hasn't changed a bit, has she?'

Ruby looked Lizzie in the eye. 'Honey, I just flew a Spitfire the week of my ninetieth birthday. There's no way you can beat that.'

'You want to see if we can take the controls of a Halifax?' Lizzie asked, as bright as she'd ever been, the rivalry still alive. 'I might just win that first bomber flight second time around. What do you say?'

They all burst out laughing, heads bent together as they linked arms and walked off to find their families. Some of her friends had lost their lives in the air, had been cut down in their prime and denied the long life they'd deserved, but she'd had the privilege of living. And she'd loved every single moment of it.

*We will not again look upon a women's flying organization as experimental. We will know that they can handle our fastest fighters, our heaviest bombers; we will know that they are capable of ferrying, target towing, flying training, test flying, and the countless other activities which you have proved you can do . . . We of the Army Air Force are proud of you; we will never forget our debt to you.*

—General 'Hap' Arnold, December 1944

# AUTHOR'S NOTE

Although this book is a work of fiction, it is loosely based on real women who dedicated themselves to the ATA and the WASP, and some of the situations they found themselves in during the 1940s as women fliers.

In the United States, two women were responsible for the creation of the WASP, and ultimately for women being accepted and encouraged to fly. Jacqueline 'Jackie' Cochran met Mrs Roosevelt and suggested that women pilots could help in the war by taking over military flying jobs, and this meeting resulted in Mrs Roosevelt writing a newspaper article stating that women pilots were 'a weapon waiting to be used'. Despite the army disagreeing at the time, Jackie refused to give up, and General Henry 'Hap' Arnold asked her to deliver a twin-engine bomber across the Atlantic. At this time, the United States still wasn't in the war, but they were sending warplanes over for use by British fliers. When Jackie successfully delivered the plane and returned home, she lunched with the president and Mrs Roosevelt, and the president himself asked her to find out how many other American women could fly well enough to handle American warplanes. General Arnold then went on to suggest that Jackie take a group of American female pilots to England to join the British women's pilot group that was already flying non-combatant missions. Given this, Jackie's career was a big part of my inspiration for the character Lizzie, and I've woven fact with fiction into some parts of Lizzie's story.

Nancy Love was the other American woman determined to fly and see women assist in the war effort. She wasn't as ambitious as Jackie in that she didn't want to run a big air corps, but she was an excellent pilot and wrote to officials in 1940, suggesting that women could ferry planes for the army. The army wasn't interested in her plan until Pearl Harbor was bombed on 7 December 1941. The army didn't have enough men to fly combat missions and also deliver new planes, and so they announced the establishment of the Women's Auxiliary Ferrying Squadron on 10 September 1942. Nobody had told Jackie of this development, and when she read about it in a newspaper, she immediately returned home to the US, shocked that a women's squadron had been established and that she wasn't the head of it!

On her return, General Arnold worked out a compromise: Nancy's squadron started at the same time as Jackie's training programme, which was called the Women's Flying Training Detachment. By the summer of 1943, both programmes had combined into one big group – the Women Airforce Service Pilots (WASP). Despite the resounding success of the WASP, in December 1944 the programme ended, much to the disappointment of its members. Earlier in the year, Congress had defeated the bill that would have finally made the WASP part of the Army Air Forces. It wasn't until 2010 that the leaders of Congress would present the Congressional Gold Medal to the WASP – the signing of the bill to award the medal was unanimously supported by Congress and signed in the presence of some WASPs by President Barrack Obama. The speech by General 'Hap' Arnold in this story, at the final graduation ceremony, includes much of what he actually said in his speech at the end of 1944.

In England, female pilots made faster progress during the early 1940s, mainly because there was such a need for experienced pilots to transport planes from a factory outside of London to Scotland. It certainly wasn't because the general public was more accepting, as these pilots faced much criticism from all fronts, and had to prove that they deserved to be in the air. But after the Battle of Britain, during which a quarter of the country's 1,000 pilots were either killed or seriously injured, they simply couldn't spare RAF pilots for any non-combat flying. That's when women ferry pilots became crucial to winning the war.

Pauline Gower, the daughter of MP Robert Gower, was an inspirational pilot who cleared the way for women in the Air Transport Auxiliary (ATA). She was a pioneer in female aviation and insisted on women being paid equally to their male counterparts after finding out their weekly pay was 20 per cent less. Pauline welcomed Jackie Cochran to fly with them when she arrived from the United States, and although they were very different women, they respected each other's abilities in the sky. This is another part of the story that is very much based on fact.

Pauline was part of the 'First Eight': the eight women pilots who were permitted to ferry Tiger Moths from London to Scotland. Each woman had to have over 500 hours' flying experience, and to start with they were only allowed to fly light aircraft. It wasn't long, though, before their numbers grew from 8 to 166 female pilots, and they were flying not only Tiger Moths, but 147 different types of aircraft, including four-engine bombers that even intimidated most male pilots. The First Eight were all highly experienced pilots, but when the squadron expanded many of the new recruits didn't even drive a car, let alone fly planes! They were also from extremely varied backgrounds, from socialites to working girls, stunt pilots to architects and even ballet dancers. These incredibly brave women often flew several planes every single day once they'd completed their training; often they had never flown the plane they were told to pilot. They received a ferry notebook that gave them instructions and specifics for the aircraft, and away they went, into conditions that were often cloudy and dangerous, and with no way of defending themselves in the case of enemy fire. And with no instrument training or radios to use.

The favourite plane of the 'Attagirls' was the Spitfire, which was light to the touch, fast and incredibly sensitive. It was nicknamed the ultimate *ladies' plane*, but it certainly wasn't easy to fly despite being loved by all the girls. After reading about the love these brave women had for the Spitfire, it was the logical namesake for this book, and I wish to honour the memory of every single female pilot – true feminists before their time and women I greatly admire. Their story is certainly one that deserves to be told.

Of the 166 female ATA pilots in Britain, 15 died serving their country. Unlike in the United States, these women *were* recognised for their outstanding efforts immediately after the war, with the entire ATA (men and women included) credited with helping to win the war. In total, the ATA ferried 308,567 aircraft, with some women personally delivering in excess of 1,500 planes during their time with the ATA.

Many events in this novel are factual; however, it is very much a work of fiction, and I have had to make exceptions to fit within the parameters of my story.

As with all of my novels, I need to thank my incredible team at Amazon Publishing – Sammia Hamer, Victoria Pepe, Sophie Wilson and Gill Harvey. Thank you also to the design and author relations team at Amazon, as well as to my agent, Laura Bradford. And finally to my amazing readers – you are the reason I can write the stories I love! Thank you from the bottom of my heart for buying my books.

Soraya xx

# ABOUT THE AUTHOR

*Photo © 2014 Carys Monteath*

Soraya M. Lane graduated with a law degree before realising that law wasn't the career for her and that her future was in writing. She is the author of historical and contemporary women's fiction, and her novel *Wives of War* was an Amazon Charts bestseller.

Soraya lives on a small farm in her native New Zealand with her husband, their two young sons and a collection of four-legged friends. When she's not writing, she loves to be outside playing make-believe with her children or snuggled up inside reading.

For more information about Soraya and her books, visit www. sorayalane.com or www.facebook.com/SorayaLaneAuthor, or follow her on Twitter: @Soraya_Lane.